HARD HEADED WOMAN

HOWARD GIMPLE

Book Cover by Tom Caggiano

Ever since the world began
A hard-headed woman
Been a thorn in the side of man

—Elvis Presley

CHAPTER ONE

Hannah Johansson stood at the lectern in front of 300 people staring at her, waiting for her to say something heartfelt and meaningful. She looked around the room. A room that was unfamiliar to her even though she'd been in it thousands of times. But that was when it was the multipurpose room at the Jamaica Bay Wildlife Refuge. She played in the large barn-like structure as a child with her dolls and toys and electric trains. She practiced her jumpshot here when her father put up a hoop after she made her junior high team. She watched him give lectures here to local schoolkids and birdwatching clubs. And when she was a little older, it was where she came when she needed to be alone with her thoughts and her guitar.

But the room that Hannah knew was gone. It was now the Axel Johansson Memorial Auditorium, renamed to honor her father's memory. Completely renovated and refurbished with rows of fluorescent lighting on the ceiling, hickory floors, new windows and doors, radiant heat and a raised stage in front, facing fifteen rows of plush theater seats. The hall was decked out like a wood nymph wedding. Plants and flowers everywhere. Trees in huge pots with fake birds in the branches. And a few real ones flitting around the rafters.

Every seat was filled. The first two rows were reserved for relatives and VIPs. Hannah's aunt Gilda and cousins Catherine and Phillip were sitting in the middle of the front row, flanked by officials from the Mayor's Office, the New York City Parks Department, the National Parks Service and local assemblymen and state senators. The second row held representatives from a half-dozen environmental organizations including the Sierra Club, the National Audubon Society and the World Wildlife Fund.

The rest of the packed hall was crammed with children from neighborhood schools, birdwatching enthusiasts from all over the city and beyond, and men and women of all ages and ethnicities who loved the beauty and tranquility of the Refuge and wanted to show their appreciation and gratitude for the man who created and nurtured it.

Two hardbacked wooden chairs were positioned a few feet in front of the rest. That's where they put Hannah and her mother, who were required to sit for the better (or worse) part of an hour and smile demurely as a parade of a few friends and a lot of strangers filed by to tell them how sorry they were for their loss.

Michael Leigh, the president of the east coast chapter of the National Environmental Conservancy and the organizer of the event, had just finished his speech, the last of a dozen tributes to her father, the man who, as the memorial pamphlet said, 'transformed a rat infested, garbage strewn swamp into one of New York City's environmental treasures, the Jamaica Bay Wildlife Refuge.'

Before Leigh left the stage he said, "Our final speaker, Superintendent Johansson's daughter Hannah, would like to say a few words." Which was a total lie. Saying a few words or any words was the last thing she wanted to do.

On one side of the podium an easel held a portrait of her father in his khaki superintendent's uniform, surrounded by a snowy egret, a great blue heron and a glossy ibis, painted by the celebrated wildlife artist Arthur Singer. On the other side was a wrought iron plant stand, but in place of a plant it held a hand-enameled aluminum urn containing her father's ashes.

Hannah searched the audience for a friendly face.

Her mother was a mess, head-down, sniffling, dabbing at her eyes with a shredded white tissue. Gilda wore her usual scowl of scorn. Catherine stared down at the phone in her lap. Phil shot her a wink and a thumbs-up. Her friend, Bette, seated towards the rear, met her gaze with a nervous smile.

Tiny pearls of sweat formed on Hannah's forehead. She felt her eyelids sag, her legs wobble. Was she just nervous or was it the Weakness? She gripped the lectern for support, cleared her throat and leaned in a little too close to the gooseneck microphone, producing a squeal of feedback that snapped her head back.

"Thank you all for coming," she said, fighting to maintain composure. "I know my father meant a lot to you. He meant everything to me. He was my hero. My mentor. My best friend. I loved him more than I could ever possibly say."

Her face contorted. Her eyes welled up.

"I'm sorry. I'm so sorry. I'm so sorry I killed him," she wailed.

Her legs went numb and she crumpled to the floor, her flailing arm knocking the urn over as she fell.

The room gasped.

Seconds later, she wasn't sure how many, she looked up to see her cousin Phil towering over her. He grasped her under her arms and slowly lifted her to her feet.

"Are you okay, kid?"

She nodded.

He helped her back to her seat and gently lowered her into it.

The room hummed with a hundred hushed conversations.

Michael Leigh sprang to his feet and strode hurriedly to the podium. For a man on the far side of both sixty years and three hundred pounds, he moved with a dancer's grace. He stood regally, waiting for the din to subside.

When the room was quiet he said, "On behalf of the Environmental Conservancy I want to thank you all for coming this morning to pay homage to our friend and colleague, Axel Johansson. Now it's time to allow his family some privacy."

The 90-minute ride from Howard Beach to Rocky Point was silent, punctuated only by Olive's sniffles, sighs and groans. That was fine with Hannah. She spent the entire time cataloging all her recent screw-ups, culminating in this latest catastrophe.

Phil dropped Hannah and her mother off in front of the house on Dogwood Road then drove away, saying he wanted to visit some friends and that he would stop by before heading back upstate.

As soon as they opened the door, Lena, Hannah's 10-year-old golden retriever, ran over to them. Olive smiled for the first time in days and grasped the dog's face with both hands.

"Have you been a good girl while we were gone, you little mischief maker?"

Finally emerging from her gloomy torpor, Olive scurried into the kitchen and started making snacks for anyone who might come calling with condolences. She filled bowls with tortilla, pita and potato chips and smaller dishes with salsa, hummus and spinach dip. She made pigs in blankets from mini hot dogs and filo dough. Threw some shrimp into boiling water and made cocktail sauce out of horseradish, ketchup and lemon juice.

When Hannah asked how she could help, her mother waved her hand and said, "Oh, no thank you dear. I don't want you to trouble yourself. You just relax. You've already been through enough today."

Hannah sat in the old oak rocking chair by the bay window. Guilt, anger, sorrow, regret and humiliation swirled in her head. A handful of people came to the house, neighbors and some of Olive's friends from the senior citizens club. Hannah thanked them somberly for their kind words.

Things got a little more lively when the 'Stewed Tomatoes' arrived. They were Olive's longtime pals from back in the days on Ashby Avenue in Flushing who, on a semi-regular basis over the past forty-odd years, through children, grandchildren, triumphs, tragedies, marriages and divorces, got together to drink wine, gossip, play cards, swap stories and recipes, to lend an ear, a helping hand, or a shoulder to cry on. They swarmed over Hannah, telling her she looked beautiful and that everything would be all right. Though that sort of indulgent attention usually made her cringe, this time it actually brought her some comfort.

After spending some time with the 'girls', Hannah grabbed her beloved guitar, a Martin acoustic that was a sweet-sixteen gift from her father, and went out to the back deck. Sitting in an Adirondack chair, she began strumming Peter, Paul and Mary's 'Where Have All the Flowers Gone' as the sun squashed itself into an orange egg as it sank into the undulating waters of Long Island Sound. The twilight sky was a Peter Max poster in vibrant stripes of purple, violet, crimson and pink. She placed her guitar gently next to the chair and closed her eyes and drifted into that tranquil state that's not quite sleep yet not fully awake.

"Hey Cuz," her cousin Phil said, jolting her up.

"Phil. When'd you get here?"

"Couple of minutes ago. I picked up Gilda on the way over. She's inside with your mom."

Hannah grimaced but said nothing. Phil pulled over a chair and sat next to her. He had changed out of his dark blue funeral suit into his usual attire, black t-shirt, cutoff shorts and flip-flops. Six-foot-six, with a shaved head, bushy handlebar mustache and thickly muscled arms and legs, Phillip 'Buzz' Buzek looked more like the swimming champ and rugby star he was back in his college days, than one of the foremost medical rehabilitation specialists in Western New York State.

He took a swig out of a bottle of Heineken and handed one to her. "How you holding up?"

"I'm fine."

His smile morphed into a scowl. "Bullshit!" he yelled. "You're not even close to fine."

Hannah reacted like she'd been slapped. Phil never yelled. He hardly talked. He usually just mumbled in monosyllables.

When he was little his parents thought he might be a slow learner until he skipped third grade. They figured it was some kind of mix-up. When they went to talk to his teacher about it, she told them he had the highest I.Q. in the school. They refused to believe it until she showed them his test scores.

Phil stood and glared down her. "I'm a doctor, I know what fine looks like. It's not losing muscle control and flopping on the floor like a flounder. How long has this been going on?"

She sheepishly said, "A little over six months."

"Have you been looked at?"

She forced a smile. "I'm a six-foot-three-inch blonde. I get looked at all the time."

"You think this is funny?"

"Of course I know it's not funny. What do you want me to do, lay down in the fetal position and die? The hell with that!"

He leaned forward. "Listen, there's something going on inside your body and it needs to be fixed. Have you seen a doctor?"

She sighed in dismay. "About a half-dozen. I've been tested for multiple sclerosis, muscular dystrophy, myasthenia gravis, Lou Gehrig's disease, chronic fatigue syndrome and a brain tumor. All negative. The last doc I saw checked my results, told me it was all in my head and sent me to a psychiatrist."

"What did the shrink say?"

"Nothing much, since I never went."

She expected him to scold her but he just shrugged. Then he turned in his chair and looked intently into her eyes.

"What happens when these episodes come on?"

"I call it the Weakness. It's like a switch gets flipped. All of a sudden my eyes get heavy. My vision blurs. My legs get squishy. My tongue feels disconnected to my mouth."

"How long does it last?"

"It varies, a couple of minutes to maybe fifteen or more."

Her cousin nodded thoughtfully but didn't say anything.

"So Doctor Phil, do you have any ideas?"

He tugged on his mustache. "I would have guessed a couple of the things you were tested for. Those Boston docs are very good. But they don't know you like I do. Let me look into it. I know a guy who specializes in this sort of thing. He really knows his stuff. We'll find out what's going on with you. I promise."

"You better do it fast. Before I kill anyone else."

Phil shook his head. "That's another thing. You didn't kill your father."

"Of course I did. Strokes aren't always fatal. He would still be alive if I didn't crash-land on top of him."

"That would only be true if he had a stroke."

"Of course he had a stroke. What else can it be? My father was the strongest man I've ever known. Then boom, he ages twenty years in a couple of months and becomes frail as a sparrow. If it wasn't a stroke, what was it?"

"That's what I'm waiting to find out."

"Waiting for what? The doctors at St. Theresa's already diagnosed it."

"I wouldn't trust the quacks at St. Terry's to diagnose a hangnail. They don't call it St. Terrible for nothing. Recovering stroke patients are a big part of my practice. I know what the after-effects of a stroke look like. Uncle Axe didn't look like that. I checked out his chart. There were some major anomalies. Bottom line, I'm pretty sure Uncle Axe didn't have a stroke."

"Then what was it?"

"My guess is some kind of poison."

She stiffened like she'd been cattle prodded. "Poison? No way."

"He worked with heavy-duty chemicals all the time, pesticides, herbicides, all kinds of toxic stuff. Accidents happen."

Hannah shook her head vehemently. "Not to my father. He wrote the Parks Department manual on the proper handling and storage of toxic material. There's no way he would accidentally poison himself."

"Could be somebody else did it." Phil thought for a moment. "Did he have any enemies?"

"Absolutely not! You saw all those people at the memorial this morning. Everybody loved him."

Phil thought for a few seconds. "Wasn't there some bad blood when the National Parks Service took over the Jamaica Bay Refuge from the city?"

"Yeah, when the feds came in they told him they didn't need him there anymore. They strongly suggested that he retire. But the local community wouldn't stand for it. As far as they were concerned my dad WAS the Jamaica Bay Wildlife Refuge. There was a big meeting with local politicians, school administrators, youth leaders and nature clubs. When it was over the feds relented. They made him Superintendent Emeritus and told him he could stay as long as he wanted. He had his own office, gave lectures, led tours. They even named a boat after him, the Axel Johansson Research Vessel. He always said the only way he'd leave the Refuge was toes up."

"Somebody agreed."

She shook her head. "You're a great doctor, but you're way off base on this."

"We'll see."

"How? He was cremated. You can't do an autopsy on ashes."

"Like I said, I was pretty sure he didn't have a stroke but I wanted to be positive. The last time I saw him at the hospital I took some blood."

"They let you do that?"

Phil grinned. "I didn't ask. I just did it. Then I sent it to a friend of mine at the Allegany County Police Forensics Lab. I'm waiting for the report. Then we'll know for sure."

"You're a rehab doc. Since when do you have access to a police forensics lab?"

"Since I became the Allegany County coroner."

"Oh?" Hannah raised her eyebrows. "When did that happen?"

"Right after they closed the Medical Examiners office for lack of funds."

"If they don't have any money, how do they pay you?"

"They don't. It's voluntary."

"I thought you volunteered on the ski patrol."

"I do that too."

Hannah smiled. "Now you're just showing off."

He laughed. "Not really. There's not a lot to do out there in the hinterlands and I like to stay busy."

"What about dating?"

"Alfred doesn't have much of a singles scene. I went out with a couple of women from the college but we didn't hit it off. I guess I'm not really the academic type. There were a couple of cute State Policewomen I met in autopsy, but it's hard to be charming while you're cutting up a dead body and reeking of formaldehyde."

"I still think you're way off base with this poison theory."

"Suppose I'm right?"

Hannah was silent for a few seconds. Could she really be off the hook for her father's death? That would be great but it would also mean that somebody poisoned him. Who? Why?

She said, "Let's wait until you get the report. If it turns out you're right, we'll figure something out. In the meantime, don't say anything to my mother or Gilda."

"Of course not." He stood up and gave Hannah a quick peck on the forehead. "I'm hitting the road. I've got a five hour drive ahead of me."

"When do you think you'll get the lab results?"

"All depends on how busy they are."

He turned to go.

Hannah sat staring at the deepening purple sky, thinking about what Phil told her. Her father couldn't have been accidentally poisoned. Safety was his biggest bugaboo. He was the first superintendent in the Department of Parks to insist on storing all toxic material in a stand-alone unit. Now it's standard procedure.

He even lectured Hannah and her mother to be extra careful when they used bug spray in the vegetable garden.

As for him being murdered? That was even more ridiculous. Axel got along with everybody. The only argument she ever saw him have was with Uncle Joe, Phil's dad. It was about who was better, Mickey Mantle or Willie Mays.

Maybe Phil was just trying to make her feel better. Convince her that her father's death wasn't her fault.

Phil would do something like that. He was more than a cousin. He was her part-time big brother. He always looked after her, even as kids. And with Uncle Joe being a police lieutenant, it figured that he would come up with this crazy poison/murder scenario.

"Hannah Marie!" came Olive's screech. "Come quick. There's a person here who wants to see you."

She fought the urge to ignore her mother. She was sure that the person was her aunt Gilda, who was the last person she wanted to deal with at that moment. But she couldn't stay out on the deck all night and who knew how long the old witch would stay. Maybe Gilda would be nice for once, out of respect for Axel's passing. And if she wasn't, Hannah would be the better person and not react to whatever demeaning comment her supercilious aunt shot her way.

"I'll be there in a minute," she yelled.

Bile rose in her gut when she saw her aunt standing imperiously in the living room. Then she realized it wasn't Gilda who was anxious to see her. Michael Leigh was sitting in her father's big blue club chair, chatting with her mother and Gilda. He smiled up at Hannah.

"Well, hello, my dear, how are you feeling?"

Hannah was taken aback that a man of his prominence would travel all the way out to Rocky Point from his duplex on Central Park West to pay his respects. She was no fashionista but she could see that Leigh's blue blazer and beige slacks were of the finest quality. In his breast pocket in place of the usual three-cornered handkerchief stood a trio of thick cigars. He had shed his stiff white shirt and wore a cream colored cashmere sweater. She felt like a street person in her tattered jeans and a sloppy sweatshirt.

Before she could answer her mother said, "Would you like something to eat, Mr. Leigh? We have shrimp cocktail, potato chips if you like or those little hot dogs."

"Bring the man a drink," Gilda commanded. "He drove all the way out here from the city. I'm sure he's parched." She smiled obsequiously at him. "Would you like a soft drink or something stronger?"

"That's very gracious of you ladies but really, a glass of water would be perfect. Then I must be on my way. I just wanted to stop in and make sure that Hannah was all right. She gave us quite a scare this morning."

Olive went scurrying into the kitchen.

Leigh stood. He engulfed Hannah's outstretched hand in both of his meaty paws. "I must say we were all very concerned about your health."

Hannah didn't know how to react. She hardly knew this man, except for what she read about him in the paper, and here he was, treating her like his favorite niece.

"Much better, Mr. Leigh. Thank you very much for asking. I'm sorry I caused a commotion this morning."

"Please, my dear. No need to apologize. As long as you're all right."

Olive returned with a goblet of water and placed it carefully on the end table next to the chair.

Leigh took a quick sip and said, "So Hannah, when will you be returning to Boston?"

Another surprise. How could this man, who dealt with heads of state and corporate titans, possibly know that she lived in Boston or anything about her little life?

"I won't be," she said hesitantly. "I'm living back here now." Please don't ask me why, she pleaded silently.

"I see." He glanced over at Olive. "I'm sure that's a great comfort to your mother."

Gilda walked over and put a hand on Hannah's shoulder. She stifled a cringe, wondering what caustic barb was coming.

"Boston is so provincial, don't you agree?" her aunt said with a smarmy smirk. "There are many more opportunities here for a young lady of Hannah's abilities."

She paused ever so slightly between the words 'Hannah's' and 'abilities' as if to indicate that she left out a word like 'meager' or 'limited.'

That wasn't so bad, Hannah thought. Maybe she's mellowing.

Leigh said, "I'm sure Hannah will do very well no matter where she is. She appears to be a very bright and capable young woman."

Hannah smiled demurely. "Thank you, sir."

He stood. "If there's ever anything I can do to help you, don't hesitate to get in touch with me."

He handed her a business card.

"But now I must be off. My family's waiting for me at our little place in Watermill. I still have a long drive ahead of me."

He turned to Olive and Gilda, bowed his head slightly and said, "Ladies, again my deepest condolences."

He strode out the door.

Olive beamed. "Wasn't that something, coming all the way out here just to see how you were feeling and to pay his respects."

"It was very nice of him," Hannah said. "But it's not like he went way out of his way. He was headed out east anyway."

"That's not the point," Gilda said. "Mr. Leigh is a very substantial person."

Olive said, "Yes I know. If it wasn't for his organization I don't think Axel would have been allowed to stay on after the National Parks people took over."

Gilda smirked. "Olive, please. Have you EVER looked at a newspaper? Michael Leigh was a high ranking official in the Bush administration. Now he's the head of a major financial organization."

Olive looked confused. "I thought he ran that environmental club."

"Men of Mr. Leigh's stature are asked to sit on many boards. I'm sure the Environmental Conservancy is just a one of several." She wagged a finger at Hannah. "Don't lose that card, young lady. This could be a big opportunity for you."

Hannah fished it out of her pocket and read aloud, "Flack & Spitz. Financial Strategies and Solutions. Michael Leigh, Chairman & CEO."

She shrugged put it back. "I never heard of them. And besides, I don't know anything about finance. My experience is in health care."

"Health care?" Gilda said snidely. "You were a receptionist at a psycho ward. That's not a career. It's hardly a job. You need something solid, like my Catherine. She's only two years older than you and she already made vice president while you've made nothing of yourself."

Hannah seethed. "Yes aunt Gilda, Catherine's amazing. I wish I was an ASSISTANT vice president at an actuarial company so I could sit around all day figuring out exactly when people are going to drop dead so I can gouge them for the most money while they're still breathing."

So much for being the better person.

"And by the way, I was a senior administrator in a behavioral health facility. We helped a lot of people. We saved many lives and improved many more. Hopefully we threw off some of Catherine's mortality calculations."

"There's no need to get snippy with me young lady," Gilda said in a huff. "I was only looking out for your best interests."

"That's right Hannah," Olive said. "Gilda always said you have a lot more potential than you're using. You should call Mr. Leigh right away. It could be a new start for you."

Hannah always felt worse after getting into these ridiculous quarrels with her aunt but she couldn't help herself. All these stupid arguments did was exasperate her and upset her mother.

"I'll absolutely call him," she lied. "But I can't tomorrow. I'm going to the Refuge to scatter daddy's ashes."

"You'll do no such thing!" Gilda bristled. "Everyone in the family is buried in our plot in Flushing Cemetery, two rows away from the final resting place of the great Louie Armstrong."

This was one issue Hannah wasn't going to back down on.

"One of my father's last wishes was to have his remains scattered at the Refuge and that's what I'm going to do, no matter what you or Satchmo think."

Gilda shook her head and glowered at Hannah. "Fortunately, it's not up to you, young lady."

She turned to Olive. "This is your decision. Axel was your husband. Tell your daughter that you and he will be spending eternity together nestled in the bosom of your family, alongside my dear Fred and me."

Olive didn't say anything for a few long seconds. Her lip quivered. She looked like she was about to cry. Hannah hoped that just this once her mother would stand up to her overbearing older sister. Olive knew damn well that Axel wanted his ashes scattered at the Refuge. He said so many times.

Olive looked dolefully at Hannah. "My dear Axel did want his ashes to go to Jamaica Bay."

Could her mother really be taking her side? This would be a first.

Then Olive turned her gaze to Gilda. "But everyone in our family is at Flushing. Our parents, your Fred, Uncle Ed and Aunt Gladys. All the Buzeks. It just wouldn't be right not to have Axel there."

Gilda smiled smugly at Hannah, who was fighting the urge to strangle the old harridan.

Then Olive bowed her head into her hands and said, "I just..I just don't know what to do."

Gilda walked over and patted her sister on the head like she was a whimpering puppy.

“There, there dear. There’s no reason to get upset. Nothing has to be decided now. Think about it for a day or two, then I know you’ll come to the correct decision.”

Olive sighed. “Yes, nothing has to happen right now. We have time.” She turned to Hannah. “Right, dear?”

Was that a furtive wink? She couldn’t be sure.

CHAPTER TWO

Long Island's Southern State Parkway is the urban equivalent of those treacherous mountain roads with narrow lanes and hairpin turns. Cars appear out of nowhere from onramps no bigger than a parking space. The crazy rush hour drivers tailgate incessantly and change lanes abruptly, swerving in and out of traffic at random with apparently no regard for other cars that might be in their way.

Hannah avoided it at all costs, but the radio said that there was a jackknifed tractor trailer clogging up the Long Island Expressway and the Southern State was the best alternative. It was also the quickest route to the Jamaica Bay Wildlife Refuge. So there she was, teeth clenched, heart palpitating, hands numb from gripping the steering wheel like it was a life rope.

She kept glancing at her father's urn sticking out of the top of her backpack on the seat next to her, hoping she put the lid on tight enough to keep it from falling off and dumping her father's ashes all over the front seat.

She wasn't used to rush hour traffic, which on Long Island started at about six in the morning. Most days she'd still be asleep. But this wasn't most days. She had dragged herself out of bed at five-thirty, dressed in a hurry, grabbed the urn off the mantel and tiptoed out of the house. No coffee. No tea. She didn't even bother to brush her teeth.

As soon as she saw her mother fall to pieces last night, she made up her mind. She would snatch the urn and spread the ashes over the East Pond. It was the only way to make sure that her father's wishes would be fulfilled.

She was sure her mother would eventually give in to Gilda. She always did. After 60 years of letting her sister dominate her, there was no reason to think Olive would change now.

The Refuge parking lot was empty when she pulled in. That was the first thing that struck her as odd. It should have been packed. It was a warm, cloudless early May morning. The kind of day that serious birders waited for all year. On days like this they would arrive before sunrise with their cameras, binoculars and notebooks .

Though he never said anything, Hannah always thought her father was disappointed that she never became a dedicated bird-watcher. She loved birds. She thought they were fascinating and exquisite in their grace and beauty. She just didn't see the point in shlepping all over the country just so you could fill your notebook with obscure bird sightings. She could probably identify a dozen or so species, but nowhere near the hundreds or even thousands that serious birders like her friend Bette could rattle off the top of her head.

Aside from yesterday's fiasco, which really didn't count because the auditorium was across the street and not inside the grounds, Hannah hadn't been back to the Refuge since her parents moved out.

She was living in Boston when her mother called and told her that the federal government was taking over and she and Axel had to give up their house. She could feel the anger welling up as she remembered the conversation.

"They're throwing you out!?" Hannah screamed into the phone.

"Oh no," Olive said. "They're giving us six months. I think that's very reasonable."

"What's reasonable about it?!" Hannah yelled. "Don't you remember what the Jamaica Bay property was like when we first moved there? It was a garbage dump surrounded by a stinking swamp. Dad turned it into what the Audubon Society called an urban nirvana. And to thank him they kick him out of his house. Our house!"

"It was never our house. You know that. The city built it for us. They let us live there all those years rent free."

"Yeah, so dad could be on call night and day, seven days a week. And we would be there too. Unpaid help."

"Please, let's not fight. We have to leave and that's all there is to it. It's not like we have no place to go. We were always going to move to the Rocky Point house once your father left the Refuge. That's why we bought Gilda's and Joe's shares. We'll just have to do it a little earlier than we planned."

As she walked towards the main gate of the Refuge Hannah noticed some changes. The parking lot was concrete instead of bluestone, which was probably a good thing. What wasn't good was the eight-foot high wrought-iron fence that blocked the entranceway. With sharp arrowhead spikes at the top, it looked like it should be in front of a prison yard not a nature park.

Her father never closed the front entrance. He put a six-foot chain-link fence around the periphery but that was to keep cats and raccoons away from the birds and prevent neighborhood kids from using the trees and shrubs that ringed the periphery as a make-out destination.

To add to the new penitentiaryesque ambiance, a scary looking guy stood guard in front of the padlocked double gate. He was well over six feet tall and weighed at least 250 pounds. He was unshaven and dressed all in black, from his wrinkled, sweat-stained, half-tucked shirt to his scuffed black motorcycle boots. Hannah thought he looked like a scuzzy bad guy in an early Schwarzenegger movie. He held a black assault rifle across his midsection and had a big black pistol in a holster at his hip. Embroidered letters over his right shirt pocket said 'GRABOWSKI'.

Hannah grabbed the backpack with Axel's urn and walked up to him.

Before she could get a word out he glared at her and barked, "Closed."

Hannah smiled and in her friendliest, most obsequious voice said, "That's all right officer..." She glanced at the writing on his pocket, "Grabowski, I don't need to go into the Welcome Center. Is there another way to get in?"

"It's all closed," he growled.

"All 9,000 acres? I don't believe it."

His nostrils flared like the bull he resembled and through clenched teeth he growled, "I don't give a rat's ass what you believe, lady. Do yourself a favor and get the hell out now if you know what's good for you."

Hannah recoiled. She still considered this place home and no one was going to stop her from going in. No even a Goliath with a massive gun.

"Who do you think you are," she yelled. "Talking to me like that! My father was the superintendent here for twenty years and it was never closed during daylight hours. Maybe some trails that needed fixing but never the entire place."

Before he could answer, a woman in an ill-fitting brown business suit scurried out of the Welcome Center and sneered at her through the gate. With her chubby cheeks, oversized front teeth, crinkly pug nose and permanent sneer, she looked like an oversized chipmunk who just chomped on a rotten acorn.

"What's the trouble here, Billy?" she said in a pinched voice that matched her face.

"She don't believe we're closed. Something about her father working here."

Hannah turned toward the woman. "My father was Axel Johansson."

Hannah couldn't believe that her father's name elicited no reaction. Axel Johansson was to the Jamaica Bay Wildlife Refuge what Babe Ruth was to Yankee Stadium.

"Maybe you don't understand," she continued. "He didn't just work here. He built this park. He planted every tree. Every bush. He was superintendent from the day it opened until the National Parks Service took over. When he was in charge it was open 24 hours a day, seven days a week, every day of the year. He would always say, 'Mother Nature never closes, neither should we.'"

She scowled and said, "I'm sorry young lady, but Mother Nature doesn't work here anymore. And neither does your father. The Jamaica Bay Wildlife Refuge is closed until further notice."

"Why is it closed and why do you need an armed guard?"

She sighed, annoyed, but answered, "A study is being conducted to ascertain the viability of this property in the expansion plans of JFK Airport." She spoke with no intonation, as if she were reciting from a script.

Hannah was silent for a few seconds, digesting what she just heard. "You're telling me they're going to pave it all over? What about the birds?"

She shrugged.

"That doesn't explain why you need Darth Grabowski guarding the place like it's Fort Knox. Who is responsible for all this Mrs...?"

"Ms. Dawson." She pronounced it Mizzzzzz. "I've answered enough of your questions. Now please leave." She turned and marched back to the Welcome Center.

As Hannah started walking away she felt the strength ebbing from her legs. She wobbled to a bench and sat down awkwardly, not sure if one of her attacks was coming on or if she was knocked for a loop by these horrible people who insulted her father and told her that his life's work was about to be bulldozed like so much rubble.

After half a minute the strength in her legs came back. She

looked over at Grabowski, who was sneering at her and fondling the barrel of his rifle in a particularly disgusting way.

Back in the Jeep, she drove out of the parking lot but she didn't turn south on Cross Bay Boulevard and back to the mainland. She went north and drove slowly up the service road. She stopped when she saw her old house on the other side of the fence. Her mother had mentioned that the National Parks people were using it to store old files and documents, but it looked like the only ones using it were birds, squirrels and feral cats. The windows were broken, the paint was chipped and peeling, and weeds and vines grew through the rotted floorboards of the porch. The trees and shrubs her father planted, now unattended and overgrown, engulfed her childhood home in leafy tentacles. Hannah didn't consider herself a sentimental person, but seeing the cozy clapboard cottage she grew up in looking like an abandoned hovel brought tears.

When she was in high school her friends would drop her off here, by the secret entrance her father made for her. He didn't like the idea of his teenage daughter walking the quarter-mile from the main entrance to the house alone late at night where some pervert could be waiting to drag her behind a bush. He cut a five-foot gap in the fence close to the back of the house with a bolt cutter so she could squeeze through and be home. He even filed down the sharp ends so she wouldn't cut herself. She wasn't overly concerned about her safety but she was happy not to have to walk on the dark, muddy footpath in good shoes.

Hannah grabbed her backpack out of the car, checked the urn and walked slowly along the the fence. Everything looked exactly the same as it was during her high school days except now the old fence had new razor wire spiraled along the top.

It took some groping, tugging and almost getting her eye poked out by a protruding branch, but after a few minutes she found the gap. Prickly vines and brambles were woven through the severed links. She reached into her backpack for her Swiss Army Knife. As she slowly sawed at the vines, she kept looking around, fearful that someone would show up and ask her what she was doing. But the traffic on Cross Bay Boulevard was sparse and there didn't seem to be any activity on the other side of the fence, so she finished her work unimpeded. She separated the links, carefully rolled her backpack containing her father's urn underneath, then squeezed through herself. She tied a red bandana to the fence next to the gap to make it easy for her to spot on the way out.

Her old house looked even worse up close than it did from a distance. She tried not to look at it as she made her way to the East Pond. She hugged the thicket of trees and brush next to the trail as she walked, alert to anyone who might be patrolling the area. After about five minutes she arrived at a small clearing at the northern tip of the pond. This was her father's favorite spot. To the west were the towers of Manhattan, to the south, the vast Atlantic, to the north, Jamaica Bay and across the bay, JFK Airport. And in the sky, in addition to the gas hawks, her father's name for the fume-spewing jetliners, there were birds by the hundreds. Herons, ibises, snow geese, egrets, ducks and terns, to name the few that Hannah could identify. Axel loved it here because it was the one spot where you could feel the energy of the City and the splendor of nature all at once.

When she got to the clearing, she found herself in a place she hardly recognized. When she was a little girl, her father would bring her to the bathtub-sized wooden platform he built at the edge of the pond. These were the times with her father that she most cherished. They would sit with their feet dangling over the side. He would tell her stories, or they would sing songs or just enjoy the view. When she was a little older he bought her a junior fishing kit, complete with a rod, a reel and a tackle box with lures and sinkers. One day she felt a tug on her line. Axel helped her pull it in. There was a tiny fish on the line about the size of her father's thumb. He told her it was called a peanut bunker. For weeks afterward Hannah told everyone she caught a peanut butter fish. Her cousin Phil told her she would have to catch a jellyfish, then she could make a sandwich.

Her beloved platform was gone. It was replaced by a boat dock, the kind you would find in many of the houses that backed onto the bay. Where the footpath used to be, there was now a gravel road, about a car-width across, leading back to the Welcome Center. It was rutted with tire tracks.

Hannah carefully took the urn out of her backpack and walked to the edge of the dock. After some serious prying and tugging at the tightly secured lid, it popped off and landed a couple of feet away. She kissed the urn, said "I love you daddy," and scattered her father's ashes into the waters he loved.

Her eyes were moist as she stood for a moment watching the ashes dissipate into the blue-green water. Then she heard muffled voices approaching. It would only be a moment before whoever it was would come around the curve. She sprinted off the dock to a thicket of trees and shrubs. As she ran, her legs weakened with every stride.

She hunkered down in the dirt behind a stand of overgrown bayberry bushes as Dawson the chipmunk woman and the apish Grabowski walked up the gravel road. She took a couple of quick shots of them with her phone.

Dawson held a clipboard in one hand and wagged a finger at Grabowski with the other. It looked like she was scolding him. Hannah strained to listen. The shrieks of the birds and the roar of overhead jets made it hard to hear. When the noise subsided she could hear Grabowski say, "Two o'clock tonight. Yeah, I'll be here."

Dawson said, "You better be. He won't wait." She bent down to pick something up. It was the urn lid.

Hannah silently mouthed, "Shit!"

Dawson held it up, examined each side. "What the hell is this?"

Grabowski shrugged.

A repulsive brown bug slithered up Hannah's leg. As she tried to shake it off her foot hit a stump.

Dawson turned. "Did you hear that? Somebody's out there. Go check it out."

Grabowski scowled. "Are you kidding? It's probably a squirrel or a raccoon or one of those pain in the ass birds that shit all over everything."

"Just go do it," she barked. "We can't let our guard down now. Not after all this."

"Okay, fine," he said, scowling and shaking his head.

As he lumbered into the thicket Hannah curled up behind some dense shrubs. Bayberry, chokeberry, autumn olive, black pine and rosa rugosa. All bore fruit that birds love, that's why her father planted them. They also had thorns, spiky needles and stubby branches that cut and gouged her like so many killer bees. The ground was a tangle of rocks, twigs, brambles, roots and vines. Hannah held her breath as Grabowski stopped in front of a tree a few feet from where she was huddled. She tried to ignore the earwig that was crawling up her neck, as well as the aches in her arms and legs and the stings and pricks of the spiky foliage.

"There's nothing here," he yelled. Then he walked behind the tree. Hannah could hear a zipper and a trickle hitting fallen leaves. Twenty seconds later he started back to the dock, pulling up his fly.

"I told you it was nothing," he said as he walked back to the dock.

Dawson said, "Just make sure you're back here before two this morning."

Then she turned, shoved the urn lid in her pocket and marched away with Grabowski tromping behind her.

CHAPTER THREE

Hannah had no idea how to conduct an airport expansion feasibility study but she was pretty sure that whatever it was, it wasn't building a boat dock in an area that sees almost no boat traffic. Or expanding a narrow dirt path into a gravel road. Not to mention the armed-to-the-teeth stormtrooper making sure no one was welcome at the Welcome Center. And why are they getting some kind of mystery shipment in the middle of the night? All of a sudden, Phil's crazy theory of her father being poisoned didn't seem quite so crazy.

But no matter what, she kept her promise to her dad.

She thought back to the evening a couple of days after she came home. She and her father were on the back deck, sitting next to each other. He was a fragment of the man she grew up with. Once tall, broad and strong like the trees he planted, he was now a spindly sapling.

He grasped her hand frailly and looked directly at her. His eyes retained the dynamic intensity that had left the rest of him, two blazing embers in a fading fire.

"I want you to promise me that when I die you won't let them stick me with those phonies from your mother's family. I didn't have any use for them alive and I don't want to be anywhere near them when I'm dead, which could happen any day."

"Stop it daddy. You're going to live a long time."

He tightened his grip. "Listen to me. I want my body to be cremated and my ashes spread in the East Pond. You know the place."

"Please, I don't want to talk about this."

He squeezed tighter. "Promise me."

"If that's what you want. I promise." She leaned over and kissed him on the forehead. "But it'll be a very long time until I have to keep that promise."

It was less than a month. Now she made another promise to her father. That she would do everything she could to protect the place that he built.

As she drove back, Hannah thought that maybe there was a perfectly legitimate explanation about what was going on at the Refuge, though she couldn't imagine what it was. She decided to talk to her friend Bette, who went there a couple of times a year with her birding club. She was also the smartest person Hannah knew.

Hannah grabbed her phone.

"Sarris & Gray Attorneys."

"Hi Gwen, it's Hannah Johansson. Is Bette around?"

There was no sound for several seconds. Hannah thought maybe she was in a dead zone. Then finally, "Uh. She doesn't work here anymore. I thought you knew."

"What? No. I had no idea."

"She resigned last week."

"Just like that? For no reason? Are you sure? I can't believe Bette would do something like that."

"Neither could we. It took us all by surprise."

"What happened?"

"She walked into Mr. Sarris's office and told him she was leaving. When he asked her why, she said that working here was stultifying."

"Stultifying? I don't even know what that means."

"Neither did most of us. But that's what she said."

"Then what happened?"

"She packed up a few things and walked out."

"Just like that?"

"Just like that."

"That's crazy."

"Yeah. We thought so too."

"Well...thanks." Hannah hung up.

It was hard to imagine Bette doing that. Compared to her, Bambi was a t-rex. Everyone took advantage of her. Her ex-husband, her parents, even her cats. And, of course, the lawyers she worked with treated her like a scullery maid. Still, the thought of her friend marching into the big boss's office and quitting was inconceivable. Just like the thought of turning the Jamaica Bay Wildlife Refuge into an airport runway.

She tried Bette's cell. It went straight to voicemail.

"Call me as soon as you can," Hannah said after the beep. "I have something very important to talk to you about." Then she texted her the same message.

A few minutes later she got a text back. "In church. Can't talk."

Hannah knew Bette came from a very religious family but she never seemed particularly devout herself. She went to church at Christmas and Easter and put dirt on her forehead on Ash Wednesday, but that was it. What the hell was she doing at church in the middle of the week?

Hannah replied, "Can we meet when you're done?"

"Mario's. 20 mins."

Hannah was there in ten.

Mario's Pizza & Pasta was in a strip mall a couple of blocks from Bette's parents' house in East Northport. There was a pizza counter in the front and six tables in the back. A yellowed clipping out of *Long Island Monthly* proclaiming that they made the best grandma pizza in Suffolk County was hanging on the wall in a fancy frame, along with a picture of the pope and a photo of a fat guy on a boat holding a big fish on a hook. Hannah assumed it was Mario. She ordered a slice with pepperoni and a Diet Coke.

She was halfway finished when a woman walked towards her table. Hannah almost choked when she realized it was her friend Bette. Her hair was dyed black and cut short and choppy. She wore a flannel shirt, ripped jeans and workboots.

Since Hannah had known her, Bette had stick-straight shoulder length medium brown hair that some would call mousy. Her wardrobe tended toward Catholic schoolgirl chic, lacy peasant tops, knee-length skirts and penny loafers.

Hannah looked her up and down. "Who are you and what did you do with my friend Bette?"

Bette smiled awkwardly. "I'm trying to make some changes."

"I can see that. But quitting your job is a lot different than changing your hairstyle. What happened?"

"I just couldn't stand it anymore."

"A lot of people don't like their jobs. But to just quit? That's a big step. What inspired you do it?"

"Actually, it was you."

"Me? I never said anything about quitting."

Bette chuckled. "It's not what you said, it's what you do. You don't let people push you around. You didn't think your marriage was working, so you left. You have these...spells, attacks, whatever they are, and you don't let it stop you. You just keep going."

"Sorry to burst your bubble, but my marriage was on the rocks for a long time before I had the courage to walk out. It was when Christopher accused me of faking my attacks just to get his attention that finished it for me. That and the fact that I'm pretty sure he was cheating on me with his grad assistant."

"He cheated on you? That's awful."

"But here's what's worse. I didn't care. That's when I knew the marriage was dead."

"You're still the toughest person I know."

"I didn't feel so tough the other day at my father's memorial service. You were there. I fell apart, literally."

"You father just died and you felt responsible. Just the fact that you stood there and faced all those people the way you did. I could never have done that."

"Look where all that toughness got me. I'm divorced. Unemployed. I'm thirty years old and living with my mother. I have no social life and no prospects for getting a job or a date anytime soon. I'm no role model for you. Or anyone."

"You'll be fine. You just need some time."

"What about you? What are you gonna do now, go back to law school?"

Bette shuddered, like she just bit into a moldy peach. "That's the last thing I want to do. If I never see another lawyer again, that would be fine with me."

"You're not thinking of becoming a nun, are you?"

Bette looked dumbfounded. "A nun? Why would you ever think that?"

"You were in church in the middle of the day, in the middle of the week. Who does that but old ladies and nuns?"

She laughed. "I was talking to Father Bart over at the Episcopal church."

Hannah did another double-take. "You really are making major changes. Do your parents know that you've switched sides?"

"I'm still Catholic. Father Bart is more like a counselor than a clergyman. I've been seeing him for a few months. He's a terrific listener."

Hannah felt a little hurt that her best friend chose to confide in a random minister and not with her.

"You never told me you hated your job."

"You had enough to deal with. Your marriage broke up. Your father was dying. Those spells you've been having. I didn't want to burden you with my troubles."

"Did you tell him that you quit your job?"

"Actually, he's the one who encouraged me to do it."

"Did he also suggest how you might be able to earn a living?"

"He said to do what makes me happy."

"You love birdwatching and playing with your cats but I don't think there's much money in that."

"I was thinking of learning acupuncture. Or maybe becoming a massage therapist."

Hannah bolted upright, eyes wide, a look of revulsion on her face. "You want to spend your day touching naked strangers?" Then she changed her expression. "I'm sorry. That just took me by surprise. If that's what you want you should definitely go for it."

"I have another surprise for you."

"Okaaay."

"I think I'm a lesbian."

Hannah, who was just taking a bite of her pizza, spit cheese, sauce and pepperoni bits all over the table.

"Whoa! Quitting your job and cutting your hair is one thing. But you can't just decide to be gay. It's something you're born with."

Bette nodded. "I agree. I think I always knew it but I couldn't admit it to myself. I grew up believing that homosexuals were perverted sinners. That they burned in hell forever."

"So I guess you haven't mentioned any of this to your parents."

"I haven't said anything to anybody. Not even Father Bart. You're the first person I talked to about it."

"You really believe you're gay?"

"I'm pretty sure."

"Have you ever been with a woman?"

"You mean like sexually?"

Hannah smirked. "No. I mean to the movies." Then, a little too loudly. "Of course I mean sexually."

The people at the other tables put down their slices to stare at them.

Bette turned several shades of red, scrunched down into her seat and shook her head.

Hannah whispered, "Sorry. Is that what this new look is about?"

Bette nodded. "What do you think?"

"I like your hair short. It suits you."

"I meant about me being gay and all."

"If that's who you are, I think it's fine. As long as you don't hit on me."

"You?" Bette cringed. "You're not my type."

"You've been gay for fifteen minutes," Hannah said, "How do you even have a type?"

"I'm sorry. I didn't mean to insult you," she said sheepishly. "You're like my sister, I could never be attracted to you. And you're so tall. I think I'd want to be with someone more my size."

Hannah didn't know how she felt about all this. Intellectually, she had no problem with homosexuality. But the thought of being intimate with another woman skeeved her out. She wouldn't even go to a female gynecologist. And what about Bette telling her she didn't find her attractive? Was she insulted? Relieved? She decided it didn't matter what she felt. Her friend was going through an existential crisis and she had to be there for her.

"I'm sorry I snapped at you. It's just a lot to take in all at once."

"But what about you? You said you had something important to tell me."

"Oh yeah. With your bombshell, I almost forgot."

She told her friend about everything that happened that morning at the Refuge.

Bette turned even paler than usual. "That's awful. We have to do something."

"I intend to. I'm going back there tonight. I heard them

talking about something happening at that dock tonight at two. Some kind of delivery. I'm going to take my Nikon D 5500 with a zoom lens. It's great for low light photography. Maybe once people get a look at what they're really doing there, they'll cancel the airport project."

Bette looked horrified. "You can't go back there, it's too dangerous. You said they have guns. They'll shoot you."

"They couldn't find me in broad daylight. They have no chance in the middle of the night. I grew up playing hide and seek there. I know every tree, every shrub and every rock to hide behind."

Bette didn't say anything for several seconds. Hannah was waiting for round two of her friend trying to talk her out of it. Then Bette looked at her with determined eyes and said, "I want to come with you."

That was the last thing Hannah expected. She shook her head vehemently.

"Absolutely not. Like you said, it's too dangerous."

"If it's not too dangerous for you, it's not too dangerous for me."

"It's not the same. The Refuge is precious to me. It's my father's legacy. It's where I grew up. This is my fight. I won't put you at risk."

"You're wrong. It's my fight too. The Jamaica Bay Wildlife Refuge is one of my favorite places on earth. I love it. And really, in the last few years I've been there a lot more than you."

Hannah felt a stab of guilt, regret and remorse. Maybe if she stayed home and had been at the Refuge with her father none of this would have happened. But even if that wasn't the case, at least she would have had more time with him. Time she'll never get back. The best she could do now was fulfill her vow to protect the place they both loved.

"It's not the same. Sure you loved to go there. But I grew up there. It's part of me."

"This is about more than just my love for the Refuge. It's

about who I really am. If I can do this, maybe I really can change. Not just my clothes or my hairstyle or even my..." She brought her voice down to a whisper. "My sexuality. Please, Hannah, let me come with you."

Hannah was silent for a few seconds. "I'll pick you up at midnight. Wear dark clothes."

CHAPTER FOUR

What are they really doing at the Refuge? Was her father really poisoned? Could those two things be related? And what the hell is going on with Bette? Could she actually be gay or is this just a phase? Those were the questions swirling in Hannah's head during the twenty minute drive from East Northport back to Rocky Point. Maybe she'll get some answers when she goes to the Refuge later. But first she has to face Gilda and her mother.

When Hannah walked in, Olive was sitting on the sofa, knitting while humming softly. Lena snuggled contentedly at her side, gnawing a piece of rawhide. The old lab jumped off the couch to greet Hannah and present her with the gooey lump of leather.

Olive gazed up at her distractedly. "Oh hello, dear."

That certainly wasn't the response Hannah expected. No 'Where did you go?' 'Where's your father's urn?' 'Why didn't you tell me what you were going to do?' Maybe her mother didn't realize the urn was missing.

"I spread daddy's ashes in the East Pond. It's what he wanted."

Olive turned to Hannah. "I thought so. This morning when you and Axel's urn were both gone I was sure that was where you went."

"You're not mad?"

"Of course not. Like you said, it's what he wanted."

"But yesterday when Gilda made a big deal about having daddy buried with the family in Flushing Cemetery, you didn't disagree."

Olive grinned slyly, "I didn't agree either. Your father never liked that side of the family. Jamaica Bay is where he wanted to be. And where he should be."

"Why didn't you say so yesterday?"

Olive shook her head. "I didn't want to get into a big to-do with Gilda."

"What is it with you and Gilda? I've never seen you argue with her. Or even disagree with her. Why do you let her push you around like that? You never let anyone else treat you that way."

Olive let out a major sigh. Hannah thought she may have stepped over a boundary. She was waiting for her mother either to deny it or tell her that it was a long story and she didn't want to go into it.

Instead Olive said, "Growing up we fought all the time. Over chores. Or toys. Sometimes over nothing at all, as I imagine all sisters do." She paused for a moment. "Then things changed."

"What happened?"

"I was in eighth grade, she was in ninth. There was this boy that she had a big crush on, Jimmy McCreedy."

Hannah could never understand how her mother's brain worked. Sometimes Olive called her Helen and called her friend Helen Hannah, but the exact name of some obscure boy from sixty years ago she had no trouble with.

"So what happened?"

"It was the spring social. Gilda was sure Jimmy was going to ask her to go with him. She talked about him all the time. But he never did. He asked another girl. Gilda went to pieces."

"I don't understand why that's such a big deal. Stuff like that happens to everybody. It's part of growing up."

"The other girl was me."

"Oh."

"I didn't go, of course, but the damage was done."

"I guess Gilda was pretty mad, huh?"

Olive shook her head. "She didn't seem mad at all. That was the problem. She didn't cry. She didn't scream. She went into the bathroom and got my father's razor. It was the old kind, that the barbers use."

"A straight razor."

"That's right."

"What did she do, shave all her hair off in protest?"

"If only that was all she did. She cut herself up and down her arm ending at her wrist. There was blood everywhere. I was afraid she was going to bleed to death."

Hannah was stunned. "Oh my God!"

"Mother took her to the emergency room."

"What did they say?"

"Say? They didn't say anything. They bandaged her up and gave her an antibiotic."

"Nothing else? They didn't mention counseling? Therapy?"

Olive shook her head. "It was sixty years ago. There was no such thing as therapy."

Hannah wanted to say that of course therapy existed back then, but this wasn't the time to discuss the history of psychology.

"Grandma took Gilda home and that was it? Nothing else?"

Olive smiled wryly. "Oh yes, there was something else."

"What?"

"When mother got home she went and got father's garrison belt. Then she beat me so hard I couldn't sit down for days."

"Why? You didn't do anything wrong."

"Your grandmother thought differently. She said I led Jimmy on. That I was scheming to steal him from Gilda. That I was a cruel, selfish little hussy."

"I can't imagine you ever doing anything like that. Even as a young girl."

"I didn't. But it didn't matter. She made me put my hand on

the bible and swear that I'd never do anything to upset Gilda. She said that if she ever hurt herself again it would be on my head."

"And all these years later you still won't stand up to her?"

Olive shook her head forcefully. "I never have. Until today."

"What? Today? How?"

"When Gilda saw that you took the urn she became very angry. Out of her head, really. She started yelling and carrying on, calling you a wild child. A spoiled, selfish, inconsiderate brat. I told her to pipe down. I said I knew you were going to take the urn to Jamaica Bay and scatter Axel's ashes there."

"But you didn't know."

"Of course I did. I could see it in your eyes."

"That must have really set Gilda off."

Olive smiled and nodded. "Oh yes. Especially after I told her that I thought it was the right thing to do."

"What did she say?"

"She called me a traitor to the family. She said you were a bad seed. A black sheep. That her Catherine was a vice president and Philip's a doctor and you're a thirty-year-old vagrant who will never amount to anything."

"What did you say?"

"I kept quiet for the longest time, hoping she would run out of steam. But she kept ranting and raving and she wouldn't stop. Finally I couldn't stand it anymore so I told her to dry up and blow away."

Hannah suppressed a smile. She knew that this was a very serious thing for Olive to say, as close to a curse as she ever got. She bit down on her cheeks to keep herself from giggling. When she was sure she wasn't going to burst out, she said, "Where's Gilda now?"

It wasn't like her aunt to miss an opportunity to put Hannah down.

"In the middle of her tantrum, Gilda noticed that the can of cat food she leaves for Perry's breakfast was still full. She lets him out every night. I keep telling her it's not safe for him out here.

That there are raccoons and stray dogs and all kinds of other wild animals roaming around at night that could hurt Perry. But she never listens. She says he's street smart. That he always comes back in the morning. And he always did. Until this morning.

"Gilda became frantic with worry. She forgot all about me and you and the urn, and started running around the house with the cat food can, opening all the closets, shouting 'Perry, Perry. Where are you?' When she was sure he wasn't here she went out looking for him."

Olive looked over at the clock above the fireplace. "That was a while ago."

"You don't think she'd do anything to hurt herself, do you?"

Olive shook her head. "Oh no. Not after all this time."

"I bet it freaked her out that you finally stood up to her."

Olive allowed herself a small smile. "You could say that."

Hannah realized she was still wearing her backpack. She took it off, removed the urn and carefully placed it back on the shelf over the fireplace. She hoped no one would notice the missing lid.

"They made quite a few changes at the Refuge. Have you seen them?"

Olive shook her head. "The only time I've been near there was for your father's ceremony yesterday. And that's on the other side of Cross Bay Boulevard so it's not really inside the Refuge." She paused for a second. "What kind of changes?"

"They put a big iron gate in front of the entrance and built a boat dock at the end of East Pond. And they expanded the footpath. Now it's a gravel road."

"Why would they do that? There are no cars allowed."

"There are now. I saw tire tracks."

Olive shook her head disdainfully. "I don't like the sound of that."

"I didn't like it much either."

As Olive dabbed her cheek with a crumpled tissue, Hannah decided that she wouldn't say anything about the scary guy with the big gun or the weaselly woman who dissed her father. She didn't want to make her mother any more upset than she already was.

As she walked to her room she said, "I'm going out with my friend Bette later tonight, so don't wait up for me, okay?"

Olive forced a smile. "That's perfectly fine. A young woman your age should get out. Have a nice time."

CHAPTER FIVE

Hannah picked Bette up a little after midnight. Her friend spent the entire drive to Jamaica Bay huddled in the Jeep's passenger seat, head bowed, quivering, sighing and chewing on her fingernails. Hannah was too busy navigating the twists and turns of the Southern State to notice Bette's state of dread. Even though there were fewer drivers, they made up for it by being even more reckless. And half of them were probably drunk. It didn't help that most of the lights on the parkway were out.

Hannah stopped at the same spot on Cross Bay Boulevard where she had parked earlier that day. The only illumination was from the half-moon shrouded by wispy clouds. The macabre hoots, cries, squeals and chirps from owls, frogs, crickets and other night creatures added to the Haunted Mansion atmospherics.

"Are you sure you want to do this?" Hannah said, "You look like you're ready to throw up."

"I'm okay," Bette said. But clearly she wasn't.

"You wanna know how you could really help me?"

Bette looked up.

"By being my getaway driver."

"What do you mean?"

"Stay in the car and wait so if we have to make a quick escape we'll be ready to go."

"Are you sure?" Bette said, trying not to look as relieved as she felt. "You're not just saying that cause you think I'm afraid? If you want me to come with you I will."

"No, really. This is better. I can go in, take my pictures and get out a lot quicker by myself. With two people, there's twice as much chance of getting caught."

"If that's what you want. Text me when you're on your way back."

Hannah shook her head. "I can't. Cell phones don't work here. My father read somewhere that the electromagnetic radiation from cell towers might be harmful to birds. He made sure that no towers were erected anywhere near here."

She handed Bette her keys. "Remember, as soon as you see me coming, start the car and be ready to move."

Hannah grabbed her camera off the back seat and was out the door. She was dressed all in black. Black leggings, a black sweatshirt and black Chuck Taylors. Her long, wavy blonde hair was crammed under a black watch cap.

She used her phone flashlight to find the bandana she tied to the fence that morning. Once through, she began to carefully make her way to the East Pond, keeping close to the dense trees and shrubs that hugged the perimeter. Minutes later she was crouched, camera in hand, behind a bushy Russian olive tree about fifty feet from the dock, where a flatbed barge was moored. It was stacked with what looked like hay bales, each about the size of a steamer trunk. They were shrink-wrapped in green plastic. They're smuggling drugs, Hannah thought.

Grabowski was loading the bales onto an all terrain vehicle, it looked like the one her father used to move heavy items like 50-pound bags of fertilizer around the Refuge.

A man she'd never seen before stood, arms folded, watching. Occasionally he would write something in a notebook. Though he was dressed in civilian clothes, a dark turtleneck and slacks, his bearing was military. Like someone who was used to giving orders and having them instantly obeyed. And the way Grabowski responded added to that impression.

Hannah clicked furiously with her Nikon, shooting the barge, the bales, the ATV, Grabowski and the man in the turtleneck.

Dawson showed up. She walked over to the turtleneck guy and started talking animatedly, pointing back towards the entrance. A minute later he strode off.

Grabowski loaded the rest of the bundles onto the ATV. Then he and Dawson got in and drove towards the front of the Refuge as the barge headed back across Jamaica Bay.

Hannah waited until everyone was gone before she started back. Her legs were numb. Was it the Weakness or from crouching for so long? She stood up gingerly, grabbing a tree branch for support. After a few minutes the numbness subsided. She made her way back to the gap in the fence. She pushed the camera carefully through, then squeezed through herself.

She waved as she approached the Jeep but it didn't start. As she got closer she couldn't see anyone inside. Maybe Bette was asleep on the front seat. She opened the door. No Bette. She checked the back. Nothing.

Hannah waited in the car for ten minutes. What the hell happened? Did Dawson and Grabowski grab her? Could some roving street gang have taken her? Hannah told herself that there was probably some reasonable explanation why Bette wasn't there and to stop concocting these horror show scenarios. Whatever happened to her, there's nothing you can do about it right now.

Her phone was useless, thanks to her father's cell tower phobia, and she had no idea how to hot-wire a car. The closest subway station was a couple of miles up the road across the Cross Bay Boulevard bridge.

She was tired, cold and tense. Her legs ached. Her back throbbed. But even if she made it to the subway, what then? She could take it to the Long Island Rail Road Jamaica station but she wouldn't have enough money left for the train to Port Jeff. Or she could sit in the car and wait. For what? For Bette? Hannah doubted she'd be back. For help? Not likely.

She hid her camera under the seat and started walking toward the bridge. After ten minutes she heard a vehicle coming up behind her and moved to the side. It was an old pickup truck. It pulled over a few feet in front of her. She balled her fists. Whoever these guys were, they weren't going to get her without a fight.

A man climbed out of the truck. He was tall and slim with a slight limp. She steeled herself for a possible attack. But as he ambled towards her she could see that he was smiling genially and looked to be in his fifties.

"Do you need some help there miss?"

She didn't let her guard down. She had seen too many TV shows where the bad guy offers to help and the next thing you know the girl is bound and gagged in the back of a panel van.

But the voice seemed familiar, as did the face.

Hannah squinted, trying to focus.

"Tom? Tom McCaffrey? Is that you?"

"Yeah, I'm McCaffrey. Who are you?"

"It's Hannah Johansson."

He walked closer and peered at her face.

"Hannah? What are you doing out here so late at night?"

"It's a long story. The short version is I went to the Jamaica Bay Refuge to do some night photography. When I got back to my car I couldn't find my keys. They must have fallen out of my pocket. I'm on my way to the subway." She paused for a second. "How do you happen to be out here?"

"I work the swing shift at one of the cargo depots at the airport. I'm just on my way home." He paused for a brief moment. "The subway is still a ways away. Where's your car?"

"About half-a-mile back."

"Why don't we see if we can get her started?"

"It's so late. And you must be exhausted. I'll be okay on the train."

"It's not safe on the subway this time of night. Besides, it's not every day a guy my age gets to help a beautiful damsel in distress."

Hannah didn't know McCaffrey all that well. He always seemed like a good guy. Her father liked him but who knows. After a slight hesitation she walked with him to his truck.

In less than two minutes they were parked behind the Jeep. McCaffrey reached behind his seat for a toolbox. He grabbed a screwdriver, a flashlight and a piece of copper wire.

Hannah watched as he unscrewed things on and under the steering column. He pulled something down behind the ignition switch that looked like a knob attached to a bunch of cables. He fiddled with the knob and all the dashboard dials lit up.

"Is that bad?" Hannah said. "The lights went on but it didn't start."

"We're almost there," McCaffrey said. He got out of the car and popped the hood.

"Once I find the starter relay you should be good to go."

He pulled the top off the fuse box and inserted the ends of the copper wire into two slots. The engine cranked twice, then started.

"There you go," he said, beaming. "That should get you home."

Hannah was amazed. "I can't believe it. Thank you so much."

"To turn it off just turn that knob counterclockwise."

"That's so awesome. Where did you learn how to do that?"

"I was a cop for twenty years. When you're out on the streets you learn to do all kinds of things."

"I didn't know you were a policeman."

"Sure was. Your uncle Joe was my lieutenant when I started out. That's how I first met your dad."

"Tom. You're a lifesaver." She leaned over and kissed him on the cheek.

"Happy to do it. I was very sorry to hear about your dad. He was a terrific guy. I wish I could have made it to the service but I was on a double shift. Give my best to your mom."

He turned and climbed into his truck.

CHAPTER SIX

Hannah stood at the edge of the dock, her wrists lashed behind her. Three sharks circled hungrily, churning the water below. Grabowski in his black SWAT gear, looking like a slovenly Darth Vader, glared at her malevolently as he aimed his assault rifle at her heart.

Dawson, chewing furiously at a huge wad of gum, sounding like the Wicked Witch of the West, said, "I told you to mind your own business but you wouldn't listen. Now it's time to..." Dawson's voice morphed into Olive's. "Wake up. It's after ten."

Hannah opened her eyes to see her mother standing over her.

"What time did you get home? I waited until almost one o'clock."

"You didn't have to wait up for me, ma. I'm not in high school anymore."

"I know, but I just figured..." Olive often drifted off in the middle of a sentence. Most of the time it was super annoying but at the moment Hannah really didn't want to know what her mother just figured.

"Your friend Bette called a couple of times."

Hannah bolted up. "When? What did she say? How did she sound? Is she all right?"

"She sounded the same as always. As a matter of fact, she wanted to know how you were." Olive cocked an eye at Hannah. "Where did you two go last night? I thought you girls were out for a night on the town."

"We went back to the Refuge."

"Back to Jamaica Bay? In the middle of the night? Why on earth...?"

"Listen ma, there are things going on there. Bad things. A scary looking guy with a machine gun patrolling the place like it was Fort Knox. Mysterious deliveries in the middle of the night. The nasty witch in charge, who didn't know anything about the Refuge or everything that you and dad accomplished there, said that they were trying to decide whether or not it was feasible expand the airport there."

Olive folded her arms in front of her. "If that's what they want, there's nothing we can do to stop them."

"That's true, except I don't think that's what they're doing. I told you about the boat dock and the gravel road where the footpath used to be, remember?"

"It could be they're using the road and the dock to bring in building supplies."

"Okay. But why do they need an armed guard? And who gets deliveries at one o'clock in the morning?" She shook her head solemnly. "There's something going on there that has nothing to do with the airport. I'm sure of it."

"What else could they possibly be doing?"

"I don't know, but I'm going to keep digging until I find out." She didn't want to mention the drugs.

Olive wagged a finger at Hannah. "You'll do no such thing. You're not a well woman. You have those fainting spells or seizures or whatever they are. And you've been in a terrible state of mind since you've been back. I can't remember the last time you said two civil words to me. It's not my fault that you and Christopher had a falling out. Or that you have these attacks. Or that your father died. But you're treating me like it is. And it's not fair."

Tears streamed down her cheeks. "My whole life has been for you and your father. Now I feel like I've lost both of you."

Hannah ran over to her mother and engulfed her in a tight hug. "I'm so sorry, ma. You're right. I've been a horrible bitch. My life is falling apart and I'm taking it out on you."

For a long moment they stood, silently weeping, snuggled in each other's arms. Finally Olive said, "That's all right, dear." She patted Hannah gently on her shoulder.

Through muffled sobs, Hannah said, "It's been so awful. These stupid attacks. Christopher turning out to be a cheating bastard. Daddy getting sick. And to top it all off, I fall on top of him, knock him down the steps and kill him. Gilda's right. I'm a total failure."

Olive stepped back and said, "You certainly are not! None of this was your fault. You can't blame yourself for what happened to your father. You had no control. It was God's hand that pushed you."

"Oh, ma. I love you." Hannah plopped down on the bed.

Olive said, "Promise me you won't get involved in whatever is happening at Jamaica Bay. It's not our concern anymore."

"But..."

"Please. I don't want to worry every time you leave the house."

Hannah sighed. "All right. I promise."

Olive nodded contentedly. "That's good."

After a few seconds Hannah said, "I better call Bette and let her know I'm okay."

"Why don't you just wait till she gets here?"

"She's coming here? When?"

"She said she had to come out this way and asked if it was okay to stop by for a few minutes. I told her to stay for lunch but she said she had an appointment at 12:30."

Hannah stretched her arms over her head and yawned prodigiously. "I really need a shower. If she gets here before I'm done, could you entertain her for a few minutes?"

"Our course." Olive shuffled out of the room.

After luxuriating longer than usual in the steamy stream, Hannah felt ready to rejoin the human race. She threw on a pair of comfortable jeans and a beige cotton top.

Bette was on the sofa in the living room, a cup of tea and a plate of Oreos on the coffee table in front of her. She was talking animatedly to Olive, who was in the wing chair next to her. Bette ran to Hannah, threw her arms around her and cried, "I'm so sorry. I thought I could help but all I did was make things worse. I left you stranded out there in the dark. Can you ever forgive me?"

Hannah patted her friend gently on the shoulder. "I'm fine." She sat cross-legged on the big ottoman in front of her father's club chair facing her friend, who sank back down on the sofa. "I was worried about YOU. The car was there but you were weren't. I didn't know what to think. Where did you go?"

"You were gone about a half-hour when a big SUV, I think it was a Hummer, double-parked next to me. A man got out. He was tall. Even taller than you. When he came up to the car I got so scared." She shuddered. "I closed the window and locked all the doors. I thought he was going to murder me right there."

Olive gasped and said, "Oh my."

Hannah said, "Go on."

"He didn't look like a mugger. He was clean shaven. His hair was combed. Actually, he was sorta nice looking, except for that scar."

"What kind of scar?"

"Across his eyebrow. Like he'd been in a car accident."

"What was he wearing?"

"A sweater. Turtleneck I think."

"What else?"

"I can't be sure. It was very dark and I was so scared."

"Wait here," Hannah said and went to her room. She came back a minute later with her camera and held the monitor screen up to Bette. It was one of the shots she took at the Refuge. "Is this the guy?"

Bette leaned in. Stared at it. "It could be. Who is he?"

"He was there last night supervising the loading. What happened next?"

He knocked on the window and flashed a wallet with a badge and an I.D. with his picture on it."

"What did it say?"

"I have no idea. I could hardly think. And he only held it up for a few seconds. I was so relieved that he wasn't going to murder me I didn't really pay attention to it."

"Then what?"

Bette made a circular movement in the air with her finger. "He made a sign like this for me to open the window."

"Did you open it?"

"Of course. He said that I was trespassing on restricted government property."

Hannah shook her head. "That's a lie. You didn't believe him, did you?"

"I sorta did," Bette said contritely. "Then he said he wanted to bring me in for questioning. He told me to get into his car. So that's what I did. "

"What's the matter with you!" Hannah yelled. "You get into a strange man's car on a deserted street in the middle of the night? A ten-year-old girl knows better than that."

"I know," she said meekly. It looked like she was about to cry.

Hannah softened her voice. "Okay, now you're in his car. Did it look like a police car? Did it have one of those two-way radios? Big antenna sticking out of the back?"

"I don't know. I was in a fog."

"What did he say?"

"He kept asking me questions. What was my name? What was I doing there? Who did I work for?"

"What did you say?"

"For a long time I didn't say anything. I just sat there whimpering. Finally I told him I was waiting for a friend."

"You ratted me out!?"

"Oh no. I never mentioned your name. I said I had a friend who was a photographer. That you were trying to get some pictures of nocturnal birds. I rattled off the names of some so he would think I wasn't lying."

"He didn't ask you for my name?"

Bette shook her head. "He didn't believe me. He called me a liar and a traitor. He said that there was a top secret operation going on inside the Refuge and I was committing a treasonous act. That's when I lost it completely. I thought I was going to prison for the rest of my life. That they'd lock me up in Guantanamo with terrorists and rapists and murderers. I was screaming, crying, I'm surprised you didn't hear me from inside the Refuge."

"What then?"

"He tried to calm me down but it was no use. He finally said maybe I was just in the wrong place at the wrong time."

"Just like that? One minute he's ready to send you to prison for life, the next, it's all good? That doesn't make sense."

"Probably not. But that's what happened. Then he drove to the Kew Gardens station. He told me to go home and never to go anywhere near the Jamaica Bay Wildlife Refuge again."

Olive said, "You poor dear. How awful!"

Hannah said, "Was it the subway station or the Long Island Rail Road?"

"It was the railroad."

"How did he know you lived on Long Island? Did you tell him?"

Bette shrugged. "I don't remember telling him. Maybe I did. I was so scared I don't know what I was saying." She paused, took a breath. "But what about you? It wasn't until I got home that I realized I still had your keys in my pocket and you'd be stranded out there. I had visions of him going back and arresting you. I was so relieved when I called this morning and your mom said you made it home."

Olive turned to Hannah. "How DID you get home?"

"Do you remember Tom McCaffrey?"

"Oh yes. An Irish fellow with a thick head of curly hair. He and your father went fishing together sometimes."

"That's him. What a sweet guy. He was driving home from his job, he works nights at the airport, and he saw me walking up Cross Bay Boulevard."

Olive looked horrified. "In the middle of the night all by yourself? That street is dangerous. You could have been killed."

"There was more chance of me being killed if I stayed where I was. I figured my best bet was to take the subway to Jamaica Station and take the train home. That's where I was headed when he saw me."

"He drove you all the way back here from Howard Beach?"

"No. He drove me back to the car and managed to get the engine started."

"That was very kind of him. You should send him a thank you note."

"Sure ma, soon. By the way, where's Aunt Gilda?"

"She said she was going out for some fresh air but I think she's searching for Perry again."

Bette, who had three cats of her own, said, "That's the Siamese, right?"

Hannah said, "Yeah. Gilda's a lot nicer to that cat than she ever is to me."

"What happened to him?"

"He went out and hasn't come home."

Olive said, "It's been more than a day. Gilda's very concerned."

"Oh I wouldn't worry," Bette said. "He's probably out exploring. One of my guys was gone for almost a week before he got tired of eating out of garbage cans. I'm sure he'll be back in a day or two."

"I hope so," Hannah said. "If anything happens to that cat, Gilda will be even more horrible, if that's possible."

CHAPTER SEVEN

Hannah sprawled, exhausted, on the living room sofa, staring at her father's ashless urn on the mantel shelf, thinking about the ash heap she made of her life since the day she walked in on Christopher and his graduate assistant huddled on the couch in their Boston apartment.

They weren't quite quick enough as they unclinched and pretended they were working. But their disheveled clothes and flushed faces would have given them away in any case.

Christopher, trying to brazen it out, said, "Hi babe. You don't look good. You okay?"

"I had another attack. My muscles gave out while I was crossing Commonwealth Avenue. It was pretty bad."

He gestured towards the young woman sitting next to him. "You know Tracy Park, my grad assistant. We were trying to get a jumpstart on these exams."

A few years younger than Hannah, she was tall and willowy with long, silky black hair and black jeans that clung to her like they were shrink wrapped.

"I'm sure we can finish tomorrow," Tracy said, as she hurriedly gathered up the blue exam booklets that were scattered across the coffee table, dumped them in an oversized tote bag and scurried out of the apartment, mumbling garbled goodbyes.

Christopher said, “How are you now?”

“I’ll live,” Hannah snarled.

She tromped into the bedroom and slammed the door. She was livid. At Christopher. At Tracy. But most of all, at herself. Whatever she had with Christopher had died months earlier. They were now more like roommates than lovers. When she first started having her Weakness attacks he didn’t seem to care. He told her to drink more water. Go to sleep earlier. He even accused her of making it up to get more attention. She should have walked out then but she didn’t want to add another failure to her list. Then when he started spending more and more time with his grad assistant she suspected they were doing more than grading papers. But she wasn’t sure. She thought maybe she was just being paranoid. Now she was positive.

When she emerged an hour later she was wearing a backpack and carrying a suitcase. With damp eyes but a calm voice she said, “I’m moving back to Long Island.”

He put down the book he was reading, stared up at her, opened his mouth slightly, then closed it again. After a few pensive seconds he said, “If that’s what you want.”

“If you can send the rest of my things to my parents’ house in Rocky Point, I’ll pay for the shipping,” she said, trying very hard to keep her voice from cracking.

She walked out. She turned the corner, leaned against the side of a building and cried. After a few minutes she wiped her tears away and walked to the Kenmore station of the T, Boston’s subway system. She took the train to the Amtrak station, then another train to Bridgeport, where she got on the the ferry across Long Island Sound to Port Jefferson, and then took a taxi from Port Jeff to Rocky Point, a journey of close to six hours. She arrived at her parents’ front door, exhausted, ashamed and depressed.

From that moment she’d been careening down a bottomless

rabbit hole of self-pity, self-doubt and self-recrimination. And dragging the people she cared for with her. She decided that this is where it ends. No more looking back at what she could have done or should have done differently with Christopher. Or how she could have avoided knocking her father down the stairs. Or trying to figure out what was really going on at the Refuge. It was time to move on. The first step would be to try to rebuild some badly damaged bridges.

Making peace with her mother was easy. Making amends with Gilda would be tougher. Even when she was a little girl her aunt always seemed to have it in for her. Hannah wasn't sorry she scattered her dad's ashes in the East Pond, but perhaps she could have handled it better. She could have stressed to her aunt that it was her father's dying wish and that she promised him she'd fulfill it. Instead she snuck out in the dark like a two-bit second-story man.

The sound of heavy footfalls trudging up the front steps told Hannah that her chance to put things right with her aunt had arrived.

Gilda opened the front door, looked around and said, "Has he come back?"

"Who?"

"Perry, of course."

"No. Not yet."

"I'm very concerned. He never stays out this long."

"I'm sure he'll show up any minute."

Gilda looked up at the urn, grimaced, then said, "Where's Olive?"

"She's over at the Knights of Columbus hall at a senior citizens club meeting. I can take you over there if you like."

"I'm very capable of driving myself if I were so inclined," she said sharply. "The last thing I'd want to do would be to listen to a bunch of old hens brag about their grandchildren and complain about their aches and pains."

Hannah said, "Aunt Gilda, I want to apologize for sneaking out of here this morning with my father's urn."

"Your mother said you went to the Jamaica Bay Refuge to dump Axel's ashes in the swamp there."

Hannah winced at 'dump' and 'swamp' but she wouldn't let herself be drawn into another argument.

"I know the Refuge wasn't your favorite place," she said, keeping her voice steady and forcing a slight smile. "But my father loved it more than anywhere in the world. It was his fervent wish that his ashes be scattered in the East Pond. I'm sure you can understand that."

Gilda folded her arms and scowled. "I understand what it means to be a close-knit family. I'm not sure you and your mother do."

"That's not fair," Hannah said. "Being a family means a lot more than spending eternity in the same pile of dirt as your dead relatives. It's caring about each other and supporting each other while you're alive. Not judging each other and snapping at everyone who doesn't agree with you or live up to your unreasonable expectations."

Hannah had to do a little more work on her bridge-building skills.

Gilda bristled. "Is it unreasonable to assume that a woman of your age and supposed intelligence could secure a decent job? Or maintain a solid relationship? You're flighty. You never follow through on anything. You quit your basketball team. You abandoned photography, which was supposed to be your passion. You went to three different schools before you finally graduated."

"I followed through on my promise to my father."

Before Gilda could answer, Olive walked in holding a package. It looked like a large shoe box, clumsily wrapped in brown paper.

"I found this at the side door. Was anybody expecting a delivery?"

Hannah shook her head. "Nothing I can remember. Who is it addressed to?"

Olive looked closely at the box, turning it over. "That's odd," she said, perplexed. "There's no name on it. Or address either."

"Someone from the neighborhood probably dropped it off. Maybe it's something of daddy's that they thought we should have. Open it. There's probably a card or a note inside."

Olive painstakingly removed the wrapping. The top was sealed with tape. "Can somebody get me a scissors?"

"Give me the box," Hannah said. She took it from her mother, put it on the coffee table, ripped the tape off and pulled up the top.

Then she screamed.

Olive and Gilda ran over to her.

Olive looked in the box and cried, "Oh my God!"

When Gilda saw what was in it she gasped, shrieked and fell back on the couch, clutching her heart.

Inside the box was the lifeless body of Gilda's cat Perry. A rope was tied around its neck. In the corner of the box, tucked under Perry's legs, was a multicolored disk-shaped object about six inches in diameter. Hannah recognized it instantly. It was the lid of her father's urn. She reached in, grabbed it and shoved it in her pocket.

Gilda was shaking and panting heavily as she lay awkwardly on the couch, her vacant eyes staring blankly at the ceiling. Hannah thought there might soon be another memorial service in her future.

After what seemed like hours but was actually a little more than a minute, Gilda pulled herself upright. As she gathered her thoughts her face clenched angrily.

Pointing at Hannah, she howled, "This is your fault. My precious kitty is dead because of you. You killed your father and now you killed my beautiful Perry. You're evil! You were a horrid little girl and you've grown to be a despicable woman." She turned towards Olive. "I'm sorry but it's true."

Now it was Olive's turn to explode.

"How dare you say such a thing about my daughter in my house!" she screamed. "If anyone's evil, it's you. You never cared about anyone but yourself. You're a selfish, self-centered old shrew. No one can stand you. Not even your own daughter. Why do you think she moved all the way to Connecticut? To get as far away from you as she could."

"I don't have to listen to this," Gilda snapped back. "No wonder she turned out the way she did. Look who raised her."

Olive yelled, "Get out of my house!"

"With pleasure," she sneered.

A couple of minutes later, swinging her small suitcase, Gilda marched to the front door.

"I shall never set foot inside this house again," she declared as she slammed it behind her.

Hannah and Olive slumped back in their chairs, emotionally drained. After a few seconds, Hannah said, "Thanks for sticking up for me."

Olive sat up, her face still crimson with rage.

"Who does that Gilda think she is. The nerve! I should have given her a piece of my mind a long time ago."

Hannah was quiet for a couple of seconds, then she said, "Did you see what else was in that box?"

"You mean the rope?"

Hannah pulled the lid out of her pocket and held it up. "No, this."

Olive squinted at it. "What is it?"

Hannah handed it to her mother. Olive stared at it. Turned it over. Held it up to the light. Then shook her head. "I have no idea."

"Look over at the mantel."

Olive looked, then shrugged.

"It's the lid to daddy's funeral urn."

Olive stared at the lid, glanced over at the urn, then back at the lid. "My God, you're right. How in the world did it get inside that box?"

"I dropped it on the dock at the Refuge when I scattered daddy's ashes. That horrible woman, Dawson, picked it up."

"I don't understand."

"They did it, Dawson and her big ape henchman. They killed Perry."

"You think those people you saw at Jamaica Bay killed Gilda's cat?" Olive shook her head vehemently. "I don't believe it."

"There's no other explanation. I saw her pick up the lid. If she or one of her stooges didn't kill the cat, how did it get in there?"

"I don't know. But I can't believe that those people would do such a thing. You said they're doing some kind of airport study."

"I told you that's what they said they were doing. I'd bet my life they're lying."

"So who are they?"

"Spies. Terrorists. Gangsters. Drug dealers. Whoever they are, they're up to no good. I've seen something on TV about sleeper cells. Enemy agents who come here and live as Americans. They raise their kids to get government jobs and steal all our secrets."

"I think you're letting your imagination run away with you. I can't believe that there's a sinister plot going on at Jamaica Bay. I'm sure there's a very logical explanation."

"What?"

"I don't know."

"I don't know either. What I do know is I definitely saw that Dawson woman pick up the lid. When I went back last night, they were getting some kind of mysterious shipment from across the bay. Probably from the airport. If you don't believe me, I have the pictures to prove it."

"Of course I believe you. But I'm sure they had a legitimate reason."

"Tell me."

"When we were there your father would get deliveries all the time."

"They came by truck during the day through the front entrance. Not in a barge in the dead of night."

"Things get delivered at night all the time. My friend Dotty lives near one of those big stores, Home Junction."

"Home Depot."

"Yes, that's it. She says they get deliveries there at all hours. It keeps her up half the night."

"Even if you're right, that doesn't explain what happened to Bette."

Olive shrugged.

Hannah said, "I'm sure that the guy who picked her up checked the license plate of the Jeep and found out it was registered to me. They had my name, address, everything. And now they send us the lid back, along with Gilda's dead cat, to make sure we know they know."

"What reason would they have to do that to poor Perry. Gilda had nothing to do with any of this."

"How could they know he was Gilda's cat. I bet they were watching the house, saw the cat come out and figured he was mine."

"Even if that's true, I still don't see the purpose."

"To send me a warning."

"For what?"

"To stay away from the Refuge."

Olive thought for a few seconds, then said "If you're right and it is a warning, I think you should take it seriously."

"I'm taking it very seriously."

"You'll forget the whole thing?"

"That's exactly what I intended to do. But now I'm not sure what to do."

"You shouldn't do anything. You don't even know if they're doing anything wrong."

"I know they killed Perry."

"You don't know any such thing. But if you really believe that, report it to the police. It's their job to deal with that kind of thing. Not yours."

"What would I tell them? That I was scattering my father's ashes in Jamaica Bay and I saw a woman pick up a lid from my father's funeral urn and the next time I saw it, it was in a box with my aunt's dead cat? And by the way, I think there's something sinister going on there, I'm not sure what, but I think you should investigate it."

Olive nodded. "All right, you made your point. It's not a job for the police. But it's not a job for you either. It's time for you to get on with your life."

"That's just what I intend to do."

"Good." Olive put a finger in the air. "With all this excitement I forgot to tell you your cousin Phil called."

"What did he say?"

"I can never understand what that boy is talking about. Something about taxes on a screen. Is he helping you with your income tax return?"

"He's not doing anything with my taxes. Are you sure he didn't say tox screen?"

"Tax, tox, what's the difference?"

"It's a big difference. What about it?"

"He said it was positive. Does that mean you're getting a refund?"

CHAPTER EIGHT

Hannah screamed at the dead phone in her hand. "Phil, where the hell are you?"

She'd been calling for a half-hour and getting his too-cool-for-the-room voicemail message. "Phil. Talk."

When they were kids, Hannah thought her cousin's James Dean persona was cool. As a grownup, it's annoying.

"Phil, it's Hannah," she said the first time she called. "I need to talk to you right away. It's about my father's tox screen and what's going on at the Refuge. Please call me as soon as you can."

Ten minutes later with more urgency. "Phil, call me. It's very important."

The next few times she didn't leave a message, just hung up and growled.

In between calls she looked at the Refuge photos on the viewfinder of her camera. She deleted more than half. A lot of shots were redundant. Many more were blurry, dark or just not very compelling. She wound up with a half-dozen usable pictures of Dawson, Grabowski, the guy in the black turtleneck, the barge and the green bundles.

Back when this was her grandmother's house, she and her cousins spent every summer here with their mothers while their fathers worked in the city and drove out on weekends. Phil and his brothers stayed in the room that was now hers. It was next to the side door, far away from the other bedrooms so that the boys' boisterous shenanigans wouldn't bother anyone else.

When Hannah's parents bought the place from her grandma they made it her room, even though she hadn't lived with them for years. But it was more like a shrine. They furnished it with everything from her old bedroom at Jamaica Bay. Her bed, her desk, her dresser and her night table. On the walls were framed posters of *Love Actually, Legally Blonde* and *Friends*. They even put out all her old swimming medals, basketball trophies and National Honor Society certificates. It reminded them of the little girl they adored who grew up to be an athletic and academic standout at John Adams High School. It reminded Hannah of all her failures, screw-ups and false starts since then.

She spent the next twenty minutes pacing, cleaning and chewing on her cuticles. Finally the phone rang.

"Phil, is that you?"

"What's going on? Are you all right?"

"I'm fine. You got the tox screen back?"

"Didn't Aunt Ollie tell you?"

"She thought you were helping me with my tax return."

He chuckled. "Good old Ollie."

"It was positive?"

"Yeah, for methyl iodide."

"I have no idea what that is."

"It's a heavy duty insecticide. Like Raid on steroids. Not a nice chemical. Did Uncle Axe ever use it?"

"I have no idea. Was it harmful to birds? He would never use anything that could hurt the birds."

"I don't know about birds, but it's bad for humans."

"How bad?"

"Very. But get this. Methyl iodide poisoning is what they call a stroke mimic."

"A what?"

"A lot of the symptoms are the same as a stroke. Slurred speech, partial paralysis, seizures. I can see how they got it wrong."

"I knew it. Those bastards murdered him."

"Whoa! Slow down," he shouted into the phone. "All we know right now is that it was in his bloodstream. We won't know how much until I get the full results. Anyway, everybody loved Uncle Axe. Who'd want to murder him?"

"The same people who killed Gilda's cat."

"Somebody killed Aunt Gillie's cat?" Phil cried. After a couple of seconds, he said, "That's awful. But what does that have to do with your father?"

"Let me start from the beginning."

She told him about all the strange and sinister goings-on at the Refuge. About Bette's brief abduction. And about dropping the lid at the dock, seeing Dawson pick it up and having it show up the next day in a cardboard box next to Perry's rigor mortised body.

After she was done, she said, "I don't know what to do."

"You've done all you can. Nothing's gonna bring your father back. My advice is to just forget about it."

"That's what I thought. Now I'm not sure. I just told my mother I was going to move on with my life. That whatever they're doing at the Refuge is none of my business."

"I think you should stick with that."

"My father's murder is my business."

"We don't know if he was murdered."

"There's no way he could have been accidentally poisoned. He was the most cautious person I ever met. Especially with dangerous chemicals. And you said it wasn't a stroke."

"I said I didn't think it was a stroke. That's far from a solid diagnosis."

"It's a better diagnosis than he got at the hospital."

"Even if I'm right, it isn't nearly enough to prove it was murder."

"It's enough for me. I'm going to the police."

"I work with the police. I have a pretty good idea of what they need to start a murder investigation. And this isn't it."

"What do they need?"

"For starters, you need to have a suspicious death. Uncle Axe was diagnosed with a stroke. Then he had an accident that in his weakened state proved fatal. Nothing suspicious there. The only thing out of the ordinary is that he died after you knocked him down the stairs. If the police investigate anybody, it'll be you."

"What about the whatsis iodide?"

"He worked with chemicals for thirty years. They'll conclude that it was either an accident or long-term exposure."

"Then their conclusions will be wrong. If he had poison in his body somebody put it there."

"All right. Go to the police. Maybe that's what you need to get all this out of your system."

"Thanks, Phil. I knew I could count on you to agree with me."

"But I don't necessarily agree..."

She hung up before he could finish.

CHAPTER NINE

Hannah had no idea what to expect as she walked up the marble steps of the Howard Beach police station. From the outside, the entrance reminded her of her old middle school, an austere limestone and brick building whose better days were behind it. But instead of black and yellow school buses parked out front, there were a half-dozen blue and white police cruisers. The large gold letters on the scarred oak doors said, 'Welcome to the 106th Precinct.' The dingy, ill-lit lobby featuring peeling paint and a bulletin board crammed with yellowing placards of wanted posters, anti-drug messages, drunk driving warnings and missing children advisories was anything but welcoming.

As she climbed the front steps her vision began to blur and with each step her legs became more leaden. The Weakness. Despondent at its return at the worst possible time, she sprawled onto a wooden bench.

After she made it through her Jamaica Bay escapade without her muscles short-circuiting she had hoped that the attacks might have vanished as abruptly as they appeared. No such luck.

After a few minutes she felt her strength slowly returning. A policewoman about Hannah's age walked over to her. She somehow managed to look feminine in her blue patrolman's uniform. Most of her hair was tucked under her cap but a few dark brown wisps poked out. Her black, penetrating eyes showed concern. Her name tag said 'Santiago'.

Mortified that she might think she was some strung-out junkie, Hannah straightened up and sat at attention.

"Are you all right, Miss?"

Hannah nodded. "Yes, of course."

"How can I help you?"

"I think my father might have been murdered."

Officer Santiago's eyes widened. "Oh."

She looked Hannah up and down, took out a black notebook and asked for her name and address. Then she took Hannah up a flight of stairs to a large room that smelled like overripe laundry. A dozen or so desks were scattered around it. About half were occupied by tired looking men and women, reading reports, looking at computer screens or talking on the phone. She walked Hannah over to a desk at the back of the room. The detective sitting at it was shuffling through papers, trying not to notice them. He had thick, dark, wavy hair with a sprinkling of white. His white shirt was in desperate need of an iron and his black slacks a dry cleaner. In his mid-forties, he was probably quite the lady's man ten years and twenty pounds ago.

"Detective Gasparino, this is Hannah Johansson. She thinks someone murdered her father."

He looked up and sighed. "Thanks, Santiago." He gave her a crooked half-smile that said 'Why do you bring me all the nut cases' then turned to Hannah. "Have a seat, Ms. Johansson." She sat facing him. "Now, tell me why you think your father was murdered."

She had rehearsed exactly what she was going to say fifty times during her drive to the station house. It would be quick and to the point. All fact and no fluff. Now, after the Weakness in the vestibule, her mind was blank. Her hands, clasped in her lap, began to shake.

Gasparino smiled benignly at her. "Take your time, Ms. Johansson."

Hannah took a breath and said, "Do you know the Jamaica Bay Wildlife Refuge?"

"Yes, of course." As he spoke he wrote on a yellow pad.

"My father was the superintendent there for nearly thirty years, until the feds took it over."

"Okay."

"He stayed on as a consultant until he was diagnosed with a stroke a couple of months ago. He passed away last week."

"Of the stroke?"

"That's what everyone thought except my cousin Phil. He's a doctor. He's also the Allegany County coroner. He didn't think my father had a stroke. He was convinced he was poisoned."

"Why did he think that?"

"He knows...knew my father. He thought that there were things that didn't add up."

"What things?"

"The way he talked. The way he moved. Things like that."

"How did that differ from symptoms of a stroke?"

"I don't know. I'm not a doctor."

"Was there an autopsy?"

Hannah shook her head. "No. My father was cremated. But Phil was able to take some of my father's blood and get it to a lab. There was a high concentration of this toxin."

"What toxin?"

Hannah reached into her pocket and pulled out a folded scrap of paper. No matter how many times she repeated it to herself she could never remember the name.

"Methyl Iodide. It's a pesticide."

"Did your father work with it at the Jamaica Bay Refuge?"

"I never saw him use it."

"Do you know every chemical your father used?"

"No."

"So it's possible that your father used that stuff and some of it accidentally got into his bloodstream?"

"Not really. My father literally wrote the New York City Parks Department manual on handling chemicals. He was obsessively careful."

"Even so. It's possible."

"It's also possible that I'll win the Miss America pageant this year. The odds of that are about the same as my dad poisoning himself accidentally."

Gasparino sighed. "Is there anything else?"

"Yes, there is. There's all this crazy stuff happening at the Refuge."

"What stuff?"

She told him everything that happened when she was there and afterwards. The machine-gun toting park ranger. Dropping the urn lid and having it show up with Gilda's dead cat. The dead-of-night cargo pickup at the dock. The fake FBI agent who threatened to arrest Bette, then put her on the train.

As she spoke, Gasparino wrote everything down on a yellow pad.

He looked over his notes.

"You said they're doing a feasibility study on whether or not to expand the airport there?"

"That's what they told me."

"Everything they're doing might be part of the study."

"I don't think so."

"Why not?"

"I didn't see anything that looked like it was part of a feasibility study."

"You're an expert on these things?"

"No, of course not."

"Then why do you think there's no study?"

"Why would they need an armed guard? And what about those secret deliveries at the dock? Why sneak in like a thief in the dead of night?"

"Maybe that's the only time everyone's available."

"More like the only time when nobody's going to see them."

Gasparino, who had been stonefaced the entire time, smiled. "Ms. Johansson, I can see you're not a crackpot and that you truly believe that there's something sinister happening at the Jamaica Bay Wildlife Refuge. But even if you're right, the NYPD has no jurisdiction there. It's now part of Gateway National Recreation Area. But just so you know that I'm taking what you told me seriously, I'm sending a copy of my report to the National Parks Police. If they think there's anything to it, they'll contact you."

"What about my father's murder? That's your jurisdiction."

He looked down at his notes.

"An unauthorized tox screen with no chain of custody that indicates traces of poison that your father may or may not have been exposed to during the course of his work isn't enough evidence to start a murder investigation."

"What about killing a cat? Isn't that against the law?"

"As a matter of fact, it is. Killing any animal in New York is a misdemeanor."

"But not something anybody's going to spend any time investigating, right?"

"Let's say it wouldn't be a priority."

Hannah stood. "This was a total waste, wasn't it?"

Gasparino shrugged. "You never know. It's on the record now. Maybe something will turn up."

"Thanks for your time." She said, her voice venomous. Then she turned and left.

CHAPTER TEN

When Hannah walked in Olive was sitting on her rocking chair, knitting. The needles clacked furiously. Lena was curled at her feet, her tail precariously close to getting squashed by the rocker.

"Hello, dear," Olive said.

"Hi, mom."

Hannah didn't tell her mother where she was going when she left the house that morning. She could see that Olive was dying to ask her, the high-speed knitting was a big tell.

"I was at the Howard Beach police station today."

"Oh?"

"I spoke to a detective. I told him what I saw at the Refuge. He didn't think it was anything to be alarmed about. He said it all could have a legitimate explanation. Then he told me it wasn't his jurisdiction."

Olive stopped knitting and sat up. "They're wrong. I remember when the police had to come into the park to talk to your father. He wasn't in trouble or anything. I don't remember what the reason was but I do remember that they were from the Howard Beach precinct."

"That was before the feds took over. Now it's part of Gateway and the national parks have their own police force."

"Why do they need special police just for the park?"

"I don't know, ma. Maybe they have to be good at climbing trees."

"Do you really think so?"

"No. I was making a joke."

"Oh."

"Not too funny, I know. The detective said he'd send his report over to the Parks Police but I bet he ripped it up as soon as I left."

"I'm sure he'll do what he said he would do."

"It doesn't matter. They'll think the same thing he did."

Olive smiled serenely. "You did everything you could. When the people in power make up their minds to do something there's nothing you can do to stop it. Your father tried when they decided to take over Jamaica Bay. He was banging his head against a brick wall. I think that's what made him sick."

This would be the time to tell her mother about her father's tox screen results but that was a can of worms she wanted to keep closed so she just nodded and said, "Could be."

Olive bowed her head and went back to her knitting.

Hannah, emotionally spent, went to her room to lie down.

Forty-five minutes later Olive barged in. "Hannah, come quick. You'll never guess who's at the door."

"The Publisher's Clearinghouse guy to give me a million dollars a week for life?"

"No."

"Then I'm not interested."

"It's two policemen. Actually a policeman and a police lady."

"Really?"

"It looks like you were right after all."

"Did they mention what it was they want?"

"No. They just asked if you were here. They're waiting."

Hannah slipped on her shoes and followed her mother into the living room. The two officers stood stiffly near the door in their blue uniforms. The younger one was an African American woman in her mid-twenties. She was almost as tall as Hannah and about twenty pounds heavier, with intense eyes and a mini afro. Her partner was older, forty-something. His reddish brown hair was cut short. He had the beginnings of a paunch. In five years it would be a fully formed beer belly. Both were in uniform: light blue shirt and navy slacks. Neither wore a cap.

Olive said, "This is my daughter Hannah. I'm sorry, I didn't catch your names."

The man said, "I'm Officer Gilman." He nodded at his partner. "This is Officer Anderson." They flashed their I.D.'s. He looked at Hannah. "Hannah Johansson?"

She nodded. "You must have gotten Detective Gasparino's report."

"That's why we're here," Gilman said.

"I'm surprised you people are really looking into this. Gasparino didn't think it was worth his time."

Gilman said, "This is a very serious matter."

"I'm glad you think so."

A look of puzzled surprise washed across his face. "You are?"

"I grew up at the Jamaica Bay Wildlife Refuge. If there's anything I can do to protect it, I will."

Gilman said, "I see." He turned to his partner. "Go ahead Kim."

Anderson walked over to Hannah and grabbed her arm over the elbow. "Ms. Johansson. You're under suspicion of violating national security statutes including sabotage, espionage and criminal trespass on a top secret government installation. Please come with us."

Hannah pulled her arm free and yelled, "That's crazy! You don't know what you're talking about."

Gilman said, "Don't make this more difficult than it has to be."

Olive cried, "Hannah, what's going on?"

"These idiots think I'm some kind of terrorist."

Olive looked horrified. "No. It must be some sort of mistake."

Gilman turned to Olive. "It's no mistake, ma'am."

Anderson glared at Hannah. "Put your hands behind your back."

"You're handcuffing me? Really?"

"Please just do as I say."

Anderson cuffed her, then walked her towards the door with Gilman trailing behind.

Hannah yelled back at Olive as they pushed her out the door, "It's okay, ma. This is all a big screw-up. Call Phil."

CHAPTER ELEVEN

Hannah sat slumped in the cramped back seat of the patrol car trying to figure out how things ever got this out of whack. All she wanted to do was fulfill her father's final wish. Now Gilda's cat is dead. Her aunt and her mother aren't talking. And she's on her way to jail. Not that her life was so great before. No job, no social life, no place of her own and a mysterious disease that caused her to kill her father. Who knew she would be thinking back on those days as the good times?

Then Axel's voice resounded in her head. 'Are you gonna sit there and feel sorry for yourself or are you gonna fight?'

She remembered back when she was in grade school. She was tall for her age. Taller than all of the boys. And her feet were enormous. She was terrified that they would never stop growing. The kids in her class noticed. They called her Bozo, Bigfoot and Gigantor. When she told her mother, Olive said to ignore them. That responding would only egg them on and soon they would get bored. The problem was when they got bored with name calling they decided they would up the ante. Instead of just calling her names, they started stomping on her feet. That was her Popeye moment, as in: *That's all I can stands. I can't stands no more.*

Hannah fought back. One of the boys went home with a

black eye, another, a fat lip. The third ran away in horror and told the teacher.

Hannah came home that night with a note saying Mrs. Kramer, the Vice Principal, wanted to meet with her and her parents. Axel came to school with Hannah the next morning. They were lectured that violence had no place in school, no matter what the reason. But because she was an excellent student and had never been in trouble before, she would be let off this time with a warning. But if it happened again the consequences would be much more severe.

Hannah was mortified. It wasn't fair. They started it and they're not in trouble. She was about to say that, but all she said was "But..." when her dad glanced sternly at her with a quick shake of his head.

On their way to the parking lot Axel said, "One more thing about the fight you had with those boys."

"Y...yes?" she said nervously.

"Good for you!" His face broke into a wall-to-wall grin. "I couldn't say so in front of the principal, but I'm proud of you."

"You're not mad at me?"

"Not at all. Your mother told me that you were being picked on. She thought maybe we should say something to the teacher. I thought it would be better if you took care of it yourself. The only way to stop bullies is to stand up to them. And I'm glad you did. You should never let anyone take advantage of you. Those boys will never bother you again because now they respect you. Respect is one of the most important things you can have. You can't buy it and nobody can hand it to you. You have to earn it. Sometimes you have to fight for it. I had to do it a lot when I was younger."

He told her about when some kids ganged up on him, calling him a squarehead. That was the first of many fights he had in high school.

"In this life, you have to fight for what you know is right, no matter what other people think."

Hannah decided that the best way to honor her father was to regain the fighting spirit that she had lost somewhere along the line. She swore that if she managed to get out of jail, she would find out who was responsible for poisoning her father and make sure they paid for it. And if no one would help her she'd do it herself.

In a little less than an hour, they pulled up in front of U.S. Park Police Headquarters in Brooklyn's Floyd Bennett Field. Long and low, it looked more like a Costco's than a police station. A couple of white and green Park Ranger cars were parked in front.

The main lobby was nothing like the one at the Howard Beach police station. The walls were freshly painted. The front desk, semi-circular of polished wood with a granite top, looked like it would be more at home in the reception area of a boutique hotel. The officer behind it, a husky, middle-aged woman with short brown hair, had the same harsh scowl as the vice principal who scolded her those many years ago.

After she was fingerprinted and photographed, Officer Anderson marched her to the Interview Room.

"Wait here," she said then left, slamming the door behind her.

There were two plastic chairs on either side of a metal table that looked like the one her dad and uncles used to play cards on, back when the Rocky Point house was still a bungalow. There was no window in the room and no mirror. A guy came in who introduced himself as Detective Leedy. He looked like a football coach, short and stocky with big arms, a blonde crew cut trending towards gray, and a sneer that he probably thought made him look tough. He wore a tan sport coat, brown pants, white shirt, no tie. He smelled of sweat and cigarettes. He motioned for her to sit, then he sat facing her. He switched on a small digital tape recorder and told her to start at the beginning.

"The beginning of what?"

He shrugged. "Whatever."

Hannah steeled herself for some intense questioning. But this guy seemed disinterested.

Relaxing a little, she talked about how her father built the Jamaica Bay Wildlife Refuge practically single-handedly and was the superintendent there until the feds took over. His last request was that he wanted to have his ashes scattered over the East Pond, his favorite spot in the Refuge. She talked about how she was shocked when she came back after not seeing the place for several years to see huge, spiked iron bars in front and a black clad guy with an assault weapon who looked like he should be patrolling a war zone not a bird sanctuary.

She went on to tell him how she had to sneak back in to scatter her father's ashes and dropped the lid of the urn on the dock. That she heard them talking about some secret mission that was supposed to happen that night that sounded very sinister so she went back with her camera and took pictures of them unloading something that looked like drugs off a small barge. By his expression, or lack thereof, Leedy didn't seem to think that any of it was a big deal. Then she told him about Bette's bogus encounter with the fake federal agent and how Gilda's cat turned up dead at their front door along with the urn lid that she dropped at the Refuge that morning. She finished with Phil's lab results that indicated that her father was poisoned.

Every once in a while Leedy asked a question or told her to repeat something, but mostly he let her ramble, punctuating her story with an occasional grunt or sigh.

She ended with, "It's not me you should be investigating but those people at the Refuge. I'm sure what they're doing is criminal."

He stared at her with vacant eyes. "Anything else?"

She shook her head.

"All right."

He left the room. A few minutes later, Anderson walked in, grabbed her by the arm and marched her to a cell about the size of a large walk-in closet with a wooden bench and stainless steel sink and toilet.

Like the little girl who got in trouble for sticking up for herself two decades earlier, Hannah was horrified at the unfairness, though she should have gotten used to it by now.

During summers at the Rocky Point bungalow there weren't any girls her age to play with. Her cousins Phil and Jerrold begrudgingly let her tag along with them. Most days they swam in Long Island Sound and played pickup basketball with some of the kids who lived in the neighborhood all year.

At first, no one but her cousins wanted Hannah on their team. They didn't want to play with a girl. But they soon found out she had game. She was tall and quick with good hands and a deadly outside shot. The cousins dominated the locals. After a while they told Phil that they didn't want her around anymore. They never said why but Hannah knew it was because they didn't want to be humiliated by a girl.

By the time her cousins were high school age, basketball was out and drinking beer and smoking pot was in. Hannah rarely hung out with them, and when she did she stood in the background sipping a Diet Coke while they smoked and drank and roughhoused. When someone passed her a joint or a beer she'd smile and say "No thanks, I'm good." Pretty soon all the guys ignored her. Her cousin Catherine, on the other hand, was very popular. Far from the prim and proper young lady her aunt Gilda made her out to be, she smoked, drank, cursed and made out with some of the older boys.

Anyone would have thought that Hannah would wind up as the most accomplished of all the cousins. In high school she was a star athlete and honor student. But as they say, 'past performance does not guarantee future results.'

Now, all these years later, Jerrold the former pothead has a successful veterinary practice, beer-swilling Phil is a doctor and slutty Catherine is doing well as an actuary, though not as well as Gilda brags. And Hannah, the goody-goody A-student, is out of work, still living with her mother, sitting in a police station waiting to be booked.

It could have been ten minutes or two hours later that another policewoman, around forty with a bad dye job, wearing a uniform a size too small, appeared on the other side of the bars. "Hannah Johansson?"

"Yes."

"Come with me."

As she walked towards the front of the building she could hear a strident voice echoing through the corridor. It sounded familiar.

"This is the most egregious example of governmental overreach that I have ever seen. Ms. Johansson is a model citizen whose only crime is trying to fulfill her father's dying wish. What exactly has she been charged with?"

Hannah walked into the lobby to see her mother standing by the front desk next to a tall man in his mid-thirties. He was wearing a dark blue pinstriped suit, powder blue shirt and yellow paisley tie. His hair was dark and tightly curled. He wore black Buddy Holly glasses and his rather prominent chin featured a dark goatee.

Leedy was behind the desk, clearly flustered. "She hasn't been charged yet."

"Either charge her or let her go."

Hannah glared at Olive. "I thought I told you to bring Phil."

"Phillip can't come down until tomorrow morning. He suggested I call Mr. Jacobson, who very kindly agreed to come."

Jacobson held out his hand. "Hello Hannah, long time no see."

Hannah glowered at him. "Not long enough." She slapped his face, sending his glasses flying across the room.

Olive gasped. The policewoman grabbed Hannah and pulled her away. Jacobson stood dumbstruck, his face flushed, his mouth agape.

Hannah turned to the policewoman. “Please take me back to my cell.”

CHAPTER TWELVE

Hannah spent most of the night pacing back and forth in the holding cell. After a couple of hours her legs tired. She collapsed exhausted on the wooden slab but her brain spun wildly, flinging questions without answers.

What are those horrible people doing at the Refuge? Why did they kill Gilda's cat? Why did they poison my father? Can Jacobson sue me for assault? Will the Parks Police arrest me? What's prison like? Where did the Weakness come from? Will I ever be rid of it? Is it real or in my head?

After squirming around on the slab (was it meant to be a bench? A bed? An instrument of torture?) for the better part of an hour, she gave up and stretched out on the concrete floor, finally nodding off. She was awakened by a young Latina policewoman whose sparkling eyes and friendly smile were a drastic contrast to the sullen dragon lady of the night before. As she escorted Hannah to the main lobby she asked her how she was feeling. All Hannah could muster for a reply was a shrug and a grunt.

The clock over the front desk read 7:30. Phil was standing in front of it, casually chatting with the desk officer, an athletic looking guy in his twenties.

Phil looked over at her and winked. "C'mon, cuz. Let's get out of here."

She turned to the officer. "I'm free to go?"

"Yes, ma'am." He handed her a plastic baggie with her phone, keys and wallet along with her empty handbag.

Ignoring the aches in her back, legs, arms and head from her concrete nap, she bounded over to her cousin and bear-hugged him.

"Thanks for coming." She planted a kiss on this cheek as they walked to his 1965 Corvair, parked in a space that said 'Reserved for Parks Department Vehicles.' He called it his poor man's Porsche. She called it the deathmobile. And she was not alone. It was the car featured in Ralph Nader's book *Unsafe at Any Speed*. Deathmobile or not, she was thrilled to be in it. The car she imagined herself being driven away in this morning was a paddy-wagon to the Tombs. Compared to that, Phil's 50-year-old rattletrap was a Rolls Royce.

Hannah said, "Was the drive horrible?"

"Naw. It was fine. Not a lot of traffic between midnight and 6 am coming from Upstate New York. You hungry?"

"Starving." She hadn't eaten anything for the better part of a day. The police offered to get her pizza or a sandwich but all she asked for was a bottle of water. Anything else would have come back up.

"I know a place."

Phil headed for the Savoy, one of Brooklyn's oldest diners and one of the few not run by Greeks. The coffee was always fresh, the burgers fat and juicy and the breakfasts would hold you till dinner. And it was just five miles down Flatbush Avenue.

The place was more an old-fashioned luncheonette than one of those stand-alone chrome and glass temples to the gods of gluttony that the Greeks erected all over the tri-state area. Tucked in next to a pharmacy on one side and a beauty salon on the other, the Savoy was long and narrow with a counter that ran from the front door to the back. The short-order cook, about three hundred jiggly pounds, sweat pouring down his shiny bald head, danced back and forth from the eight-burner gas range to the stainless steel coffee urns to the flat top grill where the eggs, home fries, bacon and pancakes were sizzling.

Eight booths hugged the wall opposite the counter. Three were occupied. The one closest to the door contained a mother with two young children. Another had an elderly couple. The third held two middle-aged men in paint spattered white overalls.

Hannah and Phil walked to a booth near the back. She wriggled, twisted and squirmed, trying to get comfortable in a seat obviously meant for either a toddler or a midget, not a six-foot three-inch woman whose back was screaming.

"Whatsa matter honey? You got shpilkes?" the waitress said as she put two cups of coffee on the table. She was skinny, bordering on bony, with black hair that looked like it was dyed with shoe polish. Her eye shadow was purple, her lipstick pink and her talon-like fingernails were mauve with white daisies painted on them. Her powder blue uniform smelled of tobacco and cooking grease. "You know what you want or do you need a minute?"

"A couple of minutes," Phil said.

"No problem," she said and went to check on the other tables.

Hannah said, "What's shpilkes?"

"It's Yiddish. It's something like ants in your pants."

"How do you know that, you're half Italian and half Czechoslovakian?"

"One of my best friends growing up was Gary Feinbaum. We spent a lot of time at his grandma's house. Besides learning a little Yiddish I developed a taste for kishka."

"And that is?"

"It's a cow bladder stuffed with chicken fat and table scraps, served with gravy."

Hannah made a face. "I hope you're not going to have that for breakfast. I'm just getting my appetite back."

Phil smiled. "I checked. It's not on the menu."

"Let's see." Hannah reached for the menu, about the size of

the *Sunday Times*, groaned and bent over. "Serves me right for trying to sleep on cement."

"Serves you right for slapping the guy who tried to get you out of jail last night. You coulda slept in your own bed."

Hannah bristled. "I'd rather sleep on broken glass than let Ron Jacobson help me."

"C'mon. I know Ronnie a long time. He's a good guy."

"He's a liar, a cheater and a scumbag," she yelled.

The elderly couple and the painters turned to stare at them.

Hannah, embarrassed, continued sotto voce. "He used me. Led me on. Brought me flowers. He told me I was the woman he'd been searching for his whole life. I was falling in love with him. Then, boom, he vanished. Not a word. No phone call. Nothing. He changed his phone number. He even cancelled his Facebook account. I thought maybe something horrible happened to him. Then I found out he's married and has a kid. I swore that if I ever saw him again I'd punch him in the nose. He got off easy with a slap on the cheek."

"You don't know the whole story."

"I know everything I need to know."

"No. You don't."

"Then tell me. What do you call someone who did what he did?"

"A guy with no good options. It was either quit you cold turkey or never see his son again."

"I don't believe it. He's a lawyer. Lawyers do that to other people. They don't get it done to them."

Phil shrugged. "I guess his ex-wife had a better lawyer."

"Where's his son now?"

"With Ron."

"And his wife?"

"Last I heard she was out of the country."

"He could have called me after his wife left."

Phil shrugged. "He was probably too embarrassed. Ashamed.

All I know is every time I talk to him he asks how you are. What you're doing."

Before Hannah could answer, the waitress came back. "Whatta yiz havin?"

Hannah said, "Two eggs over medium with bacon very crisp and whole wheat toast."

She looked over at Phil.

"A stack."

"You want bacon too?"

"I'll have sausage."

"Sure thing."

After she left Phil said, "I got the full tox screen results."

"Well?"

"There was enough methyl iodide in your father's system to kill a buffalo."

"What does that mean?"

"He was definitely murdered. There's no way that much could be concentrated in his bloodstream by accident. He'd have to have bathed in it."

"You mean it wasn't my fault? I didn't kill him?"

Phil shook his head. "Whoever fed him that poison killed him. No doubt."

Hannah was about to say something, then gasped, sniffled and started crying.

"Are you okay?"

Tears flowed down her cheeks. "You have no idea what it was like thinking I killed my father. Guilt piled on top of shame, piled on top of...I don't know. Just feeling awful all the time. You've given me myself back."

The waitress came with their breakfasts. Hannah picked up a piece of bacon. It was burnt and shriveled, like a big spent match. Just the way she liked it. She shoved it in her mouth and crunched happily. Then she took some egg and a bite of toast and washed it down with a swig of coffee. She was halfway done before Phil had finished dressing his pancakes. He liked them with dollop of maple syrup on each piece, strawberry jelly on top with a dab of butter.

While he was fussing with his breakfast, Hannah said, “Can you get a copy of the lab report?”

Phil shook his head. “Sorry, cuz. There was no report. They just called me with the results.”

“But you were always complaining about all the stupid paperwork you had to do.”

“That’s when it’s official police business. This was a favor. They went way out on a limb doing an unauthorized tox screen. Any paper trail would put me and the lab in deep doo-doo.”

“Oh, I see,” Hannah said.

Then she concentrated on finishing her breakfast.

Phil meticulously cut a small wedge of pancake.

“Why’d you get locked up anyway? What did you do besides belt Ronnie? I asked Ollie but she didn’t know.”

“Actually it’s your fault.”

“What are you talking about? I was 400 miles away.”

“Remember when I told you I snuck into the Refuge in the middle of the night and took pictures? I said I didn’t know what they were doing but I was pretty sure whatever it was, it was bad.”

“Yes. I also remember I told you not to do anything about it.”

“No you didn’t. You said I should let the police handle it so that’s what I did. I went to the Howard Beach precinct and told a detective what I saw.”

“Most people who talk to the police don’t get thrown in jail. What the hell did you say?”

“Nothing.”

“I work with the police. They very rarely arrest people for nothing. You must have said something.”

“I told him about the boat, the bundles, Dawson.”

“Who’s that?”

“She’s the woman who threw me out of the Refuge that morning. She and that steroidal sidekick of hers. I also told him about the bogus FBI guy who hassled Bette then drove her to the train."

"There must be something else."

"I told him I took pictures of what was going on."

"Did you show him the pictures."

"No. They're in my camera at home."

Phil's eyes widened, which for him was an explosion of emotion.

"Those pictures could be the key. Our proof that something shady really is going on there. I bet Axe found out about it and that's why they poisoned him." He thrust his arm out. "Hi five, cuz. We got em."

Hannah slapped his outstretched palm with hers.

"Let's get back to the house and check out those pictures."

CHAPTER THIRTEEN

A blue and white Suffolk County cop car was parked in front of the house when they drove up.

"What now," Hannah said, as she got out of the car.

Phil grinned slyly. "Maybe they missed you at the jail."

She scowled. "Not funny."

Hannah opened the door to see Olive sitting on the couch, turning a box of tissues into confetti. Her hands were trembling. A policeman stood a few feet from her, notebook in hand.

When she saw them, Olive jumped up from her chair and waved her arms frantically, like she was hailing a taxi in the rain. "Thank God you're here. We had a robbery. Phillip, please talk to the policeman. He wants to know what's missing."

Hannah bristled. "Phil doesn't live here. How would he know what's missing? I'll talk to him."

Shrinking in her chair, Olive smiled wanly and said, "All right, dear. I just thought Philip being a man and all."

This was when Hannah usually blew up about Olive's belief that men were supposed to handle things and women were there to make dinner and tidy up. But with everything that's happened lately she decided to bite her tongue and most of her cheek.

She turned to the policeman. He was about Hannah's age, a shade under six feet and stocky. His brown hair was cut short.

"Can you tell me what happened here Officer..."

"Fason." He held out his hand to shake Hannah's.

She gripped his outstretched hand hard and shook it forcefully. "I'm Hannah Johansson. I live here with my mother." She gestured at Phil, who was still standing by the door. "That's my cousin Dr. Phillip Buzek. He's in from Upstate." Phil gave the cop a quick nod. She didn't usually introduce Phil as 'Doctor' but she didn't want the cop to think that they were typical low-rent Rocky Point bozos.

Fason nodded back at Phil then turned to Hannah. "One of the bedroom windows was broken. That's how they got in."

Olive turned towards Hannah and dabbed at her eye with the shredded tissue. "I'm so sorry. I went to the market this morning. I should have stayed home. None of this would have happened."

"Don't be silly, ma," Hannah said, feeling guilty about snapping at her before. "There's no way you could have known. If you were here you wouldn't be able to stop whoever did this and they could have hurt you." She turned back to the policeman. "Do you have any idea who did this?"

He shook his head in disgust. "Kids looking for drug money. It's happening more and more around here. They didn't get much, just whatever they could carry. It was your basic smash and grab job."

"What's this world coming to?" Olive shrilled. "We never used to lock our doors. Now you're not even safe in your own home."

The cop said, "Don't worry, we'll get them. Let's see what they took." He pointed at Hannah's room. "In there."

He started walking. The others followed.

"My room? That was the only room they hit?" Hannah said.

"That's what it looks like. Like I said, a quick smash and grab."

Hannah examined the room while the others stood in the doorway. It was a mess. Dresser drawers were pulled out and turned over. Blouses, jeans, underwear, socks and pantyhose were strewn haphazardly all over the floor. Her empty jewelry box was upside-down on the bed. The nightstand drawer was open but there wasn't much in there to begin with, a box of tissues, a small flashlight, the TV remote and a small notepad and pencil. Her laptop and tablet, which had been on top of it next to the clock radio, were missing. The closet door was open. Her coats and dresses were disheveled but still hanging. Her shoes were in the shoetree, untouched.

She looked up at the top shelf of the closet and her stomach nosedived. Her cameras were gone. Her old Nikon FM2, the first serious camera she ever owned. It was precious to her. A birthday present from her father when she was fourteen. He bought it for her when she told him she wanted to be a wildlife photographer. The Nikon D5500, the one she used the other night, was also missing.

She turned to Phil. "They took my camera," she cried. "The one with all the shots from the Refuge."

Phil said, "Shit."

She glared at the policeman. "This wasn't kids. It was those bastards from Jamaica Bay. Now there's no proof."

Hannah's legs went wobbly. She staggered to the bed and flopped down on her back, staring up at the ceiling with droopy eyes.

Phil and Olive ran to her.

"Oh my God!" Olive cried. Tears streamed down her cheeks. She tried to wipe her face with one of her crumpled tissues but her hand was shaking too violently.

"C'mon, Aunt Ollie," Phil said. He gently guided her to the rocking chair in the corner of the room. "Sit here and relax. Hannah will be fine in a couple of minutes."

Fason walked over. "What's going on?"

"My cousin gets these seizures. They come on out of the blue and can last anywhere from ten minutes up to a half-hour or more."

"What's the matter with her?"

"We're not sure."

"Do you need me to call the paramedics?"

"No. She'll be all right. She just needs to lie still for awhile." Phil said, "But I don't think you're gonna get much more her today. Do you have a card?"

Fason nodded. He took one out of his wallet and handed it to Phil.

"We'll call you with a list of what's missing."

"Okay." The cop turned to go.

Twenty minutes later, Olive was in the living room knitting at breakneck speed.

Hannah had regained enough strength to slowly begin to put her room back together. Phil was doing the heavy work, moving furniture and putting the drawers back in the dresser.

It skeeved Hannah to think that those creeps from the Refuge were in her room, touching her things. She fought the urge to put everything in a pile and set it on fire. Instead she stuffed it all in two big black plastic bags, figuring she'd take it to the laundry sometime.

"I have a friend," Phil said. He was sitting cross-legged on the floor. "A guy I interned with at St. Vincent's. He's at NYU Langone now. I told him about you. He said he'd like to see you."

Hannah flumped on the bed, drained, demoralized and depressed. "I'm not interested."

"You should be."

She shook her head. "Thanks, Phil. But I told you I'm not ready to start dating again."

Phil grinned. "Neither is he. He's happily married with two kids."

She looked at him like he had three heads "Why would you want to set me up with him?"

"He's a neurologist. He's very good. I told him about what's going on with these attacks you have. He had some ideas."

"I've wasted enough time in doctors' offices. I don't need another one to tell me I'm crazy."

Phil smirked. "Of course you're crazy but that's not what's causing these attacks. He thinks it sounds like myasthenia gravis."

She shook her head. "I've been tested for that. Also Guillain-Barré, MS and chronic fatigue. All negative."

"I mentioned that to him. He told me that these neurological tests are hit and miss. He's a good man. And a great doctor. You can look him up online, Rudy Romano. Call him."

She shook her head. "Forget it. There's too much going on."

"If you change your mind, here's his number." He put a folded yellow Post-it note on her night table. "If you call, make sure to mention that you're my cousin, the one I spoke to him about. That'll get you an appointment right away. If not, you'll have to wait months. He's that good."

"I appreciate your trying to help me. I really do. But if you really want to help, work with me to find out who murdered my father."

She was ready for him to say it was impossible. He was too busy. He lived six hours away. And this was a job for the police, not a small town medical examiner and an unemployed mental health clinic administrator.

Instead he grinned and said, "You got it. I'm in."

"Really! But you said I should let the police handle it."

"That was before you got arrested. Before they stole your camera. The cops don't seem to give a crap. It's you and me against the world." He smiled broadly. "Like old times."

Hannah jumped off the bed and bear-hugged her cousin. "Thank you so much!"

"There's one condition."

She stiffened. "What?"

"Make an appointment with Rudy." He walked over to the night table, grabbed the Post-it and put it in Hannah's hand.

"All right. But I'm telling you, it won't make any difference."

"Just call him."

"Okay. I said I would and I will." After a few seconds she said, "So what's our first move?"

"Not so fast, Kemosabe. If I'm gonna do this I need to be here. I have to go back to Alfred and settle some things. I have to arrange for another doctor to cover my practice and let the Wyoming Coroner's Office know I won't be available for awhile."

"Wyoming? That's crazy. Don't they have any coroners closer than that? It's halfway across the country."

"Wyoming County, New York. It's next door to Allegany. We cover for each other." He stood. "I better get going if I want to be back here to be Tonto to your Lone Ranger."

"I was thinking more like Robin to my Batgirl."

"I didn't know Robin worked with Batgirl."

"Welcome to the era of female empowerment."

CHAPTER FOURTEEN

After her cousin left, Hannah dragged the ottoman next to Olive's rocker. She sat cross-legged on it, reached out and gently grasped her mother's wrist.

"Ma, I know how hard this has been for you. I want to apologize for making an awful situation worse. Getting into that stupid fight with Aunt Gilda. Getting arrested. Making a scene in the police station with Ron Jacobson. Today's break-in." She shook her head sadly. "I messed everything up. I'm really sorry."

Olive smiled benignly at Hannah. "That's all right, dear. You're very excitable. You're more like your Aunt Gilda than you think."

Hannah didn't know how to respond. The last thing she wanted to do was get into an argument with her mother but she had a hard time swallowing the comparison between herself and her harridan aunt. The woman was self-centered, inconsiderate, opinionated, overbearing, controlling and rude. Did Olive really believe she was that way too?

Hannah stood. "I'm going to make myself some tea. Would you like some?"

"That would be lovely. I made banana bread. It's in the fridge."

Hannah went to the kitchen, filled the kettle and put it on the electric burner. The one thing she missed about her apartment in Boston was the gas stove. There were no underground gas lines in this part of Rocky Point. Everything had to be electric. Everyone said it made no difference but she was sure that gas cooked everything better. Even water.

She took the box of Bigelow black tea from the cabinet. After she came home, Hannah convinced her mother to switch from Lipton tea to Bigelow. She thought Lipton tasted like old sweat socks. Olive couldn't tell the difference.

When the tea was ready she cut two pieces of banana bread, got forks and napkins, put everything on a tray and carried it to the coffee table.

"This is nice," Olive said. "I can't remember the last time we had the chance to have a mother-daughter tea. Lately everything's at sixes and sevens."

Like a lot of Olive's expressions, Hannah had no idea what that meant. So she smiled and took a bite of banana bread. "I should have been here when dad got sick. I could have helped. I wish you would have let me know."

"You had your own life in Boston."

Hannah smirked. "Look how that turned out."

She gazed over at a framed photo on the mantel shelf of her father at the Refuge in his superintendent's uniform with Oswaldo, Barbara and Jacqui. She felt a tinge of jealousy seeing her friend Jacqui next to her father. "If I was at the Refuge with daddy, maybe none of this would have happened."

"Don't be silly. There's nothing you could have done. Axel had a stroke. "

This was, quite literally, the moment of truth. Should she tell Olive the that her father was poisoned, which would probably upset her even more, or let her remain blissfully ignorant?

Hannah said, "Actually, he didn't."

Olive put down her tea. "Of course he did. That's what's the doctors said."

"Phillip thinks they made a misdiagnosis. He believes that daddy was poisoned."

Olive shuddered. "Poisoned? That can't be."

"When Phil saw daddy in the hospital he didn't think he had a stroke. Some things weren't right. Little things that we wouldn't notice but a doctor, especially a rehab doc like Phil, who sees a lot of stroke patients, would recognize. He wanted to be sure so he took a blood sample from daddy and sent it out to be tested. The results showed huge amounts of something called methyl iodide. It's a pesticide. And it can kill you."

Olive set her jaw and shook her head. "That can't be. How can they have made a mistake like that?"

"That's what I thought. But Phil said a lot of the symptoms of methyl iodide poisoning are the same as a stroke. It's what they call a stroke mimic. To the first responders it looked like a stroke and there was no reason for the emergency room doctors to consider anything else. And with stroke victims, getting treatment started immediately is very important."

Olive shook her head vigorously. "No. My Axel could never have poisoned himself. He was always very careful with chemicals. It was one of his, what's the word, fetishes."

"That's what I told Phil. The only other explanation is that somebody gave him the poison on purpose."

"It's not possible. Only Oswaldo, Barbara and Jacqui were there. At the end it was only Jacqui. They all loved Axel."

Oswaldo Espinosa had been at the Refuge for eight years. He was a landscaper for the New York City Parks Department. Originally from the Dominican Republic, Axel treated him, his wife and daughter like family. He left on disability a year ago after knee surgery. Barbara Ahearn was an ornithology professor at Queens College who volunteered at the Refuge as a guide and lecturer. She had moved to North Carolina to be with her daughter and granddaughter when the National Parks Service took over management of the Refuge. Jacqui Folami was Hannah's friend in high school. She worked with Hannah at the Refuge for a couple of summers. When Hannah went away to school, Jacqui, who went to St. John's in Queens, stayed on. After she graduated Axel hired her full time.

"They were the only ones there. That's why I don't believe it."

"What about all those people who were doing the airport expansion study. They were there when daddy got sick. And they're still there."

"They didn't even know your father. Why would they want to hurt him?"

"I don't know. But I'm going to find out."

"You'll do no such thing," Olive yelled. "You promised me that you were through with Jamaica Bay. That whatever they were doing there wasn't your concern."

"It's not. I really don't care what they're doing. But if someone there poisoned daddy, that's a different story."

"Even if what you say is true, there's nothing you can do. It's a matter for the police."

"I've been to the police, remember. They were more interested in arresting me than finding out what happened to daddy."

Olive started to say something but no words emerged. She grabbed a napkin off the table and began tearing it into pieces.

"Sorry ma, I know this hurts you to hear this. But daddy was murdered. I don't know who did it or why but I'm going to find out."

Olive sat quivering in her rocker, her eyes mirrors of dread.

CHAPTER FIFTEEN

The Arsenal, a 150 year-old three-story castle of a building tucked into Central Park at 64th Street and Fifth Avenue, across the street from some of Manhattan's poshest hotels, shops and apartment buildings, is the headquarters of the New York City Parks Department.

Hannah had never been to Jacqui's office. The guard at the front desk checked her name with a list of scheduled visitors and told her to go on up to the third floor. When she got there the door was open but no one was inside. She thought she might have gone to the wrong office but once she looked around it was unmistakably Jacqui's. One wall was filled with photos and mementos of her glory days as a star high school athlete. Team portraits, yellowed newspaper clippings, two Hillcrest High School Women's Basketball MVP certificates and a 'Queens County Female Athlete of the Year' plaque. Another wall was more personal. It held pictures of Jacqui with her mom, dad and two younger sisters. Also two diplomas, her undergraduate degree from St. John's and her Master of Public Administration from Baruch College. There was a framed autographed Miami Heat jersey of LeBron James, her basketball idol.

Two other photos caught Hannah's eye. One was a faded

black-and-white shot of the All-County Girls Basketball team, cut out of the sports section of the *Queens Chronicle*. It was the only sports-related item on the personal wall. The headline read: 'Queens of the Hardwood.' Hannah walked over to it. Thirteen girls stood in a semi-circle behind the two kneeling co-captains, Hannah and Jacqui.

The other photo was more recent. It showed Hannah's dad standing with his arm around Jacqui beside an osprey nest at the Jamaica Bay Wildlife Refuge. Axel was wearing his superintendent's uniform. Jacqui was dressed as a park ranger. Hannah eyes moistened as she thought about how much she missed her father. She was a little jealous that over the last few years Jacqui got to spend more time with him than she did.

Jacqui walked into the room, stirring Hannah from her reverie.

"Hello girlfriend, sorry to keep you waiting. My meeting ran late."

The two women exchanged hugs.

"Jacqui, hi. You look gorgeous."

Her hair, which was a full-blown Angela Davis afro in high school, was now done in sumptuous copper curls touching her shoulders. She looked every bit the young executive in a black blazer suit, powder blue shirt and black heels. Hannah felt underdressed in jeans, sneakers and a sweater.

Jacqui looked over Hannah's shoulder at the championship photo and said, "Yeah, we had some battles back in the day," she said with an electric smile. "White Lightning versus Chocolate Thunder."

"Yeah, but you won all those battles. I was never half the ballplayer you were."

Jacqui winked at her. "I got a secret for you. You could have been just as good as me. Maybe better. You were taller, had great hands and more range on your jumpshot. I just wanted it more. For you it was a game. For me it was my passion, my life."

"And I almost ruined it all for you."

"You didn't ruin anything. If it wasn't for my screwed-up knee I would have never met your father. Any success I have I owe to him. He took me under his wing at Jamaica Bay. Then he put in a good word for me here. I don't know where I'd be if it wasn't for him."

She paused for a few seconds. "And you. If you hadn't talked me into working there with you all those summers, none of it would have happened."

Hannah gestured to the diplomas on the wall. "Dean's list at St. John's. Then a Masters of Public Administration. No one helped you get those. You worked your ass off."

Jacqui patted her behind and grinned. "Not all of it. I put on a few pounds since our playing days." Then she got serious. "I'm so sorry I didn't make it to your dad's memorial. There was a family emergency at my sisters' in New Jersey."

"No need to apologize. The only thing you missed was seeing me make a total ass of myself."

Hannah told her about knocking over her father's urn at the service and everything that happened since.

"That's why I wanted to meet with you. You were there with my dad at the end. Who are those people? I have a hard time believing that they're doing any kind of study for the airport. What are they really doing there?"

"Good question," she said ruefully. "When the National Parks Service first took over and made us part of Gateway, everything was cool. We had a couple of meetings about their plans for the place. Basically, they said we were doing fine and we should keep doing it. They didn't want to change anything.

"Then sometime later, I forget exactly when, we got a memo saying that the Port Authority was thinking of expanding JFK and they would be conducting a feasibility study to see if it made sense to use the Refuge as part of the expansion. They said we should keep the place open but some people would be coming to do the study. They told us they wouldn't interfere with anything we were doing."

"Was that woman Dawson there?"

"Yeah." Jacqui grimaced. "Surly bitch. She introduced herself as the project manager. Some days other people showed up but mostly it was just her and that big scary looking dude with a scarier looking gun. She told Axel he was there for security. I don't know why you need security to conduct a study."

"I thought the same thing. Anything else?"

"This other guy walked around with her sometimes, checking things out. I think I heard her call him Colonel something. I didn't catch a last name."

"Tall, with a Marine-style haircut? Has a scar cutting across his eyebrow."

"That's him. How'd you know?"

Hannah told her about Bette's mini abduction.

"That's crazy," Jacqui said, wide-eyed. "He threatened her, drove her around, then took her to the railroad station? That doesn't make sense."

"None of it makes sense. Did they start building the road while you were still there?"

"What road?"

Hannah told her about the gravel road and the dock where her dad's fishing platform use to be. "Did they start that when you were there?"

Jacqui shook her head. "There wasn't any construction going on as far as I can remember. A lot of deliveries, though. Dawson fenced off an area just south of the main entrance. That's where they stored everything."

"Did you ever see what was there? Any heavy equipment? Construction material? Stuff like that."

"You couldn't see anything. The fence was high, maybe eight feet. And it was all covered with some kind of material. I tried to get a look once but that security guy was there. Him and his machine gun. Scared the hell out of me."

Hannah scanned through her phone. She showed Jacqui the shot of Grabowski. "Is this him?"

"Yeah."

"Did my dad have much to do with them?"

"Hardly anything. When they first showed up Axel was his usual friendly self. But they had no interest in anything we had to say. And they were nasty, especially that Dawson woman. I don't blame him for not wanting to talk to them. They were in charge of tearing down what he spent his life building."

Hannah's mind drifted. Flashing on her father again. Wishing she had more time with him.

Jacqui snapped her finger. "Hey girl, where'd you go?"

"Sorry. I was thinking about my dad. Where were we?"

"Talking about Dawson and her pet gorilla."

"Oh yeah. Anything else they did that seemed hinky?"

"Hard to tell. They weren't there that long when your father got sick. That's when I knew it was time for me to get out."

"That goon whose picture I showed you, Grabowski. Did you ever speak to him?"

She shuddered. "No. That guy gave me the creeps."

"That's too bad. I wanted to see if I could find anything out about him and Dawson. And maybe that other guy who took Bette for a ride."

Jacqui smiled. The same smile that lit up her face on the basketball court after she made an especially spectacular move to the hoop. "Why didn't you say so. You want their names and addresses?"

Hannah's eyes lit up. "No way. You can really do that?"

"We have something called a shared services agreement with a lot of other New York City agencies. Human Resources, Accounting, Maintenance and General Administration data for all those departments are on the same server. It's supposed to streamline the bureaucracy and save money, but the jury's still out. The Parks Department takes part in the program, I think the Port Authority does too."

"Are you sure?"

"Let's find out."

After a couple of minutes and several mouse clicks her printer spit out two spreadsheets. She handed them to Hannah.

"This is the contact information of everyone who worked at the Refuge during the past two years, including vendors, volunteers and student interns. I bet they're somewhere in here."

"Thanks. This is a big help."

Jacqui's desk phone rang. "Yes. Okay, I'll be there in a few." She turned to Hannah. "I gotta go. Another meeting. Next time you're in town we'll have lunch."

"Sure thing."

Both women stood and gave each other a hug.

Hannah walked to the door, turned and said, "One thing I forgot to ask you. Do you know if my father ever used a chemical called methyl iodide?"

Jacqui, who was gathering some folders for her meeting, said, "No, I don't think so. What is it?"

"It's a pesticide. Pretty heavy duty."

Jacqui thought for a moment. "It doesn't ring a bell. I didn't really get involved in the spraying. Your dad handled most of it himself. Him and Oswaldo. Is it important?"

"It could be." Hannah opened the door. "Thanks again, Jacqui. See you soon."

CHAPTER SIXTEEN

Hannah's phone had vibrated several times while she was with Jacqui. As soon as she was back on Fifth Avenue she checked her messages. There were three texts, two emails and a voicemail. All from Bette.

She called her friend. "Are you all right?"

"I'm pathetic. I'm a hopeless loser."

"Uh-oh. What happened?"

"I can't talk about it on the phone. Can you come over?"

"I'm in the city. I was with Jacqui. I can be there in a hour or so."

"Thank you."

Hannah speed-walked down 64th Street to the parking garage on Lexington. After the first two hours the price jumped from thirty to forty dollars. She only had a twenty, three fives, two singles and some change in her wallet. If she didn't get there in time she'd be a couple of dollars short. And her Visa card was maxed out. She'd either have to beg the attendant to let her slide for the three bucks or call Jacqui and ask her to come and bail her out. Either alternative would be totally humiliating. She checked her parking stub. She clocked in at 10:30. She looked at her watch. 12:22. She had eight minutes.

She broke into a run. Back in her playing days she could run a mile in a little under six minutes. But that was before the Weakness. The garage was only three blocks away, but her legs were wobbly. By the time she got to the cashier's booth she had to hold on to keep from falling. She peeked at the clock on the wall. 12:29. Made it with a minute to spare. The booth was empty. A pudgy Hispanic guy in a dark green jumpsuit came lumbering up the ramp. She was girding up for a fight if he tried to charge her for the extra hour when she was there on time and he was the one who was late.

He squeezed into the cashier's booth, took her ticket and inserted it into the punch clock on the inside counter.

"Twenty five dollars."

She blurted out, "I thought it was thirty."

As soon as she said it she felt stupid, like the kid who tells the teacher she forgot to give the class their homework.

"There's five-dollars off for pretty ladies."

He gave her a smarmy wink, smiled a gap-toothed smile, took a coupon from a stack next to the clock and slid it out to her.

Her first instinct was to tell him he was a disgusting pig, rip the coupon up and throw it in his face. But she quickly decided that this was no time to be a feminist crusader. Instead she thanked him, took a twenty and a ten out of her wallet and slipped it in the slot under the Plexiglas window, told him to keep the extra five and walked to her car.

She drove down Second Avenue, turned on 36th Street to the Midtown Tunnel, then got on the Long Island Expressway for the 40-odd mile trip to Bette's apartment in Huntington. She couldn't figure out why most people hated the L.I.E. They called it the Long Island Distressway and the World's Longest Parking Lot, and that's when they were trying to be nice. But to Hannah it was Long Island's best highway by far. It had three wide lanes going each way plus an HOV lane. It didn't have the scary hairpin turns of the Southern State or the dangerously short onramps of the Northern State, the two other roads that traversed the length of the Island.

But she loved it for another reason. If it wasn't for the L.I.E., the Jamaica Bay Wildlife Refuge would never exist. It was a story she heard from her father many times.

Back in the fifties, Robert Moses was the most powerful man in New York. More than the mayor. More than the governor. He was the New York City Planning Commissioner, Parks Commissioner and Construction Coordinator, the Long Island Parks Commissioner and the head of a half-dozen other commissions, departments and authorities all at the same time. And because none of those positions were elected, he didn't have to answer to politicians or the public. His admirers called him the 'Master Builder.' He was responsible for the construction of highways, bridges and major properties, including the United Nations headquarters and the New York World's Fair. Many others referred to him by different names. Tyrant and dictator were two of the gentler ones.

Moses wanted to build a highway that ran from New York City all the way out Riverhead on the eastern end of the Island. It would be one of his crowning achievements. But he had a huge obstacle. Long Island's Gold Coast was home to some of America's wealthiest families, with names like Vanderbilt, Whitney and Guggenheim. Since they didn't have to earn a living, many of the heirs to these huge fortunes devoted themselves to art, nature and ecology. They founded organizations like the Nature Conservancy and the Audubon Society, devoted to protecting the environment and preserving the natural bounty of Long Island. The last thing they wanted was a six-lane superhighway slicing through the middle of their verdant landscape like a chainsaw through a wedding cake.

The Jamaica Bay Wildlife Refuge was his compromise.

"Let me build my expressway," he said at innumerable lunches, cocktail parties and civic meetings, "And I'll build you a beautiful nature preserve right here on Jamaica Bay, where people from all over the world can come and enjoy the untouched natural beauty of New York City's last real wilderness."

Luckily for him, most of the people he spoke to had never actually seen the area around Jamaica Bay that was to be the site of this natural wonderland. Overgrown with weeds, covered with trash and smelling of airplane fuel spewing from the jets taking off and landing a couple of miles away at Idlewild Airport, soon to be renamed after JFK, Moses had no idea how to turn that murky swamp into something that would pass for a nature preserve.

One day he summoned Axel Johansson to his headquarters on Randall's Island. Johansson was a master gardener for the New York City Parks Department. He was a big man, his face ruddy and his hands calloused from a lifetime of working outdoors. His eyes, though, betrayed a gentle kindness. He shuffled back and forth nervously in front of Moses's desk.

He had seen the great man several times over the years at meetings or functions. This was his first face-to-face encounter.

"Johansson, do you know anything about birds?" Moses said matter-of-factly, as he gazed at blueprints spread across his desk.

"A little. A friend of mine is a birdwatcher and I go out with him every once in a while." He spoke slowly, trying not to sound nervous.

"Where are you living now?"

"In my mother-in-law's house. It's a two-family in Flushing. We're on the lower level."

Moses knew exactly where Axel Johansson lived, how much rent he paid his mother-in-law and, of course, that he earned an annual salary of three thousand four hundred and sixty dollars from the Parks Department.

"Suppose I told you that the City is willing to build you a house in Howard Beach and double your salary?"

Axel jolted backwards. "I don't understand."

"We'd like you to build us a bird sanctuary."

Puzzlement turned to bewilderment. "You mean like a birdhouse?"

"Not a birdhouse, a big, beautiful park, where your bird-watching friend, and thousands more like him, could go to look at the birds and enjoy the wonders of nature."

"I'm sorry sir, but I don't really know that much about birds."

"You don't need to know about birds. The experts tell me that if you want to attract birds you've got to grow plants that make the food they like to eat and plant trees that they like to nest in. And you know all about trees, shrubs, plants and grasses. You've done wonders with our golf courses. People are actually starting to enjoy playing on them, which I consider a minor miracle. Now I need you to turn the swamp next to the airport into a bird-watcher's paradise. That would be a major miracle. Do you think you can handle it?"

"I'll certainly try, sir." Axel Johansson stood at attention. It looked like he was getting ready to salute, his old army instincts coming back to him. "But I'm not sure what you meant about building me a house."

"If we're going to make this work, you've got to be there year round. Twenty-four hours a day, seven days a week. That means living there. We've already started construction on the house. It won't be a mansion but it'll be a nice home for you, your wife Olive and your little girl, Hannah, isn't it?" Moses, as always, had done his homework.

"Thank you sir, thank you very much. I feel honored that you would choose me for such an important job. But I must say again, I really don't know anything about building a bird sanctuary. I'm a gardener, a landscaper, not a bird man."

"Don't worry about that. We have access to plenty of ornithologists, bird scientists, who can tell us what to do. What we need is somebody who can actually roll up his sleeves, get his hands dirty and do it. We believe you're the man for the job. There's not a lot of money in the budget for a big staff. You'll have to make do with a skeleton crew."

"I'll do my best, sir."

Moses stood up and extended his right hand. Johansson shook it forcefully.

"Good luck, son."

Eight months later, Axel, Olive and eighteen-month-old Hannah moved into a white, one-story, three-bedroom house in the middle of a fetid swamp that was to become the Jamaica Bay Wildlife Refuge.

CHAPTER SEVENTEEN

Bette's mini apartment was on the top floor of a cute little Cape Cod, a block off Main Street in Huntington. It consisted of a small room with a smaller bathroom. A mismatched two-cushion loveseat, armless upholstered chair and imitation wood coffee table, all bought at garage sales, took up most of the space. A combination sink-fridge-stove was on the far wall.

Hannah sat on the loveseat. There were three empty cans of Bud Light on the coffee table.

"I'm such a loser," Bette said, pacing back and forth. "I can't even be a normal lesbian."

Hannah grimaced. "Normal lesbian? I don't even know what that means."

"It means I'm a big, fat failure." She plopped down on the chair.

"All right, I'll bite. Why are you such a failure?"

"I went to a club last night."

"Big deal. You've gone to a lot of clubs. Most of them with me."

"This was a different kind of club."

Hannah raised an eyebrow. "Oh? You mean..."

"It was a gay bar. Actually, a lesbian bar, the only one on Long

Island. The Henhouse, in Hauppauge." She picked nervously at her cuticles, which were already raw.

"How would you even know about a place like that?"

"I've been on a couple of Long Island lesbian message boards. There are a lot more gay women out here than I ever imagined." She drifted for a few seconds, then said, "Would you like a beer?"

Hannah looked askance at the spent cans on the coffee table. "Do you have anything besides Bud Light?"

"I might have a Heineken or two left from the last time you brought some here."

"Sold."

Bette was back with a bottle of Heineken for Hannah and another Bud Light for herself. Three beers was over her limit. Four was really pushing it.

"All right," Hannah said. "You went to this lesbian bar. Then what?"

Bette took a deep breath. That and the fourth beer seemed to calm her down.

"Just finding the place was an ordeal. It's in the middle of one of those industrial strip malls, in between an exterminator and an HVAC company. It was dark. All the other places were closed and there was no sign. There was this scary looking guy standing in front of a door. I could hear music coming from inside. He looked like some kind of Hell's Angel, with a buzz cut, leather vest and tattoos up his neck. And he was huge, close to three hundred pounds with big muscles. I didn't want to go into a biker bar by accident. I read somewhere that they take defenseless women prisoners and use them as sex slaves."

Hannah rolled her eyes. "Where'd you read that? *The Enquirer*?"

Bette shrugged.

"So that's it? End of story? You never found the place?"

"I wish that was the end of the story. I kept looking for it. I even checked my phone to make sure I had the right address. After I passed the biker a few more times he pointed at me. He wore black leather gloves where the tips of your fingers stick out. His nails were painted black. He motioned for me to come over. I didn't know what to do. My first instinct was to run but my legs were shaking so hard that I was afraid I'd fall. I walked over to him thinking maybe I could bluff my way out of getting raped or killed. As soon as I got close he looked me up and down. I thought I was dead. He asked me if I was looking for the Hen House. That's when I realized that the big scary guy was a big scary woman. When I told her I was, she said, 'First time, huh?' She looked at me the way a dog looks at a piece of steak. Then she told me there was a ten dollar cover charge, took my money and let me in."

"What was it like?"

"It was wall to wall with women. Some were young and hipster looking but there were a lot my age and even older. The music was blaring. Half of the women were smoking cigarettes. The other half smoked cigars. It was like getting stuck in the smoking car on the railroad. I had a major coughing spasm and everyone looked at me like I had the plague. Unfortunately, that's the only time anyone looked at me except for this older woman who looked like my aunt Theresa, only with a nose ring. She winked at me and asked me if I wanted a drink. I got so flustered, I stuttered 'no thank you,' ran and hid behind a potted palm near the pool table."

"There was a pool table?"

"Yeah, a nice one. There was a crowd standing around watching the women play. According to what I read, pool tables are a big deal in those kinds of clubs. You play pool, don't you?"

Hannah glared at her. "What's that supposed to mean?"

"Nothing. Just that I remembered you once mentioned that you used to play."

"My cousin Phil's parents had a pool table in their basement in Flushing. I played when we went to see them."

"Were you any good?"

Hannah scowled at her. "Forget about pool. What happened at the bar?"

"What happened? I sat there shaking like I had Parkinson's. Then I had to go to the ladies room. But two girls were in there making out. I freaked. I ran out of the ladies room door, out the front door and didn't stop until I was in my car."

"That doesn't sound so bad," Hannah lied.

"Not bad? It was awful. Humiliating. The biker woman at the door howled with laughter when I ran by. I'm sure everyone inside was laughing too. I can never show my face in there again. And it's the only lesbian club within a hundred miles of here. I am such a loser."

"You were nervous. It was your first time. I bet that happens to everyone the first time they try something like that."

Bette brightened. "You really think so?"

"Absolutely. The next time you go it'll be different."

"There won't be a next time. I can't do it again. Not alone."

"Is there anyone you know who could go there with you?"

Bette hesitated. "I really don't know any lesbians." She looked sheepishly at Hannah. "Would you come with me?"

Hannah jolted, like she'd been stuck with a cattle prod in a delicate place.

"What? Me. No way. If one of those women touched me, even by accident, I'd either belt her or throw up. Probably belt her and then throw up."

"No one's gonna hit on you. You'll be with me."

Hannah shook her head vigorously. "Absolutely not. Forget it. Change the subject."

"Okay. Sorry." Bette hesitated for a few seconds, then said, "Wasn't there something you wanted to talk to me about?"

"Oh yeah. You remember my friend Jacqui?"

Bette nodded.

"When I went to see her this morning she gave me a spreadsheet with the names and addresses of everyone who worked at the Refuge for the last few years. I bet the people I saw there the other night are on it. I was hoping that you could get some information about them. See if they have prison records. Stuff like that. Anything that might give us a clue about what they're really up to."

"Are you sure you want my help? The last time I tried to help you I made things worse."

"That's because you were out of your element, like at the bar last night. This is right up your alley. You're a great researcher. It's what you did at the law firm. And you never have to leave the apartment. You can do it all from your computer."

She closed her eyes for a few seconds. "I guess I could. I still have my Sarris & Gray I.D. I can access a couple of websites and bulletin boards that only attorneys and law enforcement can use."

"That's terrific."

Hannah handed her the sheet that Jacqui printed out for her.

"I'm interested in Dawson and Grabowski. Their names and contact information should be here." She took her phone out of her handbag. "I have some pictures of them on my phone if that helps."

Bette sat next to her on the loveseat, staring intently at the display screen.

Hannah scrolled slowly through the photos that she took when she first went to the Refuge. Many were blurry or too far away. She came to a good shot of Grabowski.

"That's the guard."

Bette cringed. "He's almost as scary as the bouncer at the Hen House."

When Hannah showed her a picture of Dawson, Bette said, "This woman looks very familiar. I think I've seen her before."

"She's that horrible woman who's in charge of the phony airport evaluation. Maybe you saw her when you were at the Refuge."

Bette shook her head. "No. I don't think so." Suddenly her eyes brightened. "She was there."

"At the Refuge?"

"No, at the Hen House."

"The lesbian bar? Are you sure?"

"I'm not one hundred per cent positive. It was very dark and smoky. I had a massive headache. But I'm pretty sure it was her. I remember her because she was one of the few women in the place who looked normal. No tattoos. No piercings. Decent clothes and haircut. I remember looking at her and thinking maybe you don't have to be a freak to be a lesbian."

Hannah brightened. "If Dawson's a lesbian, that might be the leverage we need."

"For what?"

"Who knows. But it's something. You've got to go back there and make sure it was really her."

A sly smile crept over Bette's face. "I will under one condition."

"Name it."

"You have to come with me."

Hannah's face went through several contortions. Surprise. Horror. Disgust. "Oh no. Not a chance."

"If you don't go. I don't go."

"That's blackmail."

"No it's not. It's quid pro quo. You want me to do something for you and I want you to do something for me."

"Except what you want me to do is disgusting."

"I'm not asking you to have sex with another woman or even touch one. Just to walk into the bar with me."

Hannah scrunched her face in distaste. "I don't know."

Bette folded her arms. "That's my condition."

"I'll think about it." Hannah didn't look happy. "Whether or not I go with you, are you still gonna be my researcher?"

Bette smiled smugly. "I'll think about it."

CHAPTER EIGHTEEN

When she walked into the house Hannah was shocked to see her mother reading a newspaper in her father's club chair. Olive considered the chair consecrated ground. An upholstered memorial to her husband. The back cushion was discolored and indented where his head rested. The arm covers were frayed from his elbows. Hannah could just as easily picture her mother putting a butterfly tattoo on her butt as sitting in Axel's sacred chair.

"You're in daddy's chair," she cried. "What's wrong?"

When she put the paper down and turned to face her, Hannah saw that it wasn't Olive in the chair, but Gilda. This wasn't the first time Hannah wondered how two sisters could look so alike and be so different.

"Oh, hello Gilda," Hannah said, trying hard not to show the animosity she felt. "I thought you were my mother."

Gilda cringed. "Heaven forbid." She pointed to Olive's bedroom door. "She in there suffering with a migraine. I'm sure it was brought on by your shenanigans."

Hannah forced herself not to react. She was determined not to fight with Gilda. She walked towards Olive's bedroom without making eye contact with her aunt.

"Where do you think you're going?" Gilda screeched.

"I'm going to see how mom's doing."

"Absolutely not. You'll only make it worse."

Hannah gnashed her teeth, took a breath and very calmly said, "I'm sorry Aunt Gilda, but you don't give the orders in this house. In fact, the last time you were here you said you would never set foot in here again."

Gilda glared at her. "You'd like that wouldn't you," she cackled like a geriatric Wicked Witch of the West. "Then nobody would be around to hold you to account. Certainly not your weak-kneed mother. Once she married that heathen father of yours the Christian values she was brought up with went out the window."

"That's it!" Hannah screamed. "I promised my mother I wouldn't fight with you but this is too much. My father was a better person than you could ever hope to be. You're nothing but a mean, nasty old hypocrite with no right to lecture anyone about Christian values. What about the golden rule? Do unto others. You treat everyone like crap. My whole life all you've ever done is put me down and compare me to Catherine. I'll tell you something about your precious daughter. She was a total slut in college. She had two abortions. Two! One after screwing her economics professor, which is probably the only reason she passed the course. I guess she takes after Fred. Everyone in the family knows that he was a compulsive gambler and serial adulterer. But who could blame him, being married to a horrible bitch like you."

Gilda began to shake. With rage or shock or both. She opened her mouth but no sound came out.

Olive shuffled into the room, a towel wrapped around her head. Her attempted shout was more of a raspy groan. "Quiet! Both of you."

Gilda sunk down into Axel's club chair. Hannah stood, still seething, her hands balled into fists at her side.

Olive wagged a finger at them. "You should be ashamed of yourselves. Both of you. With the passing of my poor Axel still tearing my heart apart, I thought I could depend on my sister and my daughter, the two closest people I have in this world, to help me get a little peace and comfort. Instead you're making it worse." She pointed at one, then the other. "I want you both to leave. Get out of my house. Now."

Hannah, deflated said, "But she..."

"No buts." She pointed at the door. "Go."

Hannah stormed out the door and headed for the beach. Her beach. The water was a cloudy brownish green with floating strings of seaweed and the occasional jellyfish. The sand was coarse and full of jagged stones that turned bare feet bloody. But she wouldn't trade it for the shores of Hawaii. She loved everything about it, even its name. Beech beach. Because the staircase leading down to it was at the end of Beech Road. But that was the only redundant thing about it. From languid lake to raging sea, it was different every day. On that particular cloudy spring afternoon the Sound was in a kittenish mood. Timid but a little playful. Tiny waves, more like ripples, tiptoed gingerly up to the shore, then scampered back.

Hannah walked along the pebble-strewn sand to a giant log that was deposited there by last March's nor'easter. That day the Sound was a different animal. A bellowing grizzly that destroyed everything in its path, including a rack that held ten kayaks, two lifeguard towers and a twenty-foot seawall, all reduced to splinters. A huge slab of concrete rested awkwardly at the edge of the bluff. Before the storm, it was part of a parking lot that overlooked the sound, 200 feet up the cliff.

Hannah braved the hurricane force wind and punishing hail that day to try to take some pictures of the ferocious tempest. All she got for her trouble was a series of blurry gray images, a renewed appreciation of the awesomeness of nature and a water-logged lens in her favorite camera.

She sat on the log and gazed hypnotically at the rippling water, which always relaxed her. But not this time. Her mind was a continuous loop of scenes from her personal disaster movie.

Frame after depressing frame cycled through her brain. Knocking her father down the stairs. Passing out on the podium at his memorial. Dawson and her hooligan henchman doing who knows what to her beloved Jamaica Bay Refuge. The burglary that burgled nothing but her camera with the incriminating photos. Getting hauled off to jail in handcuffs. Poor Perry's mangled corpse mingled with her lens cap. The revelation that her father was poisoned. Murdered.

The more she thought about it, the more she realized that Gilda was right. She was a total loser. No job, no relationship, no apartment of her own and not much likelihood of getting any of them anytime soon. Her body, which she could always depend on, betrayed her with some mysterious condition that doctors can't diagnose. The guy she thought was the love of her life turned out to be a lying, cheating asshole. And now even her mother is pissed off at her.

Her ringing cell phone jolted her out of her wallow.

It was Bette. She thought about not answering it. Then she pressed 'Talk.'

"Hullo," she said glumly.

"What's the matter? You sound awful."

Hannah wasn't one of those women who loved to share her deepest thoughts, dreams and sorrows with anyone who would listen. Or anyone at all, for that matter. She thought her feelings were nobody else's business.

"Just not in a great mood," she said.

"You will be as soon as you hear what I found out about those names you gave me."

Hannah perked up. "What? Tell me."

"Not over the phone. It's a show-and-tell. Are you busy?"

"Busy feeling sorry for myself."

"You didn't have dinner yet, did you?"

"No. I'm not too hungry."

"Well I'm starved. Can you meet me at the Asian Pavilion? It's usually pretty empty. We can get a table for six and spread out."

"Why do we need to spread out?"

"You'll see."

"This isn't a trick to try to get me to go to that lesbian bar with you, is it?"

"Absolutely not. Trust me, you'll want to see this."

"Okay, I'll meet you there in a half-hour."

CHAPTER NINETEEN

The young hostess greeted Hannah with a demure smile as she walked through the front door of the Asian Pavilion.

"One for dinner, yes?"

Hannah glanced quickly around the room, looking for Bette. Two of the eight tables were occupied. One by two distinguished looking older women. Hannah guessed they were professors at Stony Brook University, just a few blocks away. The other by a young couple.

"I'm supposed to meet my friend. She hasn't been here yet, has she? Short, dark hair. Glasses."

"Okay, yes. This way." The hostess walked toward the rear, signaling Hannah to follow her.

A four-panel floor-to-ceiling fabric screen with white seagulls on a pale blue background separated the main dining area from two long tables near the kitchen. At one, a boy of about twelve was folding wontons and depositing them carefully into a large bowl. A young man stood over him, arms folded, instructing him on the finer points of wonton construction. Bette was at the other table, sipping tea from a small stemless cup and munching on crispy noodles.

When the hostess brought Hannah to the table, Bette looked up and said, “Welcome to my office.”

Hannah sat, facing her. “So, what did you find out?” she said, peering at the manila folder next to the noodles.

Bette grabbed the white porcelain tea pot, refilled her cup then poured one for Hannah.

“I don’t know about you, but I’m starving,” she said with a sly smile. “I got so involved in this research that I forgot to eat lunch.”

She picked up the menu and gazed at it intently. She seemed to enjoy toying with Hannah, knowing her friend was dying to know what was in the folder. She signaled to the wonton coach, who was their waiter.

When he came to the table, Bette said, “I think I’m going to have the General Tsao’s chicken with brown rice.”

The waiter turned to Hannah. “And you?”

Hannah forced herself to smile, or at least not look so surly. “I’ll just have some fried rice with vegetables.”

The waiter grabbed the menus and was off.

Hannah glowered at her friend. “We ordered. We had tea. Is there anything else we need to do before you tell me what you learned?”

Bette grinned. “Are you ready?”

“I’ve been ready for the last ten minutes.”

“It’s all about Iraq.”

Of all the theories swirling in Hannah’s mind about what was going on at the Refuge, none were even remotely connected to Iraq.

“What possible connection could a bird sanctuary in Queens have with Iraq?”

Bette nodded. “I know. Right. That’s what I thought. But the more I kept digging, the more Iraq kept popping up.”

Hannah said, “I can imagine Grabowski being over there. He looks like just the type who would kill Iraqi babies just for fun.

But Dawson? She doesn't seem like any kind of a G.I. Jane. More like an evil librarian."

Bette took a sheet of paper out of the folder and eyed it for a few seconds. She began to read: "From June of 2003 to April of 2004 Elyse Dawson was a civilian administrator with the Coalition Provisional Authority in Baghdad."

"That sounds pretty important. Are you sure we're talking about the same woman. Mousy brown hair, beady eyes, face like a chipmunk."

Bette reached into the folder, pulled out a photo and handed it to Hannah. "Is this her?"

"Her hair's a little grayer now and she's a couple of pounds heavier but yeah, that's definitely her. If that's who they put in charge over there no wonder it was such a mess."

"Mess?" Bette yelled. "It was a goddamn catastrophe! Thousands of American soldiers dead or crippled for life. And more than half-a-million Iraqis killed. For what? Things are just as bad there now as they ever were. Worse!"

The young wonton origamist at the other side of the room stopped to look at her.

She cut herself short. Put her hand over her mouth. "I'm sorry," she said, contritely. "I get very emotional whenever I think about that terrible, useless war."

"You don't have to apologize. I got sick to my stomach every time I saw anything about it on TV. After awhile I stopped watching the news. As soon as it came on I flipped over to the Hallmark Channel. So now I don't know much about current events but I can tell you anything you want to know about The Waltons and Little House on the Prairie."

The waiter arrived with their food. Bette dove into her chicken like she hadn't eaten for a week. Hannah picked at her fried rice.

When Bette came up for air, Hannah said, "You still haven't told me what Iraq has to do with what's going on at Jamaica Bay."

"Sorry." She opened the folder. "Elyse Dawson was Assistant

Director of Logistics for the Coalition Provisional Transportation Authority."

"What exactly is that?"

"She was in charge of making sure that everything that was flown into the country got to where it was supposed to go."

"I wouldn't have thought she had the smarts for that. Or the expertise."

"She didn't." Bette scowled. "Before she went to Iraq she was a paralegal."

"You're a paralegal. Do you know how to do that stuff?"

Bette shook her head and smirked. "No. And I'm sure she didn't either."

"So how'd she get such an important job?"

"The same way incompetent people everywhere get jobs they're not qualified for. She had connections. Her father is Dick Dawson. Ever hear of him?"

Hannah shook her head. "Doesn't ring a bell."

"He was the Under Secretary of State for Public Diplomacy and Public Affairs under the first President Bush, basically a P.R. flack. But that's not what made him famous. After he left Washington he wrote a book, *The Downfall of Democracy*. It was about how liberals are turning America into a socialist state. He promoted it on Fox News and all the right wing radio and TV shows. It even made it to the bottom of the best-seller list for a week or two. That led to his having his own Fascist radio program. He was one of the earliest proponents of invading Iraq. I'm sure that's how his daughter wound up there. Back then, ideology was more important that actually knowing what you're doing."

"So she was in over her head in Iraq. I still don't see how that ties in with the Refuge."

"I'm getting to that." Bette took a sheet of paper out of the folder.

"William Grabowski was in Baghdad the same time as Dawson. He was in Special Forces but had an OTH discharge."

"What's that?"

"It means he did some bad stuff over there but never got court-martialed. He went back to Iraq as a contractor for a firm called Armstrong and Warren."

"Never heard of them."

"Neither did I. There were hundreds of companies raking in money over there. Huge multinationals like Halliburton, Raytheon and ITT. Also plenty of smaller ones that came and went. That's why I thought it was weird that A&W kept popping up."

"What did they do?"

Bette looked down at the info sheet. "Transportation and Logistics Management."

"I thought logistics was Dawson's job."

Bette nodded. "It was. That's the connection."

"Where does Grabowski fit in? I doubt he can spell logistics, much less do it."

"His job was to guard the trucks transporting the material. Are you starting to see the connection?"

Hannah shook her head. "Not really. They knew each other from Iraq. How does that help us?"

Bette took another sheet out of the folder. "I'm not finished," she said smugly. "Armstrong and Warren was involved in several lawsuits for doing shady deals over there. A lot of the stuff never got where it was supposed to go. It was a big scandal. Eventually they became insolvent."

"Is that the same as bankrupt?"

"Similar. But there's a major difference. You can't buy a business that's filed for bankruptcy but you can buy a company that's insolvent. And that's what happened."

Hannah rolled her eyes. "Enough with the finance law. I still don't see what any of this has to do with the Refuge?"

Bette preened smugly. "This is where it gets interesting. The firm that bought Armstrong and Warren is a company called Greenleaf Industries."

Hannah looked perplexed. "Greenleaf. Where have I seen that name?"

"Probably on a sign at the Jamaica Bay Refuge. They're the ones in charge of the JFK extension evaluation. Think about it. They're supposed to be trying to figure out if they can build an airport there. To do that you need engineers, architects, geologists, people like that. What you don't need are a paralegal and a security guard."

"Now we're getting somewhere."

"But wait." Bette grinned. "There's more." She grabbed another sheet out of the envelope. "Greenleaf hired an outfit called BlackAmmo to handle security for the Jamaica Bay project. Grabowski is technically employed by them."

Hannah raised her hand. "Slow down. Can you go over all these companies again? It's starting to be a big jumble."

"Okay," Bette said slowly, like she was talking to a child. "Armstrong and Warren was the company that did logistics in Iraq. Dawson worked with them over there. A&W was bought by Greenleaf, the company that's doing the airport extension evaluation. That's who Dawson works for now. Grabowski, who worked for A&W, is now employed by BlackAmmo, the security firm hired by Greenleaf."

"I'm sorry but none of this seems that sinister to me. The airport hired Greenleaf to do the project and they outsourced their security. Sounds normal. What's the problem?"

"Greenleaf is the problem. For a project as important as expanding one of the word's most important airports, you'd think the Port Authority would choose a major player."

"Wait. The Port Authority? How are they involved in this? I thought they dealt with the bridges and tunnels that go from New York to New Jersey."

"They do. But they also run the New York airports, JFK, LaGuardia and Newark."

"I never knew that. Sorry I interrupted you. Keep going."

"Greenleaf. I looked up the top 100 civil engineering firms.

Greenleaf wasn't there. They weren't in the top 500 either. In fact, they weren't listed anywhere. Not in any of the databases. Not even the proprietary ones. The only thing I managed to dig up was an address in Panama."

"Panama? Why would the Port Authority use a company from Panama? It doesn't make sense."

"It does if it's a shell company."

"Stop showing off. You know I don't know what that is."

"When you don't want anyone to know your business you set up a dummy company that's a stand-in for the real one. That way, when someone starts nosing around, all they find is an address."

"Why would the Port Authority use a company like that when they can hire the best firms in the world?"

"Good question."

"Is there any way to find out what the real company is?"

"It's difficult but not impossible. I'll have to do a lot more digging."

"I'm sorry."

Bette's face lit up. "Are you kidding? I love this stuff."

"That makes one of us. If I had to look through corporate records all day, I'd shoot myself. What about the security company, BlackAmmo? Is that also a fake?"

"No. It's a real company based here in New York, according to their website."

"Does the website say if there's any connection to Greenleaf?"

"There might be a connection but it's not on the website. Mostly there are a lot of pictures showing off their soldiers or contractors or operatives, whatever you call them. Gorgeous guys, bare chested, muscles bulging, glistening with sweat and grime, posing with long knives and huge guns. I was getting more turned on with every shot. There was one picture that really caught my attention. It was BlackAmmo's president, Stan Westbrook. He's a retired Marine colonel."

"What about him?"

"He was the guy that picked me up that night when we went to the Refuge."

"Holy shit! Really? Now we're getting somewhere." Hannah paused for a minute. "I'm glad you're attracted to guys again. Now I won't have to go to that bar with you."

"The Hen House? You were really going to come with me?"

"You did all that work for me. I figured it was the least I could do."

"I didn't do it just for you. I told you, the Jamaica Bay Wildlife Refuge means a lot to me too."

"Just so you know, I was really ready to go."

"Great! Let's go tonight."

Hannah stiffened. "I thought you were back into guys."

"Maybe, but I still might be attracted to women. I'm just not sure. If we go back, maybe I'll know."

CHAPTER TWENTY

When Hannah was a little girl, her favorite days of the year were Christmas, Easter and the last day of June, when everyone in the family gathered at Hannah's grandparents' house on Ashby Avenue in Flushing. It was a four-car caravan. Hannah and her parents in her father's forest green Ford Fairlane. Her grandparents in the big Chevy Suburban, loaded with food, toys, clothing and odds and ends from the four households. Uncle Fred, Aunt Gilda and Catherine in their fancy Buick. And Uncle Joe and Aunt Theresa with Phil and Jerrold in the Dodge Diplomat.

Hannah remembered gazing out the window at farms, orchards and fields of wildflowers, excitedly looking forward to spending the summer in the country and playing on the beach with her cousins.

That Long Island didn't exist anymore. At least not in that part of Suffolk County. No longer rural, it wasn't quite a suburb, it was a conglomeration of subdivisions and shopping plazas in search of an identity. The 20-minute drive down 25A from the Asian Pavilion in East Setauket to the Hen House in Hauppauge, featured a parade of tacky strip malls where the orchards, fields and wildflowers used to be. The gleeful anticipation of a joyous summer by the nine-year-old Hannah was replaced by the dread of being in a crowded, noisy bar surrounded by hordes of sweaty predatory women who wanted to do disgusting things to her.

She had nothing against homosexuality as a concept. She believed that sexual attraction was hard-wired at birth and that being gay or straight was no more a choice than being tall or short. It's just that whenever she pictured two women in bed together it made her slightly nauseous. Now she'd be in a place where there was a good chance they would be making out at the table next to her.

What made her feel even worse was that Bette, whose mood usually ranged from melancholy to morose, was as happy as a kid on her way to Disney World.

Bette looked over at Hannah. "I think we should start a business doing this."

"Going to lesbian bars? I don't think we'd make much money."

"No, not that. We should become investigators."

"You mean like Jack Nicholson in Chinatown. He got half his nose sliced off."

Bette shook her head. "That's not how it is in real life. Nowadays an investigator's main weapon is a laptop. Law firms hire them for all kinds of cases. My old company had three on retainer. And investigators make good money. Neither one of us has a job right now. What do we have to lose? I can handle the legal stuff and do the background checks and other research and you would do the field work. You'd be a great interviewer. People like talking to you."

"Are you kidding! My mother's not even talking to me."

Bette ignored her. "I know a lot of lawyers. I bet I could get us tons of clients."

"If it's so non-violent, how come in every detective show I see on TV someone is always getting beat up or shot at? Usually it's the investigator."

"That's because if they showed what investigators actually do no one would watch. Besides, if any rough stuff did happen, you can handle it. You took karate for a couple of years, right?"

"Not karate, muay thai."

"Isn't that a drink?"

"That's mai tai."

"Muay thai, mai tai, potato-potahto. It doesn't matter. What does matter is you're one tough lady."

"What matters is that I have this mystery condition that turns my muscles into cottage cheese. When these attacks happen, I can hardly strike a match, much less an attacker."

"How are you now?"

"Right now, I'm fine. It doesn't happen all the time. Sometimes not for days or longer."

"Maybe whatever it is, is getting better. It could be some weird virus that's running its course. Soon you'll be as good as new."

"That would be great. But I'm not counting on it."

"You'll see I'm right."

"Look at you. Miss positivity. I like this new attitude."

"The timid little mouse you know is still in there but I'm working on it. You're my inspiration. You're not scared of anything."

"Are you kidding. I'm afraid of so many things it's ridiculous. Like right now I'm terrified of going to this bar."

"That's different. You're just nervous about doing something you've never done before. I'm talking about real courage. Like the way you went back to the Refuge with that scary guy and his big assault rifle."

"I was plenty afraid. But it was something I had to do. It was the last promise I ever made to my dad."

"I couldn't do it no matter what. Even the way you stood up to your aunt. There's no way I could talk to any of my relatives like that."

"That worked out well for me. Now my aunt despises me, my mother won't talk to me and when my cousin Catherine, who never liked me to begin with, hears what I said, she'll be my mortal enemy forever."

After a few more minutes, Bette pulled into what looked like a strip mall designed by Mad Max on a hangover. The pavement was cracked and pocked with potholes. The storefronts were covered by metal grates that looked like chain mail venetian blinds. The few streetlamps that actually worked provided just enough light and shadow to make it eerie.

Hannah said, "This is it?"

"Yup."

"It's not the high rent district, that's for sure."

Bette parked between a Snapple truck and an HVAC van. They walked to the far end of a row of storefronts to the only door with no metal grille. As they approached they could hear the din of raucous music and a thumping bass. The front window was obscured by black fabric. There was no sign. A large woman was guarding the door, arms folded like superman.

As they approached, Hanna said, "Is that the same one from last time?"

Bette whispered, "Uh huh."

"She's not that scary."

"Not to you. You're Wonder Woman."

At the door, the guard looked Bette over.

"Back for more, huh?"

She turned her gaze to Hannah. "You brought a wingwoman with you. Good choice." She winked at Hannah.

Bette handed her a twenty-dollar bill. "This is for me and my friend."

Hannah didn't know what to expect after Bette's fevered description of her first encounter, maybe an all-female version of the Star Wars cantina. But at first glance it was just your basic dive bar, crowded, smoky and noisy, except for the fact that there were no men anywhere. There were some big, burly, bull-dykey women but most would have looked right at home in any of the Long Island pubs Hannah hung out in over the years.

There was a long bar with ten vinyl stools, all occupied, and many more women standing. Four brands of beer were on tap, including Blue Point, a Long Island microbrewery that Hannah was partial to. The pool table in the back was regulation size with mauve felt instead of the usual green.

Hannah and Bette squeezed between two stools at the bar and ordered. Bud Light for Bette, Blue Point Toasted Lager for Hannah. The bartender handed them two bottles. No glasses.

Hannah scanned the room looking for Dawson. No luck. There was a tap on her shoulder.

"You looking for me, honey?"

Hannah turned to face a 40-something woman with short hair, dyed a color that doesn't exist in nature and a face like a boxer (dog or prizefighter, take your pick). She wore a denim shirt with the sleeves rolled up. A cigarette hung from the side of her mouth.

Hannah was silent for a long two seconds then said, "Uh…sorry. I'm with her." She grabbed Bette's wrist.

Boxer-face shrugged and said, "Can't blame a girl for asking." Then she walked down to the other end of the bar.

Hannah downed the rest of her beer in one gulp. "Let's go. Dawson's not here and I'm totally skeeved."

"Just because that woman hit on you?"

"It wouldn't have been so bad if a nice looking one came over, but as my cousin Phil would say, she looks like she was beaten with a really big ugly stick."

"At least someone talked to you. This is my second time here and it's like I'm invisible."

Bette looked up at the clock over the bar. It was a black beer tray with cowgirl in a red dress sitting on a crescent moon, holding a neon glass of beer.

"We haven't even been here fifteen minutes. Let's stay for one more drink."

"I don't know if I can survive another drink."

"Come on. We'll sit by the pool table. Nobody'll bother you there."

"All right. Then we're even for the research you did."

"I told you," Bette said with fake indignation. "I didn't do that for you. I did it for myself. And I enjoyed it."

"Fine. One more drink, then we go."

Hannah asked for another bottle of Blue Point and headed for the pool table with Bette trailing behind.

The women at the table were doing more posing than playing, trying to look like Tom Cruise in *The Color of Money*, though a couple were more reminiscent of Minnesota Fats from the original *Hustler*.

Hannah and Bette stood silently, sipping their beers and watching the pool players.

After a few minutes Hannah said, "These women stink."

Bette said, "Why don't you go up there and show them how it's done."

Hannah shook her head. "Oh no. That'll just prolong the agony. As soon as we finish our beers, we're leaving."

"All right. But no chug-a-lugging."

Hannah had one more sip left when Bette said, "I think I see her."

"Who?"

"Dawson." She pointed. "Over there. By the door. Talking to that woman with all the tattoos."

Bette took a sheet of paper out of her handbag. It was a photo of Dawson she downloaded off the internet. She held it up to Hannah.

"See. It's her."

Hannah stared at the woman standing near the door. It looked like Dawson but it was too dark to be sure. "C'mon. Let's go over there."

Bette was suddenly skittish. "I don't know. Maybe it's not her."

"Only one way to find out."

"What are you gonna do?"

"When we get there I'll let you know."

Hannah marched over. It was Dawson. No doubt. Instead of a baggy business suit she was wearing black jeans and a white button-down men's shirt.

For a few seconds Dawson didn't notice her. She was too engrossed in conversation with the tattooed woman.

Then she looked around and saw Hannah glaring at her. It took a few seconds for it to register.

"You!" she screeched. "What the hell are you doing here?"

Hannah turned crimson. "You're a murderer," she yelled.

"Killing a cat isn't murder. And you can't prove it."

"I'm gonna prove you killed my father!"

"What! You're insane."

"I know you did it, you evil, homicidal bitch."

"How dare you talk to me like that," Dawson screamed. Then she threw her drink in Hannah's face.

Hannah slapped Dawson hard on the side of the head. She let out a high-pitch squeal, like a chipmunk caught in a steel trap. As her hands went up to her head, Hannah clubbed her in the gut. Dawson doubled over and crumbled to the floor, gasping and groaning.

The Hells Angel looking woman guarding the door ran in. She grabbed Hannah in a powerful bear hug from behind, pinning her arms to her sides.

Hannah tried breaking free but the grip was too strong. Hannah rammed her head back, into the guard's nose. She yelped but held her grip. Then Hannah stomped her heel into the guard's instep. The hulking lesbian let go, blood dripping from her nostrils.

"You broke my nose you fucking bitch," she cried, then staggered onto a bar stool, holding her nose.

The bartender jumped out from behind the bar and came at Hannah with what looked like a child-size baseball bat. Before she could swing it, Hannah kicked her in the stomach, sending her gasping to her knees.

The Hen House erupted into bedlam. Women screaming, running in every direction, knocking over tables, chairs, anything in their way. Four women brandishing pool cues, surrounded Hannah. She held her hands up in a 'truce' gesture. None of the women approached her or said anything. They just stood there forming a human barricade while Hannah leaned against the bar, gulping air, her muscles rubbery.

They stayed that way for a few minutes when a policeman pushed through the crowd. White. Mid-thirties.

He looked around at the mayhem. "What the hell's going on here."

Dawson stepped forward, a large red weal blooming on her cheek. She pointed at Hannah.

"Arrest her," she screamed. "She attacked me. This riot is all her doing. "

The cop said to Hannah, "Is that true?"

Hannah shrugged, too exhausted to reply.

He took her elbow. "You better come with me."

They marched through the hostile gauntlet.

CHAPTER TWENTY-ONE

The policeman walked Hannah to his patrol car, parked a few doors down. A few minutes later Bette stole furtively out of the bar and walked over to them.

The cop eyed them with a mixture of pity and revulsion. "I know you lesbians think you're as tough as any man, but getting into barroom brawls ain't the way to prove it."

"I'm no lesbian," Hannah said, indignantly.

He eyed her skeptically. "If you say so. I guess you just randomly wandered in that place while you were strolling through a dark, deserted industrial park in the middle of the night."

Hannah glared at Bette, then said, "It's a long story that you probably don't want to hear and wouldn't believe if you did."

He sneered. "Whatever. I need to see some I.D."

Bette said, "Are we going to be arrested?"

"Not unless somebody presses charges. And I don't think that's going to happen with that crowd." He took a leather-covered field notebook from his duty belt. "But I need your names and addresses for the incident report."

They handed him their licenses. He copied the information and gave the licenses back. He looked benignly from Hannah to Bette.

"Do yourselves a favor, stay away from here. You girls don't look like troublemakers. But if I catch you doing something like this again, things won't go so easy." He got into his car still shaking his head.

Neither woman said a word as they shambled to Bette's Prius like prisoners returning to their cell after lights out.

In the car, Hannah said, "I don't know what was worse. Getting into a brawl with a bunch of sweaty women or that snarky cop looking at me like I was some sort of degenerate." She looked over at Bette who was grinning. "What are you so happy about? That was an absolute horror show."

"Not totally."

"Why? Because we didn't get the crap beaten out of us in there and we're not on our way to jail?"

"That's one reason." She reached into her bag and took out a small notebook. "And this is another."

"What is it?"

"Dawson's daily planner. I lifted it out of her bag while you two were fighting and everyone else was watching."

"Wow. Okay. Good work. Let's have a look."

Hannah leafed through the pages. Each two-page spread was devoted to a single day. Most were filled with mundane entries. Meetings, deliveries, doctor's appointments.

She noticed that at the bottom of a few pages there were cryptic notations in red ink.

After staring at them cluelessly for a minute or so, she had a thought. She turned to the night that she and Bette went to Jamaica Bay. At the bottom of that page was: 2:00. 20M. TM/SW/BG.

She handed the diary to Bette. "Take a look at the bottom of this page."

Bette looked intently at it then shrugged. "It doesn't mean anything to me. Do you think it's some kind of code?"

"Did you notice what day that was?"

Bette looked down, then back at Hannah. "It was last week. But I don't see the significance."

"It was the night we were there," Hannah said. "When they picked up those bundles at the dock. I bet these notations are for when they get their shipments from across the bay."

"If you're right, this could be an important clue." Bette started leafing through the pages to the end. "There's only one more page with writing at the bottom."

Hannah's expression went from gleeful to glum. "It doesn't matter. Once Dawson finds out her datebook's missing, she'll change the schedule. We just blew our last chance of catching them in the act."

"The act of what?"

"Smuggling."

"What could they be smuggling?"

"I don't know, but they're going through a lot of trouble not to have to go through Customs with whatever's in those bundles."

"I'm sorry. I thought stealing her diary would really help."

"There's nothing to be sorry about. You did great. It took smarts and guts. I'm proud of you. It's just too bad we can't put it back before she realizes it was missing."

Bette grinned slyly. "Maybe we can."

She fished her phone out of her handbag and photographed the page with the red code at the bottom.

Hannah said, "What good will that do?"

"You'll see."

Bette dropped the diary in her bag, opened her door and headed back toward the Hen House.

"Wait," Hannah yelled, "Where are you going?"

Bette didn't answer. She kept walking back towards the bar. She went inside.

A few minutes later she came out, her face illuminated by a huge grin.

When Bette got back in the car Hannah said, "Are you all

right? Those women in there were pretty angry. I thought you'd be leaving there on a stretcher."

"When you're small, quiet and mousy you're practically invisible. You just fade into the woodwork. It's the story of my life. Only this time it worked to our benefit. Nobody noticed me when I came in or when I left."

"What was it like in there?"

"It was weird."

"It was weird before."

"But this was a different kind of weird. The music was turned off. It was sorta quiet, like they were trying to come to grips with what just happened."

"Did you see Dawson?"

"She was over in a corner with a couple of women around her. She was pretty shaken up but it looked like she was enjoying the attention."

"She didn't see you, did she?"

"I don't think so. But even if she did, I don't think she knew we were together."

"What about the diary? Were you were able to sneak it back into her bag."

Bette shook her head. "Impossible. She was clutching it on her lap with both hands, like it was a life preserver."

"What did you do?"

"I dropped it on the floor near the bar, close to the spot where you slapped her. I'm hoping somebody finds it and gives it back to her, thinking she dropped it in all the confusion."

Hannah nodded approvingly. "That's pretty good. Maybe you should do the field work and I'll do the paperwork."

"No thanks. Tonight was enough excitement to last me a lifetime."

"What's the date of the next red entry?"

Bette looked at her phone.

"It's this Thursday. If that first number is the time, it's at one o'clock in the morning."

"That doesn't leave much time."

"To do what?"

"I don't know yet. I'll have to figure it out when I get there."

Bette looked horrified. "No. You're not going back."

"You went back into the bar. The least I can do is go back to the Refuge. Whatever's in those bundles is the key to everything. It's why they killed my father. I'm sure of it."

Bette shook her head. "You can't. It's too dangerous. It's one thing fighting with some overweight out of shape women. That thug at the Refuge looks like the Incredible Hulk with a worse attitude. And the other guy, what's his name, Westbrook, he looks pretty tough too."

"It doesn't matter. They'll never know I'm there. I'll go in. Take some pictures. And get out. Trust me, there's nothing to worry about."

Bette put her hand to her mouth. "Oh God. That's it. We're doomed."

"What are you talking about?"

"You just put the whammy on us."

"Stop with the superstitious crap. You've been hanging out with your grandmother too much. Nothing's gonna happen, believe me."

Bette crossed herself. "I hope you're right."

CHAPTER TWENTY-TWO

When Hannah arrived home around midnight, she was totally exhausted and wide awake. The lesbian riot. Almost getting arrested. Again! Dawson's planner. Her father's murder. Sneaking back into the Refuge. It all swirled in her head, keeping her awake for hours. She finally passed out sometime between three and four in the morning.

The phone jarred her awake. She reached for it. Missed. Knocked it off the nightstand. By the time she scrounged around the floor and found it, the ringing stopped. Still groggy, she blinked several times, trying to clear her vision and get the blurry numbers on the phone into focus. The time was 9:05. The missed call was from Phil.

Her body told her to go back to sleep but her brain said no.

She called her cousin back.

"Phil, it's Hannah. What's up?"

"I'm in the hospital with Gilda."

"Oh my God. What happened?"

"She was talking on the phone with Catherine last night when all of a sudden she said her chest was pounding and she felt faint. Catherine told her to lie down. She called an ambulance. Then she called me."

Whenever anyone in the family had a medical issue their first call was to Phil. Sometimes even before their regular doctor. He always made time to help, whether it was to show up or to stay on the phone until help arrived. That more than made up for his habitual tardiness.

"Was it a heart attack?"

"It doesn't look like it. Most of the tests came back negative. We're still waiting for one more."

"Is Catherine there now?"

"No. She stayed here all night. I told her to go back to Gilda's to get some rest."

"What hospital?"

"Huntington."

"I'll get my mom. We'll be there as soon as we can."

Phil was quiet for a few seconds, then he said, "I don't think that's such a good idea."

"What do you mean?"

"I've never seen Catherine so pissed off."

"About what?"

"You."

"Me?"

"As soon as I got here Catherine started carrying on that you gave Gilda a heart attack. That you killed your father and now you're trying to kill her mother."

Hannah opened her mouth but nothing came out. Her emotions were on a runaway remote. She went from being angry at what Catherine said, to feeling guilty that she put Gilda in the hospital, to being pissed off all over again remembering how Gilda attacked her, to feeling sorry that she put her mother in the awkward position of having to choose between her daughter and her sister. After about ten seconds Phil said, "Are you still there?"

"I'm here."

"What did you say to Gilda that was so bad?"

Hannah took a breath to steady herself. Then in as calm a

voice as she could muster she said, "Gilda was in one of her bitchy moods, worse than usual, making nasty comments left and right. I had promised my mother I wouldn't let her get to me. And I tried. I really did. But you know Gilda. She kept at it. Picking at me like a scab. Telling me I was worthless. A loser. A disappointment. I wouldn't bite. I just smiled and nodded. But she wouldn't stop. Then she started saying horrible things about my dad. How my mother lowered herself when she got married. How the whole family looked down on us. That we had no Christian values. That's when I lost it."

"What the hell did you say?"

"I told her she was no one to talk about Christian values. That Catherine was a slut in college. That she had two abortions."

"No wonder Catherine's pissed off at you."

"That's not all. I told her we all knew about Fred's cheating. That nobody blamed him because he was married to a bitch like her."

"Holy shit! Were you TRYING to give her a heart attack?"

"I know. I was out of control. I wish I could take it back. Do you think she'll be okay?"

"She should be fine. Her tests were all good."

"If it wasn't a heart attack, what was it?"

"Stress can cause chest pain. What you said could certainly stress her out. But knowing Gilda, I wouldn't be shocked if we find out that she faked the whole thing."

"I hope so. If she died I don't know what I'd do. Not after everything else."

"Like what?"

Hannah told him everything that happened since the last time she spoke to him, finishing with her plan to sneak back there to see what's in the storage barn.

"I know I promised to help, but going back there is a bad idea after what you just told me. We'll have to think of something else."

"There is nothing else. It's our last chance. I'm going. If you want to come I could use the help. If you don't, I understand."

"What about your condition. Suppose you get an attack?"

"I'll deal with it."

"All right, I'll go with you. I'm not gonna let you face those thugs alone."

"Are you sure? You don't have to. It's my home they're destroying. It's my father they poisoned."

"I loved uncle Axe. If they killed him I want them to pay for it as much as you do."

"Dawson's diary said the next shipment is coming tomorrow night at one a.m. And it's the last one."

"I'm in."

"Are you sure?"

"One hundred per cent."

"Thanks. I owe you."

"Here's how you can pay me back."

"How?"

"Call Rudy Romano, my neurologist friend. Make an appointment like you promised."

"How do you know I didn't call him already?"

"Cause I spoke to him."

"All right. I'll call."

"I know you probably ripped up his number so here it is again."

He gave her the number and told her he'd be there tomorrow night after dinner. Then he hung up.

Now came the moment Hannah was dreading. Telling her mother that Gilda was in the hospital with a possible heart attack because she did the one thing she promised she wouldn't do. Olive loved her sister. She had every right to blame Hannah for what happened. To be mad at her. To never talk to her again. Her father always told her that there was only one way to face a problem. Head on. So she went to the kitchen where Olive was sipping coffee and nibbling on a blueberry muffin.

Olive looked up. "Oh, good morning, dear."

"Morning, ma."

Hannah took a mug from the cabinet, poured herself some coffee and sat facing her mother.

Olive gazed intently at her. "What's bothering you? Something's wrong. I can see it in your face."

"I just spoke to Phil. He was in Huntington Hospital."

Olive started kneading her napkin nervously. "Oh dear. Is he all right?"

"He's fine. It's Gilda."

Olive frowned. "Gilda? What's the matter with her?"

"She had chest pains. They think she might have had a heart attack."

Olive said nothing. She seemed deep in thought.

Hannah said, "I'm so sorry, ma. It's my fault. You told me not to let her get to me but I didn't listen. I lost my temper. Now she's laying in the hospital, maybe dying, and I put her there. I wouldn't blame you if you never talk to me again."

Olive shook her head disdainfully. "I thought she might pull something like this."

"You think she's faking it?"

"I guarantee it. A leopard doesn't change its spots."

"But you told me..."

"I know what I told you. And I also heard what Gilda said about you, me and especially my Axel. I'm glad you said what you said. It's about time someone put that woman in her place. Lecturing about Christian values. As you said, the golden rule is the most important Christian value. And she most certainly has never treated others the way she thinks she should be treated."

"I thought you'd be mad at me."

"At first I was very angry at both of you. Then I realized that she was the instigator. After you left she started lecturing me on what a bad mother I was for letting you get away with everything."

"What did you do?"

"I told her to leave. Right then and there."

"What did she do?"

"She said if she left she was never coming back. I heard that before so I told her good riddance to bad rubbish."

Hannah went over and kissed Olive on the cheek. "I love you ma. You're the best."

"Just be very careful when you go down to Jamaica Bay."

"How'd you know I was going back?"

"You speak very loudly when you're on your cell phone. My eyesight isn't as keen as it use to be but my hearing is still good."

"You're okay with me going back?"

"Of course not. You said those people are dangerous. I don't want you to be anywhere near them. But no one could ever stop you from doing what you put your mind to. You're hard headed, like your father. I'd rather you tell me what you're doing than going behind my back. Just be very careful. And I'm glad Phillip's going with you. He won't let you get into too much trouble."

Hannah smiled. "Your hearing IS good."

"And don't worry about Gilda. She's healthy as a horse."

Hannah stood. "Thanks for standing up for me."

"Oh, I almost forgot. You remember Mr. Leigh, the nice man from the Environmental Conservation Society."

"You mean the Environmental Conservancy? Yes. What about him?"

"His secretary called while you were asleep, looking for you."

"Did she say what it was about?"

Olive shook her head. "Just that he wanted to talk with you. I wrote down the number."

Olive walked over to the kitchen counter. There was a small notepad next to the phone. She ripped off the top sheet, folded it in half and handed it to Hannah.

"He's a very important man. Make sure to call."

"I will. Thanks."

Hannah went back to her room. She picked up her phone and scowled at it like it was an evil thing. It was bad enough she promised to call Phil's friend to make another useless appointment with another useless doctor. Now she also had to call Michael Leigh. For what, she had no idea.

Her aversion to talking to strangers on the phone went back to her first job after college. She was a receptionist at a medical practice. The phone never stopped ringing, mostly from people who were pissed off. Because they didn't want to wait months for an appointment. Because she couldn't diagnose their problems over the phone. Or when she told them their procedure wasn't covered by insurance. And they all yelled at her like it was her fault. From then on, she hated talking to random people on the phone. She didn't even like talking on the phone with her friends.

She called the neurologist's office. The receptionist told her the doctor could see her in three months. She was about to say something, then she stopped herself. She knew what it was like to be on the other side of that conversation. She jotted down the date and hung up.

She gritted her teeth and dialed Leigh's number. His assistant answered and asked Hannah if she was free to meet with Mr. Leigh Friday morning at ten at his office. When Hannah asked what the meeting was about the answer was vague.

Hannah figured that a bigshot like him didn't have to give you a reason to meet with him. If he summoned you, you came. No questions asked.

No sooner did she hang up when her phone rang.

"Good morning, partner. How are you?" It was Bette. She sounded upbeat and excited.

"My aunt Gilda's in the hospital and I put her there," Hannah said glumly.

Usually she was the positive one and Bette was morose. Like Tigger and Eeyore. She didn't like being Eeyore.

"Don't tell me you finally belted her."

"No. Maybe I should have. It couldn't have turned out much worse."

"What happened?"

"Remember those things I said to her, about Catherine being a slut and her husband cheating on her?"

"Yeah."

"It got her so upset she wound up in the hospital."

"What's wrong?"

"They're not sure yet. It might be a heart attack but it's probably just stress."

"What are you gonna do?"

"Nothing I can do."

"You're not gonna stop the investigation, are you?"

"No way. My father was murdered. I'm gonna find out why."

"Okay. I was hoping you'd say that."

"Any ideas about what we should do next, before I go back to the Refuge?"

"We should check out BlackAmmo. See if they're a real company or just a bogus front like Greenleaf."

"Good idea. Text me the address. I'll go now."

"Now!?"

"Why not? I need to do something. I can't just lay around here feeling sorry for myself."

"Do you want me to come with you," Bette said hesitantly. "I will if you want me to."

"It's better if I go there alone. I don't know what I'm gonna say when I get there. I'll have to make something up. One person can get away with faking it. It's a lot harder with two. You keep doing your research."

"Are you sure?"

"Absolutely. Without you, we wouldn't even be this far." Hannah was quiet for a second. "By the way. Michael Leigh called. I'm meeting him on Friday."

"Really? That's great. I read about him. He had a big-time position in the Bush Administration. Now he's a real mover and shaker in New York financial circles."

"Can you do me a favor and look up him and his company

and let me know what they do, so when I see him I won't look like a total idiot."

"Sure."

"Thanks. I'll call you when I get back from BlackAmmo."

"Be careful."

"Yes, mother."

CHAPTER TWENTY-THREE

The BlackAmmo office was on the eighth floor of a ten-story building on West 27th Street in Manhattan, between Sixth Avenue and Broadway. It was a bustling, commercial block that felt more like a Moroccan bazaar than a street in Midtown Manhattan. Shops on the block sold everything from mini Statues of Liberty and Empire State Buildings to cameras, toys and games, computers and peripherals, TV's and small electronics, phones and accessories, kitchen gadgets, assorted tchotchkes and dozens of other items. The common denominator was that they were all cheap and of dubious quality. Many were knockoffs with look-alike logos like Rulex, Gocci, and Panisonic, designed to catch the undiscerning eyes of gullible tourists who thought they were getting the bargain of a lifetime.

Delivery trucks and cargo vans clogged the road, parked, double-parked and triple-parked up and down the street. Young men shouted to each other in a potpourri of languages as they loaded and unloaded their wares under the watchful eyes of scowling store managers. All the while, bicycle messengers darted in and out of traffic like matadors, millimeters away from being impaled on an offending fender of a speeding yellow cab.

When Hannah walked out of the elevator she was greeted by a

sign written with a black Sharpie that was Scotchtaped to the wall facing her. There was an arrow pointing left under which was written, 'Sound Hound Studios.' Written under the right-pointing arrow was BlackAmmo. There was also a sign indicating where the restrooms were.

Hannah ducked into the semi-seedy ladies room and examined herself in the mirror, trying not to touch anything but the doorknob. She had no idea what the trendy investigator was wearing these days so she chose a blue chambray shirt and her cleanest jeans. She checked under her arms for sweat stains but her antiperspirant was holding up. She took a deep breath and strode out the door.

She didn't know what to expect the headquarters of an organization of mad dog mercenary killers to look like but it certainly wasn't this. If she didn't see 'BlackAmmo Defense And Security Solutions' stenciled on the door, she would have thought she was in an accountant's office.

The walls, the furniture and the carpet were in various shades of nondescript beige and tan. There were framed landscape prints on the walls and potted plants on the floor. The only anomaly was a plaque on the wall behind the front desk. The letters 'BADASS' were mounted in hammered steel above an ominous image of a clenched fist with the full name of the company below. Seated behind the front desk was a clean-cut African American guy in his early thirties. He would have looked like a smart, young junior executive except for his mammoth shoulders and boulder-like biceps straining the seams of his polo shirt. The nameplate on his desk said 'Pat Goldney'.

He looked up and smiled. "How can I help you, Miss?"

"I'd like to speak with someone in charge."

He reached for a pen and a yellow legal pad. "What is this in reference to?"

Hannah was surprised by the professionalism and courtesy of the young man. She expected a goon with no manners and a third-grade vocabulary, not someone who spoke like an on-the-scene reporter for the Five O'clock News.

"I visited the Jamaica Bay Wildlife Refuge the other day. At the front gate a guard, I think his name tag said Grabowski, told me it was closed. When I asked him why, he cursed at me and gestured with his gun in a crude, sexual manner."

Goldney made a show of writing furiously while Hannah spoke. He looked up and said, "I'm very sorry to hear that, Miss..."

"Johansson. Hannah Johansson."

"I'm very sorry Miss Johansson. I'll write a report and have this dealt with immediately. Thank you for bringing it to our attention," he said and looked down at some papers on his desk.

She didn't schlep all the way into the City to be peremptorily dismissed. She decided to channel her inner Emeril and kick it up a notch.

"That's not good enough," she yelled. "I thought that big gorilla was going to attack me. I was traumatized. I had nightmares. How do I know that you'll even write a report. Even if you did, it would probably go right in the garbage as soon as I left." She took a breath, then said, "I'm not leaving here until I see someone in authority."

Goldney stiffened in his seat. It was clear he wasn't used to being hollered at. It took him a few seconds to compose himself. Then he said, "I can assure you that this matter will be handled appropriately. But if you insist, I'll see if Ms. Lund, our office manager, is available. She handles our personnel issues."

He picked up his phone, punched in a few numbers and waited. About ten seconds later, he said, "Ms. Lund, I have a Miss Johansson out here. She claims to have been treated very inappropriately by one of our men at the Jamaica Bay Center."

He listened for several seconds, then said, "I am filling out a report. But she insists on speaking to someone face-to-face."

He led her into a corridor. They stopped at a door. The nameplate affixed to it said, 'Kristin Lund.'

Goldney opened it. “In here,” he said. Then he returned to his desk.

The office was small and sparse. There were no pictures on the wall. The desk was bereft of photos, mementos or anything personal. There was a phone, a computer and a printer, along with a wooden desk organizer that held two pens, a memo pad and a stack of business cards. None looked like they had ever been used.

Seated behind the desk was a woman of indeterminate middle age, anywhere from 35 to 55. She was wearing an olive green blazer and tan shirt. Her face was square. Her features flat. Her slate gray hair was pulled back in a tight bun. She had big shoulders.

She stared at Hannah with piercing hazel eyes.

“What is it, young lady, that is so important, so sensitive, that it has to be said to me in person?”she growled.

There were two guest chairs in front of the desk but Hannah didn’t sit. She leaned forward, still not sure about what she should say. “Ms. Lund, is it?”

Lund nodded.

“Do you vet your employees?”

“Of course.”

Hannah stared at her. “Not very well, I would say.”

“I beg your pardon.”

“The other day I was at the Jamaica Bay Wildlife Refuge and a man named Grabowski, who I learned was employed by your company, spoke to me extremely rudely. Then he stroked his gun in a very coarse and sexually provocative manner.”

Hannah waited for a reaction but Lund was stiff and silent.

“I did some research and found out that Grabowski has a criminal record.” Hannah had no idea if this was true but figured it was more likely than not. “I demand that he be fired immediately or I’ll go to the authorities.”

Lund’s face tightened. Her right eyebrow began to twitch. She leaned forward.

"You are in no position to demand anything. I know all about your visit to the Jamaica Bay property last Thursday." She glanced at her computer screen. "You were the one who was rude and uncooperative. Your were asked to leave several times before you finally did so. Then you trespassed on the property and you were detained by the Port Authority police for your actions. Now please leave before I call the police and have you arrested."

"Arrest me for what?" Hannah yelled. "Not believing your lies?" She took a breath. "I don't know what you people are doing at the Refuge, but I'm going to find out. And I'd bet my last nickel that it has nothing to do with expanding the airport."

"You don't know what you're talking about. Get out of here right now or I'll have you thrown out."

The office door flew open. A man stood in the doorway. His tall frame took up most of it.

"What's going on in here?" he shouted.

Lund said, "Mr. Westbrook, this is the woman who was causing trouble at the Jamaica Bay site the other day."

He walked toward Hannah. "What do you want?" he said sternly.

She pointed at him. "It's you. You kidnapped my friend. You were there that night, giving orders. You're the one in charge." She thought for a second, then her face contorted with rage and she screamed, "I bet you're the one who poisoned my father, you bastard!"

She started pummeling him with her fists.

After a few punches, he grabbed her wrist in mid-strike, spun her around, gripped her shoulder with his other hand, forced her down onto a chair and held her there.

"Let go of me!" Hannah screamed. "I'm a personal friend of Michael Leigh. After I tell him how you treated me, you'll be lucky to still have a job." She slumped back in the chair. She didn't know why she brought up Leigh's name but somehow it worked.

Westbrook released his grip. He turned to Lund. "Get Goldney in here."

"Don't you want me to call the police?" Lund said. "That woman assaulted you."

He glared fiercely at her. "Just do what I said."

Lund was about to say something, thought better of it and left, slamming the door.

Westbrook sat down in the other guest chair next to Hannah. "I don't know what happened to your father but I can assure you it wasn't me or any of my people. As far as what's going on at the Jamaica Bay site, you're correct, it's not about airport expansion."

Hannah's eyes widened. "Really! I knew it. If they're not doing the airport evaluation, what are they doing there?"

"I can't give you any more information but I can tell you that it's a very sensitive government operation. If you really do know Michael Leigh, ask him. He'll verify what I'm telling you."

"Why would Mr. Leigh know anything about this? I thought he was in finance."

"He is. But he's also Vice Chairman of the Board of the Port Authority."

"I will ask him. I'm seeing him on Friday."

"Really?" He raised an eyebrow. "I really shouldn't be telling you any of this, but with your history at the Jamaica Bay Refuge and what happened to your father, I feel you have a right to know. Of course, all of this is highly confidential."

"How do you know anything about my history?"

Before he could answer, Lund walked back into the office with Goldney trailing behind her.

Westbrook turned to him. "Please escort Miss Johansson downstairs and give her any help she needs."

Lund looked dourly at Westbrook. "But..."

He cut her off. "This is no longer your concern."

She stood, silently seething.

Goldney walked over to Hannah. "Please come with me, Miss."

Hannah followed Goldney out. Westbrook winked as she walked past him.

CHAPTER TWENTY-FOUR

Hannah felt unsteady as she walked out of the building with Goldney. She didn't know if it was from the emotional and physical stress she had just been through or another attack. She was starting to think that her constant fear of getting an attack was worse than the attacks themselves.

Among the trucks, cabs and cargo vans parked near the building was a huge black Hummer with a BlackAmmo logo painted on the door. The only difference between that Vehicle and the U.S. Army Humvees that annihilated Saddam Hussein's army in Desert Storm was that there was no 50-caliber machine gun mounted on the roof. It looked to Hannah like something out of the Transformers movies. Like it would morph into a giant black robot and destroy everything in its path.

"Goodbye Miss Johansson," Goldney said and started back inside.

"Wait," Hannah cried.

He turned.

Hannah thought for a minute. "Can I call you if something else comes up?"

"Of course." He handed her a gunmetal gray business card

with BADASS embossed in big black letters and the full name of the company much smaller underneath.

"My office number and my cell number are on the back. A pleasure to meet you." He smiled and went back inside.

As soon as he was gone Hannah switched her phone off airplane mode and called Bette.

"I've been trying to reach you all morning," Bette said as soon as she answered. "Where have you been?"

"I've been investigating."

"Really?"

"I just left BlackAmmo."

"I don't believe it."

"Why not? That was the plan."

"I know. It's just that..."

"What?"

"I didn't think you'd really go through with it. Going there all by yourself. Weren't you scared?"

"I was petrified. But my dad said either you conquer your fear or it conquers you."

"My fear conquered me a long time ago. It was total surrender."

Hannah ignored this. "Guess who I saw up there."

"Dawson?"

"Nope."

"Grabowski?"

"No."

"I give up. Who?"

"Westbrook."

"Really? The colonel? The guy with the scar? The fake FBI agent?"

"Yes. All of the above."

"He was really there?"

"Of course, he's the president of the company."

"I wasn't even sure that the company really existed."

"It's real. With offices, employees and everything."

"And you just walked right into the president's office?"

"Not exactly. I made a scene in the HR office and he came in."

"Oh my God. What happened?"

"I totally freaked out."

"What does that mean?"

"I lost it. I screamed at him. I accused him of poisoning my father."

"Holy crap!"

"That's not all."

"What?"

"I started punching him."

"You really hit him? What were you thinking?"

"Obviously, I wasn't thinking."

"Did he hit you back?"

"No, thank God. He would have put me in the hospital for sure."

"What did he do?"

"He forced me down into a chair and held me there. I couldn't budge a muscle. It was like I was encased in cement."

"Then what?"

"I started ranting. I said the first thing that came to my mind."

"What?"

"I told him I was friends with Michael Leigh."

"Michael Leigh? What does he have to do with any of this?"

"Nothing that I know of. I guess he'd been on my mind cause I'm supposed to see him on Friday. He's a big supporter of the Refuge and he really liked my father and you said he used to be a big deal in Washington. The crazy thing is, as soon as I blurted out Leigh's name, Westbrook totally changed his attitude."

"I don't understand."

"Neither do I. But all of a sudden, I was his buddy. He told me that Leigh would vouch for him. Then he admitted that what they're doing at the Refuge doesn't have anything to do with the airport."

"He admitted that? Wow, that's incredible! Did he say what they're really doing there?"

"No. He said was that it was some kind of top secret classified government project."

"Do you believe him?"

"No way. I think he said that to stop us from investigating."

"But suppose it's true? They could arrest us as spies."

"That's ridiculous! Who would we be spying for, the Long Island Birdwatching Club?"

"Yeah, you're right...I guess." Bette didn't make a sound for a few seconds, then, "Ummm..."

"What?" Hannah knew that tone in Bette's voice. It usually meant she was trying to say something that she knew Hannah didn't want to hear.

"You're gonna hate me."

"What!"

"You drove in, right? You have your car?"

"Yeah. I'm walking to the garage now."

"Do you think you could make a little detour before you come home?"

Hannah couldn't imagine what Bette was getting at.

"Just tell me what you want me to do."

"You know what LexisNexis is, don't you?"

"I've heard of it."

"We used it all the time at my old law firm."

"Okay."

"They have something called Company Alerts. Where you can get news about a specific company. I did it for Greenleaf."

"Did you find out who really owns them? We thought that would be important."

"No. Not yet. But I got an alert that they leased space in Lufthansa's cargo warehouse at JFK."

"Really? What do you think it means?"

"I'm not sure. It could be nothing. It could be important. Do you think you could swing by the airport and check it out?"

"What would I be looking for?"

"I don't know. Something to do with the Refuge."

"How am I supposed to do that? I'm sure they don't just let anybody traipse in and nose around looking at stuff."

"You'll figure something out. You're great at this. Look at how well you did at BlackAmmo."

"You want me to start punching the guy in charge and tell him Michael Leigh sent me?"

Bette chuckled. "That probably won't work twice in a row. If you don't want to do it, I understand."

"Of course I'll do it. My father was murdered. I'll do anything to get to the bottom of it. Meanwhile, see what you can find out about this Westbrook guy. Is he really a colonel? What connection does he have with Dawson and Grabowski or anything having to do with the Refuge?"

"Okay. You be careful."

"I'll talk to you later."

Hannah ended the call.

Twenty minutes later, she stood dumbfounded outside the longest building she's ever seen. It was the size of several football fields. The loading bays went on forever. Several dozen container trucks were nuzzled into them like piglets suckling on the teats of the world's most humongous sow. More trucks were lined up outside, awaiting their turn. The air reeked of diesel fumes from the trucks and jumbo jets thundering overhead.

Hannah couldn't figure out how to get inside the building. There were plenty of gates for trucks and tractors and forklifts but she didn't see an entrance for people. She spotted a man and woman in navy blue uniforms and matching hard hats walking toward the far end of the building. One held what looked like an iPad, the other had what Hannah guessed was some kind of scanning device, like the kind the UPS guy makes you sign when you get a package. She followed them.

After walking the entire length of the building, they went through a battered metal door tucked into a corner. Hannah waited about half-a-minute, then followed. She found herself in a small anteroom. Lufthansa posters were taped on walls that were badly in need of a fresh coat of paint. A middle-aged African American woman wearing a slightly rumpled navy blue Lufthansa blazer was seated at the front desk, watching a tiny rabbit-eared TV that was nestled on her desk in between her phone and laptop.

She lowered the volume and looked up at Hannah. "How can I help you?"

Hannah looked up at the posters, then back to the woman. "I'm sorry. I'm looking for the Greenleaf warehouse. This is obviously Lufthansa."

"No reason to apologize. You're in the right place. This is Lufthansa's warehouse. Greenleaf leases space from us. They got the middle section." She gestured to a door to her left. "It's through there." She turned back to her show, upping the sound.

"Excuse me," Hannah said, loud enough to be heard over the heartthrobs on One Life to Live. "How will I know when I get to the Greenleaf part?"

The woman laughed sardonically. "Don't worry honey, you'll know."

Hannah opened the door and found herself in a space the size of a half-dozen Home Depots all smooshed together. Crates and boxes, ranging from the size of a box of groceries to steel containers that you could fit a small truck into, were scattered everywhere, some on pallets, some on the floor. More were stored up on steel mesh shelves that lined the walls. All had 'Lufthansa Freight' stenciled on them.

Dozens of motorized forklifts were parked haphazardly around the facility. A few were being driven around slowly, like bumper cars looking for something to ram.

Hannah had no idea what she was looking for. Or what she would do if she found it. At least no one bothered her as she wandered around.

That changed when she came to the Greenleaf section of the

building. A wire fence separated it from Lufthansa's area. Two guards in black uniforms like the one Grabowski wore at the Refuge, complete with assault rifles and handguns, stood, arms folded, in front of it. One was a stocky woman with long, shiny, black hair and caramel skin. She wore a name tag that said 'Azar'. The other was a tall, dark-skinned guy. His tag identified him as 'Tannous'.

As Hannah stood at the gate he barked, "Who are you?" His high-pitched, strangely accented voice was so out of sync with his menacing look that she had to stop herself from smirking.

Hannah had a plan. She thought of it while she was stuck in traffic on the Van Wyck. Actually she stole it from Jack Nicholson in *Chinatown*.

She reached into her pocket and handed the snarling security guard Goldney's business card.

"I'm Pat Goldney, with BlackAmmo," she said, trying to keep her hand from shaking. "I'm here to inspect the operation and file a report. You were supposed to get a call."

He shook his head. "No call."

She shrugged. "I don't know what to tell you. They told me they would call."

The two guards looked at each other. Neither said anything.

After several seconds, Hannah said, "Listen, I'm supposed to have a look around, take a few pictures and write a quick report that they can send to some government agencies. It's bureaucratic bullshit and it shouldn't take longer than ten minutes."

He shrugged and handed the card to his partner. She glanced at it and nodded.

He scowled, opened the gate and said, "Go in."

The blue walls were now forest green. The haphazard way the Lufthansa section was arranged was replaced by an austere rigidity. She noticed that most of the crates were labeled 'TMA Cargo' with Arabic lettering underneath.

After wandering around, trying to look like she knew what she was doing, she saw an area tucked into a back corner caged within a wire fence. It was about ten feet square and eight feet high. The rear concrete wall had a metal lift gate that Hannah assumed opened to the loading dock. There was no way to enter from the warehouse. The only access was from the outside. There were stacks of green shrink-wrapped bales scattered around the enclosure. About twenty altogether. They looked identical to the ones she saw at the Refuge.

She pressed her phone against the fence and began snapping photos. She caught her hand on a sharp edge of one of the chain links and dropped the phone to the concrete floor with a crash.

"Goddammit!" she yelled, and bent to pick it up, hoping it wasn't cracked.

At that instant, a snarling Rottweiler charged out from behind the crates and leaped at her, crashing into the fence. Startled, she screamed, jerked backwards and fell on her tail bone. Pain shot up her spine. She struggled to her feet.

She turned to see the two guards running at her, pistols drawn.

"All right," the male guard said. "Who the hell are you?"

"I told you. Pat Goldney from the New York office."

He slapped her hard across the face. "You lie!"

The force of the blow knocked Hannah back but she stayed upright. Her cheek throbbed. Her jaw ached. A tiny dollop of blood formed at the end of her lip.

The woman spoke. "Greenleaf sent no one. I called. When I tell the man on the phone Pat Goldney is here, claiming to be from Greenleaf main office, he say impossible. When I ask why, he say he is Pat Goldney."

Hannah stood there in stunned silence. She couldn't think of a plausible lie. And the truth seemed more ridiculous.

When they realized that Hannah wasn't going to talk, the woman guard turned to her partner and began speaking quickly in a language Hannah didn't recognize.

After a brief back and forth, she gripped Hannah's elbow and hustled her into a large storage closet. It smelled of disinfectant and mold. There were mops, brooms, metal buckets, tool boxes, cables, plastic containers of bleach, ammonia and mineral spirits. A few empty crates were stacked in a corner. A bare 40 watt bulb in the ceiling provided the only light.

The guard took down one of the crates and pushed it to the middle of the room. "Sit."

Hannah sat.

"Hands behind back," she barked.

Hannah did as she was told. The guard bound her wrists behind her with a plastic cable tie.

She stepped back, looked derisively at Hannah and said, "We are Lebanese company. This is Lebanese soil, like embassy. You are a spy. A terrorist. We know how to deal with terrorists."

Then she took a picture of Hannah with her phone.

Hannah forced herself to sit stoically as the guard left the room. She didn't want her to see how terrified she was. As soon as she was alone she began to shake, struggling to keep images of rape and torture out of her head.

CHAPTER TWENTY-FIVE

Hannah's jaw throbbed, her tail bone ached, her head was pounding and she was queasy from the cleaning fluid fumes.

This is my punishment! I spent my whole life disappointing my father. He bought me my first camera, I lost interest in photography. I went away to college instead of going to school here and helping him at the Refuge. Then I dropped out and stayed away, leaving Jacqui to do what I should have done. Now I'm 31 years old and I have no money, no job, no social life. I am good at one thing, tearing my family apart. My mom, who never raises her voice, had a screaming fight with her sister. Catherine and Gilda aren't talking thanks to me. My aunt is in the hospital and her cat is dead. All because of me. Just when I thought my life couldn't get any worse, I'm locked in a filthy, putrid closet, waiting to spend the rest of my life in a Lebanese prison. Maybe it's exactly what I deserve.

Hannah promised herself that if by some miracle she didn't wind up getting raped and beaten on a daily basis by jihadi madmen, she'd change. She'd think before she spoke. She'd finish what she started. She'd make her father proud.

A fresh wave of nausea overtook her. She fought to keep herself from throwing up.

The door opened. The female guard was back with venom in her eyes. She was clutching a knife. Black, with a curved blade.

"Please! No!" Hannah cried.

But the guard kept coming. She was now standing in back of Hannah.

Hannah closed her eyes, waiting for the blade to slash across her throat.

The next thing she knew her hands were cut free.

"Get up," the guard shouted.

Hannah tried to stand. Her legs were jelly. She slumped back down on the crate.

"Up now!"

Hannah stood on wobbly legs.

"Let's go."

The guard grabbed Hannah's arm and dragged her across the warehouse floor to a metal staircase. She pushed Hannah up a flight of steps onto a steel mesh catwalk in front of a 40-foot long shipping container converted into makeshift offices. There were four doors cut into the side marked Personnel, Security, Maintenance and Operations. She pushed Hannah to the door marked Security.

The guard knocked twice. A male voice inside said, "Come."

She pushed Hannah inside then slammed the door behind her.

Hannah found herself standing in a cramped space, body shaking, heart pounding. She was looking at the back of a man seated at a table in front of three video screens mounted side-by-side-by-side on the wall in front of him. Each screen showed a section of the warehouse. The images changed every ten seconds. His right hand held a mouse while his left rested on a keyboard.

Most of the cramped space was taken up by a metal desk on which was a phone, a laptop and several manila folders. A bulletin board on one wall was papered with cargo manifests. The other wall was bare.

"Hello Hannah," the man said, still facing the monitors. The voice sounded familiar.

He turned around in his chair. It was Tom McCaffrey.

Hannah stood dumbly, her mouth open. After a few seconds she composed herself and said, "Tom, what are you doing here?"

McCaffrey smiled. "I work here. I'm the swing shift security supervisor. My officers reported that there was a suspicious woman snooping around the restricted area. When they confronted her, she gave them false information. They assumed she was either a thief or an industrial spy. Imagine my surprise when they showed me the woman's photo and it was you. Now Hannah, what are YOU doing here?"

He gestured at one of two molded plastic chairs. Hannah sat, still quivering, her hands clasped in front of her.

"Oh Tom," she said, tears again forming at her eyes. "I've never been so frightened in my life. They told me this was foreign soil and I would be treated as a terrorist. I thought they were going to lock me up forever in some horrible Lebanese prison."

"Sorry, that's my fault," McCaffrey said, stifling a slight grin. "We've been having a problem with theft and vandalism lately. I told my officers that if they catch someone in the act they should scare the shit...excuse me...scare the hell out of them. The Lebanese prison? I guess that was Azar's idea." He smiled. "Good touch, though."

Hannah's face was ashen. Her body tense and quivering.

He smiled. "Relax. I know you're not a thief or a spy. You're not going to jail. And nobody's shipping you off to a black site in Lebanon."

Hannah sighed. "Thank God."

"So tell me, what were you doing here?"

Hannah began to feel the tension seep away. "It's kind of a long story. I don't even know where to start."

McCaffrey leaned back. "Start from the beginning. I'm here until midnight."

She told him everything that happened from when she

knocked over her father's urn at the memorial service to the night he saw her on the Cross Bay bridge to her encounter that morning with Westbrook at BlackAmmo.

McCaffrey took some notes as she spoke. The only time he interrupted her was when she told him about Phil's tox screen results.

"You trust this cousin of yours?"

"With my life. He's more like a big brother than a cousin."

"He knows what he's doing? You said he was only a part-time coroner."

"He's a full-time doctor and a very good one."

"He said your father was murdered?"

"My cousin said he had enough toxic chemicals in him to give him stroke symptoms and that it would eventually have killed him."

"You're sure it wasn't some kind of accident?"

"Positive. He said there was no way you could get that much poison into your bloodstream inadvertently."

He shook his head slowly. "Who'd want to kill Axel? I never heard anyone say a bad word about him. Did he have any enemies?"

"No. None."

"You told all this to the police?"

She nodded. "Oh yeah. I don't know if they're in on it or they just didn't believe me, but not only didn't they help, they wound up arresting me."

After that, he let her finish her story without interruption. Until she mentioned how Westbrook's entire demeanor changed when she told him she knew Michael Leigh. Then, like Westbrook, McCaffrey's expression went from solemn to reverential.

"Michael Leigh is a saint," McCaffrey said. "I don't know where I'd be if it wasn't for him. He literally saved my life."

The name was like a magic word. Instead of Abracadabra or Shazam, all she had to do was mention Leigh's name and people changed their whole attitude towards her.

"I had no idea you knew Mr. Leigh."

He smiled. "Your father's the one who introduced us." He furrowed his forehead. "It was back when I was involved with the Baytenders."

The Jamaica Baytenders were a group of local fishing and boating enthusiasts who volunteered to keep Jamaica Bay and the waterways adjacent to it clean and safe. Most lived in Broad Channel, a middle class Queens neighborhood that was actually an island in the middle of the bay. It's connected to the rest of the borough by four bridges — two for cars, two for subway trains.

"My dad really appreciated all the work you guys did."

"We thought the same about him." McCaffrey shook his head somberly. "He was taken way too soon."

Hannah nodded sadly. After a few seconds she said, "How did Michael Leigh get involved with the Baytenders?"

"We were working on the West Pond breach after Super Storm Sandy. Mr. Leigh and some other people from the Environmental Conservancy were there to check out the damage. After awhile we all got to talking and they wound up giving us ten thousand dollars towards the repair. He'd call me every once in a while to see how things were going. He told me that if I ever needed help I should reach out to him."

"You said he saved your life."

"He saved me and my son." His face turned mournful.

"I think I met him once a long time ago. We were both very young. Tommy, right?"

"Close. Timmy."

How is he doing?"

"Not too well," he said sadly.

"I'm so sorry. What happened?"

"From the time he got his first G.I. Joe, all Timmy ever wanted to be was a soldier," McCaffrey said wistfully. "The 911 attack happened at the beginning of his senior year in high school and that sealed the deal. The day after he graduated he went to an Army recruitment office. But he had Crohn's disease and they wouldn't take him. He didn't give up, though. He was bound and determined to fight for our country one way or the other. He must have gone to a dozen more recruitment places. Air Force, Navy, Marines. Same answer. Then he tried the military contractors. Blackwater, Northridge, Triple Canopy. They all said if the U.S. Military didn't want him, neither did they. Armstrong and Warren was the only firm that gave him a chance."

Hannah perked up. The dots were starting to connect.

"A&W handled logistics for the Provisional Authority. They said Crohn's was no problem as long as he was taking medicine for it. They sent him to Baghdad to work security for truck convoys."

Hannah made a face. That was also what Grabowski did. She wondered if they worked together.

"It sounds pretty dismal, I know, but he loved it. He called once a week and he never sounded so happy. Then his truck was ambushed. Two guys died. Tim barely survived. He was hit five times. His spine was severed. They left him for dead. We didn't think he was going to make it." He sighed and wiped a phantom tear from his cheek. "Maybe it would have been better if he didn't."

"What happened?"

"He was in the hospital for months. When he got out he was totally paralyzed. He needs a ventilator to breathe. He has to have somebody to feed him and help him with his bathroom stuff. I did the best I could. But I was all alone. My wife passed away a couple of years before it happened. In a way I'm glad, because this would have destroyed her. It destroyed me. All my savings are gone. The hospital bill alone was a couple of hundred thousand. I had no way to come close to paying it. The G.I. Bill didn't cover it cause he worked for a private company. Neither did my health plan from the police department. I was desperate. I called everyone I could think of. Congressmen. Senators. The V.A. They all said they were very sorry but there was nothing they could do."

"What about the company he was with?"

"They just disappeared. No phone. No address. No nothing. It's like they never existed."

"I don't understand. How can a company just vanish?"

McCaffrey shrugged. "I don't know, but I was at the end of my rope. I seriously considered taking Tim off his ventilator and taking a razor to my wrists."

"Oh God."

"I called Mr. Leigh as a last resort. I knew he had a lot of major connections, but I didn't really think he could help. Next thing I knew he got me this job with full health insurance. It covered 24-hour home nursing care for Timmy. Somehow he even got the hospital bill paid for. Without that, I really don't think I'd be alive today. I know Tim wouldn't be."

"I'm so sorry. I had no idea."

"Thanks. And I apologize for what happened to you here today."

"No, I'm sorry I caused you all this trouble."

McCaffrey smiled. "Enough apologies. Let's get you out of here. Where's your car?"

"In a parking space on the other side of the warehouse."

He pointed to a door in the back of the office.

"That leads outside to the parking area. Come on, I'll walk with you."

CHAPTER TWENTY-SIX

"I'm really mad at you," Hannah said into the phone. Her voice was a little hoarse because she had been yelling at the traffic on the Van Wyck Expressway for five minutes.

"What did I do?" Bette said, nervously.

"You told me to go the Greenleaf Warehouse at JFK."

"I'm sorry. Was it a waste of time?"

"It was almost a waste of me."

"Oh my God! What happened?"

"I was slapped, punched, attacked by hounds from hell, tied up and locked in a disgusting storage closet that reeked of toxic fumes. They told me they were sending me to some horrible middle eastern prison where I'd spend the rest of my life being beaten, tortured and raped by a bunch of smelly, sex-crazed Jihadi madmen."

"Who? Who did this to you?"

"The guards at the warehouse."

"What did you do? I thought you were kidding when you said you were going to punch them."

"I didn't do anything. I was walking around the warehouse minding my own business when I saw a bunch of bundles that looked exactly like the ones I saw at the Refuge."

"They beat you up and threatened you just for walking around? That's hard to believe."

"Maybe I gave them a fake name and a fake I.D."

"How'd you get a fake I.D.?"

Hannah told her about making believe her name was Pat Goldney and producing his business card as proof that she worked for BlackAmmo. Then she recounted her whole harrowing experience with the crazy security guards and her surprise and relief when their boss turned out to be Tom McCaffrey. And how he said Michael Leigh saved his life.

"That's weird."

"What?"

"Don't you think it's funny that Michael Leigh's name keeps popping up. Maybe he has something to do with all this."

"You mean that he might have something to do with my father's death? No way. He loved my father and was a big supporter of the Refuge."

"I don't know. He seems to be connected to a lot of the people who are involved."

"I think you're way off base on this but I can ask him about it on Friday."

"That's right, I forgot you were meeting with him."

"I bet once he finds out that my dad was poisoned, he'll be as mad as we are. Then Dawson'll pay for what she did."

"Not so fast. We don't know for sure it was Dawson."

"Who else could it be?"

"That's what we're trying to find out."

"I know it's Dawson. I just need proof. And I bet I'll have that tomorrow night."

"You're not really going back to the Refuge after what happened today?"

"If Michael Leigh's gonna help us I need to convince him I'm not crazy. The only way to do that is to show him hard evidence. And according to Dawson's diary, tomorrow night is our last chance to get it. "

"It's too dangerous," Bette shrieked. "You almost got caught last time. And if it was anyone else but McCaffrey at the warehouse today you'd be in real trouble. Sooner or later your luck's gonna run out."

"It's different this time. Phil's coming with me. He won't let anything happen to me. By the way. Did you find out anything about Westbrook?"

"Not much. He was with the Marines in Iraq."

"Was he there the same time as Dawson?"

"It looks like they overlapped. I can't say for sure whether they knew each other over there. She was in Baghdad. He was stationed in Fallujah."

"Is that close?"

"I have no idea."

"What about after Iraq?"

"He went off the radar. Probably signed on with a military contractor. About a year ago he resurfaced as the head of BlackAmmo."

Traffic on the Van Wyck started to move.

"Okay. Gotta go. Keep digging."

An hour later, Hannah turned into her mother's driveway and parked next to Phil's red Corvair, in the spot that Olive's 20-year-old Volvo usually occupied.

When she walked in she saw tiny bits of torn paper scattered over the living room floor. Phil was sprawled on Axel's club chair, half asleep. He bolted upright when he saw Hannah.

"Hey cuz," he said drowsily, "Where ya been?"

"It's a long story." She gestured at the floor. "What's that? Did they throw you a ticker tape parade?" She looked around. "Where's my mom? Her car's not in the driveway."

"She's at the hospital."

Hannah froze. "What happened? Is she okay?"

"She's fine." Phil was up and pacing. "It's Gilda. She's having emergency surgery. Ollie wanted to be there when she woke up. I told her there was no point in rushing. Between surgery and recovery, it'll be awhile before Gilda's cleared for visitors. Your mom said the last time she saw her sister they fought. She wanted to make sure Gilda knew she still loved her."

"I don't understand. You said there was nothing wrong with Gilda. That her heart was fine."

"That's what I thought. All the docs thought so too. Her EKG was normal. Her vitals were good. There were no cardiac issues whatsoever."

"If she's going into emergency surgery, something's wrong. What's going on?"

"I don't know. When I got here Ollie was frantic. Crying, running around in circles, tearing up tissues two at a time." He gestured at the Kleenex confetti on the floor. "When I finally got her to calm down she told me that Catherine called. That they ran more tests and Gilda was on her way to surgery."

"What kind of surgery? Did she say?"

"No. I called but couldn't get any information. HPPA bullshit."

"I can't believe it," Hannah cried. "This is all my fault. First my father. Now Gilda. I'm a freaking menace."

She plopped down on the couch, legs asplay, her head slumped back on the armrest.

"Are you okay? You're not having an attack, are you.?"

Hannah shook her head. "Just exhausted."

"You sure?"

"Yeah."

"Speaking of those crazy attacks. Did you ever make an appointment with Rudy?"

She nodded.

"Good. He's the best. When do you see him?"

"In three months."

"Three months!" he yelled. "That's unacceptable."

"It was the first slot they had."

He pulled out his phone.

Hannah said, "It's late. His office is probably closed."

"I'm not calling his office." Then after a few seconds. "Rudy, it's Buzz. Remember the other day, I spoke to you about my cousin?" He listened for several seconds. "Yeah. That's right." After another pause, Phil said, "Three-months won't work. She needs to see you right away. I mean, like immediately." He looked over at Hannah, shot her a thumbs-up. "Okay, great! Thanks, buddy. Drinks are on me next time."

He turned to her. "You have an appointment tomorrow morning at 8:30. He's squeezing you in before his regular office hours so don't be late."

Hannah wanted to tell him that he's the one who's always late, not her. But she didn't have the energy so she just thanked him.

Phil stood to leave. "I'm going to the hospital to check up on Gilda. Will you be all right here?"

"I'll be fine," Hannah said. Then, when he was halfway out the door. "Are we still on for the Refuge tomorrow night?"

Phil turned back. "Are you sure you're up to it?"

"Oh yeah. Are YOU up for it?"

He grinned. "I can't wait."

CHAPTER TWENTY-SEVEN

Hannah's hands and feet were tied to the side of the bed. A skinny man dressed all in black with a skimpy beard, a jagged scar across his cheek and an evil, toothless smile stared down at her. He began to loosen his baggy trousers.

Hannah screamed, "Stay away from me, you filthy pig!"

Then she woke up, drenched in sweat.

She glanced at the clock radio. Seven-thirty. She only had an hour to get to her doctor's appointment. And after Phil badgered his friend into giving it to her, she didn't want to be late and make her cousin look bad. She had twenty minutes to get ready. Dr. Romano's office was in Stony Brook Hospital, a thirty minute drive.

She had dozed off after Phil left and fell into a deep sleep on the couch. The phone roused her around midnight. It was Phil calling from the hospital. He told her that Gilda's surgery went well. She wouldn't be cleared for visitors until she was out of recovery and in ICU, which would be several more hours. He talked Olive into spending the night at Gilda's house with Catherine and coming back to the hospital the next morning.

"How is Gilda?" Hannah asked, feeling guilty.

"She's fine, thanks to you. You saved her life."

"What are you talking about?! I'm the one who gave her the heart attack in the first place."

"She never had a heart attack."

None of this made sense to Hannah. "If she didn't have a heart attack, why did she have surgery?"

"They did an echocardiogram and it confirmed that there were no cardiac issues. That was the good news. It also showed a six centimeter thoracic aortic aneurysm. That's basically a ticking time bomb sitting on top of her heart. Anything over five-and-a-half can rupture at any minute."

"So..."

"So if you never told her off, she would never have gone to the hospital with her bogus heart attack and they never would have done those tests. If it wasn't for you she'd be dead in six months. Probably a lot sooner. You're a hero."

Hannah didn't feel heroic. But at least she felt relieved that she didn't kill her aunt.

After she finished talking to Phil she couldn't fall back to sleep, wondering what Phil's neurologist pal will tell her tomorrow morning and concocting multiple doomsday scenarios about what will happen when she goes back to the Refuge. She finally fell into an uneasy slumber around three a.m.

She took a quick shower, brushed her teeth and dried her hair in record time. She threw on jeans, sneakers and a plain white top. It was ten to eight when she got in the car.

She decided to take the back roads and avoid the morning rush hour traffic on Route 25A. Of course she got stuck behind a school bus that stopped every half block. And every mom felt compelled to wave and blow kisses at their little darlings.

"C'mon. Let's go," she yelled at the windshield, banging her fists on the steering wheel.

The school bus turned up a side street as if the driver heard her.

"Thank you!" she said with a sigh.

For the next few miles she was the only one on the road. She drove like Danica Patrick on amphetamines, screeching around turns and gunning it on straightaways.

Stony Brook Hospital was only a couple of miles away. She was feeling confident about getting to her appointment on time when she saw a temporary sign that said 'Road Work Ahead'.

"Shit!"

At the end of the block, a line of four cars were stopped, held there by a guy in an orange jumpsuit, holding a portable STOP sign. She slammed the brakes and pulled in behind them.

After a minute that seemed like an hour, he turned the sign around. It now read SLOW.

Just as the fourth car was passing him, jumpsuit man started to turn the sign back.

"Oh no you don't," Hannah yelled and gunned the engine, streaking past the startled road worker. Glancing at the rearview mirror, she saw him angrily waving his sign at her.

She got to the hospital parking garage at 8:28. That's when she saw the sign. GARAGE FULL.

She veered left to the outdoor parking lot. The first few rows were filled. She drove to the end row, which was always empty. She didn't want to waste time going up and down the aisles.

She sprinted the hundred yards to the hospital entrance. The Neurology Department was on the sixth floor. There was a crowd in front of the notoriously slow elevators so she decided to take the stairs.

She ran up the six flights gulping air. She was sweating, her heart was racing and she was feeling lightheaded when she made it to the Neurology suite. She staggered into the empty waiting room on jelly legs and collapsed onto a chair.

Her eyelids drooped and her vision was blurred and doubled. She was having an attack of the Weakness. Maybe a heart attack as well.

A nurse walked over to her. "Hannah Johansson?"

Hannah nodded.

"Follow me."

Hannah willed herself to stand and shuffled behind the nurse past a half-dozen examination rooms. They stopped a door marked, 'Rodolfo Romano, MD, FAAN.'

The nurse opened the door to a small office and Hannah staggered in. Dr. Romano was behind a desk. His head was down, looking at some papers.

As he looked up he said, "Hannah? Come in." He gestured to a chair in front of t desk.

His hair was thinning and prematurely gray. His eyes were intense.

She sat facing him.

He stared intently at her for a few seconds, then said, "You have myasthenia gravis."

Tears came to Hannah's eyes. Oh God, she thought. I'm gonna die.

"How long do I have, Dr. Romano?"

"To live?"

She nodded, mournfully.

"How old are you? Around thirty?"

"I'll be thirty-one next month."

He contemplated for a few seconds, then smiled. "With luck, I'd say about fifty years."

"Really?"

"Give or take."

"I thought Myasthenia Gravis was fatal. I read about it. It's what killed Aristotle Onassis. If he couldn't survive it with all his billions, what chance do I have?"

"Aristotle Onassis died over forty years ago. Medical science has made a lot of progress since then. We have medications that can alleviate a lot of the symptoms. And procedures that bring about total remission in some patients. But even if symptoms persist there are steps we can take to keep your quality of life close to normal."

Hannah felt like she was just given a death sentence and a reprieve at the same moment.

"That's good news, isn't it?"

"The good news is that now that we know the cause of your symptoms we can take steps to treat it. Let's go into one of the examination rooms. I'll do a couple of quick tests and we'll talk about treatment options."

CHAPTER TWENTY-EIGHT

Hannah watched a mute Guy Fieri make Korean-Mexican burritos with a heavily tattooed woman in a food truck somewhere in Los Angeles. Guy was on a TV mounted high on a wall of the Centurion diner. In addition to its glass and chrome showcases of gooey pastries and menus the size of the Suffolk County phonebook, there were a half-dozen flat-screen TV's strategically located throughout the diner, all tuned to the Cooking Channel. It was like a sports bar for foodies.

It was not quite 11 a.m. and the place was nearly empty. The breakfast crowd was gone and the lunchers hadn't arrived. Hannah sat in a booth by a window facing the parking lot. A busboy placed a menu on the table. She told him she was meeting a friend. He came back seconds later with another menu and two glasses of water.

A waitress ambled over. She was around Hannah's age, with high blonde hair, too much makeup and a nose ring. Her blue waitress uniform clung to her zaftig curves.

"Hiya, hon. You waiting for someone?"

Hannah nodded. "Are you still serving breakfast?"

"All day. Every day."

"Great."

"You wanna order now or you wanna wait?"

She saw Bette's Prius pull into the parking lot.

"I see my friend coming now. I'll wait till she's here."

"You want some coffee in the meantime?"

"Yes, thank you."

Hannah waved to Bette, who was standing by the door with a befuddled look on her face.

"Are you okay?" Bette said breathlessly when she got to the table. "You said you had news from the doctor."

Before Hannah could answer, the waitress came back with her coffee.

"Are youse ready to order?"

Hannah said, "Give us a couple more minutes."

"No problem."

Bette glared at Hannah anxiously. "What did the doctor say?"

"Let's check out the menu first. I'm starving." Giving her a taste of what she put Hannah through at the Asian Pavilion.

They opened the voluminous tomes. Hannah turned to the 'All Day Breakfast' page. Bette went to 'Paninis and Wraps.'

After a minute's perusal Hannah beckoned the waitress.

"I'll have scrambled eggs with Canadian bacon and whole wheat toast."

The waitress turned to Bette. "How about you?"

"The turkey and Swiss wrap, please."

"Okay. What are you drinking?"

Bette was thoughtful. "Can you tell me if the turkey is prepackaged or fresh?"

"It's right off the bird."

"Good. Is it possible to have thousand island dressing instead of mayonnaise?"

"No problem."

"Can you put the dressing on the side?"

"Sure."

"Do you have whole wheat wrap?"

"Yeah."

"Is it gluten-free?"

"I dunno. I'll check." The waitress's lips were still smiling but not her eyes. "What to drink?"

"Can I have an iced tea?"

"Sure."

As she turned to go Bette yelled at her back. "Is it sweetened or unsweetened?"

The waitress kept going without answering.

Hannah said, "That wasn't an order, it was an interrogation. If I was that waitress I would've dumped this water on your head."

"Why? I just asked a couple of questions."

"Never mind. It doesn't matter." Hannah thought for a few seconds. "Did you have any luck finding out about Michael Leigh?"

"Yes. It's all in here." She held up her big black satchel bag. "I'll tell you all about him in a minute. First, tell me what the doctor said."

Before Hannah could answer the waitress was back with more coffee for Hannah and Bette's iced tea.

She took a sip. "It's unsweetened. Good."

"I'll have your food in a couple of minutes," the waitress said, then breezed away.

"Okay now tell me. What did the doctor say?"

"He told me I have myasthenia gravis."

A horrified look washed across her face. "Oh my God. No!" she cried. "I'm so sorry." She reached across the table, trying to hug Hannah and almost knocked over her iced tea.

"Calm down. It's okay."

"How can it be okay?" she yelped. "I remember reading about it. It's deadly. How can that be? You're healthy, athletic. You can't die. It's not fair." She was now whimpering.

Hannah reached across the table and grabbed Bette's hand. "Stop," she said soothingly. "I thought the same thing, but luckily they can treat it now. There's medicine for it and they can do surgery. Besides, the doctor said I have a mild case. He gave me some pills to reduce the symptoms. He said they might even eliminate them completely."

"Really?"

She handed a small vial to Bette.

Bette held the bottle up to the light, examining it like it was a rare artifact. "Mestinon? I never heard of it."

"Me neither. But I've never been diagnosed with myasthenia gravis before."

"Do you think it'll work?" She handed the pills back to Hannah.

"I'll let you know after tonight."

"What's tonight?"

"Remember Dawson's diary? Tonight's the last delivery."

Before Bette could say anything the waitress was back with their food.

She turned to Hannah. "More coffee?"

"No thanks."

Then to Bette. "Another iced tea?"

Bette shook her head then gestured at her wrap. "This is gluten free, right?"

"Yeah. One hundred percent." As she walked behind Bette, the waitress shrugged and winked at Hannah.

After she left, Bette said, "I lost my train of thought. Oh yeah. You can't go back there, not with this horrible disease."

"Of course I'm going. This is our last chance, remember?"

Bette reached across the table and clutched Hannah's hand in both of hers.

"Please don't go. It's too dangerous. And even if you find something, the police aren't interested. You said so yourself."

"You're right. The police are useless. If I never see another cop again that would be fine with me. I'll take whatever we find out to Michael Leigh. They'll listen to him, won't they?"

Bette grinned and nodded. "Oh yes."

"He's some kinda big shot banker. Right?"

"You have no idea." She pulled a spiral notebook out of her bag and opened it on the table. Bette's cramped hand-written notes covered the entire page. "Big shot hardly covers it. The phrase Master of the Universe comes to mind."

Hannah's eyes widened. "Really? Tell me. What did you find out?"

"First of all, he's brilliant. He went to Princeton. Majored in Business and Economics. He was also the captain of the wrestling team. That's where he became best friends with Donald Rumsfeld. You heard of him, right?"

Hannah glared at her friend. "Of course. You think I'm a total idiot?"

"Not at all. But I know you're not too interested in politics."

"That's true. But I do pick up a newspaper every once in awhile. Let's get back to Michael Leigh."

She continued reading. "After he graduated magna cum laude from Princeton, he went to Harvard for his MBA. His first job after he graduated was as an analyst at Lehman Brothers. In two years he was head of their Risk Management Group. Then he was recruited by his pal Rumsfeld to work in the Office of Economic Opportunity in Washington.

"He spent the next decade shuttling back and forth between Washington and Wall Street, depending on who was in the White House."

She turned the page.

"About twenty years ago he started his own investment company, Rock Ridge. Of course it was super successful. A decade later, they were bought by the private equity firm Flack and Spitz. In two years he was named their CEO."

Hannah smiled. "That's all? What a lazy bum."

"Believe it or not, that's not all. His company recently bought Howard Bank and Trust. Now he's running that. A few years back he was the head of the New York State Republican Party. Now he's the Vice Chairman of the Board of Commissioners of the Port Authority."

"Here's what I don't understand. My father knew nothing about finance and he thought all politicians were crooks. I can't imagine how he and Leigh ever became friends?"

Bette nodded knowingly. "I was getting to that. Leigh's all-time hero was Teddy Roosevelt."

"What does that have to do with anything?"

"Old Teddy was crazy about birds. He built bird sanctuaries all over the country. Leigh is an avid birder. That's his connection to your dad."

Bette looked up. Hannah was staring out the window, transfixed.

"Earth to Hannah, are you still here? Have you heard anything I said?"

"Yes, of course," Hannah jerked her head back to Bette. "You were talking about Teddy Roosevelt."

"What's out there that has you mesmerized?"

"There's a black Lincoln Town Car across the street. It's been there since you got here."

"So. The driver's probably getting something to eat."

"Why didn't he park in the lot?"

"I have no idea. What do you care?"

"There was a car just like that in front of BlackAmmo. I think it followed me to the warehouse at the airport. Suppose it's the same guy?"

Bette gave a little chuckle. "You're being paranoid. Those cars are all over the city and especially the airports. All the limo services use them. I rode in one the last time I went to JFK. Besides, if they wanted to follow you they'd use an inconspicuous car like a Chevy or a Ford, not a big, black limo that stands out like a sore thumb."

"I guess you're right," Hannah said sheepishly.

"Of course I'm right. There's only room for one paranoiac on our team, and that's me. But I don't think I'm being paranoid when I tell you those people at the Refuge are dangerous."

"Don't worry. I'll be fine."

"Do you want me to come?"

"Now that would be dangerous." Hannah laughed. Then she glanced out the window. "The Town Car's gone."

"See? I told you there was nothing to worry about."

The waitress was back.

"Anything else?"

"Just the check, please," Hannah said.

As Bette reached into her bag Hannah held up a hand and said, "This is on me. You keep digging and see what else you can find out."

The check came. Hannah left a generous tip.

On their way out Hannah said, "Don't call me this afternoon unless it's really important. I'm going to try to take a nap so I'll be awake tonight."

"I still don't think you should go."

"I know," Hannah said as they got to their cars.

CHAPTER TWENTY-NINE

When Hannah arrived back home Olive was dozing in her rocking chair with her knitting on her lap and Lena at her side, her tail precariously close to the rocker rail. Hannah didn't wake her. She was in no mood to talk to her mother about myasthenia gravis or her planned return to the Refuge.

She took two Mestinon tablets and lay on her bed waiting for something to happen. The only thing that happened was that she fell asleep. When she woke up Olive was in the kitchen sculpting a big ball of chopped sirloin and pork into a meatloaf.

Hannah steeled herself for an inquisition but all Olive said was, "Hello, dear."

Hannah didn't know whether to be pleasantly surprised or concerned that her mother wasn't still mad at her.

After dinner she changed into the all-black clothing she wore the first night she snuck into the Refuge.

She spent the rest of the evening sitting on the back deck, playing Joni Mitchell songs on her guitar, gazing at the gentle waves of the Sound, trying not to think about what she'd been through the last couple of days or what might happen in the next couple of hours.

Phil didn't show up until eleven. He told her he spent the

evening catching up with an ex-girlfriend. He didn't say who and Hannah didn't ask. There was a hint of beer on his breath.

"Is that Heineken I smell? You're not drunk, are you?"

Phil smiled. "I had a couple of beers a few hours ago. It won't affect my driving." He cocked an eyebrow." "How'd you know it was Heineken? Nobody's nose is that good."

Hannah grinned. "You don't drink anything but Heineken. When I got a whiff of beer there was only one choice."

"I say, Sherlock, that's a splendid deduction," Phil said in a very bad British accent. "You might turn out to be a half-decent investigator after all."

On the ride to the Refuge Phil was his usual laconic self. The only break in the silence was when Hannah asked him what he knew about myasthenia gravis. He said he didn't have any experience with it, only that it was an auto-immune disease. He thought it might be related to muscular dystrophy.

"Now you're making me nervous."

"Don't be. If Rudy said you'll be fine, you'll be fine. He knows his shit."

They got to the Refuge at twelve-thirty. They were sitting in Phil's Corvair on Cross Bay Boulevard.

"Okay, Nancy Drew, what's the plan?"

She pointed to the fence.

"We'll go through the gap in the fence."

"I don't see any gap."

"My dad cut it for me back in high school so I wouldn't have to walk through the Refuge alone in the dark. It was still there when I went back the other day. That's how I got in."

"All right, what happens once we get in?"

"The storage barn is about fifty yards south of the Welcome Center. We'll find a good hiding place behind the trees, take some shots while they're unloading the bundles and go out the same way we came in. Easy. And they'll never know we were there."

"What good will that do? You'll have some pictures of guys

carrying bundles into a storage facility. There's nothing criminal about that."

"If they're the same bundles that I saw at the airport warehouse, it might be enough to convince Michael Leigh. I still have those shots on my phone."

"It's dark. The photos won't show a lot. Even if they look somewhat similar, there's no way to prove they're from the same shipment." He shook his head sadly. "I'm sorry Hannah, it sounds pretty flimsy."

Her face went hangdog. "You're right," she said plaintively. "I just don't know what else to do. We can't just give up."

"If only we knew what was in those bundles we'd have something to make a case."

Hannah flashed a grin. "Phil, you're a genius. That's a great idea."

Phil looked dumbfounded. "What idea?"

"C'mon."

"Hold on! Where are you going?"

She looked at her watch. "It's a quarter to one. They're not due to be here for another fifteen minutes at the earliest. We can sneak into the barn, see what's in those bundles, shoot some pictures and get out with time to spare. I'm sure it's drugs. It has to be. Cocaine and heroin come in bundles like that, don't they?"

Phil shrugged. "How would I know?"

"Wait. Hashish comes from the Middle East, I bet that's it. Whaddaya think?"

"I think if these guys are bringing in that much dope from the Middle East, they're not fooling around. Glad I brought this."

He opened the glove box and pulled out a pistol. It was big and black and scary looking.

Hannah shook her head vehemently. "No guns. Handguns are a scourge. They should be outlawed. Why do you even have one?"

"The Coroner's Office is technically part of the police force.

The department issued me this and I keep it in the car, just in case."

Hannah glared at him.

"Put it back," she said. "Or I'll go myself. You and your gun can stay here. I'm serious."

"Okay, okay. Can I at least take this?" He held up something that looked like a fat, black lipstick tube.

"What is it?"

"Bear repellent. I use it when I go hiking in the woods upstate."

"What does it do?"

"It's pepper spray on steroids. If a bear or some other wild creature mistakes you for a tasty morsel, you spray this in their face and it stops them."

"Does it kill them?"

"No. Just blinds and disorients them for a couple of minutes so you can get your ass outta there. It works on humans too."

Hannah thought for a second.

"Okay, fine. Let's go."

She was out the door and through the gap in the fence before Phil had left the car. She made her way through a wild tangle of overgrown barberry bushes, rosa rugosa, scrub pines and autumn olives that gouged her eyes and stabbed her arms and legs. Thorny weeds, roots and vines grabbed her ankles and snagged her feet. She had to hold onto the tree trunks to keep from falling.

Phil caught up with her in front of the storage barn. It was 24 feet wide, 20 feet long and twelve feet high. It had wide double-doors for tractors, wood chippers, Bobcats and other big landscaping equipment.

Phil pushed hard at the doors. They didn't budge. "It's locked. You wouldn't happen to have a key, would you?"

"I wish." After a few seconds she said, "I'm pretty sure there's a window in the back. Maybe we can get in through there."

She ran to the rear of the shed. The window was below the peak of the roof.

"Give me a boost," she said as Phil came trudging around the corner.

He knelt and laced his fingers together. Hannah stepped into his cupped hands. He stood, lifting her up towards the window.

Hannah was at the sill.

"A little higher," she yelled.

He grabbed her ankles and pressed straight up, grimacing and groaning from the strain.

"Okay. I'm at the window."

Phil's arms quivered as he struggled to hold her steady.

She pushed up on the top of the sash but it didn't budge. She jammed at it with the heels of her hands as hard as she could until her hands were numb with pain. About to give up, she gave the window one final push. It inched upward.

Phil yelled, "My arms are giving way. I don't know how much longer I can hold you."

"Hang on. I'm getting it."

Two more shoves and she was able to squeeze through. She looked down but it was too dark to see anything. She braced herself for whatever was underneath her; concrete, wood or the hard steel of heavy equipment; and dropped into the black abyss. Her fall was cushioned by what felt like giant pillows. Using her phone's flashlight, she realized she was sprawled across a pile of green bundles, exactly like the ones she saw at the airport warehouse.

"Yesssss!" she said in a whispered shout.

Her father's tools and machinery were gone. In their place was a large wooden table with two identical machines that looked like a cross between a king-size computer printer and a jumbo slot machine. The bundles, about a dozen of them, were strewn haphazardly against the back wall.

She took out her phone and clicked pictures of the machines and the bundles but she still didn't know what was inside them. She tore at the green cellophane with her fingers but it was too strong. She cursed herself for not having her Swiss Army knife. Then she remembered the nail clipper in her back pocket. When she was stressed, which lately was all the time, she picked at her cuticles until they were raw. She carried the clipper with her to snip off the jagged ends.

She jabbed the point of the clipper's nail file into one of the bundles, then sawed at it until she could jam her fingers through.

She was curious to see what kind of drugs were inside. But there weren't bundles of weed or bricks of hashish or bags of cocaine or heroin. What she found were stacks of hundred dollar bills, held together by paper wrappers. Mounds of them.

She gaped open-mouthed for a few seconds. Then she heard a rumble outside.

"Shit!"

She had lost track of the time. She looked at her phone. Five after one. It was them. Grabowski and Dawson and who knows how many other thugs. She tried the door, even though she knew it was locked. She ran behind the table and pushed it towards the door. It inched forward slowly. After the longest minute of her life, the table was against the door.

She ran to the rear of the barn. There was no way she could reach the window without Phil to give her a boost. She stacked some of the bundles under it hoping she could climb up and grab the bottom of the sill.

She took two steps and the bundles tumbled down, her legs flew forward and she landed on her butt in the center of the pile.

The rumble outside abruptly stopped.

She heard voices but she couldn't make out what they were saying.

She ducked behind some of the bundles and held her breath. It was the only thing she could think of.

She heard the lock click.

When the door banged against the table, a voice yelled, "What the fuck!"

The door rammed against it again. It moved about an inch.

Hannah scrunched down behind the bales of money as low as she could as another thud pushed the door forward.

CHAPTER THIRTY

Whoever was outside kept shoving and the door kept slowly moving forward. Hannah figured after one more push they'd be in. She held her breath.

Then she heard a shout. "Yo! Look. Somebody's fucking with the truck."

Another voice said, "Yeah, I see him." Then yelled, "Hey you! What the hell are you doing?"

The thumping at the door stopped.

"He's getting away. C'mon!"

Hannah heard the sounds of running feet. Then a pop, like a firecracker. She waited about two minutes. She crept slowly towards the door and peeked through the gap. She didn't see anyone. She did see the strange six-wheel all-terrain dump truck, loaded with more green shrink-wrapped bundles. She could hear garbled shouts fading in the distance. And more firecrackers.

She ran through the shrubs and brambles back toward the opening in the fence, ignoring the cuts, pricks and gashes to her face, arms and legs. She spotted the red bandana, squeezed through and headed for the Corvair, hoping Phil would be inside. He wasn't. Her every instinct told her to keep running. But she wouldn't leave without him. The door was unlocked. No surprise, Phil never locked his car.

She sat in the passenger seat, ready to duck down if anyone approached. Two minutes went by. Then five. She decided that if Phil didn't show up in another five minutes she would head for the subway. She was about to leave when she saw a leg coming through the fence. Then an arm. Then the rest of Phil. His left arm hung limply at his side. His right hand was pressed against his left shoulder. He jumped into the car, breathing hard.

"I haven't run all-out like that for some time. Feels good," he said between gasps.

Before Hannah could respond, he started the car, gunned the engine and peeled out down the street, right hand on the wheel, left arm dangling.

"Are you okay? What's wrong with your shoulder?"

"A scratch. It's nothing."

"What happened?"

"I was behind the trees watching the storage barn. I saw them pull up while you were still inside. When they started for the door I knew I had to do something so I snuck over to their vehicle and started banging on it like a lunatic, hoping they'd forget about you and come after me. It worked. After a quarter of a mile those guys were gassed." He grinned. "I knew my morning runs would help me live longer."

"Are you sure they didn't follow you?"

"Positive. I ran an extra half-mile just to be on the safe side. Then I doubled back. They were nowhere in sight. Probably went back to finish unloading."

They roared up Cross Bay Boulevard, across the North Channel Bridge, through Howard Beach towards the Long Island Expressway, running red lights, screeching through turns, zigzagging around the few cars on the road at that hour, nearly rear-ending a delivery truck that pulled out in front of them, all while Phil's left arm dangled limply at his side.

"Watch out!" Hannah screamed. She gripped the front of her

seat with both hands like she was on an out-of-control mechanical bull.

Phil turned onto the Expressway. They were doing ninety, but at least there were no roller coaster turns.

After a few minutes of silence, Phil said, "What did you find? Drugs? Guns?"

Hannah shook her head. "You'll never guess."

"You're right. I won't."

"It was money."

"Money? Are you sure?"

"Trust me, I know what money looks like."

"You mean like dollar bills?"

"Hundred-dollar bills. Wads of them. Tied together in packs. Bundled like bales of hay. I bet there was a couple of million dollars in there."

"It doesn't make sense that they would leave all that money unguarded. I bet it's fake."

"That's what I thought." She pulled a packet out of her jacket pocket. "So I took some to check out."

Phil glanced over. "Wow."

A dark stain was spreading down his sweatshirt sleeve.

"That's no scratch!" Hannah screeched, horrified. "You've been shot."

"I'm fine," he said through clenched teeth.

"No you're not! You're losing blood. We have to go to the hospital. Right now!"

Phil ignored her.

He drove in silence for another few minutes. Then he pulled into a service area on the side of the highway.

"You better drive," he said. "I'm not feeling so great." He got out of the car and shuffled around to the passenger door. Hannah slid over to the driver's seat. Phil slowly, awkwardly eased himself into the car.

"Where's the nearest emergency room?" Hannah demanded.

"No hospitals," he said through clenched teeth.

"Then I'm not driving." She shut the engine and folded her arms defiantly.

He turned to her. "We can't go to a hospital. They have to report gunshot wounds to the police. We trespassed. Broke and entered. And stole a bunch of money. We're talking serious jail time."

"Those crooks won't press charges. They'd have to explain what they were doing with all that money."

"It's still a crime whether they press charges or not. But even if we don't get arrested, I could lose my license."

"If you don't get some medical attention, you could lose your life. Look how you're bleeding."

Phil smirked. "It's not even a pint. I could lose twice that much and still be okay."

She shook her head. "For once in your life, drop the cool-dude crap. You don't need to be the hippest guy in the morgue. I think Huntington Hospital is the next exit."

"Okay, listen," Phil said, his voice cracking. "Go to Stony Brook. Another fifteen minutes won't make a difference. I know some of the docs there. Maybe I'll get to keep my license." He looked at her plaintively. "Please."

Hannah nodded and started the car.

Phil contorted in his seat, reached his right hand around to his left-hand pocket and pulled out his phone.

Hannah said, "Who are you calling in the middle of the night?"

"A friend who works at the Stony Brook E.R."

He hit a speed-dial number. "Yank, it's Buzzy. How are you?" After a few seconds he said. "Not great. That's why I'm calling. Can you meet me at the E.R. bay in fifteen minutes." After another pause he said, "I'll tell you all about it when I get there." He ended the call.

"Yank?" Hannah said. "I've met most of your friends. I never heard of anyone called Yank."

"It's someone I know from med school, okay? I'm not up to talking right now. Just drive."

The Expressway was deserted. Hannah pushed it to eighty-five, hoping there were no cops lurking.

Twelve minutes later they pulled into the Stony Brook University Medical Center ambulance bay. A pretty woman with long, wavy strawberry blonde hair stood at the curb, a stethoscope around her neck. Her white lab coat couldn't hide her shapely figure. Next to her was a gurney manned by two orderlies in blue scrubs.

Phil gingerly opened the car door and swung his legs out, still holding his shoulder. He smiled meekly. "Hey Yank, what's up?"

"What the hell," she said to no one in particular. "Get your ass on the gurney, Buzek."

He sat on it awkwardly. The orderlies pulled his legs up and positioned him.

Phil looked up at her. "You look great," he said, his voice thready.

She scowled down at him, shaking her head. "Wish I could say the same for you. What the hell happened?"

"Just a graze. It looks a lot worse than it is." Phil closed his eyes.

She felt his pulse. Then she sliced the sleeve off his sweatshirt with a scalpel. She wiped the wound carefully with an antiseptic pad and put a bandage over it.

She turned to the orderlies. "Room five. Stat."

Hannah walked over to her. "Is he going to be all right?"

She eyed her disdainfully. "Who are you? Wife? Girlfriend? Getaway Driver?"

"I'm Phil's cousin Hannah. Hannah Johansson."

"Ellen Yankovsky. My patients call me Dr. Y. My friends call me Ellen. Phil is the only one who calls me Yank." A glimmer of recognition flashed in her eyes. "I think we met once. Basketball player, right?"

"Use to be. A long time ago."

Dr. Y walked quickly through the ER door, steps behind the gurney. She turned back to Hannah. "You coming?"

Hannah ran to catch up.

When she got there, Dr. Yankovsky said, "Okay. What the hell happened?"

Hannah didn't know what to tell her. She didn't want to go into the whole story about her father being poisoned and everything that happened since. After hemming and hawing for a few seconds, she said that Phil wanted to see her old house at the Refuge and since he was going back upstate tomorrow they decided to go tonight. When they got there someone started shooting at them for no reason. Phil got hit in the shoulder and they came here.

"That's your story?"

"I know it sounds weird."

The doctor shook her head skeptically. "Weird is one way to put it."

She took Hannah to the ambulatory surgery waiting room. It was the size of a small ballroom with rows of theater-style seats. Two other people were there, both sprawled over several chairs, asleep.

"Wait here," Dr. Yankovsky said.

"Will he be okay?"

"Give me a few minutes. I'll let you know."

A few minutes turned into almost an hour. Hannah was exhausted but her mind was on overload. She tried to read a magazine but couldn't concentrate. She attempted to formulate a plan of action now that she knew what was in those bundles but she was too busy feeling guilty about Phil. She texted Bette that she was in Stony Brook hospital with Phil and asked her to call Olive first thing in the morning. Then she leaned back and stared at the abstract painting on the wall.

When Doctor Y finally reappeared she didn't look happy. "It's worse than we thought."

CHAPTER THIRTY-ONE

Hannah jolted upright. "Oh my God, Phil's dead!" she cried, "I knew it."

Dr. Yankovsky held up both hands in front of her.

"Whoa. Calm down. It's nothing like that. But it's a lot more than a scratch. An inch to the left and it would have hit the subclavian artery. That would have been extremely serious."

Hannah looked puzzled. "If it's more than a scratch but not extremely serious, what are we talking about?"

"Nerve damage. There's a bundle of nerves in the shoulder called the brachial plexus. The bullet pierced it."

"Is he going to be okay?"

"It depends what you mean by okay. I don't think he'll need surgery but we have to see the imaging to be sure. It's a very painful injury but Buzzy's a rugby player. He's used to pain. And he keeps himself in shape. That'll help. He won't be on a rugby pitch for awhile but with luck, he should be almost as good as new in a few months."

"That's great news. Can I see him?"

"I gave him something to help him sleep. I suggest you go home, get some rest and come back tomorrow after he wakes up."

"Please, let me stay in his room," Hannah pleaded. "It's my

fault he's here. I don't care if he's sleeping. I need to be there when he wakes up so I can tell him how sorry I am."

Dr. Yankovsky thought about it for a few seconds. "Okay. Come with me. I'm going up now to check on him."

Phil's shoulder was heavily bandaged. He was hooked up to a monitor that measured his heart rate, blood pressure, respiration and oxygen levels. His eyes were closed.

When Hannah and Dr. Y walked in, he opened his eyes and raised his head a little.

"Hey guys," he said. His voice was raspy and slurred. "Where's the beer?"

Dr. Yankovsky said, "It's coming soon. The strippers are bringing it."

Phil grinned. "That's why I love you, Yank." He turned to Hannah. "How are you holding up, cuz?"

"Oh Phil, I'm so sorry. This is all my fault. I should have never gotten you involved."

Phil looked up at her. "I loved Axe. I want to find out what happened as much as you do. I'm sorry I can't help you follow through."

Dr. Yankovsky looked up at the monitor. "All right, Buzzy. Go back to sleep. I'll stop by later to see how you're doing."

She turned to Hannah. "You can stay if you promise not to keep him up all night."

"I promise," Hannah said. Then she sat down, rolled her sweatshirt into a pillow, put it behind her head and leaned back.

Dr. Yankovsky turned off the light as she left the room. A minute later, both Hannah and Phil were asleep.

CHAPTER THIRTY-TWO

Hannah looked up into the black barrels of two assault weapons pointed at her head. Above them were the snarling faces of Grabowski and Westbrook. Elyse Dawson stood behind them, her chipmunk face twisted in an evil smirk.

"You've interfered with our plans one too many times, Hannah Marie."

With the words 'Hannah Marie,' Olive's voice came out of Dawson's mouth.

Hannah opened her eyes, not sure of where she was. Then she remembered. She was in a chair in a room in Stony Brook Hospital. Phil was asleep in the bed next to her, attached to a jumble of tubes and sensors, hooked up to a monitor. The clock read 8:45. Olive was standing in front of her, shredding the remains of several tissues.

"Hannah Marie, are you all right?" she asked, her voice filled with dread. "Your friend Betty called me early this morning and told me you were in the hospital with Phillip. What happened?"

"Hi ma," Hannah said while trying to collect her thoughts. "You know there's something fishy going on at the Refuge."

Olive nodded.

"Phil thought so too. We went there last night to investigate.

All of a sudden we heard shots. We ran like hell. I didn't even realize Phil was hit until we got back to the car."

"Why would anyone there want to shoot you?"

"No reason I can think of. Maybe they were trying to rob the place and thought we were the police."

"I never thought of that. What did the police say when you told them?"

"We didn't report it. If the police find out, Phil could lose his medical license."

"That doesn't seem right. Why should he lose his license for getting shot?"

"Technically, we were also trespassing. That's a crime."

"Oh, I see," she said solemnly.

Phil stirred.

"Hi Aunt Ollie. How are you?" he slurred.

"Never mind how I am. How are you?"

"I'm fine. You know these doctor types. They're always making a bigger deal about things. Probably just trying to pad the bill."

He winked at Olive.

"Now Phillip," she scolded. "I don't believe that for a minute. You always were one to take unnecessary chances. You and Hannah both. You do what the doctor says without your usual wiseacre shenanigans. You're still not too big for me to take you over my knee."

Then she winked back.

"Okay auntie, you're the boss."

Dr. Y walked into the room.

"Good morning. I'm going to do a quick exam and change the dressing."

"When do you think he can come home?" Hannah asked.

"If all goes well he could be out of here by this evening. But right now I'll have to ask you both to wait outside for a few minutes."

Hannah and her mother went to a small waiting area opposite

the nurses station. There were well-worn padded chairs along with a small sofa. An ancient TV was mounted on the wall playing the Long Island local news station with the sound off. Subtitles scrolled underneath. Olive sat, mesmerized by the muted news. Hannah paced in front of her, silently berating herself.

Catherine walked out of the elevator to the nurses station. She was in the middle of asking which room Phil was in when Olive saw her and yelled, "Yoo hoo, Catherine dear. In here."

Catherine walked over to where Olive was sitting. She kissed her aunt lightly on the cheek. "Hello Aunt Olive, it's so good to see you." She kept her eyes riveted on Olive.

Hannah, who was a couple of feet away, said, "Hello Catherine."

Catherine stared straight ahead.

After a few seconds of strained silence, Hannah said, "I guess you're still mad at me."

Catherine balled her fists at her sides. She turned and glowered at Hannah. Her face flushed. Her teeth clenched. Her arms quivered at her sides.

"Are you trying to kill our whole family?!" she screamed. "First your father. Then my mother. Now Phillip. Who's next on your hit list?"

Hannah turned away. In a small way she agreed with her cousin. She was at least partially responsible for her father's death and for Phil's getting shot. She wasn't ready to take the blame for Gilda's heart condition but she could see how Catherine could feel that way.

Olive jumped off her chair and stood nose-to-nose with Catherine.

"How dare you say such a thing!" she yelled, wagging a finger inches from her niece's face. "Hannah had nothing to do with any of those things. If anything, she saved your mother's life. Now you take back what you said this instant."

Catherine screamed, "Get away from me you old witch!" Then she shoved Olive with both hands.

Olive stumbled, backpedaled a couple of wobbly steps, then fell, landing with a thud on her backside.

Hannah looked on in horror as her mother hit the floor. She launched herself at Catherine. They both went down in a heap with Hannah on top of her smaller cousin. She straddled her and began wildly punching her head and shoulders.

Olive, still on the floor, pushed herself up into a sitting position. She screamed, "Stop it. I'm all right. Please Hannah. Stop!"

Two orderlies rushed in. They yanked Hannah off Catherine, dragged her across the room and shoved her roughly onto a chair. Everyone at the nurses' station crowded into the room. Two of the younger nurses gently helped Olive into another chair while others tended to Catherine, who was dazed and bleeding. They walked her over to the small couch.

A security guard appeared in the doorway, hands on hips. A large woman. Her cornrowed hair was pulled back in a bun, held together by a light blue scrunchy which matched her uniform. Everyone in the room froze.

"What the hell happened here?" she shouted.

Hannah and Catherine both spoke.

"She attacked me."

"She assaulted my mother."

The guard said, "One at a time." She pointed to Catherine. "You first."

Catherine's face was red and puffy.

"She knocked me down and beat me." She gestured at the orderlies. "If those two men hadn't come in and pulled her off of me, she might have killed me."

She turned to Hannah. "What do you have to say?"

Hannah pointed at Catherine. "She attacked my mother. Knocked her to the ground. My mother's close to eighty years old. I ran over to protect her. What would you do if someone did that to your mother?"

The guard looked over at Catherine. "Is this true?"

Catherine was shaking. Her lips quivered. "It –w-w-was an

accident. She was in my p-p-personal space. I just wanted her to move back a little. I hardly touched her. I didn't think she would fall."

Hannah screamed, "That's a lie. She shoved her. Hard."

The guard glared at Catherine, then at Hannah. She turned to one of the older nurses. "Does that one," she jerked a thumb at Catherine, "Need to be seen by a doctor?"

"That's probably not a bad idea," the nurse replied. "At minimum she has facial contusions that need to be looked at." She turned to Catherine. "Can you walk?"

Catherine nodded and stood up slowly.

The nurse held her by the upper arm as she walked her slowly out of the room.

When she was at the door Catherine turned and pointed at Hannah.

"This isn't over."

The only ones left in the waiting area were Hannah, Olive and the security guard.

The guard looked at Hannah, "I'm going to have to report this to the authorities."

Before Hannah could say anything, Olive said, "But officer, my daughter was defending me. You can't arrest her."

"Nobody said anything about anyone being arrested. There was an altercation here that resulted in a hospitalization. By law, I have to fill out an incident report and send it to the Suffolk County D.A. They'll decide what to do."

At that moment, Dr. Y walked in, not looking very happy. Ron Jacobson was next to her.

"What the hell happened?" the doctor said.

"This girl," the guard glared at Hannah, "And some other girl decided to stage a WWE wrestling match in here. From the look of the other one, I'd say she's the winner."

Yankovsky looked quizzically over at Hannah.

Hannah shrugged. She was slumped in her chair. She ached from head to toe. She was humiliated and exhausted.

Olive stood. Her voice was shaky. "It wasn't Hannah's fault. We came in here to wait until you were finished with Phillip. Then Catherine came in and started yelling at Hannah. Hannah didn't say a word back so I told Catherine she was barking up the wrong tree, blaming Hannah for everything. Then Catherine pushed me, I lost my balance and fell. That's when the fracas started."

The guard looked at Hannah. "Is that what happened?"

Hannah nodded.

The guard said, "I'm still gonna have to send a report to the D.A."

Jacobson stepped forward. "Excuse me, miss. I work in the D.A.'s office." He held up an open wallet. On one side was a gold and blue badge that read "Suffolk County District Attorney's Office." The other side held a photo I.D. "I can handle it from here, if you like."

A wide grin spread across the guard's face. "I sure would like. You just saved me about two hours of paperwork."

Jacobson walked over to where Hannah was sitting.

"Come with me, miss," he said severely.

Hannah followed him out.

Just when she thought things couldn't get any worse, she was now in the custody of a guy she recently assaulted.

CHAPTER THIRTY-THREE

Hannah stood at the back of the crowded elevator, head down, shoulders slumped. Jacobson was next to her. People got on and off at almost every floor. Visitors, holding flowers or balloons. Ernest nurses, doctors and other hospital staff in white coats or blue scrubs. One woman held a huge tray of fancy breakfast items: bagels, croissants, donuts, fruit, yogurt. Several people gazed hungrily at it, others stared intently at their phones. No one smiled. Why do you people look so miserable? Hannah thought. At least you're not on your way to jail.

The elevator doors opened to a hospital lobby that would not have looked out of place in a four-star hotel, with a polished oak and granite information desk, travertine tile floors, oil paintings on the walls, lush upholstered chairs and sofas, luxuriant potted palms, an upscale gift shop and a Starbucks. The only indication that she was in a hospital were the signs indicating the way to Ambulatory Surgery and Patient Relations as opposed to ballrooms and luxury suites. No wonder health care costs so much.

She and Jacobson were the last ones out of the elevator. She turned to him and said, "Would it make any difference if I apologize for hitting you the other day?"

He smiled. "Would it make any difference if I apologize for the way I treated you?"

She was confused. "You mean just now?"

"No. Before."

Hannah gaped at him, open-mouthed. "I don't understand."

"Back when we were seeing each other I should have told you that I was separated and going through a horrible divorce. Then, out of the blue, I shut you out. I didn't answer your calls or respond to your texts. I never told you why. That was totally wrong and I'm sorry. I never even mentioned that I had a son."

"Phil told me."

Did he tell you that my ex-wife threatened to take him out of the country if I ever spoke to you again?"

"Not in so many words." She gave him half a stink-eye. "Anything else you think I should know?"

"Only that I thought there was a real chance we could have had something special."

Hannah scowled. "And you thought the best way to demonstrate that was to lie to me, then vanish from my life. No goodbye. Nothing. I agonized for weeks trying to figure out what I did to you to make you treat me that way."

"I know. I treated you terribly. But at the time I didn't think I had a choice. It was either cut you off completely or lose my son."

"If you were separated and in the process of getting a divorce, why can't you see anyone you want?"

"It's a complicated story." He gestured towards the Starbucks. "Why don't we go in there and sit down. I'll explain."

Hannah didn't know what to think. Minutes earlier she was preparing to be arrested by someone who hated her. Now a guy who she despised, and who she thought despised her, was taking her for coffee instead of to jail.

They sat at a table by the window, looking out at the lobby.

"What would you like to drink?" Jacobson asked.

"Coffee."

"Just coffee? Are you sure? It's on me so you can have anything you want. Espresso, cappuccino, latte, chai."

"I've never been in a Starbucks before. I don't know what those other things are."

Jacobson rolled his eyes and smiled. "Never been in a Starbucks. That's practically un-American."

Hannah didn't know where this was going. Was he serious or was this flirty-cutesy contrition act a ploy? Maybe he was buttering her up to get a confession. To what? Assault? Disorderly Conduct? Disturbing the Peace? Still, if he wanted to keep up this banter, she would play along.

"I never understood why people would pay so much for a cup of coffee?" she said, forcing a smile. "You can get really good coffee at a lot of places for a lot less."

"Must be the ambiance," he said. "What kind of coffee would you like?"

"Black."

"Dark roast or regular?"

She shrugged. "I don't know. Dark."

"How about something to eat?"

"What do they have?"

"Do you want healthy or tasty?"

"Do they have anything that's healthy and tasty?"

"I like their egg white and turkey bacon."

"Okay. I'll try it."

Jacobson went to get the food.

Hannah checked her phone. There was a text from Bette.

'Where are U?'

Hannah texted back: 'Starbucks SB hospital lobby.'

'Are you all right?'

'Not sure.'

'Wait there for me. Big news.'

Not as big as my news, Hannah thought.

But her news brought as many questions as answers. She knew that Dawson and the others were using the Refuge to smuggle huge amounts of money out of the airport. Probably from somewhere in the Middle East. Where was it going? Did her father suspect what they were doing? Was that why he was killed? If he did suspect, why didn't he report it to the police? He had plenty of time to do that.

Before Hannah could come up with any answers, Jacobson was back with breakfast on a cardboard tray.

"Black dark roast and a turkey bacon and egg white sandwich, as requested," he said, placing it in front of her.

"Thank you. How much do I owe you?"

He shook his head. "I told you, it's on me, to commemorate this special occasion."

Hannah looked puzzled. "What special occasion? Phil getting shot? Me beating up Catherine?"

"Your first time at Starbucks."

Her first inclination was to insist on paying, then she decided not to.

"Thanks. That's very kind of you." She glanced over at his side of the table. "What are you having?"

"I decided to try something healthy myself. A spinach, feta and egg white wrap. Want a taste?"

She hesitated, then said, "Okay."

He cut off almost half his sandwich and put it on her plate.

"That's way too much," she said.

"I already had breakfast this morning. This is more than enough for me."

Hannah finished her sandwich and almost done with Ron's half before he was halfway through.

"Do you always eat this fast or are you in a hurry to get out of here?"

"I'm not in any hurry. Actually, my friend Bette is on her way to meet me."

She took a sip of coffee then scrunched up her face. "It's bitter."

"Their dark roast is not for the faint of heart."

"Is that latte you're drinking?"

"Cappuccino."

"What's the difference?"

"I'm not sure. Different cups." He smiled. "I think latte might have more milk or less foam or vice versa. My first time in Starbucks I tried the cappuccino, liked it and stuck with it."

Hannah had enough coffee talk. "By the way, thanks again for not arresting me."

"To tell you the truth, I couldn't have arrested you even if I wanted to."

"I thought district attorneys have the power to arrest people?"

"They do. But technically, I'm not a district attorney. I'm a consulting attorney employed by the D.A.'s office. I have the badge and I.D. but if you look closely you'll see 'Consulting' in a bar at the bottom of the badge. That means I have no law enforcement authority."

"I'm just happy you showed up." She paused for a few seconds. "Come to think of it, why did you show up? How did you know that Phil was in the hospital? He was too out of it to call you. My mother didn't call you, did she?"

He smiled. "I really like your mom, but no, we don't talk on a regular basis. Actually, Yank called me. Dr. Yankovsky."

She looked perplexed. "How do you know her?"

"Buzz, Yank and I hung out together in college. We were on the University of Buffalo swim team. We were from the City. Everyone else on the team was either from upstate or out of town. They made fun of our Noo Yawk accents. That bonded us. After graduation, we went to different schools but stayed in touch."

Hannah sipped her coffee while Jacobson finished what was left of his wrap.

After a quiet moment, she said, "What is a consulting D.A.? I never heard of it."

"Back when Suffolk County was still a backwater, they had one district attorney and he had one assistant. Now, the population has exploded and the crime rate has quadrupled but the district attorney's budget has hardly increased."

"Really? How come?"

"Citizens won't complain too much about paying policemen who protect them and keep them safe. But everyone hates lawyers. And politicians hate to raise taxes. So while the law enforcement budget has been able to keep up with the times, the D.A.'s has lagged. So they bring on consultants to make up the difference."

"How can they afford to pay you?"

"We're funded by a different budget. And there are no benefits to cover. No health insurance. No retirement. No sick days or vacation. We only get paid when we're on an active case. It's a good deal for the county."

"What about for you?"

"All the C.D.A's all have their own practice so the county work is like a bonus."

"How many of you are there?"

"Right now, there are four, each with a different specialty. Matrimonial, financial, employment. I handle immigration."

A look of dread came over Hannah's face. Before she could stop herself she said, "Don't tell me you're one of those horrible people who prosecute undocumented workers and separate them from their children." So much for getting on Jacobson's good side.

Instead of being angry, he smiled and shook his head. "On the contrary. Suffolk County is a sanctuary jurisdiction. Most of what I do is to keep the people that ICE arrests from being deported."

"Oh." She smiled in approval.

"Speaking of separating people from their children, I need to explain why I cut you off cold turkey."

"You said you had to choose between me or your son. That sounds crazy."

"I'll tell you what's crazy," Jacobson said, getting agitated. "My ex-wife. She had me followed by some sleazy private detective who took pictures of you and me together. Did I mention she was

Israeli? A sergeant in their army? She said if I ever saw you again or even spoke to you she would take Josh and go back to Israel and never let me near him."

"Can she do that?"

"Legally, no. At least not without a court battle."

"You're a lawyer. You could stop her."

"Probably. But nothing could stop her from getting on a plane with him. Once they were over there, U.S. laws don't apply. It would be next to impossible to get him back."

"Why would she care if we were seeing each other?"

"Because she's an evil, vindictive bitch. She's a miserable person and she wanted me to be miserable too. Still, I should never have let her manipulate me like that. I've regretted it ever since."

Hannah couldn't tell if he was sincere or just making excuses, but in the end it didn't matter. The damage was done.

"I spent weeks trying to figure out what I did or said to make you dump me like that. Then, when I heard you were married, I figured you were a sleazy dirtbag cheating on your wife."

He slumped in his seat and looked hangdog at her. "I'm so sorry for that and I understand why you would hate me."

Then he sat up and cocked his head. "But there is something I don't understand. You're about the straightest person I ever met. You're the only person I know who when she gets too much change gives it back. All of a sudden, you're in jail, you're brawling in the hospital waiting room, not to mention belting me." He made a show of rubbing his cheek. "And let me tell you, that hurt. You've got quite a left hook." He took a sip of cappuccino. "What happened to the goody two-shoes I used to know?"

"It's a long story." Hannah took a deep breath. "Okay. Here goes."

She went through the entire tale.

She was just about finished when she saw Bette at the door. It was a different version. Not the punk model but not the corporate career girl either. Bette 3.0 was a modified flower child. Her spiky hair was now a short bob. The black, skin-tight, ripped pants were replaced by stonewashed Levis. And she wore white Keds slip-ons instead of black Doc Martens boots. Slung over her shoulder was a messenger bag decorated with cartoony images of birds and daisies.

Hannah waved. Bette saw her, came over and sat at their table.

Hannah didn't say anything about Bette's transformation. She didn't want to make her friend any more self-conscious than usual.

"This is Ron," Hannah said. She turned to Jacobson. "This is my friend Bette."

Jacobson smiled. "Hannah was just telling me about your adventures. You're her Watson."

Bette looked confused. "Thanks for the compliment, but I'm no supercomputer."

Jacobson chuckled. "I wasn't talking about IBM's Watson, I was referring to Dr. Watson, Sherlock Holmes's partner."

"I'm more familiar with IBM than Sherlock Holmes," she said sheepishly. "I'm no detective, either. I do research. I look things up online."

"According to Hannah, you do a lot more than that." He stood up. "I'll be off. I'm sure you two have a lot to talk about."

He took a business card from his wallet, scribbled on the back and handed it to Hannah.

"This has all my contact information, including my personal cell phone number. Call me anytime of the day or night for any reason."

"Thanks."

He turned to Bette. "It was a pleasure to meet you."

As soon as he was out the door, Bette said, "Ron? Was that Ron Jacobson, the guy you hit at the police station the other day?"

"Uh-huh."

"I thought you hated him."

"I thought so too. Now I'm not so sure."

"That's good. Cause he's really cute."

"Cute?" Hannah scowled. "Boys stopped being cute after eighth grade." She took her last sip of coffee. "Forget about him. What's the big news you were going to tell me."

"You first. What happened last night? How did Phillip wind up in the hospital? And what does Ron Jacobson have to do with it?"

"We went back to the Refuge last night as planned."

"You, Phil and Ron?"

"No, just me and Phil. Ron comes later."

Bette leaned in. "Go on."

"I snuck into the Storage Barn. You'll never guess what I found inside."

Bette smiled. "I bet it was money. Bundles of money. Am I right?"

Hannah's eyes bugged out. Her mouth dropped open.

"How on earth did you know that?"

"I'll tell you in a minute." She stood. "I haven't had Starbuck's chai in a long time."

"What the hell is chai?"

"It's tea."

"Why do they call it chai?"

"So they can charge three times as much as for tea."

Bette smiled and was off to the counter.

CHAPTER THIRTY-FOUR

Bette put two containers on the table and slid one over to Hannah.

"I got you another coffee."

"You didn't have to do that."

"Yes I did. I hate to drink alone."

Both women busied themselves with their drinks, taking the lids off the containers and taking little sips of their beverages.

They started to speak at the same time.

Hannah said, "How did you know about the money in the Barn?"

Bette said, "You first. Tell me what happened to Phil. Then I'll explain about the money."

Hannah nodded. "He got shot. The bullet missed the main artery. The doctor thinks he'll make a full recovery. Another inch and it could've been a whole different story."

"What happened? Who shot him?"

Hannah took a breath. Then she recounted everything that happened last night. At the Refuge, on the road and at the hospital, ending with her knock-down-drag-out with her cousin Catherine and Jacobson's intervention.

Bette looked horrified. “You could’ve been killed. Both of you. You were lucky this time. Don’t let there be a next time.”

“No way I’m giving up now that I’m sure my father was murdered. You can quit if you want to. It’s not your fight.”

“Who said anything about quitting. I’m in this all the way. I just meant you need to be more careful.”

“You really want to keep going with this?”

“Absolutely. This is the best job I ever had.”

Hannah smiled. “Is it still considered a job if you don’t get paid?”

Mike Bloomberg was the mayor of New York for twelve years and didn’t get paid. It was still his job.”

“Mike Bloomberg’s a billionaire. You’re not.”

“I have enough saved up to last me a few more months.”

“Okay now tell me. How did you know about the money?”

Bette pulled a yellow pad out of her bag and rifled through the first few pages. They were crammed full of notes in her tiny, cramped handwriting. She turned back to Hannah.

“Do you remember, at the beginning of the Iraq war, there were news stories about all the money that the government sent over there?”

Hannah thought for a few seconds then shook her head. “Not really.”

Bette took another quick glance at her notes. “Once Saddam Hussein was gone, Iraq was a complete disaster. There was no electricity. No water. No police. No telephone. Nothing. Most importantly, no banking system. The Americans arrested anyone who was in Saddam’s party, which was just about everyone who worked in any government agency. They had to start from scratch. And the few Iraqis left in the system demanded to be paid in cash. American dollars. The Iraqi dinar was worthless.”

Bette took a quick sip of her chai.

“Some of the money they used was from Saddam’s vaults, but most of it was flown in from the U.S. in shrink-wrapped bundles like the ones you saw. And no one kept track of any of it.”

"You're saying there were millions of dollars floating around Iraq?"

"Not millions. Billions."

"And it was all up for grabs?"

"Basically, yeah. It was a free for all."

"Where does Dawson fit in? You said she was in transportation logistics, not banking."

"There were no banks, remember. Her department was in charge of delivering the cash to where it was needed."

"And you're saying it didn't get there."

"Nobody knows where it went."

"Somebody must know. Who kept track of it all?"

"She did. Or at least she was supposed to."

Hannah grimaced in disgust. "Where were the accountants, bookkeepers, bankers?"

Bette shrugged.

Hannah said, "That doesn't make sense."

"A lot of what went on over there doesn't make sense." Bette turned to the second page of the pad. She studied it then said, "A guy named William Franklin was brought in to be Dawson's boss for a little while. He was from the Department of Transportation in the George W. Bush administration."

Hannah nodded slowly. It was all starting to come together. Except for one thing.

"All this happened about a long time ago. Why is this stuff happening now?"

"Good question."

Bette turned back to her notes.

"Here's what's really weird. After all the reports of the money being mishandled, and sometimes out-and-out stolen, the Treasury Department put some kind of marker on the bills. If the money stayed in Iraq like it was supposed to, no problem. But if for some reason it got back here, or anywhere other than Iraq, it would be immediately flagged as counterfeit."

"How?"

Bette shrugged. "How should I know. Invisible ink? Ultraviolet etching? Voodoo? It's the U.S. government. They can do anything."

"If the money is useless over here why are they going through all this trouble to smuggle it in?"

"That's a good question. Maybe the most important question. The answer to that might be the key to this whole thing."

"What about this guy Franklin? Is he involved too?"

"Doesn't look like it. He was gone after a few months. The next time his name came up was as a plaintiff in a Whistleblower suit against Armstrong and Warren. Him and some other guy."

"Did they win?"

"Yes and no."

"What does that mean?"

"They won in lower court, but the A&W lawyers kept appealing. It dragged on and on. Franklin died before anything was settled."

Hannah slumped in her seat. "Poor guy. Looks like he was the only one trying to do the right thing. You said there was someone else."

Bette glanced down. "Yeah. Isaac Robertson."

"What happened to him?"

"I don't know. His name popped up once or twice in connection with the lawsuit. After Franklin's death there's nothing else about the lawsuit or Robertson."

Hannah made a noise somewhere between a yawn, a sigh and a groan. "Another dead end."

"Maybe not."

Hannah sat up. "Oh?"

"Their lawyer was a guy named Graham Allendale. He's up in White Plains. His sister is in the New York State Assembly. She's running for State Senate this year. He's in charge of her campaign."

"How does that help us?"

"Do you remember my brother Dominick?"

Hannah did. He was a total sleaze. He 'accidentally' groped her once or twice when she was at Bette's parents' house. She never mentioned it to Bette. What was the point?

"Short, skinny, thinning hair."

"That's him."

"How is he involved in any of this? Was he in the Iraq War?"

Bette chuckled. "Dominick? No way. That's the last place he'd ever be. He didn't even like playing soldiers as a kid."

"I don't get it. How is he connected to any of this?"

"Dominick lives in Rye Brook, up in Westchester. He's very active in local politics there. He even ran for mayor once. I asked him if he knows Allendale. He says they're friends. He gave me Allendale's phone number."

"Great! Let's call him."

"You mean right now?"

"Yes. We don't have much time. Lawyers' offices are very busy. Who knows when we might be able to see him."

Bette grimaced. "What should I say?"

"Ask him if we can come to his office sometime and talk to him."

Bette scrunched up her face. "Can you do it? You're better at that kind of thing."

Hannah shook her head. "Absolutely not. It's your brother who knows him. You spent the last couple of years in a law office. You should be the one to speak to him."

Bette was quiet for a few seconds. Then she hesitantly said, "Okay."

She dug into her bag for the slip of paper with Allen's address and phone number and punched the number into her phone.

"Hello, is this Mr. Allendale?"

She covered the phone and mouthed to Hannah. "It's him."

"My name is Bette Guglielmetti. I believe you know my brother Dominick. I wonder if you have any free time on your calendar to speak with my associate and me."

She listened for about a minute then said, “Really? Today? Two o’clock? Yes, I think we can make it.”

After a few more seconds, she said, “Thank you. I look forward to meeting you too.” She ended the call.

Hannah gave her a thumbs-up and said, “Good job.”

Bette shrugged. “I didn’t really do anything. Dominick had already reached out to him.”

“You told your sleazebag brother what we’re doing!”

Then, before Bette could reply, Hannah said sheepishly, “I’m sorry. I know you love your brother. I just feel uncomfortable having people know my business.”

Bette smiled. “No apology necessary. I do love my brother but that doesn’t mean I don’t know who he is. All I told him was that I was doing some investigating for my office. He doesn’t know that I quit. And he certainly doesn’t know anything about our investigation.”

“Oh, okay, good. Do you know how to get to Allendale’s office?”

“I’ve been to Dom’s house lots of times. He said Allendale’s office is only about ten minutes from there. It shouldn’t be too hard to find.”

Hannah stood.

“Let’s go.”

CHAPTER THIRTY-FIVE

"If you don't need me to help you find Westchester," Hannah said as she reclined her seat. "I'm gonna close my eyes for a couple of minutes."

"It's not the myasthenia, is it?"

"No, I'm just tired. The only sleep I've had in the past two days was a few hours dozing in Phil's room at the hospital. And those chairs aren't exactly made for great snoozing."

"After everything that you've been through, it's no wonder you're exhausted. At least you didn't have an attack."

Hannah hadn't thought about it, but in the last day she did everything that usually triggered the Weakness. Intense physical activity, strong emotion and high stress. Could this new medicine really be working? Before she could decide, she nodded off.

The blare of a truck horn jolted her awake. She shot upright. Her neck ached and she felt slightly queasy. She looked around and slowly came back to herself.

Shaking her head, trying to knock the fuzzballs out, she said, "How long was I out?"

"Almost an hour. We'll be there soon."

Hannah sat up and lowered the passenger-side sun visor to have a look at herself in the interior mirror. She was startled by what she saw. Who was that zombie staring back at her? One side of her face was covered with indentations from the seat. The other side was pale and puffy. Her eyes were bloodshot. Her hair was sticking out in all directions. She looked like Elsa Lanchester in Bride of Frankenstein. And that wasn't the worst of it. She was still in her all-black ninja outfit from the night before, but now the leggings were scuffed and torn, her sweatshirt grimy and stained and her Chuck Taylor high-tops were caked with dirt.

"Turn around!" she screeched. "Why didn't you tell me I looked like a Rocky Horror Show reject."

Bette glanced over at her. "You look fine."

"Are you crazy? I look like something the cat dragged in and threw up on. I don't know what I was thinking, going to see some fancy lawyer looking like the limping dead. He'll take one look at me and throw us out of his office." She turned her head towards her armpit, sniffed and grimaced. "And I smell even worse. Turn around, we're going home."

Bette pulled over. She glared at Hannah.

"Absolutely not! You're not going on a date. You're meeting with a lawyer. Lawyers deal with addicts, thugs and criminals every day who look a lot worse than you."

Hannah shook her head vehemently. "You talk to him. I'll stay in the car. You know what to ask. And besides, you know him."

"I never met the man in my life. I heard my brother mention his name once or twice."

"You worked in a law firm. You know how to talk to these kinds of people."

"I hate talking to people I don't know. I'm not that great with people I do know."

"Maybe this wasn't such a good idea."

"We came all this way to see him. You can't chicken out now."

"I'm not chickening out. I just don't think I have any credibility looking like this."

"You're going to talk to him and you'll do fine," Bette said commandingly. "Case closed."

Hannah was shocked into silence by Bette's authoritative tone. She had never seen her friend so assertive. She liked her newfound spunk but it would take a little getting used to.

Hannah smiled, gave her a three-finger Girl Scout salute and said, "Yes, chief."

A few minutes later they were on a street that couldn't make up its mind if it was commercial or residential. Storefronts with neon signs in the window stood next to quaint homes with basketball hoops and swing sets. They parked in front of a two-story brick office building in the middle of the block.

Allendale's office was on the second floor. The first floor was split between Glam Tips Nail Salon and Tarot Readings by Josephine. An impressive sign above the second floor window proclaimed 'Graham Allendale Attorney at Law' in silver letters on a dark background. Next to it was a vinyl banner, slightly askew, with big blue block letters on a white background reading, 'Sandy Greenstein for New York State Senate.'

They walked up the front steps to two red doors. A sign on the left door read Nails/Tarot. The right one said 'Allendale/Greenstein.'

They walked up a flight of stairs. A brass plaque on the door announced 'Graham Allendale, Attorney at Law. A 'Sandy for State Senate' handbill was taped under it.

The door opened to a conference room with a long table in the center of the room covered with stacks of flyers, post cards and pamphlets touting the heroic efforts of Assemblywoman Sandy Greenstein. Well worn plastic chairs that looked like castoffs from a high school cafeteria were scatted around the table, covered with more Greenstein propaganda.

On the other side of the room was another door, slightly ajar. They heard a man's voice in heated conversation. Bette looked inquiringly at Hannah who shrugged.

After a few seconds hesitation Hannah walked over, eased the door open and tiptoed in with Bette hovering behind her. The room smelled like burnt tennis shoes. The walls were covered with 'Sandy for Senate' posters.

A middle-aged man they assumed was Allendale was seated behind a large desk under a window. His flip-flopped feet were sprawled on top of it. His rotund face sprouted five days worth of stubble. The hair at the side of his bald head was salt and pepper. His gaudy Hawaiian shirt's three top buttons were open. He held a stubby brown cigar between his almost-as-stubby fingers. It had an inch of gray ash hovering precariously at the tip that stayed put even as he waved the cigar to motion them to come in as he hung up the phone.

Hannah's anxiety about her appearance dissipated. In fact, with the office in a semi-shambles and Allendale looking like he was three days into a low-budget cruise to nowhere, she fit right in.

Allendale gestured at two chairs in front of his desk. They were the same lunchroom castoffs as the ones in the outer office. He walked around the desk and brushed the election flyers covering the seats onto the floor.

"Please ladies, sit ."

They sat.

He looked down at Bette. "You must be Dom's sister. I can see who got the good looks in the family." He turned to Hannah. "And you are?"

"I'm Hannah Johansson, Mr. Allendale. Thanks for seeing us on such short notice."

"My pleasure." He leered lasciviously at her, then caught himself and switched to his lawyerly posture. "Dom wasn't very clear about what it is you ladies need my help with. Something about the whistle-blower suit, wasn't it?"

"Well, uh..." Hannah wasn't sure what exactly she wanted to say. She didn't want to talk about the Refuge or her father. "We'd like to ask you about..." She paused, trying to collect her thoughts.

Bette jumped in. "Ms. Johansson and I are financial investigators. Our client is considering a venture with a firm that at one time was partnered with Armstrong and Warren. During our inquiries we came across the name William Franklin and his action against A&W. Then the trail went cold. As you were the plaintiff's attorney, we thought perhaps you could shed some light."

Hannah was really starting to appreciate the new assertive Bette.

Allendale leaned forward, and in a conspiratorial voice said, "This has to be off the record. I'll tell you anything you want to know but you can't use my name for attribution."

Bette sat up stiffly. "Of course. We're ethically and contractually prohibited from revealing our sources unless required by a court order. We just need facts so we can advise our client accordingly."

"Okay. But you never heard this from me."

Allendale looked furtively around the room, as if searching for hidden cameras or someone lurking in the corner with a tape recorder. Assured that they were alone, he continued.

"I'm sure I don't have to tell you that the war in Iraq was total clusterfuck...pardon my French. Everyone knew there were never any WMD's there. And do you think the U.S. government gave a crap that Saddam was killing his own people? We backed dozens of dictators all over the world who did a lot worse. It was all a money-grab by that bastard Dick Cheney. The blood of the four thousand Americans who died over there is on his hands."

"And God knows how many Iraqis," Bette chimed in.

"Damn right." Allendale slammed his fist on the desk for emphasis. "Cheney figured he could get his hands on Saddam's oil. But when that didn't happen, he still raked in tens of millions. He handed out dozens of bogus contracts to his pals at Raytheon, Halliburton and who knows how many other blood sucking companies. And he got a piece off the top from every one."

"What does that have to do with Will Franklin?" Hannah asked, impatiently.

Allendale held up a hand. "Hang on, sweetie, I'm getting to that."

Hannah bristled at 'sweetie' but kept her mouth shut.

Allendale tapped his cigar on the rim of his coffee mug, dislodging the recalcitrant ash.

"When Cheney was Secretary of Defense in the Bush administration, the first one—not the idiot son, Marc Armstrong was his DIA liaison."

Hannah said, "You mean CIA?"

"No, DIA, the Defense Intelligence Agency. The CIA reports to the President, the DIA works for the Defense Department."

"I never heard of them," Hannah said.

"They're not as well-known as their big brother but they're every bit as vicious and corrupt. A bunch of jackbooted fascists the whole lot of them."

Allendale fished a book of matches out of his desk drawer and relit his cigar. The burnt tennis shoe aroma intensified.

Hannah shot Bette a quick sidelong smirk. Her friend grimaced. Hannah wasn't sure if it was because of the cigar or Allendale's diatribe.

The lawyer leaned forward. "After he left the DIA, Armstrong married Cheney's sister's daughter." He grimaced. "I'm pretty sure it wasn't for love. She had a face like a bullfrog."

He waited for a reaction, got none.

"He and one of his buddies, Jimmy Warren—he was some kind of Green Beret hotshot—went to Baghdad early on in the war. They rented a small office in the Green Zone. They were in business less than a month when they were awarded a 20 million dollar no-bid contract to provide logistics and transportation support for the Coalition Provisional Authority. The only qualifications they had was that Armstrong was Cheney's nephew-in-law."

Bette tsk-tsked. "That's just awful."

Allendale smiled. "The awfulness is just beginning. There

were no municipal services of any kind in the whole country and the Iraqi dinar was crap."

Hannah wondered if they should tell Allendale that they already knew the history and just wanted to hear about Franklin. She looked over at Bette who was staring at Allendale in rapt attention, so she decided to keep her mouth shut and let Allendale tell his story in his way.

"Washington flew billions of dollars into Baghdad in cargo planes. Bundles of hundred-dollar bills as big as hay bales stacked on pallets. Armstrong and Warren were supposed to unload the money, separate it and deliver it where it was needed. It wasn't long before our government realized that the money wasn't getting to where it was supposed to go. That's where Franklin comes in. They sent him to fix the problem."

Bette said, "Why Franklin?"

"He was one of the few people to go over there who was actually qualified. Back in D.C. he was the Assistant Inspector General for Acquisitions and Procurement for the Department of Transportation."

Hannah said, "That sounds like a big job. Why would he leave it to risk his life in that hellhole?"

"Are you kidding? He was thrilled. He was getting paid triple what he was making back in the States and he had no expenses. They provided him with a great apartment in the Green Zone and covered all his meals."

Bette said, "But it was so dangerous."

Allendale shook his head. "The Green Zone was a fortress. And he had a full-time security detail. You have a better chance getting killed crossing Times Square than he did in Baghdad. He figured he'd set up a couple of basic systems, install some simple accounting and tracking programs, be out of there in six months and come back as a hero to a fat bank account and a nice promotion."

"Sounds like a good opportunity."

"It should have been, except that's not how it turned out."

Allendale gestured around the room. "You see this mess in here. It was ten times worse over there. Only instead of brochures and flyers, it was money. There were stacks of hundred-dollar bills scattered everywhere. On the floor. The desks. In the bathroom. They actually played football using bricks of cash as the ball. And it wasn't just in one place. It was everywhere. Who knows how many millions of dollars just laying around like yesterday's laundry, with nobody guarding it or keeping track of it."

"What did he do?" Hannah asked.

"Not much he could do. He was the brakeman on the gravy train. Instead of cooperation he got death threats. Not from the Iraqis but from the Americans. The ones who were supposed to be on his side."

Bette said, "That's terrible."

"It sure was. He had to hole up in his office with a 24-hour guard. He asked them to send a heavy security detail and a team of forensic auditors. Instead, they sent Elyse Dawson."

Hannah scowled. "We met her."

"She was useless. Worse than useless. Franklin kept trying. He sent letters, made phone calls. Nothing happened. Three weeks later they shipped him back home. He sent a scathing ten-page report about what was going on over there to everyone in the government who he thought could do something about it, up to and including Cheney, Rumsfeld and Colin Powell. He finally got an appointment with a lawyer from the DOD."

Hannah said, "What happened?"

Allendale shook his head sadly. "Franklin thought he was finally going to get some help. Instead they asked him to sign a non-disclosure agreement. When he refused, they fired him on the spot. That's when he came to me. We sued the government under the Whistleblower Act and went after Armstrong and Warren as government subcontractors. We won in the D.C. district court. They appealed and we were preparing for circuit court when Franklin died."

Bette said, "I could see how all that stress would make you sick."

"He wasn't sick," Allendale replied. "He crashed into a concrete abutment at 80 miles an hour."

Both women gasped.

Bette said, "Oh my God. That's awful. How did it happen?"

"He had three times the legal limit of alcohol in his system."

Hannah said, "He was an alcoholic?"

"Actually, I never saw him take a drink." Allendale shrugged. "Who knows."

"What a terrible thing," Bette said. "A life up in flames."

"Yeah. And the lawsuit flamed out too."

"Didn't I read that there was another person involved in the suit?"

"That would be Ike Robertson. He was a mid-level administrator in the Office of Management and Budget. A&W brought him over to deal with government paperwork. He had about five people working under him, Fed lifers who came over with the promise of a huge payday for a couple of months' work. Three weeks into the job, Armstrong gave him fifty employment contracts to sign. Robertson wanted to know why there were fifty contracts when he only had five staffers. They told him not to worry about it. That he would get a thousand dollar bonus for each contract he signed. Robertson refused. He said he wouldn't be part of defrauding the government." Allendale rolled his eyes and grinned. "Who knew there were so many honest men around Washington? Go figure."

Neither Hannah nor Bette knew how to react so they nodded and smiled benignly.

"Armstrong told him the government knew all about it. That's the way business was done in Iraq. Robertson wouldn't budge. The next thing you know they marched him out of Baghdad at gunpoint. When I got in touch with him about our lawsuit he was all gung ho. But after Franklin died he changed his mind."

Hannah said, “Did he say why?”

Allendale shook his head. “He just stopped returning my calls. The last time I tried I got a message saying that the number was no longer in service.”

Bette said, “What do you think happened?”

Allendale shrugged. “I’ve given up trying to figure out why people do what they do.”

“That’s too bad,” Bette said. “I was hoping we could talk to him.”

Hannah brightened. “Maybe we can. It’s easy to change your phone number. It’s a lot more complicated to change where you live.” She turned to Allendale. “Do you still have Robertson’s address?”

“I should have it somewhere.”

He pulled open a drawer, rummaged through it, pulled out an envelope and waved it like a little flag.

“Here it is. I sent him a representation agreement. It came back unopened.” He handed it to Hannah. “Keep it.”

Hannah looked at the envelope. “Mount Kisco. Is it far from here?”

“About a half-hour. Take the Saw Mill.”

She turned to Bette. “You know where that is?”

“Vaguely. Ms. Garmin will guide us.”

Hannah looked puzzled. “Who?”

Bette grinned. “My GPS.”

“Cute.” Hannah paused for a second. “You wanna try to see him?”

Bette said, “Absolutely!”

She stood and turned to the lawyer. “Thanks so much, Mr. Allendale. We really appreciate all the help you’ve given us.”

Hannah said, “Yes, thank you.”

“Don’t mention it, ladies. It was a pleasure to meet you. You’re welcome here anytime.”

He leaned forward and extended his hand. They both shook it and headed for the door.

CHAPTER THIRTY-SIX

Before they got on the highway Hannah made Bette stop at a Walgreens where she picked up some makeup and a hairbrush. Then they drove to a diner. While Bette ordered sandwiches and Diet Cokes to go, Hannah ducked into the ladies room where she made herself look if not beautiful, at least presentable.

When she came out Bette grinned. "I like it. Grunge chic. Very trendy."

The GPS guided them to the Saw Mill River Parkway in three minutes. A lazy river of a highway with languid straightaways, soft curves and lush, green foliage lining both sides, it was nothing like the Southern State, which you could describe as the white-water rapids of highways.

As soon as Bette hit the entrance ramp she turned to Hannah. "Well, what do you think?"

"I don't know what to think. I don't want to quit but I don't know what else we can do. I thought Franklin was our last chance and he's dead."

"Let's see what Robertson has to say."

"Just how are we going to get him to talk to us?"

"We'll tell him the same thing we told Allendale. We're financial investigators looking into Armstrong and Warren. It worked once, no reason why it shouldn't work again. I think we're doing really well."

They lapsed into silence. Bette concentrated on her driving. Her eyes darted back and forth from the road to the GPS.

Hannah gazed out the window, watching the miles rush by. And with each mile she became more convinced that they were wasting their time. All they had was a cockamamie theory about billions in stolen money that wasn't really money.

What made matters worse was that as depressed and demoralized as Hannah felt, she'd never seen Bette more upbeat. Whether it was coming out as a lesbian, pretending to be an investigator or both, it seemed to have jolted her out of her perpetual gloom. And Hannah, who always thought of herself as a positive person, had turned into Double Debbie Downer. Hannah didn't like this personality switch and she willed herself to snap out of it.

Hannah sat up. "Okay, partner, what's our plan?"

"Didn't you see All the President's Men? Their mantra was 'Follow the Money.' We need to connect Dawson and Westbrook with the money."

"But it's not real. Do you think Woodward and Bernstein would have followed Monopoly money?"

"Robertson was there. Maybe he can tell us why they're going through all this trouble for useless currency."

"Suppose he doesn't want to talk to us?"

Bette turned to her and smiled. "You'll think of something."

Hannah said, "I was hoping you'd come up with an idea. You've been doing a lot better than me lately."

"Whatever it is, we better do it fast. Mount Kisco is the next exit ."

They drove through a busy downtown and quiet tree-lined streets, following the strident directions of Ms. Garmin. They wound up in front of a small single-story house at the end of a cul-de-sac. Two large white pines shrouded it from the street. A big, black BMW polished to a high sheen was parked in the driveway. A red and white 'For Sale' sign stood high on two wooden posts in the middle of the front lawn. An 'Open House' banner was next to it.

They parked down the block.

Hannah looked askance at the sign. "Are you sure this is the right address? This house is for sale."

Bette glanced down at the envelope Allendale gave her. "Yup this is it, 27 Hickory Lane."

Hannah shrugged. "I don't have a good feeling about this. But let's go in and see what's going on."

When they opened the door a pretty Asian woman greeted them. About thirty, she wore black silk pants, a skin-tight black sweater and black high-heel sandals that made her almost as tall as Hannah. Her shoulder length hair was honey-blonde.

"Welcome. I'm Tiffany. Thank you for coming, ladies." She extended her right hand. Her nails were long and expertly lacquered in crimson. Then she handed Hannah a glossy photo of the house with a list of specifications. Paperclipped to it was a business card. 'Tiffany Leong. Licensed Realtor. Homeright Properties.' She handed it to Hannah.

Hannah took it. "I think we're in the wrong place."

Leong smiled benignly. "Not at all. I think you'll find that this is the perfect place for you and your partner. This is a very welcoming community. Very diverse. Very liberal. Very accepting. In fact, a gay couple lives right up the block. They're very happy here. I'm sure you both will be too."

Before Hannah could say anything Bette said, "You don't understand. My brother is good friends with the owner, Isaac Robertson. When he found out we were looking for a house he told my brother he would grant us the right of first refusal."

The realtor looked perplexed. "I'm sorry. No one mentioned it to me."

Bette said, "I'm sure Mr. Robertson can clear this up. Will he be back later?"

"He won't be back at all. He moved out more than a month ago."

"Do you know where he is?"

"I'm sorry but I have no idea. To tell you the truth, no one in our office has ever actually met Mr. Robertson."

Bette said, "Don't you need to contact him about certain matters?"

"We're working with his lawyer."

"That's concerning. My brother hasn't heard from him either and he's a little worried. Can you tell us the lawyer's name?"

"I'm afraid I can't. Mr. Engle, the head of our office, is the only one who has been in contact with the lawyers."

Hannah said, "Can we speak to Mr. Engle?"

Leong shook her head again. "He just left for a conference in Florida. He'll be back in a few days. But why don't you have a look around while you're here. I'm sure Mr. Robertson will be thrilled to know that you were here."

Bette said, "That would be lovely but we really have to go. There are so many things you have to take care of when planning a wedding." She took Hannah's hand in hers and held it tenderly.

Hannah stiffened for a second, then smiled sweetly back at Bette. She turned to Leong and said, "So true. We have an appointment to meet with a caterer. Then we're going see the Salsa Dolls perform. It's an all-female Salsa band. Very exotic." She sighed and put a hand histrionically to her forehead. "So much to do in so little time." She winked and blew a kiss at the patently uncomfortable real estate agent. Then turned to Bette. "Let's go, darling."

CHAPTER THIRTY-SEVEN

On the way to the car, Bette said, "I thought you were gonna kill me when I pulled the gay couple routine."

Hannah smiled. "I was annoyed for a split second. Then when I saw the way that woman cringed when you grabbed my hand I thought I'd rub it in a little."

"Thanks for playing along. I know you're not into the whole gay thing."

"I'm starting to warm up to it."

"Really?"

"For you, not for me," Hannah said quickly. Then, after a moment's hesitation. "Don't you think it's strange that the two people suing Armstrong and Warren wind up dead?"

"She never said Robertson was dead. She just said she didn't know how to get in touch with him."

Hannah smirked. "Don't be naïve. She's never seen him. No one has. Nobody can get in touch with him. People don't just disappear, especially when they're trying to sell a house. I bet he's somewhere on the bottom of Jamaica Bay, swimming with the fishes. And do you really believe Franklin died in a car accident?"

"Of course."

"Allendale told us he never saw Franklin have a drink.

Suddenly he's a major alcoholic? C'mon. Even you can't believe that."

"So what do you think happened?"

"They poured liquor down his throat and crashed him into that abutment. I'm sure of it. That's how they tried to kill Cary Grant in North by Northwest."

"You've been watching too many movies. This isn't The Godfather or North by Northwest. In real life the simplest explanation is usually the right one. Have you ever heard of Occam's Razor?"

"No. Who's in it?"

"It's not a movie. Occam was a philosopher. He came up with the rule that the simplest explanation is usually the right one."

"I don't care about Occam or his shaving habits. I do know that my father's bloodstream was filled with toxic chemicals. What's the simple explanation for that?"

"I can't think of one," Bette said as she walked around to the driver's side of the car.

Hannah eased herself into the front passenger's seat. "I can. The money. It's the same reason Franklin and Robertson are dead."

"But no one can spend it. The first time they try to pass one of those bills they'd be arrested."

"Maybe they don't know that."

"Of course they know. They were in Iraq at the time."

"Then why is everyone who could tie them to the money dead or missing?"

Bette's features contorted into a mask of dread. "Everyone except us."

Hannah put a hand on Bette's shoulder.

"I know. It's scary. Like I told you before, this isn't your fight. You've been terrific. I couldn't have gotten this far without you. And you're right, we're the only ones left who know what's really going on at the Refuge. Maybe it's better if I go it alone from here on. There's no reason for you to risk your life to help me."

"It's not about that. I told you I'll be with you on this to the end and I meant it. But I really don't know what else we can do. There's no one else to talk to. No other leads we can follow. The only thing we know is that they're ferrying worthless money from the airport to the Refuge and taking it somewhere. It doesn't make any sense but I'm pretty sure it's not a crime. And even if it is, we have no proof."

"I have the bills that I took from the storage barn, that's proof."

"You could have gotten them anywhere. There's nothing that connects those bills to Dawson or the Refuge." Bette shook her head sadly. "I know that's the last thing you want to hear but I'm afraid our investigation has hit a dead end."

Hannah hated to admit it but Bette was right. It was over. Now what did she have to look forward to? Struggling with a mysterious disease? Looking for a job that she was sure to hate? She had no social life to speak of and her prospects for ever meeting anyone, especially now that she was essentially damaged goods thanks to her disease, were about the same as winning the lottery.

Hannah forced a half-hearted smile. "It was fun while it lasted, except for me getting robbed, arrested, beat up and shot at."

Bette beamed. "It was the most fun I've ever had."

"So I guess we're back to being two unemployed losers."

"We're not losers," Bette said, forcefully. "Maybe we didn't prove who poisoned your father, but we were pretty awesome just the same. I was thinking we could actually start our own agency, like a modern day Cagney and Lacy."

"More like Laverne and Shirley. Only I don't know who's the schlemiel and who's the schlimazel."

The car was quiet as they followed Ms. Garmin's directions to the Hutchinson River Parkway. It was rush hour. Traffic coming out from the city was at a standstill. Their side was moving slowly, but at least they were moving.

After awhile Bette said, "Have you heard from your cousin Phil? I wonder how he's doing."

"No. I keep meaning to call him."

She took her phone out of her bag and switched it off Airplane Mode. "I have three texts."

Bette said, "From Phil?"

"No, they're from Jacqui. She said she has something important to tell me."

"What are you waiting for? Call her."

Hannah put the phone on speaker.

"Hi."

"Hannah. Where've you been? I've been texting you all afternoon."

"I'm in Westchester. Driving back to the city."

"What are you doing in Westchester?"

"I had a meeting with a lawyer."

"Why'd you go all the way to Westchester? Not enough lawyers on Long Island?"

"It's a long story. You said you had something important to tell me."

"I've been thinking about my last couple of weeks at the Refuge. When the Feds took over, we got a memo saying that they wanted all our files for the past five years digitized so they could be stored on the cloud." Jacqui chuckled. "After he read it, your dad looked up in the sky. We didn't even have a computer."

"Yeah, he hated technology. He thought the waves interfered with the magnetic fields that the birds use to navigate." Hannah remembered the time that she and her father argued when she wanted a cell phone. He finally relented after she pointed out that millions of people had cell phones and birds all over the world seemed to find their way home.

Jacqui said, "Hannah, are you still there?"

"Yeah, sorry. I was thinking about my dad. So what happened with the files?"

"Axel asked me to handle it. I brought in my laptop and

scanner from home. It was the middle of January so hardly anyone was there. It took almost a week but I got it all done. I haven't thought about it since. Then I remembered you asking me about methyl iodide. I was pretty sure I never saw anything like that but since all the files were still on my laptop, I double-checked the inventory. I found an entry for a fifty-pound bag of iodomethane. It sounded pretty close so I checked it out. Guess what I found."

"What?"

"They're the same thing. Iodomethane is a brand name of methyl iodide. Also that it's some serious shit. It's banned in a lot of places. It causes cancer and a lot of other horrible stuff."

"I know. It's what killed my father."

"What! I don't understand. I thought he had a stroke. Are you sure?"

"Positive. His blood was full of it. Do you remember him ever using it while you were there?"

"I don't think so. There were all kinds of old bags of fertilizer and pesticides and herbicides stacked in the back of the barn. A lot of them looked like they were ready to fall apart. When I asked Axel about them he said the Parks Department gave him a bunch of surplus chemicals when he started at the Refuge but he never used any of it because he didn't know how it would affect the birds."

The line was quiet for a few seconds then Jacqui shrieked, "Oh my God! Now it makes sense."

"What?"

"That bitch Dawson."

"What about her?"

"She never wanted anything to do with me. She never looked at me. Never spoke to me. Nothing. I knew I never did anything to piss her off so I figured she wasn't fond of black people. Then one day she calls me into her office like I'm her new best friend, asking me about my life, my family, if I have any boyfriends. She wants to know all about the Refuge. What kind of birds do we see here? How do we attract them? How many visitors come each year? I remember it because it was the first time she showed any interest in me or in what we did there. She wanted to know what kind of equipment and supplies we had."

"What did you tell her?"

"I told her everything she wanted to know. I thought if she took an interest in the place maybe she wouldn't turn it into an airplane runway."

"What did you tell her about the supplies?"

"I didn't tell her anything. I made a copy of the inventory and gave it to her. A Xerox machine was the only piece of technology that your father would allow there. Next thing you know I see that big ape, Grabowski rummaging around in the storage barn."

Hannah was quiet for a few seconds, then she cried, "Oh my God!"

"What? Are you okay?"

"Jacqui, that's the missing piece."

"Of what?"

"Of how my father was poisoned."

"Really? How?"

Before Hannah could say anything, Jacqui said, "Oh shit! I'm sorry babe, I gotta go. I'm late for our staff meeting. We'll talk soon and you can tell me all about it."

"Of course."

"Okay, bye."

The line went dead.

"Did you hear that?" she said excitedly to Bette. "Now we have proof that Dawson and her gang poisoned my father."

Bette shook her head vigorously. "What proof?"

"Weren't you listening? Dawson knew about the methyl iodide. That proves she poisoned my father."

Bette pulled the car over to the shoulder. She turned to Hannah.

"Jacqui giving her the inventory list doesn't prove anything. We don't even know if she read it. And if she did, what makes you think she knew if methyl iodide was toxic? She was a logistics manager not a toxicologist."

"So what was Grabowski doing in the barn?"

"Who knows. He could have been looking for cement or tools or a million other things."

Hannah said, "He never went there before. He was looking for the methyl iodide. I'm sure of it."

"Even if he was, there's no way to prove it."

"I'll find a way. The investigation's back on. Are you with me?"

"I'll help you any way I can. But I still don't see what else we can do at this point." Bette was quiet for a few seconds, then she said, "By the way, don't you have an interview tomorrow?"

"Oh yeah. I wouldn't really call it an interview. I have an appointment to see Michael Leigh. I don't know anything about finance. He probably just wants to wish me good luck."

"A man like that doesn't take time out of his day just to wish you luck."

"So what do you think he wants?"

"I don't know. But it could be important."

"Or it could be a huge waste of time."

Both women were quiet after that. Bette concentrated on her driving while Hannah stared out the window. After what Jacqui just told her she wasn't ready to give up but she had no idea how to proceed. Maybe she needed to step away from the investigation for a little while to refresh her brain. If nothing else, her meeting with Leigh would be a good distraction.

CHAPTER THIRTY-EIGHT

Hannah's phone alarm woke her at six. She showered, dried her hair and dabbed on a little powder and lip gloss. She put on her tried-and-true Ann Taylor navy blue interview suit and her fresh-out-of-the-box dress flats. She was out the door in twenty minutes.

She decided to take the Long Island Rail Road instead of driving to the city. She wanted to avoid the stress and angst of rush hour traffic and inevitable delays.

As she drove up to the Port Jefferson train station, she felt like she had stumbled into a war zone. The harsh rat-tat-tat of workmen ripping gaping holes in the sidewalk and parking lot with jackhammers, as front end loaders dumped slabs of concrete into dumpsters with a deafening thud. A sign on the fence said 'Thank you for your patience while we work to improve your commuting experience.'

So much for avoiding stress and angst.

Hannah had two choices. She could either drive all the way into Manhattan or go to the Ronkonkoma station, fifteen minutes away and hope that she would get to New York at a reasonable time. She opted for Ronkonkoma and hoped the schedule was kind. She found a parking space at the far end of the huge lot and jogged what seemed like half-a-mile to jump on a train just as the doors were closing.

By dumb luck, the train was an express. It only made two stops and flew into Penn Station in about an hour, as opposed to the two-plus hours that the Port Jeff would have taken. Instead of being late as she feared, she was way early. Since it was a nice spring morning she decided to skip the subway uptown and hoof it.

The pavement was jammed with gawking tourists gazing up in awe at the towering skyscrapers, sweaty workmen unloading double-parked trucks as cabbies honked and cursed at them, haughty executives with perfectly coiffed hair in thousand-dollar suits strutting to the day's first meeting, harried office workers from the outer boroughs rushing out of the subway to their cubicles, homeless men hawking free newspapers through rotted teeth.

Her route took her across 34th Street, where Macy's block-long windows were decked out in floral displays and the latest spring fashions. She headed north up Fifth Avenue past the majestic spire of the Empire State Building, the lush greenery of Bryant Park and the awe-inspiring St. Patrick's Cathedral. It never occurred to her that walking nearly two miles to Madison Avenue and East 60th Street in new shoes would turn her feet into chopmeat.

Flack and Spitz was on the 15th floor of a gleaming glass and chrome tower. A uniformed guard sat at the front desk as Hannah limped into the lobby looking slightly disheveled from her trek. He asked her name and where she was going. She told him she had an appointment with Michael Leigh. He eyed her skeptically and called upstairs. After hanging up his demeanor morphed from officious to respectful. He called her ma'am, escorted her to the elevator and bowed his head slightly as he wished her a very pleasant day.

The elevator opened directly into the reception area, which was abuzz with intense men and women in dark suits, bustling frenetically in and out of offices, hands full of phones, folders, tablets and coffee mugs. After being announced at the front desk, a tall, elegant woman of early middle age introduced herself as Mr. Leigh's Senior Executive Assistant and ushered Hannah down a long corridor into a small conference room.

The walls were covered with photos of Michael Leigh with a Who's Who of Washington's Republican luminaries. Henry Kissinger, Donald Rumsfeld, Dick Cheney, Colin Powell, both Bushes. A white oak conference table with six plush chairs dominated the center of the room. A matching credenza held an assortment of yellow legal pads, pens and file folders emblazoned with the Flack & Spitz logo, bottles of artesian water and a stack of plastic glasses.

Hannah declined the offer of coffee or tea and spent the next twenty minutes thinking and worrying. About Phil's shoulder. About whether Catherine would sue her for assault, which is just the kind of thing Catherine would do. About her myasthenia gravis and whether or not she should have the operation that Dr. Romano said involved cutting her chest open. And about her Murphy's Law investigation into her father's death and all the screw-ups and disasters that happened along the way.

As these thoughts bombarded Hannah's brain she gnawed on her cuticles until they bled. As she dug into her handbag looking for a tissue to stanch the blood flowing from her thumb, Michael Leigh strode into the room. She glanced up at the clock on the wall. It was exactly ten o'clock. She stood and extended her hand. He engulfed it with both of his and shook it firmly. If he noticed that she was bleeding he didn't react to it. He seemed larger than the man she remembered from her father's memorial. His navy blue suit with the thinnest of pinstripes was exquisitely tailored around his broad shoulders and even broader waist.

"I'm so pleased to see you," he said with a practiced smile. "Thanks for coming." He sat down opposite her. "How have you been? You didn't look at all well the last time I saw you."

Hannah smiled faintly. "I'm fine, thank you."

"Fine enough to return to work?"

"Absolutely. If I had a job to return to."

"That's why I wanted to see you. I think we may have a position for you here at Flack & Spitz."

Hannah squirmed in her chair. She desperately needed a job. It made her sick to her stomach to be leeching off her mother for the last few months. But she would never accept a job that she didn't deserve just because Leigh liked her father.

"I really appreciate the offer, Mr. Leigh, but I can't see how I'm qualified to do anything in your company. I don't know anything about banking or finance. I have a hard time balancing my checkbook."

Leigh smiled benignly. "A company like ours employs hundreds of highly qualified people, many, but not all of them, specialists in finance and economics. Our workforce has a whole host of talented individuals in a multitude of disciplines."

"I'm sure that's true. Still, I can't imagine that I'm one of them."

"I beg to differ. You see, I did a little research on you." He opened one of the folders on the table and glanced at what was written inside.

"You were the Adult Patient Outreach Manager for the South Boston Behavioral Health Clinic. You started as an administrative assistant and within six months you were running the program. I think that's very impressive."

Not that impressive, Hannah thought. There were only three people in the department. Maureen, her supervisor, was a disaster. She believed that being nasty, rude and obnoxious to everyone she came in contact with would hide the fact that she didn't know what she was doing. Word was that the only reason she was hired was that she and the head of psychiatry at the clinic were sorority sisters at Wellesley. Sisterhood only went so far though, and she was fired for a long list of transgressions, including physically and verbally abusing patients, excessive lateness and drinking on the job. Phyllis, the other woman on the staff, was everything Maureen wasn't. Smart, experienced and hard-working. She cared about the patients and treated them with respect and dignity. She would have been perfect to head the department except that she didn't have a college degree, which was one of the requirements for a supervisory position. That left Hannah, who was named manager by default.

Everything Hannah knew about mental and emotional treatment and care she learned from Phyllis. There was no way she could supervise her, so she didn't. They worked as equal partners. Phyllis dealt with the patients and Hannah took care of the administrative details.

"Thank you," she said, amazed that he knew her background in such detail. "But I still don't see how my experience in a small mental health clinic qualifies me to work at a company like this."

Leigh smiled and emitted a sound halfway between a snort and a chortle.

"I think you're perfectly qualified for the job I have in mind for you."

Hannah didn't say anything. She fought to keep the doubt that she felt from showing on her face.

"A large portion of our staff is comprised of economists, analysts and mathematicians from top-tier schools. Harvard, MIT, Columbia. Many are high-strung, anxiety-ridden and socially inept; more comfortable with spreadsheets, charts and algorithms than humans. What we need in our HR department is someone who knows how to deal with them about issues that they can't come up with a formula for. To my mind, a person who has the judgement, sensitivity, patience and charm to work with high-strung, socially inept mental patients would be perfectly suited to be the Employee Satisfaction Manager on our Human Resources team. Believe me, your patients here, and I use that word advisedly, will be even more challenging than the ones you dealt with in Boston."

Hannah wasn't sure how to react to Leigh's comparing his key personnel to mental patients so she just sat there and smiled benignly.

"The salary starts at 85K per annum and the position comes with fully paid medical and dental coverage," Leigh continued. "There is also a $10,000 signing bonus payable as soon as your initial paperwork is completed. Is that satisfactory?"

Satisfactory? Hannah shouted inwardly as she tried remain calm on the outside. It's a freaking miracle! A lifesaver. Her savings had run out weeks ago and Olive had been supporting her since. And although her mother never said anything, Hannah was sure that she didn't have much money herself. What little savings her parents managed to accumulate was used up to buy the Rocky Point house from her aunt and uncle. That meant that Olive was living on Axel's small life insurance policy, her pension from the New York City Parks Department and her meager social security check. That was just enough to pay the bills and keep food on the table. Hannah wasn't even sure how she could afford the medicine that Dr. Romano prescribed when the samples he gave her ran out.

When Hannah first came back home, she applied for every job opening she could find. When she heard back at all, she was informed that she was either overqualified or underqualified. Her father's death and everything that happened since, put her job search on hold but she knew she had to start working soon or she and her mother would be destitute. If this job offer was for real she could pay for her medicine, have the surgery and pay her mother back everything she owed her and then some.

"Well, Hannah," Leigh continued, "Would you like to join our team?"

"Absolutely."

Leigh beamed and said, "Wonderful." He brought his hands together in a muffled clap. "The position has been vacant for quite awhile. We'd like you to start as quickly as possible. Is Monday too soon?"

"Monday would be great."

"Of course," he said. "You'll have to discontinue your forays into the Jamaica Bay Refuge."

Whoa, she thought. Where did that come from? She began to shiver, like somebody dumped a bucket of ice on her head. She sat up stiffly.

"If you don't mind my asking, how could you possibly know about that?"

"I'm Vice Chair of the Port Authority Board of Commissioners."

"I'm aware of that. But I'm surprised that someone in your position would concern himself with a minor incident like that."

"Given my history with the Jamaica Bay Refuge, I was asked to chair the JFK expansion evaluation committee. I get daily reports on the progress of the project."

"You know everything they're doing there?"

"Of course."

"And you're okay with it?"

Leigh's brow furrowed. He leaned in towards Hannah. "You know that I'm a big supporter of the Jamaica Bay Refuge. And a great admirer of your father and all he accomplished there. But I'm also a firm believer that the needs of the many must outweigh the needs of the few. JFK was once one of the world's premier airports, but that hasn't been true for quite awhile. Runways need to be expanded. New facilities need to be built. That requires space, which as you know, is very limited in New York City. The Jamaica Bay Wildlife Refuge has the needed space and is in the right location. And the needs of the millions of air travelers and cargo shippers outweigh the needs of a few bird lovers like you and me."

He extended a meaty, manicured hand across the table and grasped Hannah's.

"I know how much the Jamaica Bay Refuge means to you. It was your home and all that entails. It was your father's legacy. His gift to the world. A gift that gave me and many, many others great joy." He fixed his eyes on her. "Believe me, if there was any other way to expand the airport we would do it. You must understand that."

"I do understand that. I just don't understand what Dawson and her gang are doing there."

He sat up, pulled his hand away and said, "I recommended Elyse Dawson to head the airport expansion project. I've know her for years. Her father is an old friend of mine. She and I worked together when she was Assistant Logistics Manager for the Coalition Provisional Authority in Baghdad."

Another bolt from the blue.

"You were involved in the Iraq war?"

He nodded glumly. "I was there for a short while. As you may know, financing the transition after the fall of Saddam was extremely problematic. The dinar was virtually worthless. In order to keep the country afloat, billions of dollars were hurriedly shipped over there. Unfortunately, there was rampant fraud, theft, corruption and misappropriation of funds."

He pointed to the photo on the wall of himself with Dick Cheney.

"The Vice President asked me to go over there to get things under control." He smiled ruefully. "Iraq was teeming with gangsters, thugs and con men. Eventually Elyse Dawson and I cleaned up the mess but not without a fight. She stood up to all kinds of intimidation, including the threat of physical violence. I believe she is every bit a hero as the men and women in uniform during Desert Storm."

"If she's such a hero, why is she ferrying bundles of money from the airport across Broad Channel into the Refuge?"

Leigh glared at Hannah. "Are you accusing Elyse Dawson of smuggling currency into the country? That's a very serious crime."

"Even if the money can't be spent?"

"Hannah, you're not making sense."

"None of it makes sense. I think the money is from Iraq. The kind that was treated with some kind of special coating that makes it useless over here."

"Coalition currency. I instituted that program," he said with a small smile of self satisfaction. “It was instrumental in putting a stop to all the fraud and theft over there. Spendable in Iraq but nowhere else.” He looked quizzically at Hannah. “You must be mistaken. There would be no reason for anyone to take the trouble to smuggle it back to the United States. It’s of absolutely no value here.” He eyed Hannah skeptically. “Where did you hear such a farfetched story?”

“I didn’t hear it anywhere. I saw it.”

“I’m sorry. I find that hard to believe.”

“I have proof. These were taken in the storage building at the Refuge.”

She took her phone from her bag and showed him the pictures she took in the barn.

“Can I see that?”

She handed him her phone. He stared intently at the shots.

“I’m sorry but these photos don’t prove anything. Those bales could be anything. Fertilizer. Pesticide.”

“What about this?” She took a hundred-dollar bill out of her wallet and handed it to Leigh.

He stared at it intently. “Where did you get this?” he demanded.

“I opened one of the bundles. This was inside.”

“Who else was with you?” he said.

Hannah hesitated for a few seconds. “No one.” She didn’t want to get Phil into trouble if Leigh pressed charges.

“This could mean something if it is in fact coalition currency. May I keep it?”

“Of course.”

He took two fifties out of his wallet and handed it to Hannah.

“Take this in exchange.”

He held the counterfeit bill up to his face and examined it carefully.

“It’s impossible to be sure with the naked eye. We have ultra violet scanners that can verify if this is coalition currency.

Consider the hundred dollars a down payment on your signing bonus."

"You mean you still want to hire me?"

"Of course. One thing has nothing to do with the other. As long as you give me your word that you'll stay away from the Jamaica Bay Refuge from this day forward, the position is yours."

Since the investigation had come to a dead end anyway, there was no reason for her to go back there.

"You have my word."

He smiled and said, "Then you have the job."

"Thank you, sir."

Leigh stood. "You're most welcome." He thrust out his hand.

Hannah stood and shook it.

"There's a packet for you at the front desk. It will tell you everything you need to know before you start on Monday."

He strode out of the room.

CHAPTER THIRTY-NINE

Hannah slumped down in her chair. Her legs felt disconnected from her body. The photos on the wall were out of focus. Though the conference room was air conditioned, tiny droplets of sweat formed on her forehead. It was the Weakness. But at least now she had a name for it. Myasthenia gravis. And, more importantly, she had a drug for it. Mestinon. Unfortunately, she forgot to take it before she left the house. She looked through her handbag hoping it would magically appear even though she was sure the bottle was sitting on the bathroom shelf.

After ten minutes, the symptoms began to subside. She stood, steadied herself and walked slowly out of the conference room. The woman behind the front desk called to her as she walked by and handed her a white manila envelope.

Between her lacerated feet and wobbly legs there was no way she could walk to Penn Station. She decided to splurge on a taxi. She was able to hail one as soon as she walked out of the building. She couldn't remember the last time she was in a New York City cab. She did remember that it was grungy, with greasy fast food wrappers on the floor and the stench of stale sneakers, body odor and dried vomit. And that the driver spent the entire ride honking at every car that passed buy and yammering on his phone. She was pleasantly surprised that this time the cab was clean, smelled fresh and sported a video screen showing the midday news and the fare total, which increased by the second.

It always amazed her that no matter what time it was, it was always rush hour at Penn Station. She joined the throng staring up at the big board in the main concourse and saw that the next Ronkonkoma train was in forty-five minutes. She ambled over to the small waiting area between the rest rooms and the escalator to the street. She looked around the room to see that the only empty seats were on either side of a guy who looked and smelled like he just finished a hard day of dumpster diving.

She did a quick about-face and dragged herself to the terminal's rear corridor, which was also much cleaner and brighter than she remembered. The smells of the eateries triggered her appetite that the stress of the last few days suppressed. She followed her nose to Rose's Pizza where she ordered a Margherita and a Diet Coke. She was thrilled to see that there were tables in the back with empty seats. As soon as she got her huge slice—Rose's is famous for pizza slices the size of manhole covers—she headed for the rear seats. The only thing on her mind was the heavenly combination of pizza dough, mozzarella cheese, tomato sauce and basil. She ate slowly, savoring every bite. After she was done she ambled back to the concourse, looked up at the board and saw that her train was on Track 16.

Once she was on the train her mind gushed with a million unanswered question. Why did Leigh offer me the job? Does he really think I'm qualified or does he just want me to stop investigating the Refuge? What's really going on there? Westbrook said what they're doing there is a secret government program. Leigh said it's the airport expansion. Who's lying? What about Dawson? Jacqui said she knew all about the poison. Leigh thinks she walks on water. If Dawson didn't poison her father, who did? Can I handle this job? Can I deal with the commute every day? It's more than two hours door-to-door. What about my myasthenia? Suppose it gets worse? Will the Mestinon keep working? Should I consider the surgery? Dr. Romano said the surgery has a fifty-fifty chance of remission. It's a pre-existing condition, would health insurance cover it? How long would I have to be working before I could do it? If I'm out of the house for twelve hours every day, who will look after Olive?

She bolted upright. Olive! She hadn't heard from her mother since she left the hospital. Or Phil, for that matter. She called the house. No answer. She texted Phil. No response.

She tried Bette, who answered on the first ring.

"How'd the interview go? I was dying to call but I didn't want your phone to ring while you were with Leigh."

Hannah ignored the question. "I haven't heard from my mother or my cousin Phil today."

"I'm sure they're fine. Your mother had a pretty hectic day yesterday. My guess is she's asleep in her bedroom with the phone buried where she can't hear it."

"I'm worried about Phil. The doctor said he'd be released yesterday if all went well. Suppose it's worse than they thought. Maybe I should go back to the hospital."

"Don't be silly. From what I know about Phil, there's a better chance he went to see an old girlfriend and turned off his phone."

"You're probably right." Hannah said, not really believing it.

"Of course I'm right. Now tell me what happened at your meeting with Michael Leigh."

"He offered me a job."

"Oh my God! That's great! Tell me all about it."

"Hang on a minute."

Hannah looked around. She wanted to be sure she wasn't followed. There were only a few other people in the car. A couple of students in private school uniforms glued to their phones, a mother with her young daughter asleep on her lap and some weary workmen looking drowsily at the *New York Post*.

"Are you still there?" Bette's voice chirped.

"I was just checking to make sure no one was listening," Hannah said.

"You're really getting paranoid in your old age."

"You know what they say, just because you're paranoid it doesn't mean they're not out to get you."

"Very funny." Hannah saw Bette's smirk in her mind's eye. "Now tell me about this job."

She kept her voice low. "It's in the HR department."

"Human resources? What do you know about human resources?"

"Absolutely nothing."

"That doesn't make sense."

"That's what I thought. But he said his research said I was perfect for the job."

"Research? What kind of research?"

"He knew all about me. It was a little creepy, like he's been stalking me. He mentioned my job in the behavioral clinic in Boston. "

"What does that have to do with HR?"

"He said if I can work with mental patients I'd be the perfect person to deal with his employees."

"He said that about his own staff? Weird."

"I know. And I'll tell you what's even weirder. He knew that I was investigating the Refuge. He said the one condition to get the job was that I stop going there."

There was no sound for a couple of seconds. "How the hell did he know about that?" Bette hardly ever swore, part of her Catholic school upbringing.

"He's on the board of the Port Authority. They're the ones who authorized the airport expansion project."

"So what. Board members don't get into minute details like that. There must be more to it."

"There is. He's good friends with Elyse Dawson."

"What?!"

"Yeah. He knows her since she was a kid. Her father is one of his best buds."

"Whoa. Really?"

"Not only that. They were in Baghdad together during the Iraq War."

"Michael Leigh was in Iraq?" Bette said incredulously. "He doesn't seem like the soldierly type."

"He's not. Dick Cheney sent him over there to deal with the money mess. I don't know about Dawson. Maybe he brought her over with him. He did say he got her the job at the Refuge."

There were several seconds of dead air.

Hannah said, "Hello Bette, did I lose you?"

"I'm still here." After another beat, Bette said, "It's starting to make sense."

"What?"

"They destroy the money so they can keep it."

"Now you've gone completely bonkers. Is this some new Buddhist philosophy you've taken up?"

"No. But I have been looking into the U.S. monetary system."

"Okaaaay."

"You've heard the term money laundering, right?"

"I've heard it but I don't really know what it means."

"It's when crooks put their money into a legitimate business to make it look like they earned it fair and square. It's how they clean up dirty money, hence laundering."

"Is that what you think this is?"

"It's the only answer. But no business could launder billions of dollars. Except maybe a bank. A really big bank. And there's only one person connected with this who runs a bank."

Hannah thought for a minute, trying to process everything Bette was telling her. Then she winced and shook her head. "You're telling me that Leigh is behind what's going on at the Refuge? No way."

"It's the only thing that makes sense."

"He already has a ton of money. Why would he want to risk it?"

"People like that always want more. More money. More

power. More prestige. And we're talking billions. Not millions. That can buy a lot of power and prestige."

"Even if you're right, which I still have a hard time believing, why would he want my father killed? He liked my father. I'm sure of it."

"I don't know. Maybe your dad found something out about the operation."

"If he did, he would have told someone. If not the police, he definitely would have said something to my mother. I'm sorry. You're the smartest person I know, but I think you're way off base on this one."

"It's the only lead I can think of. If Leigh isn't involved then we're at a dead end."

"Let's meet later and talk about it."

"I can't. It's my brother Dennis's birthday. The whole family's going to my mom's house in East Northport. She's been cooking for three days. And she ordered dessert from La Roma. Cannolis, zeppoles and rainbow cheesecake. Why don't you come. My parents would love to see you. And you could probably use a good meal."

"I'd love to but I'm exhausted. And I want to check on my mother and Phil."

"Okay. How about lunch tomorrow?"

"Sounds good. Tell Dennis happy birthday from me."

"I will. See you tomorrow."

CHAPTER FORTY

Hannah closed her eyes after the train left Jamaica Station and fell into a deep sleep. She jerked herself awake a half-hour later from a dream that she was plummeting down an endless elevator shaft. She glanced up to see that the train was pulling out of Central Islip. The scratchy loudspeaker announced 'Ronkonkoma. Next and last stop.'

The drive from the train station to Rocky Point was six exits on the L.I.E. then ten miles on the back roads from the center of the Island to the North Shore. Traffic was light on the expressway and she made good time. She saw a big black truck in her rearview mirror. Was he following her? Could it be the Hummer with the Badass lettering that was in front of Westbrook's building?

"Stop it!" She scolded herself. Bette was right. She had to stop with the paranoia. Long Island drivers love SUV behemoths. Hummers, Toyota Sequoias, Chevy Suburbans, Ford Expeditions, Nissan Armadas. They weren't all following her.

She went back to thinking about whether Bette's theory about Leigh being the mastermind of the funny money business at the Refuge was feasible. He did have the wherewithal to do it. But why? He didn't need the money. He was wealthy and powerful already. He loved the Refuge. And he was a huge fan of

Axel. It was inconceivable that Leigh would agree to his murder. And why would he offer her a job—a job, by the way, that she desperately needed—if he was a murderer and a crook?

Maybe it was time to stop this crazy quest, and move on with her life, especially now that she had a good job to move on to. Her father was gone. Whether he was poisoned or had a stroke, nothing would bring him back. And like her mother said, whatever they were doing at the Refuge was none of her business anymore.

She turned off at Exit 66 onto the back roads that zigzagged up to the North Shore and home, passing through Long Island's underbelly. It was the Eisenhower era's version of the American dream gone to seed. Returning World War II vets from New York City, armed with low-interest loans from the newly created G.I. Bill, trekked east to the then wide open spaces of eastern Long Island, and built small bungalows and cottages, right out of Tom Sawyer's America, with clapboard siding and white picket fences. Many were now ramshackle, with peeling paint, torn shingles and once pristine front lawns overgrown with weeds and strewn with junk.

The route also took her past the Pine Barrens, where she went on nature walks with her father. And the Carmans River where she and her cousins went kayaking.

She glanced up at the rearview. The big, black SUV was still behind her. She tensed. The road was deserted. Woods on both sides. Why was it following her? What did they want with her? Were they going to kill her like they killed her father?

Stop it! she yelled silently at herself. She wasn't even sure it was the same SUV that she saw on the L.I.E. And even if it was, there was no reason to think there was anything sinister going on. She slowed down. The SUV sped up behind her. She veered to the shoulder to give it room to pass.

It slammed into the back of the Jeep, knocking it into a stand of scraggly shrubs on the side of the road. The airbag deployed, enveloping Hannah in a gigantic marshmallow.

The SUV screeched to a stop a few feet behind her. The door opened and Grabowski stepped out of the Hummer. He was sneering malevolently as he started towards the Jeep. Just then, a beat-up old pickup truck came rattling around the curve from the other direction. It was loaded with lawn mowers, string trimmers, rakes, shovels, wheelbarrows and big green plastic barrels. The lettering on the side said 'Hernandez Landscaping.' It pulled over to the shoulder across the road from Hannah. Three workmen in soiled coveralls and work boots caked with mud scrambled out. Two were in their early twenties. The third was Hannah's age.

"Miss, you need some help?" the older one shouted.

"Yes, please!" Hannah yelled.

Grabowski looked over at the landscapers, who were running over to Hannah. He hesitated for a few seconds, then climbed into the Hummer and drove off.

Hannah squirmed out of the deflated airbag. One of the younger landscapers helped her out of the car. Her legs were wobbly. Her entire body was shaking. Her chest, arms and legs ached. Her eyes were hazy. She leaned against a tree. The three men stood around the Jeep. The older one, obviously the boss, began speaking animatedly in Spanish, pointing to the car and the road.

He got into the driver's seat and cranked the engine. It didn't turn over. He tried it again. Same result. It started on the third try. The other two ran to the rear and began pushing and grunting as the car rocked back and forth, spewing clods of dirt on them. After three or four tries the Jeep was back on the road.

"Thank you so much," Hannah said.

All three waved her thanks away. "De nada," the boss said. "It's nothing."

She reached into the car and grabbed her handbag. She took a twenty out of her wallet.

"Here, for your trouble."

"No, no," he said, shaking his head. "No es necessario. Not necessary."

"Please." She extended her hand with the bill. "It'll make me feel better."

He reluctantly took it.

"Thank you," he said.

"No. Thank you. You literally saved my life."

He smiled and took a slight bow. The two younger men nodded sheepishly behind him.

"You sure you're okay?"

Hannah said, "Yes. I'm fine."

"Then we go. Good luck."

They waved as their truck pulled away.

Hannah grabbed her phone and called 911. She told the operator that a truck forced her car her off the road into a ditch then left the scene. No, she didn't need medical attention. No, she didn't get the license number. She was somewhere on Rocky Point Yaphank Road, a couple of miles off L.I.E. The operator told her the police would be there soon.

She called home. No answer. She tried Bette. Straight to voicemail. She walked around the car and checked it for damage. The rear bumper had a large crease where the Hummer slammed into it. Other than that there were just a few scratches on the fender and some shrubbery stuck in the grill. She got back in the car to wait for the police.

With every passing minute she got more panicky. She needed to talk to someone. She tried Phil again. It rang and rang. She redialed Bette. Same result. She thought about calling Jacobson but she wasn't sure she wanted to open that can of gummy worms. Her vision began to blur. She checked herself in the rearview. Her eyelids were sagging. An attack. Why now, she thought. Of course it would happen now.

A blue and white Suffolk County police cruiser pulled up. Hannah stepped shakily out of the Jeep. A young policewoman walked over to her. She was short and stocky. Her nametag said 'Bowman.'

"Are you the one who called 911?"

"Yesh," Hannah said, her speech slurry.

"Can I see some I.D.?"

Hannah reached through the window and grabbed her handbag off the front seat. As she opened it she dropped it. He wallet, phone, keys, Tic Tacs, lipstick, a comb and an emery board were scattered on the ground. Moving slowly with quivering fingers, she picked it all up and put everything back in her bag but her wallet. She handed her license to the officer.

Bowman examined it then glared at Hannah.

"Ms. Johansson, have you been drinking?"

"No. Absolutely not. A truck pushed me off the road." She pointed to the shrubs.

"What kind of truck was it?"

"A Hummer. A big one."

"What color was it?"

"Black. It followed me off the L.I.E."

"A Hummer followed you then drove you off the road? Why would anyone do that?"

Hannah didn't have the strength to go into the whole story about the Refuge and fake money and everything else. And she was sure the officer wouldn't believe her anyway.

Instead she said, "Maybe it was road rage."

"Did you do something to provoke him?"

"Not that I remember but I've been preoccupied. Maybe I cut him off and didn't realize it."

Bowman shook her head skeptically. "Ms. Johansson, will you submit to a breathalyzer test?"

"I'm not drunk," Hannah said. "I have a disease. Myasthenia Gravis. It affects my muscles."

"If that's true the test with exonerate you."

Bowman held the breathalyzer up toward Hannah.

"Please breathe into the tube."

Hannah did.

After about fifteen seconds there was a beep.

Bowman stared at the readout. She looked surprised. "No alcohol."

"What happens now?" Hannah said, biting back 'I told you so.'

"You're free to go."

"What about the truck that hit me?"

"You can file a complaint. But without a license plate number the chances are slim that we'll find the other driver. Would you like to do that?"

"No."

"Have a nice day," Bowman said and walked to her cruiser.

Hannah got back into her car, put her head in her hands and bawled. Loud, racking sobs that erupted volcanically from deep inside her and shook her to her core. It took her totally by surprise. She never cried. Not even when her father died. Maybe it was because she grew up surrounded by boys, her cousins mostly, and was always trying to prove she was as tough as they were. Maybe it was because she couldn't stand women who used their tears to manipulate their friends, boyfriends and others. Whatever the reason, she had trained herself not to cry. Until now.

She had no idea of how long she'd been at it. It could have been a minute. Or five. Or ten.

After awhile she was all cried out. She felt cleansed. Of guilt. Of fear. Of the past.

She had tried her best to honor her father's wishes. And his memory. To find out who or what really killed him. But all she found was some crazy smuggling scheme that had nothing to do with her father. And caused a lot of collateral damage in the process. That ended now. On Monday she would start her new job and, hopefully, her new life.

CHAPTER FORTY-ONE

On the way back to Rocky Point Hannah kept glancing at the rearview mirror looking for the Hummer or any other threat.

Thankfully, all she saw was a school bus, a florist's van and a couple of small sedans. She drove past pine woods punctuated by old houses, some with chickens, ducks or even horses lolling in the yard. It was the last stretch of tranquility she would experience for awhile.

As soon as she turned the corner to Dogwood Road she could see that something was wrong. A car she didn't recognize was in the driveway. A white four-door BMW. She didn't know anyone who drove a BMW. That was odd but not upsetting. What really spooked her was that the front door was wide open.

Olive never used the front door. She thought the front steps were slippery and was afraid she'd fall and break a hip. But even if she opened the door to talk to a Jehovah's Witness or buy cookies from the sweet Girl Scout who lived down the block, she was scrupulous about closing and double-locking it.

Hannah bounded up the front steps and through the open door, slamming it behind her.

"Ma!" she yelled.

No answer.

"Ma, where are you?"

She ran through the living room to Olive's bedroom. Drawers were open, their contents scattered haphazardly on the floor. A box that held old family photographs was tipped on its side, the photos rummaged through.

Stay calm, she told herself. Maybe there is a legitimate explanation.

She went to her room. It was a disaster. Her clothes, books, jewelry, photos, even stuffed animals were scattered to the four corners. The mattress and box spring were off the frame. The TV was face-down on the floor.

Now it was time to panic. She ran from room to room shouting her mother's name, knowing there would be no answer and petrified that she'd open a door and find her dead on the floor.

She went out and searched in the backyard and around to the side of the house. Nothing. As she walked back towards the street she saw a black and white Suffolk County Sheriff's car pull up. Oh God, she thought, Olive's dead and they're coming to tell me in person.

A deputy sheriff got out of the car. He was short with chubby cheeks and buzz-cut receding gray hair. In his black uniform and dour expression he looked like a pudgy messenger of death. Hannah began to shake. He walked towards her.

She ran over to him, screaming. "My mother. Have you found her? She's not dead, is she?"

He seemed not to hear her. "Are you Hannah Johansson?" he said, stone-faced.

"Yes.

"This is for you." He thrust an envelope into her outstretched hand.

She stared at it. "What's this?"

He didn't answer. He turned and walked back to his car.

She ran after him. "Where are you going?" she screamed. "My

mother's missing. The house was trashed. You have to do something."

"I'm sorry miss," he said, getting into his car. "I can't help you with that. Call your local precinct." He drove away.

She ripped open the envelope. It was a summons. Catherine was suing her for assault and battery.

She held the paper in front of her. She screamed at it. "Are you freaking kidding me!"

She started to crumple it, then changed her mind and jammed it into her pocket.

She began to hyperventilate. She felt her legs weaken. She stumbled back into the house and plopped down, panting, in the club chair. After a few minutes she went to look for her myasthenia medicine, hoping that whoever wrecked the house didn't dump it in the toilet. The bathroom cabinet was open but the medicine bottles were untouched. She found the Mestinon and took a two pills. She had researched the drug online and it said that it takes a half-hour to an hour for it to start working and it would last from four to six hours.

She paced up and down in the living room, worried about Olive, furious at Catherine, trying to figure out what to do next.

She tried Phil again. Still no answer. She wanted to call Catherine and have it out with her but she didn't have her number and she knew it was unlisted. There was a small bulletin board on the wall in the kitchen with business cards and phone numbers on torn strips of paper tacked on it. Catherine's number wasn't there but Gilda's was. She was in no mood to hear one of her aunt's lectures but she had no other options.

She dialed the number.

"Hello Aunt Gilda, it's Hannah."

"Oh, hello." Her voice was chilly. "Why are you calling?"

"I actually wanted to speak with Catherine. Is she there?"

"No."

"Can you give me her number?"

"Where are you?"

She wanted to ask what difference it made but she just said, "I'm home in Rocky Point."

"Catherine should be there. She left with your mother several hours ago."

"Well, they're not here."

"Are you sure?"

"Yes."

"Then I have no idea where they might be."

"Why did Catherine drive my mother home? Olive drove to the hospital herself. Why didn't she drive back herself?"

"Olive sustained a hairline fracture in her wrist during that unfortunate altercation at the hospital."

Hannah pressed her lips tightly together knowing that if she opened her mouth she would wind up screaming about what a spoiled, self-centered, sociopathic bitch Catherine was. How dare she knock a 75-year-old woman to the ground. And then has the gall to sue ME. So she kept her mouth shut.

Gilda said, "The hospital decided to keep her overnight. We went there this morning to check on her and Phillip."

"Did you see Phil?"

"For a few minutes. His wound was infected. The doctor put him on intravenous antibiotics to protect against sepsis. He'll have to remain there for a few more days."

At least now she knew that Phil was all right. One worry off the list. Only a hundred more to go.

"Was my mother released?"

"Yes. Catherine was kind enough to offer to drive her back to Rocky Point."

Hannah wanted to say that it was the least she could do since it was Catherine who broke her wrist in the first place. But she said nothing.

Gilda said, "Are you absolutely sure they're not there?"

She took a deep breath and told Gilda she was positive. Then she asked if Catherine drove a white BMW.

"She has a white car. New. Very luxurious. I don't know the model. Why do you ask?"

"It's parked in the driveway."

"So she is there. Look again. This time more thoroughly. You never were very good at paying attention to details."

Hannah bit her lip. "Can you just give me Catherine's phone number, please? I can call and find out exactly where she is."

Her aunt sighed loudly into the phone. "One minute."

It took about three times that long for Gilda to find the number.

Hannah wrote it down and hung up.

She dialed her cousin's number.

"Hello." Catherine's voice was a halting whisper.

"You're suing me!" Hannah screamed. "After you knocked my mother down and broke her wrist, you have the nerve to sue me. How dare you!"

"Hannah, it's you. Thank God."

This was not the response she expected.

"Catherine, did you hear what I said? You have to rescind this bogus lawsuit immediately."

"That's not important now."

"Maybe it's not important to you. It's very important to me."

"Hannah, you don't understand. They have us. You have to come here immediately."

"What? Where? What are you talking about?"

"Listen to me." Catherine's voice was measured. "I drove Olive home. We were in the kitchen having a cup of tea when a man came to the front door. He had a gun. He made us go with him to the Jamaica Bay Refuge."

"Why did he take you?"

"He thought I was you."

"You don't look anything like me."

"I kept telling him I wasn't you but he wouldn't believe me."

"Where's my mother? Is she okay?"

"She's right here."

"Let me speak to her."

After a moment Olive said, "Hannah?"

"Ma. Are you okay?"

"I'm fine. Catherine and I are in the old storage barn. These terrible people are here, watching us. They have guns." Then Olive yelled, "Don't come here. It's you they want. They won't hurt us. Call the pol..."

Hannah heard her mother gasp. Then what sounded like a scuffle for a few seconds. Another voice came on the phone. Hannah was pretty sure it was Dawson's.

"You've been a major pain in the ass. Now's your chance to make things right and help your mother and whoever this other little bitch is."

"Just don't hurt my mother. I'll do whatever you say."

"Those coalition currency bills you took from here. We want them back. And your phone with the photos of the bills and the currency counter. Bring that too."

Bette was right. Michael Leigh is one of them. There's no other way Dawson could know about those photos.

Dawson said, "Don't screw up. Your mother's not a very strong woman."

Hannah exploded. "She's stronger than you'll ever be! If anything happens to her, you're dead."

"Shut up!" Dawson shouted. "You're in no position to threaten anybody. Just do what I said and everything will be fine. You have until eight o'clock."

The call ended. Hannah checked the time on her phone. Five-thirty-three. It took more than an hour to get there with no traffic. And this was Friday night, so with the weekend crush it would be more like two hours.

She needed Phil. He'd know what to do. But he was hooked up to an antiseptic drip in Stony Brook Hospital.

She paced around the living room staring at her phone, wishing there was an app that would give her the perfect plan. Then it rang and startled her. It was Bette.

"Bette. I'm so glad you called."

"What's wrong. There were three missed calls from you."

"Can you talk now?"

"Yeah. I'm in the bathroom. I needed a break from my family. I checked my phone and saw all your calls. Are you all right?"

"No."

"What's wrong?"

Hannah told her everything from getting run off the road by Grabowski to her phone call with Dawson.

When she finished she said, "You were right. Leigh was in on it from the beginning."

"It doesn't matter who was right. They have Olive. What are you gonna do?"

"I don't know. You're the brains of this operation. Do you have any ideas?"

"Call the police. Tell them what you just told me."

"Absolutely not!" Hannah screamed. "Every time I talk to a cop things get worse."

"I know you think you're Wonder Woman but you can't just swoop in, grab Olive and Catherine and fly away. You have to call the police."

"And tell them what? That Michael Leigh, one of the most powerful and respected men in the city, abducted my mother and my cousin? Sure. They'll believe that."

"All right, I see your point. Have you heard from Phil?"

"He's still in the hospital."

What about Jacobson? He works for the D.A. And he likes you. I bet he would help."

"I don't need a lawyer. I can see him being much help in a situation like this."

"Then I'll come. It'll be you and me, just like always."

This made Hannah smile. "That's very brave of you but, no offense, you'd be more of a hindrance than a help. And besides, if anything happens to me, you're the only one who knows the real story."

"I guess you're right," Bette said dejectedly. "What are you going to do?"

"I don't know but I have to do it soon. I only have until eight o'clock."

"Please be careful. I love you...like a sister."

"Ditto." Hannah hung up.

She stopped pacing and slumped into a chair. Bette was right. She couldn't just go in by herself, Dawson's thugs were trained killers. But who could she call. Phil was always the one she turned to in situations like this but he was out of commission. She checked the time again. A quarter to six. She grabbed her back-pack and looked inside. There was her Swiss Army knife and the bear spray Phil gave her. As she passed the bulletin board in the kitchen she saw Tom McCaffrey's card pinned on it, the one he gave her at the warehouse. He's an ex-cop and an ex-Marine. He was friends with her father. He lives near the Refuge. And he did say she should call him if she ever needed help.

She dialed the number. It was his office at the warehouse. It went to voicemail. She had already told him about some of the goings-on at the Refuge so she made her message short and to the point.

"Tom, this is Hannah Johansson. They're holding my mother and my cousin hostage at the Jamaica Bay Refuge. I'm going to try to get them out. I could really use your help. Please meet me there if you can. It's a life and death situation. Really!"

CHAPTER FORTY-TWO

Traffic was miserable on the L.I.E. Every couple of exits it slowed to a crawl for no apparent reason, then sped up, again with no discernible cause until the next blockage. Then the whole process started over.

Hannah banged her fist on the steering wheel.

"Come on!" she screamed, going five miles an hour as she passed Exit 56.

Three exits later she turned onto the Sagtikos Parkway, which would take her to the hated Southern State. But she figured it couldn't be any worse.

She figured wrong.

Traffic was moving fine for a few miles. Just as she was about to congratulate herself on her smart, decisive move she saw the overhead electronic highway sign flashing 'ACCIDENT AHEAD'. Her head throbbed. Her stomach somersaulted. A mile later traffic slowed, then came to a dead stop. She saw flashing lights in the distance.

As she sat helpless and frustrated she pictured her mother captive in the cold, dark storage barn, frightened and confused. Would they really hurt an old lady for no reason?

She tried to come up with a plan. Nothing came to mind. She

had put her Swiss Army knife and Phil's bear spray in her backpack, not much of a defense against heavily armed trained killers but it was all she had. She didn't even know if her mother and Catherine would still be in the barn. She'd have to improvise when she got there.

Catherine, ugh! She was still seething at her cousin. For attacking her mother. For that ridiculous lawsuit. And for being hateful and mean to her from the time they were toddlers forced to play together whenever their parents visited each other.

But Catherine's life was in danger and it was Hannah's fault. She'd have time to sort out her jumbled feelings about her cousin when they got out of this mess.

If they got out of this mess.

After fifteen minutes of inching along on the Southern State she finally made it to the accident scene where two mangled cars, one turned over on its roof, three police vehicles, two flatbed tow trucks and an ambulance were spread across both lanes of the highway and most of the shoulder. A highway patrol officer guided her through the tight squeeze that remained.

Once free of the clog, she screeched through hairpin turns, changed lanes with wild abandon and roared past cars at eighty-five miles an hour on the straightaways. Doing all the things she cursed other Southern State drivers for doing.

It was a little before eight when she pulled up next to the chain link fence on Cross Bay Boulevard. The sun was setting. Somewhere close by was the bandana.

After some frantic searching in the fading light she found it. Staying hidden in the trees, she Groucho-walked through rocks, ruts and divots towards the storage barn. Every few steps her feet got tangled in brambles. Thorny branches added to the scratches on her arms and face that hadn't healed since the last time she was here. Her back ached from stooping, her face was blood-streaked and her thighs were screaming.

And this was the easy part.

It was totally dark by the time she reached the back of the

barn. A dim light shone through the window. Hopefully, that meant that Olive and Catherine were still inside. Hannah furtively crept around the building, hugging the wall. She hoped the roar of the jets overhead and the cries of the night birds would drown out any noise she made. When she got to the front she peeked around the corner and saw Grabowski sprawled across an old wooden bench under a clump of Russian olives about twenty feet from the door. His eyes were shut. This might be easier than she thought. No one else was around and Grabowski was asleep. Maybe she could tiptoe in the front door, free her mother and cousin and sneak back out while Grabowski snoozed.

No such luck. The double doors were secured by a padlock.

She retraced her steps to the rear of the barn. The window she climbed through the other day was still open, except Phil wasn't here to give her a boost. She looked around to see if there was anything she could stand on. She spotted a green tarp on top of a pile of some sort. She yanked it off and dozens of brown bugs that looked like tiny armadillos scurried out. One crawled up her arm. Hannah jumped back, barely able to stop herself from screaming. Under the tarp were some old pallets in pretty bad shape. Most had broken, loose or splintered slats. All of them were streaked with black mold. She thought if she could move two or three under the window she might be able to reach up and pull herself inside.

When she pulled the first pallet off the pile it hit the ground hard and half the slats cracked. She dragged it under the window figuring she could still use it to anchor the others. The next pallet was sturdier. Unfortunately, that made it harder to lug along the rutted ground. With a lot of pushing, pulling, lifting, shifting and shoving she was able to drag it on top of the broken first pallet, then pull it diagonally up the wall creating a rickety ramp.

Standing precariously on the edge of a slat, she could just about touch the window sill. She'd have to jump, grab it and pull herself through. Back in her playing days she could do more pull-ups than any of the other girls on the team. Her personal best was eight, but that was a long time ago. Still, she was fairly confident she still could manage one.

As she pushed off, her foot broke through the rotted wood. She crashed to the ground, landing on her wrist, wrenching her ankle. She yelped in pain.

She lay sprawled on the ground amid mangled wood, dirt, rocks and weeds, disgusted with herself. A hulking figure came lumbering towards her from the other side of the barn. It was Grabowski.

Hannah sat up.

He glared down at her and snarled. "You caused me a lot of trouble, bitch!" He slapped her hard where her ear met her jaw. Her head snapped back and she blacked out for a few seconds. When she opened her eyes she was staring down the barrel of a gun only inches from her forehead.

CHAPTER FORTY-THREE

Hannah held her hands out in front of her. "Please, no!"

"Shut the fuck up!" Grabowski screamed. He brought his hand back as if to slap her again. She jerked back. He put his hand down and curled his lip in a sadistic smirk.

"You're lucky the boss wants to talk to you. When he's done your luck runs out."

He gripped her wrist and yanked her to her feet, triggering a flash of pain that shot up her arm.

"Let's go." He jabbed the barrel of the gun into her spine and prodded her toward the front of the barn.

Hannah ached all over, her wrist, her ankle, her back and several other places. But nothing was broken or even badly sprained. And the good news was, there was no Weakness. Maybe the Mestinon was actually working.

Grabowski unlocked the double doors and shoved her inside. The barn was lit by a battery-powered work lamp. Olive and Catherine were sitting on the floor against the back wall. Olive's eyes lit with joy as soon as she saw Hannah. Catherine didn't seem to notice. She stared silently at the ground.

"Hannah, dear. I didn't think I'd ever see you again."

Hannah was limping slightly and there was a trickle of blood at the corner of her mouth.

"You're hurt! That filthy brute hurt you."

Grabowski glared at Olive. "Shut the fuck up, you dried up old bag."

"No you shut up, you uncouth ape," Olive snapped back. "You should be ashamed of yourself for acting this way. Do you think your mother would be proud of you if she saw you right now?"

"Don't go talkin about my mother."

"Does she know you spend your days beating up women and cursing at old ladies?"

"My mother's dead. And you will be too if you don't shut your trap."

He glared at Hannah. "Get your ass back there with your friends."

Hannah sat down next to her mother, reached over and took her hand. Everything that was in the barn the other night was gone. The bundles of money, the big counting machines, even the table that held them. In their place was what had been there before, the equipment that her father had used to build and maintain the Refuge, most of it hand-me-downs from his days as a Parks Department supervisor. An ancient John Deere lawn tractor, dented and rusty; a gnarly old wood chipper and a well-used power auger. Shovels, hoes, rakes, axes and pitchforks, hung from hooks on the wall like salamis in an old-time deli.

"Ma, are you all right?" she whispered. "You must be scared to death."

Olive shook her head. There was no fear in her eyes, only defiance. "I'm fine, dear. These people don't frighten me. I've had to contend with bullies and blowhards my whole life." She put a gentle finger to Hannah's cheek, wiping away a trickle of blood. "But you look hurt."

"I'm okay. Just a few scratches."

Catherine sat facing away from Hannah. She was shaking

violently. Her hands covered her face, muffling the sobs, sighs and guttural blubbering that she couldn't seem to control.

Grabowski waved his gun at them. He shouted, "Everybody shut the fuck up!"

He grabbed the intercom off the wall. Because there was no cell service at the Refuge Hannah's father had installed an intercom system.

"Yeah, Ms. Dawson. I got the blonde bitch here."

He listened for awhile then he said. "Fifteen minutes? No problem. Should I do anything in the meantime?"

Another pause. "Okay I'll check."

He pointed the gun at Hannah.

"Awright, Blondie, where is it?"

"Where is what?"

"The money you stole from us." He waved the gun at her. "If you don't got it, too bad for you." Then he leveled it at Olive. "And your friends."

Catherine looked up at Grabowski, sniveling, tears streaming down her cheeks.

"I'm not her friend," she cried, pointing at Hannah. "I hate her. You see these marks on my face. She did that to me. Whatever you do to her, I'm sure she deserves it. But I don't." She took a deep breath and wiped her eyes with her hand. "I don't know who you are or what you're doing. And I don't care. Just let me go. I won't tell anyone."

Grabowski walked over to her. She looked up and smiled at him through bleary, hopeful eyes.

"I said shut the fuck up." He smacked her across the cheek.

She shrieked in pain.

He glared over at Hannah. "Where's the stuff I want?"

"It's in my backpack. I have to stand up to take it off."

"Do it fast."

The coalition money wasn't in her backpack. It was tucked away in her underwear drawer at home. She had to do something and do it now. Grabowski was unhinged. He could shoot them all.

She stood and carefully loosened the straps on her backpack. With her back to Grabowski she reached inside for the bear spray. She turned quickly and shot a yellow stream at his face. He howled in pain, dropped his gun and clutched his eyes. Then he charged blindly at her.

Before Hannah could react he had her pinned to the ground.

He grabbed for her neck. "I'll kill you, you fuckin bitch," He screamed. "I'll kill you right now!"

She tried to fight him off but he was much bigger, heavier and stronger. As his grip tightened around her throat she fought for breath. She reached around for her backpack to get the Swiss Army Knife, but it was inches from her grasp. She began pummeling the side of his head but it had no effect. Her blows got weaker with every strike. She willed herself to keep fighting but her strength was gone. As she felt her consciousness ebbing she thought, I can't believe I'm going to die with this filthy, disgusting pig on top of me.

Then she heard a dull thud. Grabowski bellowed. His grip loosened. After another loud clunk he collapsed. His dead weight fell on her. Hannah pushed him off and slowly stood up. Grabowski was sprawled awkwardly on the ground. He wasn't moving. There was a bloody gash on the side of his head. Olive stood over him, holding a shovel, quivering.

"Ma, you...you...you saved my life." She stood on wobbly legs and hugged her mother, shovel and all. "Thank you."

"I just couldn't sit there and watch that horrible monster maul you," she said resolutely. "You know I'm not a violent person by nature but this was a horse of a different color. He was choking my little girl. So I took that shovel and clobbered him. And I'm not sorry I did." Olive looked down at Grabowski's prostrate body. "He's not dead, is he?"

"I don't know," Hannah said. "But we can't wait around to

find out. The others will be back soon. We can't be here when they come."

Hannah retrieved her backpack. She noticed Catherine huddled against the wall. She actually forgot about her cousin in the melee. Catherine was staring blankly into space. Hannah didn't know if she was in shock or just stunned. She tugged at her arm.

"We gotta go."

Catherine looked up at her with glassy eyes. "You want me to come with you?"

"Yes, of course. But we have to go. Right now."

Catherine nodded blankly and slowly rose to her feet.

"C'mon," Hannah prodded.

Hannah let the other two go before her. She surveyed the barn to be sure she didn't leave anything behind. Glancing at Grabowski lying motionless on the floor she wondered if he was dead. And she wasn't sure if she wanted him to be or not.

Olive and Catherine were waiting for her outside.

"Follow me," she said, and headed back towards the gap in the fence.

CHAPTER FORTY-FOUR

Hannah led the way, favoring her gimpy ankle. Olive followed slowly behind. She had to stop every few steps to catch her breath. Catherine shuffled along behind Olive, still sniffling and sighing. Whatever sparse moonlight there might have been was obliterated by trees, making it hard to see more than a couple of feet ahead. The uneven ground was a tangle of rocks, weeds and briars that grabbed at their ankles like zombie fingers reaching up from the grave. The distance was only thirty feet but it felt like thirty miles.

Hannah began to feel that they might actually get away. They were getting close but they still had to move slowly through a thicket of snaky vines, gangly shrubs and trees with low-hanging, branches that scratched their faces and gouged at their eyes.

"Just a little farther," she said softly. "We're almost there."

Then she heard loud voices coming from the direction of the barn.

Catherine, who seemed to be sleepwalking up to that point, tensed up and started to yell, "They're coming. They're coming to kill us."

Olive turned around quickly. Her foot got tangled in a vine. She lost her balance and fell awkwardly to the ground.

Hannah kneeled next to her, cradling her mother's head in her hands. "Ma, are you all right?"

"It's my darned hip. Been giving me trouble for months."

"Can you walk, it's only a few more steps?"

"I think so. Standing up is the hardest part."

Hannah turned to Catherine who was a few feet away, whimpering.

"Help me pick my mother up."

"I'm so sorry, Olive," Catherine said. "I didn't mean to startle you."

"I know, dear. It's not your fault. I really should be more careful."

Hannah bit her tongue. Her first instinct was to yell at Catherine, asking her if she wanted them to get caught. But she realized that it wouldn't do anything but make the situation worse.

"Let's just get out of here," she said. "We'll each take one of my mother's arms and lift slowly. You ready?"

Catherine nodded.

After they helped Olive stand up she was able to hobble to the gap in the fence. Hannah grabbed a fistful of chain link in each hand and yanked it towards her. She grimaced as the steel wire bit into her fingers.

"I'll hold it open and you two squeeze through. It might be a little tight but I made it through and I'm bigger than either of you."

Olive looked at Hannah and said, "I'm sorry, dear. I can walk a little but I can't bend down like that. Not with this hip. You two go on. I'll stay here. I'm an old woman. There's not much they can do to me."

Hannah let go and the fence snapped back.

"Absolutely not. I'm not leaving you. There's an old gate down by the East Pond boat ramp."

"Yes. I remember you and your cousin Phillip begging us to let you water ski there. Your father thought it was too dangerous."

"He was right. A couple of months later a jet ski crashed into a canoe and sent three people to the hospital."

Olive looked old, frail and exhausted. Catherine was listless, dead on her feet.

"Let's go. It's only a little ways farther," Hannah said with as much enthusiasm as she could muster.

"I'll just slow you young people down. Don't worry about me. You go. I'll be fine."

"No way. You're coming with us," Hannah said emphatically. Then she turned to Catherine. "I'm sorry you got stuck in the middle of this. This isn't your fight. I'll hold the fence and you can get out here. The subway's half-a-mile up the road."

Catherine stared at the ground for a few seconds. Then she looked up at Hannah. "I'd rather stay with you and Olive if that's all right."

"Are you sure?"

She nodded.

"If that's what you want." Hannah turned back to her mother. "Put your arm around my shoulder."

They trudged along through the trees and undergrowth, stopping every few feet so Hannah could readjust her hold on Olive.

After the longest five minutes of their lives, they came upon the old ramp gate. It was densely covered with a thick blanket of ivy and several spiny vines. She could barely see where the gate ended and the fence began. She couldn't even see if there was a lock.

While Olive and Catherine leaned on a nearby tree, Hannah started hacking away at the foliage with the Swiss Army knife.

While she worked she heard Olive say to Catherine, "I don't think he was serious about setting the place on fire, do you?"

Catherine replied, "He sounded pretty serious to me."

Hannah stopped what she was doing.

"What did you just say? They're going burn down the Refuge?!" she shrieked. "Didn't either one of you think that might be something worth mentioning?"

Neither woman said anything.

Hannah glared at her mother. "Who told you that?"

"That horrible man."

"Grabowski?"

"Yes. I told him that my husband built this place from scratch. Every blade of grass. Every plant. Every tree. I told him that Robert Moses, himself, was in charge of it. He didn't even know who Robert Moses was. He thought I was talking about Moses from the bible. He said Moses was going to have a lot more burning bushes because they were going to burn the Refuge to the ground." Olive shook her head. "They'd never do that. I'm sure he was just trying to scare us."

Hannah turned to Catherine. "Is that what you think?"

Catherine shook her head emphatically. "He meant it. He showed us a couple of canisters in front of the barn. He said they would destroy the barn and everything in it."

"He doesn't know what he's talking about," Olive said. "He said they were termite grenades. Termites eat wood. They don't burn it."

Hannah said, "Termite grenades. That doesn't make sense. Even for a Neanderthal like Grabowski."

She turned to Catherine. "Is that what he said?"

"It sounded like it. I can't be sure."

Hannah thought for a minute. "Oh my God. I bet he said thermite. Not termite."

Olive said, "Thermite? I don't know what that is."

"It's what they make fire bombs out of. It can burn through anything. Even steel. This place is nothing but dry brush and leaves. It'll go up in a flash."

Olive looked confused. "I can't imagine that they would do that. There's no reason."

"Of course there is. It'll destroy all the evidence."

Hannah turned back to the gate and slashed at the vines in a wild frenzy. In a few minutes she had cleared enough to reveal an old rusty padlock. It looked like it was ready to fall apart. She pushed at the gate but it held fast. She kicked it a couple of times. Still no luck.

"Shit!" she shrieked. "This damn thing is tougher than it looks."

She stared at the gate for a few seconds then started digging in the ground. She picked up a rock the size of an orange, hefted it in her hand and threw it back. She grabbed another one, this one a little bigger, gauged its weight like she did with the first, then discarded it too. She went through several rocks this way, some were too flimsy, some too unwieldy. She finally found one the size of a cantaloupe. She held it with two hands.

"What on earth are you doing?" Olive said.

"You'll see."

She lifted the rock over her head and smashed it against the lock. Nothing.

"Goddammit!" she cried.

Catherine cried, "It's no use. We'll never get out of here."

That spurred Hannah. She hit it again. Harder. It wouldn't open. She was starting to lose hope when she noticed the rusty hasp that secured the lock to the gate was beginning to loosen. After a few more strikes, the lock, the hasp and the screws that attached it flew off into the dirt. Hannah kicked at the gate and it creaked open. She leaned against the fence, sucking wind.

"Okay," she gasped through heavy breaths. "Time to go."

Catherine held Olive's arm as they walked through onto Cross Bay Boulevard. Hannah followed. She handed Catherine a set of keys.

"My Jeep is where we first tried to get through. Take my mom to Jamaica Hospital. You both need medical attention."

"What about you?" Olive said. "If anyone needs a doctor, you do."

"I have to get rid of the thermite. Do you remember what they looked like?"

Olive glared at Hannah. "Oh no. I'm not letting you go back there. It's too dangerous."

"I'll be fine. They're out searching for us right now. The last place they'll look for me is back at the barn. I'll find the canisters, throw them into the pond and be back here before anyone notices. Trust me. I know what I'm doing. Now what did they look like?"

Olive stood, face taut, shaking her head silently.

Catherine said, "They were gray with red letters. About the size of an oil can."

Olive pressed her hands together as if praying. "Please don't go back there, Hannah. I'm begging you."

"I have to. I couldn't live with myself if I let them burn it down."

Olive nodded slowly, sadly. "All right. I never could stop you once you put your mind to something. Promise me you'll be careful."

"Of course. Now go. I'll see you soon."

After Hannah squeezed through the gate she looked back to see Catherine and Olive walking listlessly towards the Jeep.

CHAPTER FORTY-FIVE

Hannah was nowhere near as confident as she pretended. In fact she was terrified. But she knew that if she didn't get rid of those incendiary grenades a big part of her soul would be incinerated along with the Refuge. It was her father's legacy. And his burial place. But it was more than that to her. For more than half her life it was her home, her church, her neighborhood, her world. The trees, the ponds and the bay were imprinted on her soul. The birds were her only playmates when she was a child, alone in a 9,000 acre solitary wilderness where the nearest kid her age was more than twenty miles away. The Refuge was her sanctuary as a gawky teen, taller than all the girls and most of the boys at school. It was the one place where nobody made fun of her or shunned her. Most of all it was where she and her father bonded in a way that most fathers and daughters never do. The thought of having it all reduced to an ashen wasteland was more than she could bear.

She raced back through the trees, shrubs and vines, stumbling several times but not falling. What took more than fifteen minutes with her mother and Catherine, she covered in less than five. Back where she started, hidden behind a stand of Russian olives, the storage barn was ten yards in front of her. Ten yards of open space with no cover, no place to hide. Was anyone inside the barn or standing guard at the front? Were there snipers in the trees? At that moment she could be in some killer's gunsight.

Stop making yourself crazy, Seal Team Six isn't out there, just Dawson, Leigh and Grabowski.

She saw something on the ground. It was big but it wasn't moving. A dead animal? An old garbage bag? The remnants of a rotted tree? It was too dark to tell. She crept closer. She threw a rock at it. It didn't budge. She inched toward it a bit more. It looked like a body. She scrambled to the prone human figure, bear spray in hand. It was Grabowski. But he wouldn't be assaulting her or anyone else ever again. He looked like a broken mannequin. His head was caved in, at an odd angle to his body. His face was misshapen, like a discarded rubber Halloween mask. This didn't happen when Olive hit him with the shovel. This was different. More violent. Did he come to, stumble out here, fall and crash his head on a rock? If that's what happened, where was the rock? Where was the blood? She couldn't think about that now. She had to get rid of the thermite and get the hell out of there.

She checked her surroundings one more time then sprinted through the clearing to the barn. She spotted the canisters easily. Two of them. Big, battleship gray cans with pink writing and some kind of handle on top. She looked for more but didn't see any.

Over the din of the birds and the jets she heard something else. Footsteps? She ran behind a tree. Her heart pounded. The darkness, which had been her enemy for most of the night, was now her ally.

A tall figure lumbered up the footpath. As he approached the barn the blurry shadow came into focus. It was Tom McCaffrey. He was in his work uniform. His duty belt held two holsters. A large one for his gun and a smaller one for his phone.

Hannah ran over to him. "Tom. Thank God you're here. I wasn't sure you'd come."

"I didn't get your message until the end of my shift. As soon as I heard it I jumped in my car. Are you all right?" He looked around. "Where's your mother and your cousin? You said something about them being held hostage."

"They were. They're safe now. I was able to get them out."

"All by yourself?"

"I had a little help from my mom. This guy Grabowski was guarding us."

"I met him once or twice. A big, dumb ape of a man. I can't believe you overpowered him."

"I sprayed him with bear spray and my mother clubbed him with a shovel."

"Impressive."

He looked around. "Where's the rest of them? I can't believe he was doing this on his own."

"He's the only one I saw. But he did talk to Elyse Dawson on the intercom. She seems to be in charge. There could be others. Did you see anyone when you came in?"

"No. No one."

"They're probably out looking for us."

She didn't want to say anything about Leigh being involved, knowing how McCaffrey idolized him.

"Why didn't you escape with the other two? I hope it wasn't to meet me."

"Oh no." Hannah pointed to the canisters. "I came back to get rid of those."

McCaffrey looked puzzled. "What the hell are they?"

"Thermite grenades. Those bastards were gonna use them to burn down the Refuge. I was about to throw them into West Pond."

She heard a noise behind her. "That's very noble of you, Ms. Johansson." It was Leigh. He was with Dawson. "But I'm afraid this is one example of when no good deed goes unpunished. And your punishment will be quite severe."

Hannah pointed at Leigh and Dawson. "They're the kidnappers. They took my mother and my cousin. They've been smuggling money in from Iraq and using the Refuge to avoid Customs.

Leigh is the ringleader. I didn't want to tell you because I know how much you admire him. But he's not the saint you think he is. He's a crook and a murderer. He killed my father."

The last accusation shook Leigh.

"That's a lie!" he barked. "I was very fond of Axel Johansson. He was a good man. I would never agree to his murder."

Hannah pointed at Dawson. "Then she did it. Maybe he didn't know about it, but it was her. She poisoned my father with methyl iodide to make it look like he had a stroke."

"You're crazy," Dawson shrieked. "I don't even know what menthol iodine is."

McCaffrey stood silently, arms folded in front of him, as if he were watching street theater.

Hannah turned to him. "Tom, you have a gun. Arrest them or something."

Leigh smiled sardonically. "Yes Tom, do something."

McCaffrey took out his gun and walked toward Leigh and Dawson. Standing beside them, he turned and leveled the gun at Hannah.

"I'm sorry, kid. I was hoping it wouldn't come to this."

"You're with them? I can't believe it." Her legs buckled. She couldn't tell if it was myasthenia or terror.

Dawson said, "This crazy bitch has been screwing up our operation for too long. It's time we put an end to it. Shoot her now. We'll throw her in the pond and by the time they find her we'll be long gone."

Leigh shook his head. "Not until we know who she spoke to and what she did with the photos and the coalition currency. Until we find that out our entire plan is jeopardized."

Dawson bristled. "Give me five minutes with her. I'll find out everything we need to know."

Leigh said, "Don't be stupid. You have no experience extracting information. Grabowski is perfect for that task. He's a sadist and a sociopath. Where is he?"

McCaffrey said, "Did anyone try calling him?"

Hannah held her breath. Thank God she didn't tell McCaffrey that she found Grabowski's body.

Leigh shook his head. "Cell phones are useless here. You'll have to find him. He can't be far. Start at the truck in the loading dock parking lot. If he's not there check the office."

Dawson said, "What about her?"

"We'll hold her here until we find out what we need to know." He turned to McCaffrey, "Do you have handcuffs?"

"We don't use them." He reached into his back pocket and took out a double-loop zip tie. "This'll do the job."

McCaffrey walked over to Hannah.

"Put your hands behind your back."

Hannah looked at him with doleful eyes. "I'm very disappointed in you, Tom. I thought you were better than this."

He shrugged and slipped her wrists through the zip tie loops but he didn't tighten them. Then he gave her back two quick taps. Was it some kind of sign?

"This should hold her," he said to the other two.

He reached down, took a small black pistol out of his ankle holster and handed it to Leigh. It looked like the water guns Hannah and her cousins played with as kids.

"It's my backup gun. It's small but it packs a punch, trust me. I doubt you'll need it but take it just in case."

He turned to Hannah and winked. Then he walked out of the barn.

CHAPTER FORTY-SIX

Leigh held the small pistol with two fingers at the trigger guard, a look of revulsion on his face as if he were holding a dead rodent.

"I hate guns," he said. "But is this even a gun? It looks more like a toy. I wonder if it really works."

Dawson said, "Take a shot at the bitch and we'll find out."

He glared at her. "That will be enough, Elyse."

His hand quivered as he stuffed the gun in his waistband.

He turned to Hannah. "None of this had to happen, you know. I don't understand why you kept coming back despite all the warnings. If you had just left it alone, everything would be fine. You'd have a job in my company and be on your way to building a good life for yourself. Instead..." He shook his head slowly, sadly.

"How could I leave it alone? You killed my father. You or one of your goons. And the police didn't care. Either that or they were on your payroll. Either way they weren't going to do anything. So I had to."

"You're wrong," he said stridently. "As I told you before, I was very fond of Axel. I would never sanction his murder even if he had suspicions about what we were doing. But he never did. There was absolutely no reason for us to do him any harm. He had a stroke. Why can't you accept that? If anyone's responsible for his death it's you. You admitted as much at his memorial. I guess you just couldn't accept that and needed someone else to blame."

"My father never had a stroke. He was poisoned. My cousin did a tox screen. He's a coroner upstate. My father's blood was loaded with methyl iodide. It's a deadly toxin. The symptoms are a lot like a stroke. That's what killed him." She glared at Dawson. "She infected him. I don't know how she did it, but she did."

Dawson walked up to her, so close Hannah could smell her fetid breath. "You're crazy. I don't know anything about any poison."

"Liar. You knew all about it. It was in the inventory that Jacqui showed you."

"You don't know what you're talking about. I never saw any inventory."

All the while, Hannah had been working her hands free of the slack zip ties. When she was finally able to wriggle them free she faked a sneeze so they wouldn't see her arms jerk.

Her plan was to wait for an opportunity to get to Dawson, hopefully take her out quickly, then take her chances with Leigh and the tiny gun. Then she got a break. A barn owl screeched.

Leigh yelled, "What was that?"

They both turned.

Hannah leapt at Dawson, punched her in the side of her face. Dawson staggered. Hannah grabbed her head with both hands and kneed her in the jaw. Dawson crumpled to the ground, blood spurting from her mouth.

Leigh was wide-eyed. His hands shook uncontrollably as he fumbled for the pistol tucked into his waistband. It caught in his belt. He juggled it awkwardly and dropped it on the floor. Hannah dove for it as he stood gaping at it, transfixed.

Still on the ground she pointed the gun up at Leigh.

"Don't move! I don't want to shoot you but I will."

He put his hands in the air.

"Please. That won't be necessary."

Hannah slowly got to her feet, keeping the gun leveled at him.

"Get down over there, on the floor, next to her."

Leigh appeared to shrink as he eased himself down next to Dawson, who was doubled over on her side, groaning. No longer a haughty, imperious Master of the Universe, Leigh looked old, tired and scared.

As Hannah stood with the gun trained on them, her mind raced. What should she do? Whatever it was it had to be quick. McCaffrey would be back any minute. She wasn't sure if he was on her side or with them. He winked at her and kept the zip tie loose, allowing her to break free. But he was still part of their gang.

She decided that she would get the thermite canisters, throw them in the water then run like hell back to the boat ramp.

"You're dead! You're a dead woman," Dawson screamed through bloody lips. "Even if you get away tonight, we'll find you and we'll make you pay. You'll wish you never set foot on this place."

"Maybe. But I'm here now. And I'm the one with the gun."

From behind her she heard McCaffrey's voice.

"But I'm the one with the bigger gun."

She froze. A jet roared overhead. Would that be the last sound she would ever hear?

She turned slowly to face him. If he was going to shoot her he'd have to look at her while he did it.

Something in McCaffrey's eyes. A gleam? A glint? Reassured her. She relaxed. A little. He wasn't going to shoot her. At least not at that moment.

"I believe that belongs to me." He held his hand out towards Hannah, palm up. "Please give it back."

She held the small pistol by the barrel and handed it to him. He put it back in his ankle holster. Then he pointed to the far side of the barn, where the wood chippers, lawn tractors and other equipment were parked. "Go over there and don't do anything stupid."

Dawson struggled to her feet and glowered at McCaffrey. "It's about time you got back," she said. "What the hell took you so long?"

"I was gone for five minutes. I figured two people and a gun was enough to guard a woman with her hands tied behind her back. When I come back she has the gun, he's cringing in the corner like a scared rabbit and you look like you went ten rounds with Mike Tyson."

"This is your fault," she screamed. "She got loose. What did you tie her up with, spaghetti? You were a goddamn cop, you're supposed to know how to restrain someone."

"I don't know how she got loose but it was still two against one and you guys had the gun."

Leigh got slowly to his feet. "It was my fault. When she broke free and attacked Elyse I panicked. I dropped the gun. I'm not used to operating firearms. I'm sorry. I thought I ruined everything. But thanks to you we're back in control so no harm done."

"No harm done!" Elyse screamed. "Look at me. If I had that gun instead of you none of this would have happened."

Leigh reacted like he'd just been slapped. The arrogant Master of the Universe came roaring back. In his world underlings never dared yell at their superiors. Especially in front of others.

"Who the hell do you think you are! If you had the gun we'd never know what kind of jeopardy we'd be facing. Jeopardy that you put us in with your constant carping and bullying. If you would have simply allowed her to scatter her father's ashes none of this would have happened."

"I couldn't let her near the dock."

"Why not? It was empty. She would have seen nothing. But you had to play the petty dictator in your little fiefdom. I'm starting to regret ever bringing you into to this."

She sneered at him. "You could have never done this without

me, sitting up there in your fancy midtown office while I do all the dirty work in this shithole."

"Shut up. Both of you," McCaffrey shouted. "You can yell at each other later. Right now we gotta go."

"We can't go. We need Grabowski." Dawson said. "You were supposed to find him and bring him back. Where the hell is he?"

"He's not coming."

"What do you mean he's not coming?"

"I changed the plan."

Dawson said, "Who the hell are you to change the plan?"

"I'm the one with the gun."

He pointed it at her.

She took a step toward him. "Listen to me you son of a..."

"I'm tired of listening to you."

He shot her in the middle of the chest. She fell backwards and crumpled to the ground, a crimson stain spread across her tan shirt.

CHAPTER FORTY-SEVEN

Hannah gaped open-mouthed at Dawson's inert body. She felt numb. With what? Fear? Shock? Revulsion? Relief?

She hated Dawson. She held her responsible for her father's death. And Dawson was going to burn down the place she loved. She wanted her to be held accountable. She wanted her to pay for what she did. But not like this.

She glanced over at Leigh. He looked lost. Confused. He looked plaintively at McCaffrey. He opened his mouth to speak but no sound came.

"Why?" he finally said in a throaty whisper.

McCaffrey glared at him. His eyes steely. "That was for Tim."

"Tim? Your son? I don't understand."

"Yes you do. He's stuck in a wheelchair. He can't walk, talk, move or even breathe on his own. His life's a living hell. And you put him there."

"Are you out of your mind!" Leigh said, regaining some of his swagger. "I'm the one who saved him. Who saved both of you. Those were your exact words."

"That's what I thought. Then I found out the truth."

"That is the truth. You were drowning. I threw you a lifeline."

"The truth is that Armstrong and Warren put my boy into a

broken-down truck and sent him on a 500-mile trip through a godforsaken desert. The engine blew after a hundred miles. They were stuck in the middle of nowhere. Then they were ambushed. It was almost like the bastards knew they were coming. My boy never had a chance. The other guys in the truck were killed and Timmy might as well have been. Sometimes I think it would be better if he was."

As he spoke he got angrier and angrier. He started walking slowly toward Leigh.

"Armstrong knew the truck would never make it through. They knew how dangerous that route was. They knew Timmy wasn't trained for that kind of mission. And they sent him out anyway. They're just as guilty as if they'd shot him themselves."

"I know all that," Leigh said, his voice gaining strength. "What does any of it have to do with me?"

"I'll tell you what. They were headed to Lebanon. A top secret mission they were told. To deliver vital material. No one would say what it was. But you knew because you issued the order. You sent my boy on that journey to hell."

"You don't understand," Leigh said. "It was chaos over there. Pure chaos. I may have assigned the mission, but..."

"Shut the fuck up," McCaffrey yelled, then slammed the gun barrel into the side of Leigh's face. Leigh staggered backward and fell. Blood trickled from his mouth. He was conscious, but barely.

Hannah yelped, trying to comprehend what was happening. This was not the Tom McCaffrey she had come to know. Her father's fishing buddy. The man who rescued her on the Cross Bay Bridge and saved her at the airport warehouse. Did the stress of dealing with his son's issues finally make him snap?

McCaffrey turned to her. It was like he read her thoughts.

"Don't worry Hannah, I'm not going to hurt you," he said, his voice now gentle. "I think you deserve to know why I'm doing this."

He lowered his gun, holding it at his side, keeping an eye on

Leigh, who was curled up in the corner, groaning like a wounded animal.

"After Timmy got home I spent months trying to find Armstrong and Warren. They needed to answer for what they did to my son. But they disappeared. It was like they never existed. There was no record of the company in Iraq or here or anywhere else. I called the Pentagon, the State Department, my congressman. Nobody knew anything. Finally I gave up. Then I heard from this lawyer. He was filing a lawsuit. I don't know how he got it, but he had a list of everyone who worked for Armstrong and Warren in Iraq. He told me they were bought by a big company. Some kind of bank. That's who he was planning to sue. That company was Flack and Spitz."

He swung his gun over at Leigh. "His company."

Leigh jerked back. He lifted his hands, palms out, in front of his face. He shook his head. His eyes were wide with terror.

"No. Please. I beg you," he cried.

"Not such a big shot now, are you," McCaffrey said. Then he turned back to Hannah.

"Once I knew the connection between Armstrong and Warren and Flack and Spitz, I was able to find out a lot more. Dawson was in Baghdad running logistics. Armstrong and Warren reported to her. And she reported to him." He turned and glared at Leigh. "They were ripping off the government, stealing billions of dollars. Tens of billions. Money that should have gone to protecting our boys over there. To protect kids like Timmy."

He glared at Leigh. "And you know who was the brains of the whole scheme. Him."

He cocked the weapon. It was pointed at Leigh's chest.

Leigh said, "You're wrong. I went over there to stop all that."

McCaffrey scowled at him. "All those truckloads of money I've been ferrying over here, where did they come from?"

Leigh said nothing. A tear trickled down his cheek.

"I'll tell you where. That dumb ape Grabowski told me all

about it one night over a beer. A lot of beers." He sneered at Leigh. "You're a smart one, I'll give you that."

He turned back to Hannah. "They stashed all that money in some warehouse in Lebanon. They kept it there all these years, waiting for the right time. My Timmy was massacred trucking his dirty money across the desert."

"You don't have to kill him," Hannah cried. "We can call the police. Or the FBI. We have the evidence. The Coalition money is in the truck in the parking lot. They can trace it back to him."

McCaffrey shook his head and sneered. "Don't be naïve. People like him never pay for their crimes. It's always some low-level slob. Remember the big recession a couple of years back? There were bankruptcies, suicides. People lost their homes. Their life savings. The banks caused that. You know how many bank presidents went to jail? I'll tell you. Zero. They never even paid a fine. They just got richer off everybody else's misery. But this time somebody's gonna pay."

"What are you going to do?"

"What do you think I should do? It's because of this bastard that my son is paralyzed. But you have as much reason to hate him as I do. Maybe more. He's responsible for killing your father every bit as much as if he fed Axel the poison himself."

He handed the gun to Hannah.

"Go ahead. Pull the trigger. Avenge your father's death."

She shivered, clutching the gun nervously, like it was a rabid rat that would bite her hand if she moved it.

"No. I could never."

As she slowly handed it back to him she noticed that he was wearing skin toned latex gloves.

McCaffrey glared down at Leigh.

"Our girl here thinks we should hand you over to the authorities and let justice take its course. What do you think? Should we call your friends in the FBI? Or the NYPD, who you bought and paid for? How about your cronies in the Justice Department? Do you think they'll make you pay for what you did to my son? Or killing her father?"

"You're wrong," Leigh shrieked. "I had nothing to do with Axel Johansson's death. And I was nowhere near Baghdad when you son's accident happened."

"Accident!" McCaffrey bellowed. "That was no goddamn accident. He was shot five times. His spine was severed. Left in the desert to die. You weren't there but you were in charge, giving orders from thousands of miles away. Safe and comfortable in your fancy office."

He leveled the gun at Leigh who cringed in the corner.

"How does it feel to know the bullets are coming and there's not a damn thing you can do about it? That's what you put my boy through."

Leigh looked up at him, his eyes pleading. "I didn't know. I swear."

"You knew," McCaffrey sneered. "And you didn't give a shit."

He fired. Again and again and again, until he was out of bullets.

CHAPTER FORTY-EIGHT

Hannah's skin grew clammy. Her gut churned and twisted. She doubled over, retched then threw up until there was nothing left but spittle and phlegm. The stench of bile and vomit enveloped her. She collapsed to her knees, gasping. A thread of saliva dangled off her lower lip. After a few minutes she struggled to her feet.

McCaffrey stood, arms folded, surveying the scene, admiring the mutilated corpses of Leigh and Dawson, like an artist pleased with a recently completed painting. His spent handgun lay on the ground at his feet.

In a voice barely above a whisper she said, "Why?"

He turned to her. "These people decimated my son. They murdered your father. They deserved what they got. Don't you agree?"

Hannah had no answer.

After a moment McCaffrey said, "I'm not sorry for what I did. But I am sorry for what I have to do now."

He reached down for his ankle pistol. He pointed it at Hannah.

"Move over there," he said, gesturing toward the two bodies in the rear of the barn.

Hannah didn't move. "I don't understand."

"I like you Hannah. I really do. You're a great kid. And I admired your father. I wish there was another way but there isn't."

It took her a few seconds to process what was happening.

"You're...you're going to shoot me too?"

"I can't go to prison. I have to take care of Tim. He'll die without me. You're the only person who can implicate me."

"I would never do that. I owe you my life. They were going to kill me. You stopped them."

"I can't take that chance. With you here with them, the murder weapon in your hand with only your prints on it, it's open and shut. The cops won't look any further."

Hannah glanced at his gloved hands. That's why he gave her the gun. He knew she would never fire it. He did it so her fingerprints would be on it. This was obviously his plan from the beginning. Her best bet was to stall and hope that Olive and Catherine called 911.

"Tom, you're a good man. I can understand why you did what you did. I hate those people too. But you're not the kind of person who can kill someone in cold blood. Especially someone you have a history with."

As she spoke she inched toward where the shovels were hanging on the wall. If all else failed she could throw a shovel at him and run.

"I'm no threat to you," she continued. "Everyone knows I hated Dawson. The police have a report of me fighting with her in a bar. And my prints are on the murder weapon. I'm the prime suspect. Even if I told the police what happened they wouldn't believe me. Especially since you used to be a cop yourself. Can't we just throw the guns in the bay and leave? It'll look like they fought among themselves and killed each other."

She pressed her palms together in front of her. "Please, Tom. Please don't do this."

McCaffrey shook his head. "Sorry, Hannah." He motioned at the gun on the floor. "Pick it up."

As she bent down she heard the door creak open. The next thing she heard was a vaguely familiar voice.

"Freeze! Secret Service."

McCaffrey lifted him arms slowly to shoulder height. His right hand still held the small pistol.

It was Patrick Goldney, from BADASS. He held a pistol in one hand and an I.D. wallet in the other. She saw 'Secret Service' in big letters next to his photo. Was he really in the Secret Service or was it a fake I.D.?

Before she could say anything, McCaffrey said, "Calm down buddy, I'm on your side. Park Security. I got here right before you did and I found this woman standing over these two bodies."

"He's lying!" Hannah screamed. "He killed them. You know me, Patrick. You know I couldn't have done this."

Goldney glared at McCaffrey, then over at Hannah.

"All I know is I heard gunshots and find you two holding weapons and two dead bodies."

McCaffrey said, "Hear me out, Mr..."

"Special Agent Goldney."

"Hear me out, Special Agent Goldney. I'm former NYPD, out of the 103 in Jamaica. I was patrolling the grounds, heard shots, hauled ass over here and found this woman. I told her to drop her gun, next thing I know you show up."

"That's not true," Hannah said. "He's with them. They were smuggling counterfeit money from Iraq to JFK, then ferrying it across the bay. He shot them and he was about to shoot me. You've got to believe me."

Goldney shook his head. "I don't have to believe anybody. I'll take you both in and sooner or later we'll see who's telling the truth."

As Goldney reached for his phone McCaffrey whipped his gun around. Hannah rammed her shoulder into his side as he fired. His arm flailed. The shot was wild. Goldney turned and leveled his gun at McCaffrey's chest. McCaffrey grabbed Hannah, wrapped his left arm around her neck. He shoved the pistol into her ribs with his right.

"Drop it or she dies."

Goldney didn't move.

McCaffrey jammed the gun harder. Hannah winced but wouldn't allow herself to cry out. Her eyes were moist with pain and fear.

Goldney said, "She dies. You die."

McCaffrey grinned. "Looks like we have an old fashioned Mexican standoff."

"That's all right. I've got plenty of time. I have backup on the way."

McCaffrey shook his head. "I don't think so. If you did they'd be here by now. My guess is you got short-strawed on surveillance. You heard something. Wasn't sure what it was. Gunshots? Car backfiring? Fireworks? Wasn't worth calling it in until you checked it out."

"You really want to bet you life on that?"

"If I'm wrong I spend the rest of my life in jail. That means my boy Timmy's as good as dead. My only chance is to walk out of here."

Hannah said, "It doesn't have to be that way, Tom. We can figure something out. Put the gun down and let me go. I'll make sure your son gets the care he needs."

McCaffrey shook his head. "Nice try but I don't think so." He moved Hannah so she was between him and Goldney. "I'm thinking your pal Patrick doesn't want to risk hitting you. I don't have that problem."

Goldney said, "You're gonna have a lot more problems than you can ever imagine."

Hannah was getting more and more panicky as the minutes dragged on and no backup arrived. Eventually one of them was going to do something, but no matter who fired first, she was the monkey in the middle. A dead monkey.

She decided to take matters into her own hands or at least her elbow. She dug it hard into McCaffrey's ribs. The hand holding the gun jerked up and she chopped at it with both hands. McCaffrey lost his grip and it fell to the ground.

McCaffrey leaped at Goldney before he could get a clean shot off. The two men wrestled fiercely, each with a grip on Goldney's gun. McCaffrey's pistol was about six feet from Hannah. As she dove for it she heard a gunshot. Goldney howled in pain but held onto the gun. He head-butted McCaffrey, who let go. McCaffrey bent over and bit Goldney on the heel of his thumb. Goldney dropped the gun.

Now Hannah was the only one with a weapon.

She yelled, "Stop!"

No effect.

She fired into the air and screamed as loud as she could, "Stop! Or the next one is at you."

They froze. She was stunned that they did. They stood and moved an arm's length apart, panting with exhaustion.

Goldney smiled at Hannah. "I guess you were telling the truth." His left hand was pressed tightly against his bloody left thigh.

"Yes I was," she said. "You're hurt. Are you all right?"

"I'll live."

McCaffrey stared down at Goldney's gun. It was on the ground three feet in front of him.

He stepped toward it.

"Don't move," she said and leveled the pistol at him. "I'll shoot. I mean it."

He shook his head. "No you won't. You couldn't shoot Dawson and you couldn't shoot Leigh. You can't shoot anybody. You don't have the stomach for it."

"I will." Her voice cracked as she said it.

He took another step. The gun was at his feet.

"Please," Hannah pleaded. Her hands were trembling.

McCaffrey smiled malevolently. Still staring at Hannah, he kneeled to pick up the gun.

Hannah pulled the trigger.

Blood oozed from McCaffrey's midsection. Though obviously in pain, he made another move for the gun. Hannah fired twice more. Both shots hit him in the middle of the chest. He fell to his knees.

"I never thought you would do it," he rasped, and collapsed to the ground.

Goldney kneeled slowly and put two fingers on the side of the McCaffrey's neck. After a few seconds he looked up at Hannah and shook his head.

Shaking uncontrollably, she handed him the pistol, then dropped to her knees, sobbing and heaving.

CHAPTER FORTY-NINE

Hannah stood transfixed, gaping at McCaffrey's lifeless body, reflecting on what just happened. She killed a man. A man who had a severely disabled son who was totally dependent on him. What would happen to him? She told McCaffrey she would make sure he would be taken care of. How could she do that? She had no money and she didn't know the first thing about caring for a person like that. But McCaffrey was a murderer. He killed Leigh, Dawson and Grabowski. He would have surely murdered her too. She had no choice. It was self defense. But he wasn't holding the gun, he was just reaching for it. Maybe she could have wounded him. Shot him in the leg. But she never fired a gun before. She could have missed. Then she and Goldney would both be dead too. Was she a murderer?

A voice jarred her out of her macabre reverie.

"Miss Johansson, are you all right?"

It was Goldney. She forgot for a moment that he was there.

"I'm okay," she said, trying to settle herself down. "Just shaken up. I never shot anyone before. I imagine you get used to it after awhile."

"No, you never do," he said solemnly. "And that's a good thing."

He sat on the seat of her father's ancient lawn tractor. His hand was pressed against his thigh. Blood oozed through his fingers.

"Oh my God," Hannah said. "You're hemorrhaging."

"It's not as bad as it looks," he said, calmly.

She ignored him. With the memory of Phil's near fatal 'scratch' still fresh in her mind, she ran to the first aid kid mounted on the wall. White metal, dented and rusted from use and age, it was about the size of an attaché case with a small red cross in front. She yanked it open, grabbed a handful of alcohol wipes, a tube of antibiotic ointment, several square bandage packets and a roll of adhesive tape.

When she got back to Goldney she flipped open the blade of her Swiss Army knife.

"Whoa. No way I'm gonna let you dig into my leg."

"I'm not going to touch your leg. I have to cut a hole in your pants to clean and bandage the wound."

As she cut a jagged flap in the fabric, he said, "Are you sure you know what you're doing?"

"Don't worry. I worked in a clinic for two years."

She neglected to tell him it was a mental health clinic and all the wounds her patients suffered from were emotional.

"I have to contact Brooklyn HQ," Goldney said.

"Cell phones don't work here," Hannah said, as she swabbed the wound with the antiseptic.

He held up a stubby black phone. "This one does. It's a satellite phone. Works everywhere."

As he tapped the keypad, she patted the wound with alcohol, slathered ointment on it, layered three of the square bandages over it, then grabbed Goldney's hand, the one that wasn't holding the phone, and placed it on the bandages.

"Press down hard," she said.

She crisscrossed several layers of adhesive tape over the dressing.

"That should hold you until help arrives. How long until they get here?"

"Should be about an hour."

She tried not looking at the dead bodies sprawled on the floor but it was impossible. With every glance she got more nauseous.

"Is it okay for us to go outside? I really need some fresh air. That is if your leg can handle it."

"Don't worry about me."

She headed for the door. Goldney followed.

They walked over to the bench where Grabowski was dozing when she first got there. It was only a couple of hours earlier but it seemed like a lifetime ago, when she was a different person. Someone who never killed anyone.

They sat next to each other, looking to all the world like a young couple enjoying a pleasant spring evening.

"Can I borrow your phone?" Hannah said.

He handed it to her.

She called her house. It went straight to voicemail. She tried her mother's cell with the same result. Then she called Bette, who answered immediately. After assuring her several times that she was all right, she gave her a brief summary of what happened. Bette interrupted her constantly with questions and exclamations. When Hannah mentioned that she'd given her car to Catherine and Olive, Bette volunteered to drive to the Refuge and pick her up. Hannah said it wasn't necessary but her friend wouldn't take no for an answer.

As she handed the phone back to Goldney she said, "There wasn't any backup, was there?"

"No, he was right. I was bluffing," he said sheepishly. "With the noise of the jets taking off and landing next door, it was impossible to tell exactly what I heard. Our field office is in Downtown Brooklyn, an hour away. I had to be damn sure it was gunshots before I dragged everyone out here on a wild goose chase or I'd never hear the end of it. The only way to do that was to check it out."

"Thank God you did."

For an agnostic, Hannah was invoking God's name a lot lately.

She was quiet for several seconds, then she said, "Are you really in the Secret Service?"

"Yeah."

"I thought the Secret Service guarded the President and his family."

"That's the Protection Division. I'm in Investigations. We look into financial crimes."

"I had no idea the Secret Service did that."

"Most people don't. Protection gets all the publicity. It's glamorous. Guarding the world's most important people. Putting themselves in the line of fire, like in the Clint Eastwood movie. Most of the work we do is boring. Checking out counterfeit money, credit card fraud, bogus charities, internet scams, things like that. A lot of our time is spent sitting in front of a computer or talking on the phone."

"Is that how you found out about this?"

He shook his head. "It wasn't our case at first. It started in Iraq with DCIS. They had Leigh and Dawson on their radar for awhile. We've been working with them for about a year."

"DCIS?"

"It's like NCIS. But they work directly with the Defense Department. NCIS is Navy. Did you ever see that show?"

"Once or twice. I don't really like those kinds of shows. Too much violence."

As she said it she realized that she was just involved in as much violence as she had ever seen on TV. Four people dead. One from her own hand. She shuddered as she thought about it.

Goldney said, "Are you all right?"

"I'm fine. If it was a DCIS operation how did the Secret Service get involved?"

"Like I said, we deal with financial crimes. Once they discovered that the bogus bills were being shipped over here it became our case. The Brooklyn field office covers JFK. Stan Westbrook is my boss. He's the Special Agent in charge."

"Really? I thought he was one of the bad guys. What about Black Ammo or Bad Ass or whatever you call it?"

"The Secret Service set that up to get inside their operation."

"You're kidding. It was all phony? I can't believe it. Even that nasty HR woman?"

Goldney grinned. "Kristin Lund. She's one of our top forensic accountants. It was her first time in the field."

"She was scary."

"She's really a sweetheart. She does a lot of community theater. She played Nurse Ratched when her group did 'One Flew Over the Cuckoo's Nest.' We told her that her character was Ratched on steroids."

"And Grabowski? Was he with you too?"

"Oh no. He's a genuine bad guy. He was with Dawson in Iraq. I guess they hit it off. Two sociopaths."

"I still don't understand why they were smuggling in all that worthless money."

"For a long time neither did we. We knew they were doing it but we couldn't figure out why. It was Kristin Lund who solved the puzzle. You know about Coalition Currency, right?"

"Yeah. Leigh actually told me about it when I was at his office."

"After the Iraqis took over from the Provisional Authority in 2006 they printed new Iraqi dinars without Saddam's face on them. Overnight, the double-C's, that's what they called the Coalition Currency bills, lost all their value, like Confederate money after the Civil War. They were phased out and earmarked for destruction. Dawson was running logistics out of Baghdad. She was ordered to ship them to an industrial incinerator just outside Beirut. It's the only one operating in that part of the world. Instead she shipped them to a big warehouse near the Lebanon airport."

"But at that point it's just worthless paper. Why go to all that trouble?"

"That's where Leigh comes in. He figured out a way to turn that worthless paper into billions of dollars. We haven't done a final tally yet."

"How?"

"What most people don't know is that tons of old currency are destroyed every year and replaced by new bills. In New York, banks ship their used bills to the Federal Reserve Bank in New Jersey where a machine counts, inspects them and separates the bad ones, ripped bills or ones that are just too old and worn. Then the machine shreds it into confetti. The shredded bills are replaced with new ones from the mint. The counterfeit money is destroyed but not replaced."

"If the machine knows that Leigh's bills are counterfeit, why take them there?"

"The Double-C's never get to the machine. They're already shredded."

"I bet that's what the big machine in the barn was there for."

"Probably. We'll have to find it to be sure."

"Still, how does he get away with it?"

"Leigh's trucks check in, they skip the inspection and shredding stations and go straight to the disposal area. Then they pick up clean currency."

"And no one caught them. How is that possible?"

"Easy. Leigh gave each guy in the process a hundred thousand dollars. The guy at the front gate who checks the trucks in. The guy who runs the counting machine. And the shredder operator. We have them all in custody."

"Why would someone like Leigh take that kind of risk? He's already very wealthy. How much money does one man need?"

"He's not as rich as you think. He lost big in the Great Recession. His company went all in on mortgaged backed securities. His company lost billions. He lost millions. He was on the verge of bankruptcy. Then he figured out this Double-C scam."

"I don't understand why they decided to route the money through here. Wouldn't it be a lot simpler to just drive the money from the warehouse at JFK straight to New Jersey?"

"That's what they'd been doing until about a year ago. The police uncovered a huge money laundering operation at the airport. The Russian mob was sending money to JFK to finance their North American operations. Deutsche Bank was involved. It's still being sorted out. That's when we were called in."

"The Secret Service?"

"Yeah. We installed 24-hour inspection stations at all the terminals. We would have caught the Double-C's the first day. Then Leigh came up with the Jamaica Bay Refuge scheme. He used his position on the Port Authority Board to put through that bogus feasibility study. I think you know the rest."

"Last question."

"Okay."

"If you knew about this for so long, why did you wait until now to bust it?"

"Leigh's a big deal financier and a former high level official in government. If we were going to have any kind of a case against him, we needed to catch him here with the money. If it wasn't air tight it wasn't going to happen. We knew that they had an idea that we were close. They had planned to do one final run then quit while they were ahead. And we knew Leigh wanted to be here to make sure that nothing could be traced back to him. We're pretty sure that they knew Westbrook was a plant, which is why we didn't know the exact date. That's the reason I was posted outside.

"You were the last loose end. They needed to find out what you knew and what evidence you had."

He paused for a moment. "I have a question for you. Why did you get involved in this? You were this close to getting killed." He put his thumb and forefinger a quarter-inch apart. "Why do you care about a currency smuggling operation?"

"I don't."

"Then why?"

"Those people poisoned my father. I had proof. And when I went to the police, instead of going after them, they arrested me."

She began telling him about her father's misdiagnosed stroke, Phil's tox screen, her first encounter with Dawson and Grabowski on the day that she scattered her father's ashes, Gilda's dead cat, Jacqui giving Dawson the inventory that had the methyl iodide and seeing Grabowski in the barn looking through the old chemicals.

She was just about finished when she saw flashlight beams streaking through the tree branches and heard sounds of heavy footfalls, muffled voices, sporadic grunts and groans. She looked askance at Goldney.

"I thought you said it takes about an hour to get here from your field office."

"It does."

"It hasn't even been a half-hour," she said nervously. "Who's that?"

"I don't know." He grabbed his gun. "Get behind me."

CHAPTER FIFTY

Goldney leaned against the tree, keeping his weight off his injured leg. He held his gun straight out in front of him. Hannah stood behind him, ready to steady him if he lost his balance.

A woman in a dark blue uniform emerged into the clearing. She had a small orange duffle bag in one hand and a flashlight in the other. She was short and stocky, in her mid-thirties. Her hair was reddish purple with black roots, pulled back in a tight ponytail. She had dark, vibrant eyes, a hairline scar on her chin and a wry, seen-it-all expression.

Behind her was a man, in the same uniform. He was younger, twenty-five at most. He was a little over six-feet tall and built like a linebacker, with close-cropped brown hair and the beginnings of a beard that wasn't going well. He was carrying what looked like a large beach chair.

At the sight of Goldney's gun she stopped short, dropped her bag and threw her hands in the air.

"Whoa! Don't shoot. We come in peace. New York City EMS." She pointed to a patch on her shoulder. "We got a call from the Secret Service about an agent with a gunshot wound. That you?"

Goldney lowered his weapon. "Yes. Special Agent Patrick Goldney"

"I'm Salazar. That's Ferris."

Salazar looked at Hannah. "Are you Secret Service too?"

Hannah shook her head.

Goldney said, "She's a civilian."

Salazar stared at the stained flap on his pants.

"Okay. Let's have a look." She turned to Ferris. "Put it right here."

He unfolded the chair.

Salazar patted the seat. "Park it."

Goldney eased himself down.

She unfolded a small leg rest from under the seat and gently lifted his leg on top of it. She inspected the bandage through the flap Hannah cut in his pants then turned to her.

"Not a bad job, civilian. You got a name?"

"Hannah. Hannah Johansson."

"Nice to meet you Hannah-Hannah Johansson." She gazed over toward the bench. "Why don't you go over there and relax. We'll check you out after we're done with this one."

Salazar took a pair of scissors out of her bag and cut off Goldney's pant leg well above the thigh. She glanced quickly at the exposed bottom hem of his blue and red plaid boxer shorts.

"Cute," she said.

She ripped off the blood soaked tape and bandage that Hannah applied earlier, taking a clump of Goldney's leg hair with it.

"Oww!"

"Don't be a baby," she chided. "You want pain? Try getting a bikini wax." She gave Hannah a quick wink.

A tiny spec of a smile crossed Hannah's face.

Salazar examined the wound.

Then she cleaned it and applied some ointment.

"It's through and through. That's good. But you're still bleeding. Not so good. It might have nicked the femoral artery."

She grabbed what looked like an Ace bandage out of her case and wrapped it tightly around his leg, hooking it into a kind of clamp directly over the wound.

"This is called an Israeli bandage. It should keep you kosher till we get you to the hospital."

Goldney said, "I can't leave. It's my crime scene."

"If we don't get you to the hospital in a hurry, it could be your death scene. You're not bleeding out on my watch."

"I have to brief my A.I.C."

"Who's that?" Hannah asked.

"The Agent in Charge. Westbrook."

While Salazar dressed Goldney's wound, Ferris kneeled next to Hannah under the tree. He took her pulse and blood pressure with a digital cuff and got her temperature with a forehead thermometer. He entered the readings in a handheld digital device. He didn't say a word during the process. Hannah guessed he left all the talking to Salazar.

"I'll stay here and wait for Westbrook," Hannah said after Ferris was through. "I can tell him what happened."

"You don't look so great either," Salazar said.

"I'm fine. Just tired and hungry. I can't remember the last time I had anything to eat or drink." She hoped that was all it was. She was feeling very weak and wobbly. It could be exhaustion and dehydration or it could be that the Mestinon had worn off.

Salazar glanced over at Ferris who gave her a quick nod. Then she took a bottle of yellow Gatorade from her bag and handed it to Hannah.

"Drink this."

Hannah gulped it down.

Goldney said, "She can't stay here by herself. It's not safe."

Hannah said, "I grew up here. I'll be fine."

Goldney shook his head. "We don't know who else might be out there."

Salazar said, "Give me your gun. You won't need it in the hospital. I see anyone who doesn't look right, I'll cap his ass."

"You know how to use it?"

"I was a combat medic in Afghanistan. Qualified Sharpshooter in pistol and rifle."

"Okay." Goldney handed the gun to Salazar.

"After we get you to the ambulance, Ferris will stay with you on the ride. I'll come back here." She looked over at her partner. "That work for you, Ryan?"

He responded with a nod.

"Okay, let's move. We've wasted too much time already."

Salazar helped Goldney stand up while Ferris reconfigured the chair into a stretcher.

"I don't need that," Goldney said.

He took an unsteady step and his leg buckled. Salazar caught him.

"Stop giving us a hard time. Get on the damn stretcher."

Goldney complied. He said to Salazar, "Don't let anything happen to this woman. If it wasn't for her I'd be on a slab, not a stretcher.

"I'll guard her with my life." She turned to Hannah. "Don't go anywhere."

The two EMT's lifted the stretcher and headed to the parking lot.

Still sitting on the bench, she leaned her head back against the tree and closed her eyes. The movie in her head played a continuous loop of the faces of Leigh, Dawson and McCaffrey. She flashed on Olive. She was sure her mother was frantic with worry. Maybe Bette was able to get in touch with her. What about Phil? Will he be okay?

Hannah heard people approaching. She stood slowly, hoping her legs wouldn't let her down.

Salazar emerged into the clearing. "Howya doin, Hannah-Hannah?"

"Never better."

Behind her, a man in a police uniform stared intently at Hannah.

"What are you doing here?" he demanded.

It was Gilman, the Parks cop who dragged her to jail.

Salazar said, "You know her?"

"We brought her in last week."

"Why? What did she do?"

"Criminal trespass at a top secret government installation, for starters. Then she assaulted her own lawyer."

"I don't believe it."

"I don't give a rat's rump what you believe," he said, sneering at Salazar. "This woman is dangerous. We have reason to believe she's part of a plot against the government."

"You're wrong," Hannah screamed. "There was a plot but it wasn't me." She pointed to the barn. "It was them."

Gilman said, "Who?"

Hannah realized that in her frenzy to defend herself, she made her situation a hundred times worse. Now this cop, who already thought she was some kind of terrorist, would find three dead bodies in the barn and a gun with her fingerprints on it. And the only person who could vouch for her was in an ambulance, maybe headed for surgery and incommunicado for who knows how long.

Hannah had no idea what to say so she just stood there dumbly.

After a few seconds Gilman said, "Who or what is inside there?"

She couldn't tell him not to go into the barn. She figured she might as well warn him so he wouldn't be shocked at what he saw.

"There are three dead bodies in there."

The cop stiffened. "Inside. Let's go." He waved his gun at her. "You first."

Hannah walked unsteadily into the barn. Gilman and Salazar followed. It was eerily quiet after all that had happened there a short time before. The three bodies were sprawled on the ground, Leigh and Dawson against the wall, McCaffrey in the middle of the floor.

Gilman drew his gun. He pointed it at Hannah and shouted, “Don’t move.”

CHAPTER FIFTY-ONE

"Stop waving that thing around," Salazar scolded Gilman. "It might go off and hurt somebody."

"I'm placing this woman under arrest for murder."

Salazar stepped between Gilman and Hannah.

"You don't know what the hell you're talking about. She's a freakin' hero. She's been through hell tonight. And she needs to go to the hospital."

"Get out of my way or I'll arrest you too."

"Get over yourself, Ranger Smith. Why don't you go back to Jellystone Park and chase Yogi Bear and let real law enforcement people deal with this."

Gilman seethed. "Who the hell do you think you are, talking to me like that."

"I'll tell you who I am..."

But before she could elaborate on who she was and what she thought of him, a voice from outside shouted, "Secret Service. Whoever is in there, come out slowly with you hands where I can see them."

Gilman and Salazar walked out of the barn. Hannah followed.

Stan Westbrook stood in front of the barn, his right hand on his holstered gun. He wore a navy blue golf shirt with the Secret

Service insignia where the polo player or alligator logo usually sits, a five-pointed star with small circles blunting the points. Behind him was a tall athletic looking woman in a similar shirt. She had short dark hair and a severe expression. They were followed by two women and a man, wearing what looked like white full-length rain slickers.

"I'm Special Agent Stan Westbrook, Secret Service. This is my colleague, Agent Christine Eller. Who's in charge of this crime scene?"

Both Gilman and Salazar said, "I am."

Westbrook smiled wryly. "I'm happy to see that everything's under control." He turned to Hannah. "Hello Ms. Johansson."

Gilman, startled, said, "You know this woman?"

"Yes, we've met."

"Do you know what she did?"

Before Westbrook could answer, Salazar said, "This woman is my patient. She's been through hell tonight. She's on the verge of collapse. And this bozo was about to cuff her and drag her to jail."

Gilman gestured at the barn. "There are three people dead in there. One of them is Michael Leigh." He pointed at Hannah. "All the evidence points to her." Then he glowered at Salazar. "And she's obstructing my investigation."

She sneered at him. "You wouldn't know evidence if it bit you on the ass, you fucking douchebag."

Westbrook lifted his hands in the air and shouted, "Okay, that's enough! Calm down. Both of you."

Hannah said, "I'm not a murderer. You've got to believe me."

"Don't worry, Hannah," Westbrook said soothingly. "Pat Goldney called me from the hospital. He told me everything that happened here tonight. I know you're not a murderer. As a matter of fact, according to him you deserve a medal."

"Oh," Hannah said sheepishly. She glanced over at Salazar who was sporting a Cheshire Cat grin.

Gilman slumped against the barn, deflated like a Macy's float the day after Thanksgiving.

Westbrook said to Hannah, "Are you up to talking to Agent Eller about what happened tonight?"

"I guess so," she said.

He faced Eller. "I'll be inside with the crime scene team if you need me."

Eller nodded. Then, notebook in hand, she walked over to Hannah.

"I know you've been through a lot today," she said in a voice much gentler than her stony demeanor. "I've had a long day too. How about we both sit on that bench and talk about it."

"Thank you," Hannah said with a sigh.

They sat.

"Okay, take your time and tell me as much as you can."

"From the beginning or just what happened today?"

"Whatever you're comfortable with."

Hannah gave Agent Eller a quick synopsis of everything that happened leading up to her mother's and Catherine's abduction and how she was able to help them escape. Then returning to the storage barn to dispose of the thermite canisters and her capture by McCaffrey, Dawson and Leigh. As she spoke she racked her brain trying to decide what she should say about shooting McCaffrey. If she described it exactly the way it happened, she might be arrested for murder. Or at least manslaughter. If she fudged it, Goldney could implicate her when he gave his report. Then she'd look even more guilty because she lied. Thankfully, it was a decision she'd never have to make.

The sound of voices and footsteps coming down the path brought Eller to her feet and Westbrook running out of the barn. Both assumed the shooter's position with their guns out.

Bette walked into the clearing, followed by three women and a man holding a professional looking video camera. She froze when she saw the guns pointed at her and threw her hands in the air.

Westbrook grinned, holstered his gun and cocked an eye at Bette.

"Please don't shoot," Bette pleaded. "Don't you remember

me? You picked me up outside here the other day and drove me to the railroad station."

"Yes, I remember. What are you doing here now?"

"I came to drive Hannah home. I'm her partner."

"Partner? Do you mean you two are in a relationship?"

Hannah was about to protest when Bette said, "Oh no. It's nothing like that. We're business partners. Johansson & Guglielmetti Investigations."

She thrust a business card at him.

Westbrook glanced at the card skeptically and shoved it in his pocket. He gestured at the people standing behind Bette.

"Are they with you?"

Bette shook her head. "They're reporters. I guess we all got here at the same time. I met them in the parking lot. I was telling them how we broke a huge counterfeit money laundering conspiracy."

One of the reporters marched over to Salazar.

"Are you Hannah Johansson?"

Salazar smirked. "Yeah. I guess my Nordic features and flaxen hair gave me away."

The reporter was nonplussed for a moment, then she shot Salazar a dirty look and hurried over to where Hannah was talking with Agent Eller.

She put her phone in Hannah's face. "Ms. Johansson, how did you uncover this conspiracy?"

Hannah smiled perfunctorily. Excuse me, Ms/"

"Cooper. Channel One News."

"I'm not really up to talking to you right now. I'm sure my...uh...colleague, Ms. Guglielmetti will be happy to tell you everything you need to know. She's in charge of press relations."

"She wasn't here. You were."

Before Hannah could answer, Salazar hustled over. "Back off, Lois Lane. After she's done here, Ms. Johansson needs to go right to the ER. She really should be there now. You don't want her condition to deteriorate, do you?"

"Just a couple of words."

Salazar scowled. "Absolutely not. I got a couple of words for you but I don't think you want them on TV."

Cooper was still for a few seconds, then she turned and walked over to where Bette was animatedly regaling the other reporters about how she and Hannah single-handedly solved a multi-billion-dollar money laundering and counterfeiting scheme.

Salazar said, "We're going now. Do you need a wheelchair?"

"No. I'm okay.

"There's an ambulance waiting for us in the parking lot. Follow me."

"What about Bette? She came here to drive me home. I can't just leave her here."

"Look at her. She's having the time of her life. She'll be fine."

CHAPTER FIFTY-TWO

Olive rushed into Hannah's room, hands waving wildly in the air. "Hannah, Hannah," she cried. "I'm sorry to wake you, but you have to do something. They're everywhere. On the front lawn, in the driveway, all over the street."

Hannah lifted her groggy head. "Wait. What? Who's everywhere?"

It took her a few seconds to get her bearings. She was home. In Rocky Point. In her own bed. No one was trying to kill her. No one was going to arrest her. No one in a white coat was probing and poking her.

The docs at the E.R. told her she didn't have any serious injuries. She was suffering from dehydration and exhaustion and had some minor cuts and scratches. They put her on an I.V. drip and gave her some pills to help her relax. Bette was waiting for her when she was done. When she got home, sometime after midnight, Olive was standing at the front door. She hugged Hannah, asked her if she was all right, if she wanted a cup of tea, something to eat, a shot of whiskey. Hannah told her all she wanted was to sleep. She couldn't even deal with a shower. She zombie-walked to her bedroom, peeled off her clothes and plopped into bed. She was asleep in seconds.

Now it was morning.

She propped herself up against the headboard and reached for her phone on the bedside table to check the time. Nine-sixteen.

"All right ma, now slowly, who's outside?"

Olive took a breath. "Television people with microphones and cameras. And from the newspaper too. They're ringing the bell. Knocking on the door. Shouting questions."

Hannah shook the last of the cobwebs out of her brain.

"What do they want?"

"They're asking for you."

"Tell them I can't talk to them now."

Olive started shaking. Her face contorted in horror. "I can't go out there."

"I'm sorry. Of course you can't. And you shouldn't have to. This is my problem. I'll deal with it. Try not to let it upset you."

Olive nodded. "Okay." And shuffled out of the room.

Hannah hit Bette's speed dial number.

"There's a bunch of newspeople outside. They're calling the house, banging on the door. My mother's in a tizzy. What did you tell them last night?"

Bette said, "Check your phone."

There was a text from Bette, a story in the Daily News.

The headline blared, 'FUNNY MONEY RING SMASHED'.

Under it, 'Billionaire Mastermind Killed' with an old photo of Michael Leigh.

It went on to say how operatives from Johansson & Guglielmetti Investigations along with agents of the Secret Service broke the case. There was a rough summary of the Coalition Currency scheme and the events of the previous night, including the deaths of Leigh, Dawson and McCaffrey. But it was short on detail.

"Johansson & Guglielmetti Investigations? There is no Johansson & Guglielmetti Investigations. You made it up."

"We need to have a serious talk about that."

"Later. Right now I have a mob of crazy reporters outside my house. What am I supposed to do about that?"

"Don't do anything. Eventually they'll get bored and leave."

"Absolutely not!" Hannah yelled. "We can't be prisoners in our own home until that mob decides to go bother someone else. My mother's on the verge of a nervous breakdown. They're scaring the neighbors. Parking on lawns. Stomping on shrubs. Get your butt over here and deal with this. Now!"

"How?"

"I don't know. You were in your glory talking to the press last night. Figure something out."

"I'll be there as soon as I can."

Hannah headed for the shower. She scrubbed away the mud, dust, filth and stench of last night's nightmare, languishing under the steamy water for a good five minutes before she even reached for the shampoo. Then she put on her most comfortable jeans and favorite peasant top.

The aroma of bacon and coffee greeted her as soon as she hit the kitchen.

"I hope you're hungry," Olive said as she poured coffee.

"Starving."

Hannah gobbled her scrambled eggs and bacon with two pieces of twelve grain toast. She chug-a-lugged her first mug of coffee, then poured herself a second. She was halfway through mug number two when her phone rang. It was Bette.

"I'm in my car at the end of the block. What do you want me to do?"

"Whatever it takes. Just get rid of them."

Bette turned slowly into the driveway. A crowd formed around her as she got out of the car, holding a sheaf of papers. Cameras rolled and clicked. Phones and mics were thrust in her face. Questions were shouted at her.

She began handing the typewritten sheets to the reporters closest to her, then gave the entire stack to a young intern from *Newsday* and asked her to pass them around.

The letterhead read: 'Johansson & Guglielmetti Investigations. Specializing in Financial Forensics.' The 'Media Advisory,' as it was titled, had the same information that she told the reporters last night at the Refuge along with some additional tidbits.

The journalists glanced at the brief then started firing questions at her.

Bette thrust her hands in the air and yelled, "Please. Everything we can tell you right now is in the advisory. The Secret Service is in the process of investigating. They asked us to maintain media silence until they complete their investigation. Once the gag order is lifted, Ms. Johansson and I will be happy to answer any and all of your questions in detail. Thank you all for your concern."

She smiled weakly, got back into her car, drove down the block and turned. As soon as she was out of eyeshot of the reporters she stopped and texted Hannah.

– Can we meet?

– Where are you?

– Around the corner on Hickory.

– Go to the Hallock steps.

In the fifties and sixties there was a concrete boat ramp at the end Hallock Landing Road leading to one of the most popular beaches on the North Shore. Every summer, the blue-green water of Long Island Sound was filled with anglers fishing off canoes and row boats, water skiers gleefully being dragged behind roaring power boats, and men, women and children in a melange of colorful floats, tubes and rafts basking in the gentle undulations of the Sound.

A small stand adjacent to the ramp sold ice cream and candy to kids, and bait, tackle and cigarettes to grownups. The pebble strewn sand was chock-a-block with beach chairs, blankets and umbrellas. Parents played cards and gossiped, young kids built castles and forts with pails and shovels, older ones played catch and body surfed, and teens preened and flirted.

Hannah's half-brother Karl and her cousin Toni would tell her how, when they were kids, they scampered out the backyard and half-ran half-slid down the 200-foot bluff to the beach below.

Then the brown tide came. The fish died. The turquoise water turned a rusty brown. The shoreline was befouled with dead sea life and smelled of offal. Families and boaters disappeared. Lowlifes and druggies took their place. The unused ramp became littered with broken beer bottles, greasy fast food wrappers, spent condoms, used hypodermic needles and other disgusting detritus. Cracks and fissures in the concrete widened with time, making for hazardous footing.

Decades later the brown tide disappeared as mysteriously as it arrived but Hallock Beach remained desolate.

After years of trying, the Town secured a FEMA grant to upgrade the area in the hope of bringing it back to its former glory. The treacherous concrete ramp was demolished and in its place was a wooden deck with a couple of built-in benches. A half-dozen steps led down to the beach.

Hannah peeked out a rear window to see if any reporters were lurking in the backyard. The coast was clear. She snuck out the back door and made her way carefully to the top of the bluff. It looked a lot steeper than when she was a kid. Instead of careening down with wild abandon as she did in the old days, she sat on the sand and slowly slid to the bottom. She walked the quarter mile down the beach to Hallock Landing, where Bette was sitting on one of the wooden benches.

Hannah walked up the steps and sat next to her.

"I can't remember if I thanked you for picking me up at the hospital and driving me home last night. I was pretty out of it."

"Actually you did. I told you it was the least I could do."

"The press people left. What did you tell them?"

"I told them that the Secret Service put a media gag on us. I also gave them a copy of this."

She handed a sheet of paper to Hannah.

MEDIA ADVISORY

For Immediate Release

FEMALE SLEUTH HELPS CRACK BILLION DOLLAR MONEY LAUNDERING SCHEME

Hannah Johansson of Johansson & Guglielmetti Investigations, working alongside the Secret Service, broke up a years-long money laundering operation at the Jamaica Bay Wildlife Refuge. Masterminded by Michael Leigh, a prominent financier and former government official, billions in unaccounted for U.S. currency that had been airlifted to Baghdad by the Federal Government during Operation Iraqi Freedom was absconded by Leigh's associates in Iraq and flown in small shipments to JFK Airport. To avoid customs inspection, the fraudulent funds were ferried across Jamaica Bay to the Jamaica Bay Wildlife Refuge where, under the auspices of Leigh's bank, Howard Bank and Trust, the questionable money was labeled unfit currency, destroyed, trucked to the Federal Reserve Bank and replaced with new bills.

The bodies of Leigh and several of his associates were discovered by the Secret Service at the time of the raid. The cause of their deaths remains under investigation.

CHAPTER FIFTY-THREE

Hannah read the Media Advisory twice. She looked up at Bette .

"Not bad. Very professional. How'd you learn how to do this?"

"My old law firm had a freelance PR person. She sent these out from time to time on behalf of our clients. Every once in awhile, when she was busy or out of town, they asked me to write one. There are templates on the web. It's easy once you get the hang of it."

"I'm impressed. If I didn't know better, I'd think Johansson & Guglielmetti really was an agency."

"We can be. We should be. We did great. We're a terrific team," Bette said with more exuberance than Hannah had ever seen in her. "We solved the case when nobody else could. And it's not like you have some fantastic job that you're dying to go back to."

"I'm dying to stop worrying about dying. In the last couple of weeks I've been beat up, tied up, shot at, arrested, run off the road and almost got peed on."

Bette grinned. "At least you were never bored."

"At this point a little boredom sounds wonderful."

"That's today. But I bet after a few weeks you'll be raring to go. It'll be fun, exciting. And the money's good. Some investigators earn over $100,000 a year."

"I don't believe it. But even if it's true, we're not investigators."

"Of course we are. We broke the case, didn't we?"

"What case?"

"Leigh and Dawson's money laundering, of course."

"I didn't even know what money laundering was when this all started. I'm still not 100% sure. All I wanted to do was find out what happened to my father. And anyway, we don't know the first thing about being investigators."

"I do. I worked with our investigators all the time at my job. It was one of the few things I did there that I actually enjoyed. They told me what they found out, I'd figure out how it affected the case and write a report. It's not like the old private eye TV shows like Rockford or Magnum. Those days are over. Today most investigation is research, working the computer and the phone. It's what I'm good at."

"What would I do?"

"People like talking to you, especially men. You can do interviews like we did with that lawyer in Westchester. But your most important job would be branding."

"I know less about branding than I do about investigating."

"You don't have to know anything about it. You are the brand. You're the face of the franchise. You're tall, blonde and athletic. And now you're famous. You broke a big case when the NYPD and Secret Service couldn't, whether you meant to or not. We'll put your picture on our brochure along with all the headlines. We'll have more clients than we'll know what to do with."

Hannah was quiet for a few seconds. Then she said, "That's a nice fantasy, but I need a real job with a real salary and real health insurance. Don't forget, I have this stupid disease and I need medicine and I'll probably need surgery. Nobody's going to provide that for us while we make believe we're investigators."

Bette held up her phone with the screen facing Hannah.

"See these? I've already gotten emails from a few companies asking if we might be interested in working with them. One is Manhattan Mutual, they're a major insurance company. I bet we can get them to provide us with health insurance as part of our retainer agreement."

Hannah scrunched up her face. "I don't know," she said thoughtfully. "It still sounds farfetched to me."

"I'll tell you what. Give this a shot while you're looking for your real job. If we don't have a couple of clients by time you get a job offer, we'll call it quits. Whaddaya say?"

"I say let's go back and see if the reporters are still there."

When they turned the corner on Soundview Drive, the news vans, TV reporters and newspaper and journalists were gone. In their place was a police cruiser parked in front of the house.

"Shit," Hannah said, "I thought I was done with cops for awhile."

Bette said, "What do you think they want?"

"I have no idea. But that's an NYPD car. If they came all the way out to the middle of Suffolk County, it's not to give me a commendation."

"What do you want me to do?"

"Drive past the house and pull into Rocco's driveway next door."

Rocco Marchetti was in his eighties and still mowed his own lawn and chopped his own firewood. He recently bought himself a used log-splitter, his one concession to his age.

"What are you going to do?" Bette asked, nervously.

"I'll cut through Rocco's backyard, hop over the fence and sneak in the back door. I don't want them to know I was outside."

"Why? What difference does it make?"

"I don't know. It's just a feeling."

"Do you want me to come with you?"

"No. Go home. I'll talk to you later."

"Are you sure?"

Hannah shrugged. "At this point, I'm not sure of anything."

"Okay," Bette said. "But listen, don't say anything to the police. Even the most innocent remark can come back to bite you. I've heard our lawyers tell their clients that hundreds of times."

"Okay. Thanks."

Bette pulled into Rocco's driveway. Hannah jumped out. She stopped to give Buster, Rocco's big old German Shepard, a pat on the head. He looked up, lifted his tail in recognition then put his head back down between his huge folded front paws. She raced past the wooden coop that Rocco built for his racing pigeons to the four-foot picket fence that separated the two yards. She had vaulted that fence hundreds of times as a teenager without a thought. It never occurred to her that it would be a problem this time. But her foot caught on one of the pickets and she tumbled over, landing awkwardly on a juniper bush.

"You clumsy idiot!" she yelled at herself.

Some face of the franchise, she thought. The star investigator going ass over teakettle trying to climb a fence that any ten-year-old could handle with ease. She gathered herself, stood up slowly and brushed herself off. Her knees, hips and elbows ached, her ankle—the one she hurt the night before at the Refuge—felt squishy.

She glanced around to make sure no one had seen her embarrassing pratfall. The coast was clear. She limped across her yard, tiptoed through the backdoor into the kitchen. The house was quiet. Olive was nowhere to be seen, probably huddled in her bedroom, still hiding from the media throng. The front doorbell was chiming.

Was this it? she thought as she padded slowly to the door. Her fingerprints were on the gun that killed McCaffrey. Agent Goldney saw what happened. He could swear that it was self-defense. But was it really?

When she opened the door she was surprised to see a familiar face. It was the cop who interviewed her at the Howard Beach police precinct. The one who treated her like she was an escaped mental patient.

"Hello Ms. Johansson," he said.

"Oh, hello Officer..."

"Detective Gasparino."

"How can I help you, Detective Gasparino?"

"I want to talk to you about what happened last night at the Jamaica Bay Wildlife Refuge."

"I thought the Secret Service was handling that."

"They're dealing with the money laundering issue. I want to talk to you about the four bodies we found there."

Four? There were three dead people in the barn. Leigh, Dawson and McCaffrey. Then she remembered Grabowski on the ground with his head bashed in. What should she do? Bette told her not to say anything but she couldn't just stand there like an idiot. So she changed the subject.

"The last time I spoke to you, you said that your department had no jurisdiction there. That it was the Parks Police."

"There's some confusion about that right now. The Parks Police say that the Port Authority Police have jurisdiction. The Port Authority won't get involved because one of the deceased suspects in the money laundering case was on their Board of Directors. So it got kicked back to us."

"When I told you what was going on there the last time, you didn't want to be bothered. Now all of a sudden you're interested?" she said, he voice tinged with resentment.

"The last time you told us about a dead cat. This time there are four dead people. It's a very different situation."

"What about my father?"

"What about him?"

All the pent up anger about her father's death erupted. Suddenly, she didn't feel nervous about being arrested. All she felt was rage.

"He's dead," she screamed. "I told you he was poisoned at the Refuge and you didn't care."

"There was no proof."

"You could have looked for proof. You should have investigated. Isn't that what the police are supposed to do? Instead you blew me off."

"I sent a report to the Parks Police."

"And they arrested ME."

"I had nothing to do with that."

"Of course you did. If you would have listened to me in the first place and not treated me like some crazy lunatic, maybe those four people would still be alive."

"I'm listening now."

"Too late!" she cried. "If you want to know what happened last night, talk to Secret Service Agent Patrick Goldney."

"I intend to. But right now I want to talk to you."

"Well I don't want to talk to you!"

She slammed the door in his face.

CHAPTER FIFTY-FOUR

Hannah dragged herself over to her father's club chair. Her ankle was throbbing. Her head was spinning. She was trying not to throw up.

She really screwed up this time. She was sure Gasparino would be back any minute with an arrest warrant and drag her back to jail. Only this time she wouldn't be home the next day. She might never come home. Why didn't she listen to Bette and keep her stupid mouth shut.

Olive came shuffling into the living room.

"There was a police car out front. Is he the one who got rid of the newspaper people?"

"No. That was Bette."

Olive looked puzzled. "Your friend Bette? How did she do that? Where is she?"

"She went home."

"If Bette went home and the newspaper people are gone, who were you talking to?"

"The cop from the police car."

"What did he want?"

"He wanted to know what happened at the Refuge last night."

"But he was only here for a few minutes. You couldn't have told him much."

"I didn't tell him anything. I screamed at him and slammed the door in his face."

Olive was aghast. "You didn't."

She nodded contritely. "Yeah, I did."

"Why on earth would you do that?"

"I just lost my temper."

Olive gently took Hannah's hand in both of hers. "I'm sure it'll be fine. The main thing is you're safe and it's over."

Hannah stood. She wrapped her mother in a tight hug. Tears welled in her eyes.

"It's not over," she wailed. "Oh ma, I'm so sorry. I messed everything up."

"That's not true."

"You don't understand. They're all dead."

"Dead? Who's dead?"

"Michael Leigh, the Dawson woman, that goon Grabowski."

Olive looked bewildered. "Michael Leigh? The man from your father's memorial who was here the other day. Isn't he the person you went into the City to see the other day?

"Yes, that's him."

"He was so nice."

"It turns out he wasn't so nice. He was a horrible, evil man. And Tom McCaffrey. He's dead too."

"Tom? My Axel's fishing friend? He helped you with your car the other day."

Hannah nodded.

Olive shook her head in disbelief. "This is all too much."

"It's a long and complicated story that I don't have the strength to go into right now. What I will tell you is McCaffrey killed the rest of them."

"Who? Mr. Leigh? And those other people? I don't believe it."

"I saw him do it."

"Are you sure?"

"Of course I'm sure."

"How can that be? He used to be a policeman."

It was usually at this point when Hannah would snap at her mother in frustration and say something like 'So you never heard of a crooked cop?' But she realized that Olive had gone through just as much angst and stress as she had in the last few weeks and soon she would see her daughter accused of murder and dragged off in handcuffs.

Hannah gently said, "Ma, sit down. There's something else I need to tell you."

Olive eased herself into her rocking chair. "Yes, dear."

"Remember I told you that Tom McCaffrey was dead, too?"

"Yes."

"'I'm the one who killed him."

"You did not!"

"I did. I shot him. I had to or else he would have killed me."

Olive shook her head vigorously, as if trying to keep the words from entering her ears.

"That's why the policeman was here," Hannah said. "I'm pretty sure he'll be back soon to arrest me."

"I don't understand. None of this makes sense."

"Nothing that happened last night made sense. I called Tom McCaffrey before I went to the Refuge. I asked him to help me. When he got there he turned his gun on me. I thought he was gonna shoot me right then and there. But he had a different plan." Hannah paused for a beat. "You know about McCaffrey's son Tim, right?"

"Yes, poor child. Stuck in that wheelchair day and night. The poor thing can't even breathe on his own. But what does that have to do with the price of tea in China?"

"It all goes back to the Iraq War. McCaffrey blamed Leigh and his gang for what happened to Tim over there. He's been planning his revenge for a long time."

"I thought Michael Leigh was a banker. Why would he be in Iraq? "

"He was sent there by the government. Please don't ask me to go into the details."

"All right, dear. But even if all that is true? Why would Tom McCaffrey want to shoot you? You had nothing to do with what happened to his son."

"I saw him kill those other people. He was afraid I'd talk to the police about what he did. He was about to shoot me when the Secret Service agent showed up."

Olive looked bewildered. "The Secret Service? What were they doing there? The President wasn't involved in this, was he?"

Hannah explained about the Secret Service and everything else that happened after Goldney arrived.

After she was finished, her mother sat silently for awhile, trying to process what she just heard. Then she walked over to Hannah and placed a hand gently on her shoulder. "I'm sure everything will turn out all right."

Hannah burst into tears. "I don't think so. Not this time." She stood and hugged her mother. "I'm so sorry. Please forgive me."

Olive patted her gently on the back. "There's nothing to forgive."

"I love you for saying that but you know it's not true. Your fight with Gilda. Phil getting shot. Even Gilda's dead cat. All my fault. I've been a walking disaster to the whole family."

They both sat back down.

Olive said. "You're wrong. Thanks to you I had the talk with Gilda that I should've had fifty years ago." She paused for a moment. "As for Phillip, if you ask me, I think he sees that wound he has as a badge of honor. And Gilda should have never let that stupid old puss Perry roam around outside. He had absolutely no street sense." Olive pondered for a few seconds, then she said, "Perhaps if you called the police station and apologized, they'd forget about the whole thing."

"It's a murder investigation, ma. They don't just forget it if you make nice to them."

"Of course you're right, dear. But there must be something you can do."

Hannah shook her head disconsolately. "I can't think of anything."

She kissed her mother on the forehead and walked out onto the back deck. She sat on one of the rattan chairs, gazed at the gentle waves.

After a few minutes she called Bette.

"What did that cop say? I've been dying to call you but I didn't dare, in case he was still there. How are you? Is everything all right?"

Hannah took a breath. "No. I totally screwed up."

"Why? How?"

"It was the same detective that I spoke to at the Howard Beach police station."

"That could be a good thing. At least he knows you're not a criminal."

"No. He thinks I'm a homicidal madwoman."

"I'm sure you're exaggerating."

"I screamed at him. I told him that if he listened to me the first time none of this would have happened. I practically blamed him for the murders. Then I slammed the door in his face."

"Oh."

"My mother thinks maybe I should call the precinct and apologize."

Bette was silent for a few seconds. "I don't think that's a good idea. It won't help and it might make things worse. Just leave it alone. What you did is perfectly understandable or at least excusable. You just went through a terrifying ordeal. We could claim PTSD."

"Really?"

"Yes. Do you want me to come over?"

"Thanks but no. I'd be terrible company. I'm better off being by myself."

"Okay. Call me if you need me."

"I will."

Hannah went back into the house, got her guitar and her well worn Joni Mitchell songbook out of her closet. She sat down on her bed, turned to page one and started playing.

She had picked her way through all the songs on *Clouds* and *Ladies of the Canyon,* and was about to start on *Court and Spark* when her phone rang. Caller I.D. said 'Unavailable'.

She usually didn't answer those calls but thought it might be the police.

"Hello."

"Hannah? It's Patrick Goldney, Secret Service."

"Patrick, how are you?"

"I'm good.

"Are you still in the hospital?"

"No. They patched me up and sent me home. How are you?"

"I'm fine." The last thing she wanted to do was tell him how she really felt.

"Good. First of all, I want to thank you again. If it wasn't for you, I wouldn't be here."

Hannah smiled. "I could say the same about you. If you hadn't shown up when you did, I'd be another of McCaffrey's victims."

"Speaking of McCaffrey, I got a call today from a detective Gasparino."

Hannah's stomach turned over. "He was here too."

"Yes, he told me about your conversation." There was a smile in Goldney's voice. "He said you hollered at him."

"That was stupid, I know. Now I suppose he's coming back to arrest me."

"Arrest you? Why would he do that?"

"I shot McCaffrey. He was unarmed. That's homicide."

"First of all, it was a classic case of self-defense. Second, there's no proof."

"My fingerprints are on the gun that killed him."

"So were mine and Leigh's. So there's nothing directly connecting you to the shooting. But just to be on the safe side, I told Gasparino that I shot McCaffrey during the struggle."

"You mean I'm not going to jail?"

He chuckled. "No, of course not. If anything, you might get a commendation from the mayor or the police commissioner. But I wouldn't hold my breath."

"Oh my God! That's the best news I've heard in a long time. If you were here right now I would kiss you."

"Hold onto that thought. As soon as I'm done with the After Action Review and the rest of the paperwork I'd like to take you out to dinner. It's the least I can do to repay you for saving my life."

"I'd love that."

"Great. Take care."

He ended the call.

She picked up her guitar and began to play 'Free Man in Paris.'

CHAPTER FIFTY-FIVE

It was Sunday morning. Hannah slept for ten hours. No nightmares. No waking up in the middle of the night drenched in clammy sweat. The Refuge was safe. The bad guys were gone. She wasn't facing a murder charge. And she had a date coming up with the good looking Secret Service guy. She should be feeling terrific. So why did she still feel uneasy? Something was gnawing at her and she didn't know what it was. Like an itch that she couldn't quite reach.

She went into the kitchen. Olive was sitting at the table sipping coffee. Hannah poured herself a cup and sat facing her.

"I have good news."

"That's wonderful. What is it?"

"I'm not going to jail."

"That's nice, dear," Olive said nonchalantly as she took a sip.

"Didn't you hear what I said? The last time I spoke to you I was sure I was going to stand trial for murder. There was a good chance I'd be going to prison for a long time. Maybe the rest of my life. And when I tell you that it won't happen, all you can say is 'that's nice?' "

"I knew they were never going to arrest you. The police don't arrest innocent people."

Hannah didn't want to argue. She didn't mention that if Patrick Goldney hadn't lied about who shot McCaffrey, she'd probably be behind bars right now. That cops arrest innocent people all the time. And that technically, she wasn't innocent. She did kill McCaffrey. Whether it was self defense or homicide would have been for a jury to decide.

Instead she said, "I guess you're right."

Olive smiled benignly. "Of course I'm right."

After a few minutes of silent sipping, there was a knock at the door.

Olive said, "Who can that be?"

Hannah jumped up. "I'll get it."

She opened the door to see her cousin Phil, wearing a new Hawaiian shirt that was two sizes too big. The left sleeve dangled armless at his side. His bandaged left arm and shoulder bulged underneath. His right hand was holding two large floral bouquets. One was purple with lavender roses, violet carnations and mauve lilies. The other featured roses in various shades of pink.

"You're out of the hospital."

"Obviously." His stint in the hospital hadn't made him any less obnoxious.

She gestured at the flowers. "Who are those for?"

"You'll see." He winked.

Olive jumped up as they walked into the kitchen.

"Phillip, it's so good to see you. Are you all right?"

"Never better."

"What about your shoulder?"

"It'll be fine." He walked over to her and held out the bouquets. "The pink one is for you. Happy Mother's Day, Aunt Ollie."

She took the bouquet. "Oh Phillip, they're lovely. Thank you so much."

Hannah's jaw dropped. She put a hand to her mouth.

"Oh ma, I'm so sorry. I totally forgot it was Mother's Day. I'm a horrible daughter."

"Don't be silly. You had so much on your mind."

Phil thrust the purple bouquet at Hannah.

"These are for you."

"Why? I'm not a mother."

"They're for making me go to the hospital. If you remember, I didn't want to go. But you fought me on it. The docs said you saved my arm. Maybe my life."

Hannah thought that it was the least she could do since it was her fault that he got shot in the first place. But all she said was, "Thank you."

"I didn't see you as a pink kinda girl so I got the purple instead."

"They're perfect. I love them."

Hannah got Phil a cup of coffee. They all sat at the kitchen table not saying much. Phil was his usual laconic self. Olive stared out the window, looking wistfully at the sparrows, finches and chickadees perched on the bird feeder. Hannah was deep in thought, her face was pursed in a scowl.

Finally Olive broke the silence.

"Phillip, when are you going back upstate?"

"I'm not. I'm staying here for awhile."

Hannah's eyes widened. "What happened? Are you okay? Is there something you're not telling us?"

Phil grinned impishly. "It's nothing like that. Actually, I think I might be in love."

Hannah said, "You've been in the hospital the whole time you've been here. Who'd you fall in love with, your nurse?"

"Close. It was my doctor."

"Doctor Y?"

"Yeah. There was always something special between me and Ellen, but other things always got in the way: school, work, we were seeing other people, we lived too far away...whatever." He shrugged. "These past couple of days we've spent a lot of time with each other and it looks like the chemistry is still there so we decided to give it a real shot."

Hannah said, "What about your practice? Your work with the medical examiner? Your apartment and all your stuff?"

"All taken care of. I already spoke to the guy who's covering for me. He's happy to get my patients full time. And M.E.'s office can always find another consultant. I even found someone who wants to sublet my apartment up in Alfred, one of the new residents at Jones Memorial. I convinced him to box up my things and send them to me down here in exchange for a month's free rent."

Hannah leaned over and gave Phil a quick hug and a peck on the cheek.

"That's great news. She seems terrific. She'll have to be to put up with you."

Olive said, "Congratulations. I hope we'll be seeing a lot of both of you."

"I'm sure you will. We're both useless in the kitchen. We'll be coming here for home cooked meals."

He turned to Hannah. "I'm thinking congratulations are in order for you, too."

"Me? What did I do?"

"Are you kidding, you're famous."

"What are you talking about?"

"There's not a lot to do when you're stuck in bed, convalescing. Daytime TV sucks. So I've been reading *The News*, *Newsday* and *The Post* every day from cover to cover. And all of a sudden, there you are in big headlines. Hannah Johansson, Ace Investigator. You saved the Jamaica Bay Refuge and cracked a billion-dollar counterfeiting scheme. Not to mention starting your own hotshot detective agency."

"That was all blown out of proportion," Hannah said. "The Secret Service solved the case. I just happened to be there when it happened. And there is no agency. Bette made that up. All I ever wanted to do was find out who poisoned my father."

Phil said, "Mission accomplished."

Hannah scowled. "I'm not so sure."

Phil jerked forward. "What do you mean? It was Dawson and that big goon, Whatshisname."

"Grabowski."

"Yeah, him. The only thing we didn't know was who was calling the shots. Now we know it was Leigh. And they're all dead so we don't have to worry about his fancy Wall Street lawyers getting them off."

Olive said, "I still find it hard to believe that a man like Michael Leigh would be a party to anything like that. And besides, he was genuinely upset when Axel passed away."

Hannah said, "I agree. The more I think about it, the more I think he didn't do it. When I accused him of poisoning dad, he denied it vehemently. He had no qualms about admitting being part of the money laundering scheme so it's not like he was worried about his reputation. But he seemed really upset that I even thought he had anything to do with dad's death."

Phil thought for a moment. "Maybe Dawson did it and she never told Leigh."

"I thought of that," Hannah said. "But I don't think so. When I confronted her about poisoning my father, she denied it too. She said she never heard of methyl iodide."

"The prisons are full of criminals who swear up and down that they're innocent."

"She had no reason to lie. She thought I would be dead any minute. And she hated my guts. If she killed dad it would have given her great pleasure to make sure I knew about it. I can't imagine Grabowski doing it on his own. But if he did, it wouldn't be with poison. He's a blunt instrument kind of guy."

Olive's forehead furrowed. "If those people didn't do it, who did?"

Hannah shrugged. "No one that I can think of. That's what's been bothering me." She turned to Phil. "Maybe the tox screen was wrong? Maybe he really did have a stroke."

Phil shook his head. "No way. Science doesn't lie. Uncle Axe died of methyl iodide poisoning. I'm one hundred percent certain."

The room went silent.

After a few seconds Hannah turned to Olive.

"Ma, do you remember exactly when daddy started to feel bad?"

Olive thought for a moment.

"It was about a week before Christmas. We were putting up the tree. Axel could hardly lift it. I had to help him. That's when I knew something wasn't right."

There was another awkward silence.

Phil stood. "Guys, I really have to get going. I've still got a ton of things to do. Happy Mother's Day again, Aunt Ollie." He planted a kiss on her forehead. He turned to Hannah. "Don't worry, you'll figure it out. You're the ace detective." He winked, then left.

Hannah said, "I'm so sorry I forgot about Mother's Day."

"You're here and you're safe. That's the best Mother's Day present I could possibly have."

Hannah hugged her. "I love you ma. You're the best!"

She went to her room and fired up her laptop. She checked the JFK Airport news archives.

CHAPTER FIFTY-SIX

Hannah walked along Central Park South towards Fifth Avenue. It was chockablock with joggers, walkers, gawkers and bike riders. Tourists were window shopping or taking selfies with human statues or hansom cabbies and their steeds. Office workers were heading into the park for a quick picnic lunch. Pushcart vendors lined the street, hawking everything from t-shirts to cell phone chargers to souvlaki sandwiches. Plus dog walkers, unicyclists and Manhattanites simply enjoying a sunny spring day.

Hannah had taken the 10:36 train from Port Jeff to Penn Station. Then caught the number 2 subway at 34th Street and rode it to 59th. Since the trains were more or less on time and the weather was good she decided to walk to Jacqui's office. She checked her phone. Google maps said it was about a quarter mile and should take 15 minutes to walk the two long avenue blocks from 7th to 5th, then up five short streets to the Arsenal on 64th Street. Unlike her previous hike from Penn Station to Leigh's office, which resulted in bloody blisters and shredded toes, this time she was dressed for comfort not fashion, with cushiony running shoes, loose-fitting jeans and a flowy peasant top.

It was Friday. Except for walking Lena on the beach, it was the first time she'd been out of the house all week. She spent most of the week thinking about what really happened to her father and trying to figure out what to do with the rest of her life. She played her guitar on the back deck, rearranged her drawers and closet several times and watched all the Nora Ephron DVD's in her collection, some more than once.

She had turned off her phone after being inundated with media requests, crank calls, spam and texts from people she hadn't heard from in years and didn't especially want to hear from now. Bette kept texting her about starting an investigation agency so Hannah finally begged her to back off for a few days. The only person besides her mother she spoke to was Jacqui and that was only by texting. Jacqui played a part in the Refuge investigation and Hannah wanted to fill her in on the latest details. When her friend suggested they meet for lunch, Hannah texted back: *Yes*

Jacqui replied: *Friday?*

After a thumbs-up emoji from Hannah, Jacqui texted: *Arsenal@12:30.*

Even though Hannah dawdled, stopping every few minutes to gaze at the gaudy store windows and ritzy hotels along Central Park South, she was still fifteen minutes early. The last time she was at the Arsenal, she was so caught up in the nefarious goings-on at the Refuge that she didn't pay much attention to the old, austere building that seemed oddly out of place in its Central Park setting, tucked in next to the delightful Children's Zoo and the whimsical Delacorte Clock, a gigantic music box, that marked every half-hour by playing old-timey tunes while cartoony bronze animals danced a mechanical jig.

The foreboding Arsenal, on the other hand, looked like a castle out of the Middle Ages with high red brick towers on either side of the entrance with gaps where she imagined archers would be positioned, ready to repel barbarian invaders from Madison Avenue.

A huge framed poster on the entranceway wall, complete with photos and illustrations, detailed the building's illustrious history. It was built in 1851, ten years earlier than the park that surrounded it. In addition to a short stint as an armory for the New York City militia, the Arsenal served time as a police precinct, the site of the first American Museum of Natural History and the home of a menagerie of exotic animals. Today it was the headquarters of the administrative offices of the New York City Department of Parks and the Central Park Zoo. It also housed an art gallery and a rooftop garden for any aesthetes who might wander in. What the poster didn't mention was that it was where Olive Buzek, who supervised the Parks Department permit office on the building's ground floor, first met Axel Johansson, who had frequent meetings with the Buildings and Grounds Division on the second floor, when he was a master gardener for the City's parks and golf courses. That meeting blossomed into a romance and then a marriage.

Hannah tried to imagine her parents' flirtatious banter as she waited for the elevator to take her to the fourth floor. Jacqui was waiting when Hannah walked out of the elevator. As opposed to the business suit she wore the last time, she was dressed in jeans, an orange and blue New York Knicks t-shirt and Nikes. She was carrying a big Bloomingdale's shopping bag.

Jacqui said, "Hey girlfriend, I've been reading about you. You're all over the web. Who figured you to be a crime busting superhero?"

Hannah shook her head. "Not hardly. You know you can't believe anything you read online."

She glanced over at the shopping bag. "You need to return some things to Bloomies?"

Jacqui shook her head and grinned. "That's our lunch. I thought we could have ourselves a picnic up on the roof garden. I figured we'd celebrate you cracking the case. But if that doesn't work for you we can celebrate the first casual Friday of the season."

"I was wondering why you were so dressed down today."

Jacqui led Hannah down a corridor, through a door with a sign that read 'Exit to Roof' then up a flight of stairs and into an amazingly lush, green and beautiful space. A combination arboretum and picnic area, it featured dozens of wooden planter boxes and ceramic flower pots of all sizes and shapes that held a stunning variety of colorful flowers, luxuriant shrubs and small trees. Hannah recognized many of the plants but some were new to her. Interspersed among them were a dozen green picnic tables.

They sat at a table near the castle turrets with a spectacular view of the park and the towering buildings of Central Park South. Jacqui started pulling containers and small wrapped packages out of the shopping bag until the table was covered with them.

Hannah said, "What's all that?"

"Lunch."

"For who, the whole building?"

"I didn't know what you liked so I ordered some choices. Believe me, whatever we don't eat, the piranhas downstairs will gobble up. They can smell free food from three floors away."

She took the receipt out of the bag and studied it for a few seconds.

"We have grilled chicken, avocado and pepper jack cheese on a spinach wrap. Fresh turkey with brie on a whole wheat wrap. Bacon, tomato, avocado, fresh mozzarella and sun-dried tomato on a honey oat wrap. Then there's potato salad or sweet potato fries to go with it. Vanilla, chocolate or red velvet cupcakes for dessert. And a couple of different kinds of water."

"This must have cost you a bloody fortune. You have to let me pay half."

"Don't be silly. This is on the Parks Department."

"Are you sure?"

"Absolutely. They owe me. Now what'll you have?"

"To tell you the truth, I'm not super hungry. How about half of the grilled chicken wrap and just some plain water?"

Jacqui looked at her quizzically. "What are you, on some kind of diet? You don't look fat to me."

"I just haven't had much of an appetite lately."

"You don't know what you're missing. This is from Angela's. She makes the best sandwiches in the City." She patted herself on the hip. "See these fifteen extra pounds. Most of them are because of her."

She handed Hannah her half grilled chicken wrap and took the bacon wrap for herself.

While they ate, Hannah did most of the talking. Filling Jacqui in on everything that happened on that climactic night at the Refuge and in the days that followed. Jacqui stopped her every so often with a question or a comment but mostly let her speak uninterruptedly. She seemed more interested in Hannah's feelings about Patrick Goldney than she was about the money laundering operation or the shootings.

"You know what happens once you go black," she said with a grin.

"I know. But I haven't gone black, white or any color in-between for a long time."

"It's time for you to get back in the game. You're a great catch. You're smart, you're good looking and you're famous. And you don't have that whole mess with your dad hanging over your head. Those bastards who poisoned him are all dead."

Hannah didn't say anything. She concentrated on the red velvet cupcake in front of her, peeling the paper wrapper off slowly then revolving it to savor every millimeter of caloric lusciousness.

Finally she looked up and said, "I don't think they did it."

Jacqui looked puzzled and a little upset. "What do you mean?"

"They denied it. Both Leigh and Dawson."

"You believed them?"

"They had no reason to lie. I was their prisoner. They were sure that I'd be dead soon. They were just waiting for Grabowski to come back and finish the job. They admitted everything else, why not admit to poisoning my father?"

"Murder is a lot worse than money laundering. Maybe they were ashamed."

"I don't think so. Dawson hated me. She would have shot me herself but Leigh wouldn't let her."

"Why?"

She told her about the lesbian bar debacle.

"If she had anything to do with my father's death she would have loved to throw it in my face. And besides, there was no reason for them to want my father dead."

"What about the whole money laundering scheme? Maybe Axel figured it out."

Hannah shook her head. "He would have said something."

"Maybe they thought he knew about it even if he didn't?"

"Then why would they use a slow acting toxin to kill him? My father was sick for weeks. He would have had plenty of time to talk to the authorities. If they wanted to keep him quiet they would have killed him immediately."

Jacqui concentrated for a few seconds. "Maybe they just screwed up and didn't know how long it would take."

Hannah shook her head. "I know Leigh and Dawson didn't do it."

"I don't understand. How could you know that?"

"My mother told me he started showing symptoms almost a month before Dawson and her goons showed up at the Refuge. So you see, they couldn't have poisoned him. The timing doesn't work."

Jacqui pursed her lips and stared intently at the trees.

After a few seconds she said, "If they didn't do it, who did?"

"That's what I've been racking my brain trying to figure out. It has to be someone close to my father. Someone who knew about methyl iodide and where to get it and how to somehow get my father to ingest it."

Jacqui said, "I can't think of anybody who fits that description."

Hannah glared at her.

“I can.” Hannah stood and glared at her. “You!”

CHAPTER FIFTY-SEVEN

Jacqui jumped up. "That's crazy! I loved Axel. He was like a second father to me."

Hannah stood, facing her. "That's what I thought. But you're the only one it could be."

They glared at each other across the picnic table.

"What about Oswaldo? Or Barbara?"

"Barbara didn't have a key to the chemical shed. And she was long gone before my father started showing symptoms. Same with Oswaldo. He retired months earlier. In the end it was only you and my dad."

"The National Parks Rangers. They were there when he starting getting sick."

"What possible reason could they have for poisoning him?"

Jacqui was silent. She was thinking. Concentrating.

Hannah leaned forward. "I know you did it. I just want to know why."

Jacqui screamed, "You're insane. You must have PTSD from the other night. You need to see a doctor."

"I don't need a doctor. I need an answer. I wish there was another explanation. But there isn't. I loved you. My father loved you. We treated you like family. He helped you get this job. And you repay us by killing him. How could you?"

Jacqui's face contorted with rage, hatred.

"How could I!" she bellowed. "You ruined my life once. I wasn't going to let your father do it to me a second time."

"What are you talking about?"

"Like you don't know," she sneered. "I was a fucking superstar. The best baller in the city. More scholarships than I could count. Maybe the pros. You took it all away with that one dirty-ass play."

"That was an accident and you know it. If anything, you caused it. You were totally out of control. I just stood my ground. They never even called a foul. And if they did it would have been on you."

"Bullshit!" Jacqui screamed. "You low-bridged me. You couldn't wait to take me out. You were always jealous of me. You wanted me out of the way so you could be the queen bee."

"You know that's not true. I'm not like you. I never wanted the limelight. After you got hurt, I quit. I never played another game. You still got a scholarship."

"A bullshit scholarship. I was finished as a player and everybody knew it. I couldn't run. I couldn't jump. I could hardly walk. They stuck me at the end of the bench like the team lawn jockey. It was great PR for St. John's, taking pity on the broken hometown girl when no one else wanted her."

"What about us? My family opened our home to you. My father gave you a job."

"Some job. Shoveling shit in a swamp. I was a slave on the Johansson plantation. The house nigger."

Hannah was stunned. Who was this person, seething with rage? Could she have been harboring this horrible resentment the whole time?

"My father loved you. He treated you like a daughter. And now you're telling me you hated him."

"I didn't hate him." Jacqui clenched her body like a fist. She bared her teeth and screamed, “I hated you! I still hate you. You made me a cripple. Then you made me an addict.”

“What are you talking about?”

“Oxycodone. I needed it after the surgery. It was the only way I could deal with the pain. The pain you inflicted on me. I could never get off it. You did that to me.”

“You got hooked on drugs and you’re blaming me?”

“You put me in the hospital. That’s where it started.”

“Even if that’s true, you didn’t poison me. You poisoned my father.”

“I had no choice. He found my stash. I said it wasn’t mine but he knew it was. He said if I didn’t quit he was gonna turn me in to the police. I would have lost everything. Again!”

“You killed him,” Hannah cried. “You admit it.”

Jacqui shook her head, vehemently. “No. I never wanted Axel to die. I just wanted him to get sick. The airport expansion was coming and I figured we’d all be gone in a few weeks. I already had this job offer. I was set. I had to stop him. I remembered reading a bulletin about methyl iodide. How it could make you sick. How it looked like a stroke. And that you could be exposed through skin contact. I put some inside his work gloves every day. I wanted him gone. Out of the way. I never meant to kill him. I’m sorry about that.”

“You’re sorry! You’re gonna be a lot sorrier after I call 911.”

Hannah pulled her phone out of her pocket and hit the digits. She put the phone on speaker. She wanted Jacqui to know she wasn’t bluffing.

When the operator answered Hannah said, “I want to report a homicide.”

Jacqui shrieked, “No you don’t. You wrecked my life once. Not this time.”

She leaped across the table at Hannah, knocking it over, along with both chairs, and sending the phone skittering across the floor.

The two enraged women thrashed around on the ground,

punching, kicking, scratching, biting. Toppling flower pots, benches, light stands. Hannah's head crashed into a huge wood planter box. She blacked out for a few seconds. When she came to, Jacqui was bent over her, her hands wrapped around Hannah's throat.

"I'm gonna kill you, you fucking bitch!" Jacqui roared. "You're gonna die knowing I killed your father because of you!"

Hannah jerked her head from side to side and hammered her fists into her attacker's ribs. Jacqui roared in pain but kept squeezing. With her last ounce of strength Hannah hooked her leg around Jacqui's knee and yanked it down as hard as she could, bending it at an angle nature never meant for it to bend, re-rupturing tendons and ligaments that were already weak. Jacqui let out an agonized bellow, let go and collapsed to the ground. Hannah pinned her to the floor. She began pounding her fists into Jacqui's face and head.

Suddenly she felt strong hands gripping her arms. She was yanked roughly to her feet. Two burly men in green New York City Parks Police uniforms held each arm tightly. They were both a little shorter than Hannah's six-foot-three but twice as thick. One was Latino, the other African American. Another uniformed guard, also black, was helping Jacqui to her feet, a lot more gently.

"She attacked me," Jacqui yelled, pointing at Hannah. "She's a psycho racist. She called me nigger. She tried to kill me. They all saw it."

A crowd people had surrounded them. Hannah hadn't noticed them before. She was too busy trying not to be choked to death. They must have heard the commotion and run up to the roof to see what was going on. They were all staring at Hannah with expressions ranging from disdain to disgust to hate.

Hannah felt the grip on her arms tighten.

"That's not true," Hannah cried. "She poisoned my father. She tried to kill me."

"The NYPD is on the way," the Latino guard holding

Hannah said. "You'll get to explain everything to them. For now don't move, don't talk, don't give us no trouble."

Hannah noticed her reflection in one of the windows. Her face was scratched and bloody. Her clothes were ripped, filthy and disheveled. She was the picture of a violent street person. Of course no one believed her. The way she looked she hardly believed herself.

It couldn't have been more than five minutes when the NYPD arrived in the person of a plainclothes female. Mid-thirties, shortish dark hair, neither fat nor thin but solid, dressed like an office worker except for the badge pinned to her belt. She walked directly over to Jacqui, who was seated at a picnic table, sipping a bottle of Dasani water, looking forlorn. A security guard hovered behind her. Hannah hadn't been offered a seat or a drink but that was the least of her problems.

The cop spoke for a minute with Jacqui and the guard. Hannah couldn't hear everything that was being said but she heard enough to know that she was being accused of all kinds of despicable acts as Jacqui pointed venomously at her.

After she was finished with Jacqui, the policewoman walked over to Hannah, who immediately began to tell her side of the story.

"Hold on," the cop said, raising a hand. "You'll get to tell it all at the station."

Hannah pointed at Jacqui. "What about her?"

"Don't worry about her. Right now I want you to come with me."

"Am I under arrest?"

"Not yet."

CHAPTER FIFTY-EIGHT

Hannah was becoming quite an expert on police stations. From the depressingly decrepit Howard Beach station with its peeling paint and thrift shop furniture to the pristinely sleek and modern National Parks Police headquarters in Floyd Bennet Field in Brooklyn. Her latest destination was the 22nd Precinct, which was responsible for policing all of Central Park. It was both New York's oldest and newest police station. A century and a half ago, the two long buildings that comprised it were stables, home to the park's horses and the buggies they pulled. Fifty years later the barns were converted into the home of the park's blue clad constabulary, proverbial horses of a different color.

As 150-year-old structures tend to do, the buildings succumbed to the ravages of time with crumbling brickwork, leaking ceilings and the pervasive stink of mold. It was home to many unwelcome guests, including rats, roaches and myriad other disgusting denizens of decay.

Then a few years ago, the mayor gave it a $61 million facelift. While maintaining the look of the original, the building was completely rejuvenated, renovated and retrofitted with the latest high-tech equipment. The old, exposed courtyard was replaced by a bullet-proof glass-roofed atrium, turning the creaky old station house into a Central Park showpiece, a must-see on many tourist guidebooks. It was a destination Hannah would rather have left off her itinerary.

She was sitting in the Interview Room, a charming space that could have passed for a modern corporate conference room with a carpeted floor, rubble stone wall and comfortable office chairs. Unlike most conference rooms, it also featured a two-way mirror and a tripwire alarm running along its entire circumference, to be activated in the event of a violent outburst by one of its guests.

The policewoman, who identified herself as Detective Morici, said very little on the quick ride to the station. After escorting Hannah to the Interview Room she asked her if she wanted something to drink. Hannah asked for an orange juice. Morici spoke to someone on her phone and within minutes a young policeman arrived with a half-pint of Tropicana.

The detective asked if there was anything else she wanted. After Hannah said no, Morici left the room. Time passed. A half-hour. An hour. Hannah wondered if they forgot about her. If she would be there for days before anyone remembered.

Panicked and exhausted, she finally settled into a thoughtful malaise. Then into her usual fallback mode. Self-recrimination.

How could she have been so wrong about Jacqui? How could she have not seen the searing hatred that had to have been there all along? Was she so consumed with guilt after the basketball accident that she was blind to any clues about Jacqui's real feelings?

Detective Morici walked into the Interview Room after what seemed like half-a-day but was a little over an hour. She was holding an iPad and smiling wryly.

"You've been a very busy woman these last couple of weeks."

Hannah stared silently at her. She had nothing left physically or emotionally.

The detective glanced at the tablet and began to read: "Trespassing on U.S. Government property. Involved in a barroom brawl. Assaulting your own attorney at a police station. A person of interest in several homicides."

She paused for a beat. "Oh yes. You also played a major role in solving the biggest money laundering operation in U.S. history and are credited with saving the life of a Secret Service agent. I'm not sure if I should arrest you or pin a medal on you. But right now all I'm interested in is what happened today at the Arsenal."

Hannah was quiet for a moment. Then she calmly said, "Jacqui Folami poisoned my father. She admitted it to me today. When I told her I was going to report her to the police she attacked me."

Morici glanced at the tablet. "That's not what the report says."

"What report?"

"The one the guards at the Arsenal gave me."

"What does it say?"

It says that you assaulted Ms. Folami in an unprovoked racist attack and you were in the process of beating the hell out of her when they intervened."

"That's crazy," Hannah said, a little more animatedly than she should have. "We've been friends since high school. She was like a sister to me, or at least I thought she was. She lived with my family to finish her senior year after her parents moved to the Midwest. My father gave her a job working summers at the Jamaica Bay Wildlife Refuge then hired her full time after she graduated. He really cared about her."

Morici raised a quizzical eyebrow.

"If that's true, why would she poison him?"

"She was addicted to oxycodone. My father found out. He begged her to get help. When she refused, he told her he'd have to fire her for cause and be required to report that her addiction was affecting her job performance. I don't think he would have done it. I think he was just trying to scare her, to make her go to rehab. She poisoned him to stop him."

"That's quite a story. You wouldn't, by any chance, have any proof to go with it, would you?"

"She admitted it to me on the roof. Are there cameras up there? Maybe they picked it up."

"As a matter of fact we're in the process of getting the CCTV footage. But there's only video, no sound."

"Maybe my phone picked something up."

"You have a voice recorder on your phone?"

"No, but I was making a call right before Jacqui attacked me."

Morici shrugged. "Anything's possible. Let's hear what you have."

Hannah reached into her handbag. Her wallet was there, her keys, a packet of tissues, a nail clipper, a small tube of hand cream. Everything but her phone. Where the hell was it? She fought to tamp down the panic but it wasn't working. Her hands began to shake. She looked in the little pockets of her bag in case the phone magically shrunk and jumped into one of them. She even looked inside her wallet.

"It's not here," she said dismally.

"That's too bad because..." She glanced down at her iPad. "Ms. Folami claimed you assaulted her because she was black. That bumps up the crime from third to second degree assault. You could go to jail for a year and pay a pretty hefty fine."

"That's ridiculous! She attacked me."

"The guards said you had her pinned to the ground and were pounding the hell out of her."

"That's because they came at the end. Before they got there, she had her hands around my neck and was choking the life out of me. I really thought I was going to die. When I somehow managed to get her off of me all I could think about is making sure she wouldn't try to hurt me again. I was fighting for my life."

"So far the evidence doesn't look that way. Let's see if the video tells a different story."

"It will."

"I hope so for your sake. You don't seem like a white

supremacist homicidal madwoman to me. But I've been wrong before."

Hannah said, "You're not wrong this time."

Morici took out her iPhone and started texting furiously.

After she was finished Hannah said, "Can I make a call?"

"You're not under arrest. You can make as many calls as you like...if you had a phone."

"I thought police stations had pay phones."

"They did...back in the stone age. Most of the precincts have gotten rid of them. The ones still around don't work. When they renovated this place they didn't bother putting any back in." She handed Hannah her iPhone. "Here. You can use mine but make it quick."

"Thank you."

Hannah dialed her house.

"Hello?" Olive said hesitantly.

"Ma, it's me."

"Hannah, where are you? I was worried sick. It's after eight. You were supposed to be back hours ago. I tried calling your phone but no one answered."

"Something happened. I'm in the Central Park Police Station."

"Oh my God. Don't tell me you were mugged? Are you hurt?"

"I'm fine. But I'll probably have to be here a little while longer."

"I don't understand. What happened?"

"It's a long story. I'll tell you all about it when I see you."

"When will that be?"

"I don't know. But right now I have to go."

"Hannah, are you sure you're all right?"

"Yes. I'm really okay. But I have to hang up. This isn't my phone. I love you."

"Thanks," Hannah said as she handed the phone back to the detective.

Morici left the room again. This time she was gone less than half-an-hour.

When she returned she said, "I just looked at it."

"What?"

"A copy of the CCTV video. It looks like you're not a homicidal racist lunatic after all."

Hannah sighed and slumped back in her chair.

"Thank you," she said.

Morici shot her a quizzical glance.

"You were having what looked like a pretty heated but non-violent conversation when all of a sudden you made a call and she went bonkers. Who the hell were you calling that set her off like that?"

"She finally admitted to me that she poisoned my father. I dialed 911. Then she jumped me."

"You called 911?"

"Yeah. That's what set her off."

Morici yelled, "Why didn't you say so before?"

Hannah shrugged. "I don't know. I guess I didn't think it made a difference."

"It could make a huge difference. The 911 system records every phone call. If Folami really did admit to poisoning your father it might still be on the audio."

"I didn't call until after she said it."

"Did she say anything after that?"

"I can't remember. I was too busy trying not to get strangled to death."

Morici stood and headed for the door. "Stay here," she said and slammed it behind her.

Do I have a choice? Hannah thought.

She leaned back in her chair, closed her eyes and tried to wrap her mind around the realization that her ordeal was finally over. She wasn't going to jail. She wasn't going to be branded as a violent racist. She solved the mystery of who poisoned her father. She thought she would feel great, relieved, satisfied. But all she felt was empty. She didn't even hate Jacqui. She felt sorry for her. Jacqui's life was wrecked in that split-second when they collided on the court. She went from being a superstar athlete with an unlimited future to a hobbled opioid addict. And whether Hannah liked it or not, she had to bear some responsibility. Could she have done something differently? Could she somehow have avoided the collision that altered both their lives forever? She'll never know.

After another 45 minutes Morici came back. She was smiling. "Got it."

"You mean the 911 recording?"

She patted her iPad. "I downloaded the MP3 file. After Folami knocked the phone out of your hand, the operator stayed on the line. She could hear some kind of altercation in the background. The sound quality isn't ideal but it's clear enough."

"What's on it?"

"You really don't remember?"

"Like I told you. I was fighting for my life."

"Listen."

Morici tapped the screen and a scratchy voice said, "911. What is your emergency?"

Hannah's voice: "I want to report a homicide."

The next sound on the tape is Jacqui yelling, "No you don't. You wrecked my life once. Not this time." Then came a loud clunk.

Morici stopped the recording. "That must have been when Folami knocked the phone out of your hand."

Hannah nodded.

Morici said, "For the next minute or two the only thing you can hear is a lot of banging and crashing. I guess that was when you were having your cat fight. I'm gonna fast forward to the next sound bite."

She tapped the screen, waited a few seconds then tapped it again.

Jacqui's voice came on.

"I'm gonna kill you, you fucking bitch! You're gonna die knowing I killed your father because of you!"

Morici tapped *Stop*. She grinned at Hannah. "There it is. We have her on tape admitting she killed your father and trying to murder you. You won't have to worry about her troubling you or your family anymore."

A troubled look washed across Hannah's face.

Morici stared wide-eyed at her. "What's the matter? I thought you'd be thrilled. A half-hour ago you wanted her drawn and quartered. Now you look like you lost your best friend."

"In a way, I have," Hannah said glumly, "Like I told you, she was the closest thing to a sister I ever had."

Morici said, "She poisoned your father. She tried to kill you. When that didn't work she called you a racist and tried to have you arrested for a bias attack. Those are crimes. Serious crimes."

"I know. But somehow I feel like I'm partly responsible."

Morici looked at her like she had three heads and none of them had a functioning brain. Then she softened.

"You've been through a lot lately." The detective reached across the table and grasped Hannah's hand. "I can understand how right now your emotions are all over the place. But I can assure you of one thing. None of this is your fault."

"Thank you," Hannah said quietly.

"It's not my job to figure out why Jacqui Folami did what she did. That's up to a court or maybe a shrink. It is my job to make sure she's held accountable. And that's what I'm going to do."

Hannah said, "Can I go now? If I hurry, I can catch the 9:40 to Port Jefferson."

Morici glanced at the clock on the wall. "It's late. You're beat-up and exhausted. I don't want you wandering around Penn Station in this condition. You might pass out and fall down on the tracks. I don't want to have to deal with that guilt. I'm calling Uber to take you home, courtesy of the NYPD."

Hannah smiled faintly. "Thank you."

Five minutes later Morici walked with Hannah out of the

station. A Toyota Camry was waiting at the curb. It was totally black. The door handles, the wheel covers, the bumpers, the windows, even the Toyota logo were all tinted black. It looked like a mini Batmobile.

As Hannah opened the back door she turned to Morici. "Thanks for believing me."

"My pleasure. Home safe."

CHAPTER FIFTY-NINE

Hannah squeezed her six-foot three-inches into the cramped back seat. She sat sideways, stretched out her legs but kept her feet on the floor. She tried to relax. To not think about anything. Maybe play a song in her head. 'Midnight at the Oasis' popped up for no special reason. The car started moving.

Hannah said, "Rocky Point, right? You know how to get there?"

The driver mumbled "Uh-huh."

Hannah was thankful that the driver wasn't the talkative type. She closed her eyes. Her mind drifted into that fuzzy space between sleep and wakefulness.

A few minutes later the car stopped abruptly. Hannah sat up. She looked out the window. They should be in the middle of Manhattan headed for the Midtown Tunnel. It was Friday night. There should be honking horns, squealing brakes, theaters, store-fronts and office buildings ablaze with lights and activity. And the streets should be crowded with people.

Instead it was dark, silent and deserted. They were in some kind of open space. Shadows of trees on the periphery.

"What's going on?" Hannah said. "Where are we?"

The driver turned around.

"Hello Hannah," she said malevolently.

It was Jacqui.

Hannah shook herself, to make sure she wasn't still asleep, having another nightmare. Unfortunately what was happening was very real."

"Get out," Jacqui barked.

Hannah didn't budge.

She pointed a small black pistol, not much bigger than her palm, at Hannah.

"Move!" she shouted. "Or I'll shoot you where you sit."

Hannah slowly got out of the car. Her legs were stiff. She looked around. They were next to a black, eight-foot high chain link fence. On the other side of the fence was a basketball court. Four hoops with white half-moon backboards. Park benches all around. The ground was littered with broken bottles, crushed beer cans, cigarette butts, spent hypodermic needles, used condoms, fast food boxes and other junk.

Jacqui stood facing Hannah. "Let's go."

"Go where?"

"In there." She gestured towards the open gate. "Time to finish the game."

"What game? What are you talking about?"

"I want to finish what we started on the roof. I thought it should happen on a basketball court. That's where it all began. That's where it should end."

"I won't fight you, Jacqui."

"Then I'll fight you."

"I'm not angry at you anymore. I don't blame you for what happened to my father."

"Too bad. Cause I still blame you. Now move!"

Hannah stood her ground.

"No."

"All right. We'll do it here."

She leveled the tiny gun at Hannah's chest.

"No! Please! Don't!" Hannah shrieked.

"Then get your ass in there now."

"Why are you doing this? My father's dead. Nothing's going to bring him back, no matter whose fault it is. Why can't you just let it go? It's over."

"Over for you, not for me. Once I saw you walk out of the station house with that detective arm-in-arm like she was your big sister I knew they'd be coming for me."

Hannah's mind was racing. She didn't want to fight but if she refused she had no doubt that Jacqui would shoot her.

Hannah decided her best chance was to stall and hope that somebody, anybody, would show up.

"They didn't believe me. They just didn't have enough to charge me."

"That's bullshit. They could have kept you there for 24 hours if they thought you were guilty."

Hannah had no idea if that was true or not. She tried to change the subject.

"How did you even know I'd be there?"

"I'm an Uber driver thanks to you. I need the extra money for the oxy. As soon as the police finished questioning me I started watching the app. When they said they had a ride from the Central Park precinct to Rocky Point I knew it was you so I took it."

"Oh," Hannah said. She couldn't think of anything else.

Jacqui waved her gun at Hannah. "Enough chit-chat. Move."

Hannah walked slowly onto the court. Actually it was more of a shuffle. Her legs were weak. Her eyelids droopy. The Mestinon she took in the morning had long since worn off. This wasn't just tiredness. A full-on myasthenia gravis attack was coming on.

She stopped at the fence and held on.

"I said move it, bitch!" Jacqui screamed.

"I can't. My legs don't work. It's myasthenia gravis. I told you about it. Remember?"

"You're lying! You're a chickenshit coward. You got five seconds to get on that court."

Hannah shook her head slowly. The Jacqui she knew didn't have it in her to shoot someone in cold blood. But was this the same person? Could being in the grip of opioid addiction change someone so drastically?

At that moment they were drenched in light. Two blue and white New York City Police cruisers and a black Chevy Impala converged on the basketball court.

Morici stepped out of the Impala. Her hands were empty. Not so the other officers. They stood beside their cars with guns drawn.

Morici walked towards Jacqui.

"It's over, Ms. Folami," she said calmly. "Please put down the gun. There's no reason for anyone else to get hurt."

"Why? So you can throw me in jail?" Jacqui said, still pointing her pistol at Hannah.

"It doesn't have to come to that. You have an addiction. You need help. We can get it for you."

"You're lying!" Jacqui shrieked. "I know how this works. The only help you'll give me is in an eight-by-eight cell."

She turned the gun around and jammed the barrel into the middle of her chest.

"Not this girl."

Morici and Hannah both screamed, "No!"

Jacqui fired. Then she crumpled to the ground.

Morici ran to her. She put two fingers on Jacqui's throat just below her jaw to check her carotid pulse. After a few seconds she turned to Hannah and shook her head sadly.

CHAPTER SIXTY

After the Uber fiasco Morici didn't want to take any chances. She called a limousine service that she knew and trusted. It was the heart of prom and engagement party season and most of the cars were booked. The only one left on the lot was a big, black double-stretch.

Just hours before, Hannah imagined that she'd be sitting in a rickety bus alongside junkies, hookers, muggers and others on their way to the Women's House of Detention. Instead she was being chauffeured back to Rocky Point in a luxurious Lincoln Continental limo. The seats were plush and roomy. There was a mini-bar and refrigerator with bottles of wine, beer, liquor and champagne and an array of glasses below. Hannah asked the driver if she could take some wine. He told her that's what they are there for. She had a glass of pinot grigio. After she finished it she kicked off her shoes and stretched across the seat. She dozed off. She didn't wake up until the driver told her they were approaching her house.

When Olive saw the big, black behemoth turn into the driveway she ran frantically out the side door. Her legs flip-flopped disjointedly, her arms flailed wildly, her head shook like a bobble-head doll with a loose screw. As she ran she wailed, "Oh no! Oh no! Oh no!"

As Hannah groggily got out of the limo, still half asleep, Olive crashed into her, wrapped her arms around her and squeezed her so tightly that it took her breath away, wailing, "Thank God you're all right. I thought you were dead."

As Hannah extricated herself from her mother's grasp she said, "Why would you think that?"

Olive, still panting furiously, said, "I was watching the 11 o'clock news on television and they said a young woman was fatally shot in Central Park. The police were investigating. I knew you were there in the police station. I got worried. Then when I saw that hearse come into the driveway, I thought it was you."

"That's not a hearse. It's a limousine. The police didn't want me taking the train so late."

Olive dabbed her teary eyes with a crumpled tissue. Then she blew her nose. She was still gasping and trembling.

Hannah said, "Mom, calm down. Take a breath. You'll have a heart attack."

Olive closed her eyes and stood still for a few seconds, trying to settle herself.

"With all those people getting killed, Mr. Leigh and Tom McCaffrey and the others, I was afraid you'd be next."

"Actually ma, there's no need to apologize." Hannah put her thumb and forefinger a quarter-inch apart. "You were this close to being right."

Olive jerked back in horror. "What do you mean?"

"Let's talk inside."

They went into the living room. Hannah sat in her father's club chair and Olive settled into her rocker. Hannah slowly went over the day's events.

When Hannah was finished Olive said, "I just can't believe that Jacqui would poison your father. She lived with us. Her Christmas stocking is still in the closet with our holiday decorations. Are you sure there wasn't some kind of mistake?"

"I'm positive."

"It's just hard for me to imagine our Jacqui doing those terrible things."

"It was hard for me too until she admitted it, then tried to kill me."

"I know dear." Olive smiled benignly.

The thought of her daughter being strangled seemed not to bother her. Hannah wasn't sure if her mother didn't believe her or she just couldn't process it.

"The main thing is you're safe now." Olive paused for a moment, then said, "Are you finally finished with whatever it is that you've been doing at Jamaica Bay?"

"Absolutely," Hannah said emphatically. "You won't have to worry about that anymore. I'm officially out of the detective business. No more running around pretending to be some kind of overgrown Nancy Drew. I've had it with people pointing guns at me, fighting with me, running me off the road. I can't wait to get back to my old, boring life."

"You don't know how happy I am to hear that."

Hannah smiled. "Not as happy as I am to say it."

Olive got busy in the kitchen, scrubbing dishes and silverware that were already clean, rearranging things in the cabinets that were fine where they were, polishing the countertop to a glasslike sheen.

When she was finished she asked Hannah if there was anything she could get for her. Coffee? Tea? A drink?

Hannah had a sour stomach from the wine she had in the limo on an empty stomach. She took a glass of diet ginger ale and a piece of toast. When she was done, she kissed her mother lightly on the forehead, told her she loved her and went to bed.

Olive woke her up a little after eight the next morning. She was holding her old flip phone like it was a precious artifact.

She handed it to Hannah. "It's your friend Bette."

Hannah said a drowsy hello.

"Are you okay? I read about what happened to you last night."

"What? Where?"

"Today's *New York Post*. Did you see it?"

"No. I never read the *Post*. It's a total rag."

"You might want to have a look this morning. Go to their website. Call me back after you see it. Just remember, I had nothing to do with it."

Hannah fired up her laptop and navigated to the *Post's* website. An old photo of her was at the top of the page. The headline under it read: "Sexy Sleuth Solves Father's Murder."

The article went on to say that Hannah was the investigator with the firm Johansson & Guglielmetti who solved the Michael Leigh money laundering case. It then went on to describe the fight on the Arsenal roof and the final confrontation with the police in Central Park. There were quotes from the guards about the rooftop brawl and one from Morici describing how Jacqui admitted poisoning Axel on the 911 tape. It ended with Jacqui being fatally shot after a confrontation with Hannah and the police but it didn't say that the wound was self-inflicted.

Hannah was mortified at the story. She wasn't a hero. She wasn't an investigator. And she dreaded the notoriety that was sure to follow. She was also afraid that Jacqui's parents would see the story. Losing a daughter was bad enough. They didn't need any more pain and heartbreak.

But what really enraged her was the photo next to the article. They copied a picture from her Facebook page that was a few years old. In the original photo she was on the beach at a Fourth of July party with Phil and some of his friends. They were laughing, horsing around and a little bit schnockered. Everyone else was cropped out of the shot. What was left was Hannah in a bikini, standing in the sand with the surf behind her, looking like the classic shot of Ursula Andress in Dr. No. Only instead of holding a big conch shell, Hannah was clutching a Margarita in a huge green goblet.

She shuddered thinking about how every lowlife, dirtbag and pervert in the tri-state area would be sending that photo to all their degenerate friends with accompanying disgusting comments. She was happy that her phone number was unlisted or she would probably have to change it.

She called Bette back.

"Are you sure you had nothing to do with this?"

"No! Really! I swear."

Hannah believed her. Bette, good Catholic that she was, believed that if you swore to something that wasn't true you'd burn in hell for all eternity.

"So how do you think they got the story?"

"Reporters listen in to police radio calls. One of the *Post* stringers probably heard your name and remembered it from the business with Leigh and Dawson. Then it would be easy to track down the guards and give the detective a call. But it's not all bad news."

"It looks all bad to me."

"Remember I told you that a couple of companies contacted me about hiring our agency?"

"There is no agency," Hannah yelled into the phone. "You made it up."

Bette ignored her. "A big time law firm contacted me this morning after reading the story in the Post and offered to put us on a ten thousand dollar a month retainer."

"I don't believe it. Why would anyone want to do that?"

"Because of you. Whether you like it or not, you're one of New York's most famous private investigators."

"That's crazy. I'm not an investigator at all."

"I know that and you know that, but these companies think you're a combination of Sherlock Holmes and Batwoman. I don't know about you, but five thousand dollars a month sounds pretty good to me. And that's just the first offer. I haven't heard from Manhattan Mutual yet. I bet I can get another nice retainer from them. That would mean some real money."

Hannah didn't answer for a few seconds.

"It still sounds ridiculous."

"Ridiculous or not, that's what's happening. Let's face it, we're both out of work without a lot of great prospects. And like I told you, most of the work is computer research and making phone calls, which I'll handle. All you'd have to do is be the beautiful, blonde, brave, ballsy ace investigator."

Hannah sighed. "I don't know."

"I don't have to get back them right away. Think about it. Then we'll talk."

"Okay."

Hannah ended the call.

She got her guitar, went out on the deck, gazed at the rippling current of the Long Island Sound and began to play 'Sitting on the Dock of the Bay, Wasting Time.'

www.ingramcontent.com/pod-product-compliance
Lightning Source LLC
Chambersburg PA
CBHW070542310726
48982CB00010B/1441/J
* 9 7 9 8 9 9 0 7 6 1 5 9 9 *